ENEMY WITHIN

ALSO BY ROBERT K. TANENBAUM

FICTION

True Justice
Act of Revenge
Reckless Endangerment
Irresistible Impulse
Falsely Accused
Corruption of Blood
Justice Denied
Material Witness
Reversible Error
Immoral Certainty
Depraved Indifference
No Lesser Plea

NONFICTION

The Piano Teacher: The True Story of a Psychotic Killer
Badge of the Assassin

ROBERT K. TANENBAUM

ENEMY WITHIN

POCKET BOOKS

New York   London   Toronto   Sydney   Singapore

POCKET BOOKS, a division of Simon & Schuster, Inc.
1230 Avenue of the Americas, New York, NY 10020

Copyright © 2001 by Robert K. Tanenbaum

Library of Congress Cataloging-in-Publication Data

Tanenbaum, Robert.
    Enemy within / Robert K. Tanenbaum.
        p. cm.
    ISBN 0-7434-0342-8
    1. Karp, Butch (Fictitious character)—Fiction. 2. Public prosecuters—
Fiction. 3. Police corruption—Fiction. 4. Police shootings—Fiction. 5. New
York (N.Y.)—Fiction. I. Title.

    PS3570.A52 E53 2001
    813'.54—dc21   2001029133

First Pocket Books hardcover printing August 2001

10   9   8   7   6   5   4   3   2   1

POCKET and colophon are registered trademarks of Simon & Schuster, Inc.

Printed in the U.S.A.

DEDICATION

To those most special, Rachael, Roger, Billy, and Patti
and
to the memory of my boss, Frank S. Hogan

Acknowledgments

Again, and yet again, all praise belongs to Michael Gruber, whose genius and scholarship flows throughout and who is primarily and solely responsible for the excellence of this manuscript and whose contribution cannot be overstated.

ENEMY WITHIN

1

THEY WERE HAVING LUNCH AT FOUR IN THE MORNING, SITTING IN THE unmarked, a black Dodge Fury double-parked on the south side of Forty-seventh Street just west of Tenth. Nash, in the driver's seat, had a couple of chili dogs and a can of Pepsi. Next to him, Cooley was eating an Italian hero and drinking a large white coffee. It was early March and chilly, with a persistent rain, and they had left the engine running and turned on the wipers and the defroster. The car was warm, the windows were clear.

Infrequently, for it was a Sunday night, a car came down the street, slowing to pass the unmarked, and when that happened, both men stopped eating. Nash checked the rearview, and Cooley craned his neck and looked behind him and followed the vehicle as it splashed past. They were looking for a particular car, a van actually, dark blue with white lettering. It belonged to a guy—whom some other guy had told a third guy about—who was planning to run in tonight from Virginia with a big load of pistols and automatic rifles to a place on Forty-seventh between Ninth and Tenth. Three other cars were stationed at various places around this part of Manhattan, so that if the guy slipped past the anticrime team that was setting up to make the grab, and ran, there would be cars in position to block the escape.

Nash stole a glance at his partner, who had not said five words since coming back to the car from the all-night joint with their meal. Cooley's brow was flexed, and his jaw was working rather more than crushing an Italian hero strictly required, indicating a certain tension. Cooley did not like being in a blocking car. No, Detective Cooley preferred to be the first one through the door, pistol out, yelling "Freeze, freeze!" or some other hearty police exclamation. While Willie Nash considered himself as brave as it was necessary for an NYPD detective to be, and while no one had ever accused him of not pulling his load, he freely conceded that his partner was in a different class altogether in the guts department. Not exactly crazy, because Nash, who had a wife and three, would not have worked with a nut, but definitely on the unusual side. At thirty-two, Nash, though four years older than Cooley, operated as the junior partner, which he did not mind, really. It suited his flamboyant personality, and he liked the reflected glory and the lush collars you got when you hung around Cooley. Nash told himself that his part of the deal was watching Brendan's back—a full-time job in itself—and keeping something of a lid on the younger man's more outrageous impulses. He wondered now if Cooley was pissed at him for not doing something about the Firmo disaster, that failure being one reason why they were not on point tonight, but really, Nash thought, as he completed his first chili dog, what could he have done? First of all, Cooley had been—

"Jesus! That's him. There's that motherfucker!" cried Cooley. Nash looked to his right, startled. A late-model SUV was slipping by, red, an Explorer or a Jeep.

"Who?"

"Lomax, who do you think? Let's go!"

"Cooley, we're supposed to stay here until—"

"We'll be right back. Come on! Roll!" Cooley tossed his coffee out the window and the remains of his sandwich down into the footwell. Nash put the car in gear and headed after the SUV, which he now saw was a Cherokee SE with New York plates.

"Nice car," he observed. "You sure it was Cisco?"

"I stared the fucker right in the face. Look at him! He's pretending nothing's wrong, just driving along under the limit in a car that's got to be fucking hot as hell. Give him the lights and siren."

Nash stuck the red flasher on the roof and goosed the siren, a quick moan. The next sound they heard was the scream of spinning tires slipping on wet pavement. The Jeep took off, fishtailing down Forty-seventh Street. Without thinking, Nash tromped on the gas, and the Fury leaped forward, dumping his chili dog and soda all over the front seat.

The light was red at Eleventh, but it was clear that the Jeep was going to run it, not a big surprise, and Nash did not brake either as they, too, shot through the intersection, drawing an outraged honk from a taxi. The Jeep made a big skidding right at Twelfth and headed uptown, Nash and the Fury on his tail, keeping a couple of lengths back, Nash now trying, through the pumping adrenaline, to take stock of the situation, gain some control. He should tell someone what they were doing. He should call for some backup. This was crazy. It was turning into a high-speed chase, on trail-slick roads; someone was going to get hurt, and not after some armed-bank-robber, mass-murderer type, but an asshole car-thief snitch . . .

Thinking thus, he still accelerated, now to ninety miles an hour. At Fifty-third right by the little park, they passed two blue-and-whites parked nose-to-tail for a conversation, and seconds later both of those radio patrol cars joined the pursuit, the radio crackling with demands to know what was going on. Nash did not respond because he was driving too hard. Cooley did not either, although it was his job. The Jeep screamed up onto the Henry Hudson. It suddenly became damply cold in the Fury. Out of the corner of his eye, Nash saw that Cooley had rolled his window all the way down.

"Closer!" he yelled over the wind blast.

Nash saw the needle pass a hundred miles an hour, the car shaking like a blender on the scabbed asphalt typical of the city's arterials, bits of chili flying around, his hands locked tight on the shuddering wheel, and then he saw that Cooley had his gun out, and he wanted to yell out something to make Cooley stop, but he had all he could do to keep the Fury from flying off the elevated highway. He should have stopped, he should have taken control, but he didn't, and he could not really have told anyone why, except that every cop in the world would have understood why not.

Nash brought the unmarked within five yards of the swerving Jeep, and Cooley began to shoot. Nash could hardly hear the flat crack of the shots, the wind filled the car so, and he lost count. He saw the rear window of the Jeep fly to pieces though, and the right rear tire come apart. The rear of the Jeep started to shimmy violently. Cooley was reloading. The Jeep drifted right, struck the guardrails, bounced back, went into a long sideways skid. Nash stepped on his brake and whipped the wheel over hard and felt, sickeningly, his rear tires break loose from the road and felt the tail of his vehicle proceed northward independently of the steering wheel. There was a grinding, metallic thump, a shudder, the scenery revolved, another crash. An enormous boom. The windshield of the Fury starred, buckled. Nash felt sharp things strike his face.

"Brendan! What the fuck . . . !" Boom. Cooley was firing through the windshield whenever the red shape of the Cherokee came into sight. Both vehicles were out of control, bouncing across the highway and past each other like dogfighters over blitz-time London. Then a louder crash and the red car disappeared—no, there it was again for an instant—another crash, and Nash saw a shower of sparks. After a time, Nash was able to bring the Dodge to a stop.

"Let's go!" Cooley shouted, and leaped from the car.

"Cooley! Goddammit! Will you wait?" Cooley did not, but ran into the dark. Nash left the unmarked, too, and found his shaking knees could barely support his weight. Shots, a bunch of them. Now he saw the Cherokee resting sadly on its right wheel rims against the left-side median barrier, with its snout pointed downtown. He saw that Cooley was running toward the stricken car in a combat crouch, firing as he went. Nash pulled out his own pistol and took in the scene. He thought he had time for that because no one seemed to be firing back at him. The unmarked had come to a stop north of the wreck. To the south, one of the blue-and-whites had stopped in the center lane, illuminating the scene with its flashing bubble-gum lights. The other blue-and-white had parked across the center lane, blocking traffic a hundred yards to the south. Good, Nash thought, at least *someone* was using his brain.

Then he heard the *whick* of a bullet flying by his head and the sound of a couple of shots not from Cooley's gun. He crouched instinctively and fired twice into the Cherokee. He saw that Cooley was creeping around the rear of the wreck, toward the passenger side. More shots. This was the negative part of being Brendan Cooley's partner. Bent almost double, with his pistol out in front of him, Nash trotted gamely toward the left side of the vehicle. Another shot cracked past, right in front of him, and the driver's-side rear window starred around a fat hole. Three more shots in rapid succession, and the windshield splintered. Oh, great! He screamed at the two cops in the blue-and-white to stop firing, nor was he polite about it.

An instant later he had his right shoulder pressed tight against the wet metal of the Cherokee's flank. He worked the door latch and swung the driver's door out, his pistol pointing. The upper torso of a man slumped down, its lower end held in the car by the seat belt. Nash stared at the face. It was, in fact, the well-known thief, fence, and general no-goodnik Cisco Lomax, Nash was relieved to observe, or rather the ex-well-known. The front of the man's tan sweater was black with blood, and big wads of distressed tissue bulged from his face and neck. The back of the driver's seat showed nearly a dozen little puffs of exploded filling, some still white, others as red as wound dressings; the windshield was a spiderweb, sagging in its frame.

Nash looked up and met the eyes of his partner through the passenger-side window.

"How is he?" asked Cooley.

"He's dead, Cooley."

"Are you sure?"

"He took one through the head and one through the neck. That usually does the job, plus about ten or so through the back of the seat. Hey, where are you . . . ?"

Cooley had dashed off, back to their Dodge. Nash saw that he had the radio mike in front of his face. Calling it in. Good. And here were the two cops from the first blue-and-white.

"He's dead, huh?" said one of them. He was a slight, dark kid who looked about seventeen, hatless, his hair glued to his forehead by the rain. Franciosa was the name on his tag.

"Yeah. Was that you doing the shooting?"

"My partner. I didn't get one off."

"Good for you." Nash crooked a finger at the kid's partner, who seemed to be hanging back. The man came forward. He was a light-skinned black man a little older than Franciosa, inclined to be overweight, with a neat mustache. He stared at the hanging corpse.

"Is he . . . ?"

"Dead," said Nash, "Yeah, who are you . . . Higgs? Higgs, why were you shooting bullets at me?"

"I wasn't shooting at you, Detective."

"You were, son. You might not have been aiming at me, but you were shooting at me. Did they train you on that weapon at the Academy?"

"Sure. But the way it was . . ."

"Well, when I was there, the instructor said, 'Always make sure of your target and what is behind it.' I recall it because he said it about five hundred times. I guess they left that part out when you went through. Did they?"

"No." Sullen now.

"I'm glad to hear it. That last shot of yours missed my head by about two feet. What were you firing at?"

"At the . . . at the car, you know, I thought . . ."

"At the *car?* You thought the vehicle was a danger to yourself or the public?"

"I mean the driver. Your partner was shooting like crazy, and I thought, you know . . ."

"That you would join in the fun. Well, you did put one through the passenger window, maybe killing the hostages back there . . ."

The cop gaped. "Oh, shit, I didn't now . . ."

"No, you didn't." A long pause. "But in this case there weren't any, which is your dumb good luck."

Why do I bother? Nash thought; let their sergeant give them the nickel lesson. Cooley was approaching, his head down, the collar of his blue nylon jacket up against the rain.

"You call it in?"

"Yeah." Cooley looked at the corpse and shook his head. "The bastard tried to ram us. I had no choice. He spun the car around and headed right toward us. A big fucking car like that would've gone through that Fury like a ball bat through a cream pie. Christ, the two of us would've both been strained through the fucking radiator grille. Stolen car, too. We saw the little fuck-head in a stolen car, and we pursued. And he tried to kill us."

Nash saw the two uniforms exchange a glance. He could see that they knew who Cooley was and that a subtle transformation was going on in their minds, the little neural charges deposited by memory being overwritten by the story Cooley was spinning now. They were recalling how the fleeing vehicle *had* spun around and become a deadly missile heading toward the unmarked, until Cooley had shot the life out of its driver, and look, the SUV had come to rest conveniently pointing south, the proper direction. Nash, too, was making the story happen in his mind, rather more self-consciously than were the two young cops, mainly because he had enough experience to understand how vulnerable the story was.

But . . . but just maybe it *had* happened that way. There had certainly been a lot of swerving around on the slick black road, and he had been totally consumed with keeping the Fury under control. He would go with it. The car had been stolen, the chase was legit. There was no point in dwelling on the fusillade Cooley had let off during the pursuit, or the shots fired after the car had stopped. Nash just prayed that some of the bullets had hit the son of a bitch from the front.

Afterward, it was the usual mob scene. The ambulance arrived first, and then the crime-scene people crawling around, marking and retrieving shell casings and taking photographs. Five minutes later there arrived a couple of extremely unlucky homicide investigators from the Twentieth Precinct, within whose jurisdiction the event (technically a homicide) had occurred. The two of them, a thin, scholarly-looking fellow with horn-rims and a small Hispanic man built like a fire hydrant, examined what they were supposed to examine—the corpse, the corpse's vehicle, the surrounding highway, and the cops involved. The scholarly looking one grabbed a CSU photographer and directed her along the roadway, taking photographs of skid marks and guardrail scrapes, and of the bits of metal and glass lying on the road. He also pulled a big surveyor's tape measure from the trunk of his car and took a remarkable number of measurements. Meanwhile, his partner was directing another CSU person with a camcorder and light. They were walking slowly up and down the highway. The camcorder light beam pointed downward, and both men were bent slightly, as if making a nature film about the lives of roadway insects.

Soon after this investigation had begun, Cooley and Nash's shift lieutenant, Robert Maguire, drove up and looked around, carefully avoiding any contact with the two homicide detectives. He had a conversation with the four officers involved and then called the zone captain, James P. Robb, who was responsible for all detective work in a fat band across the West Side midsection of Manhattan. Robb had, of course, been in bed, and it had been a while since his last visit to a graveyard-shift crime scene, but he had driven in from the Rockland County suburb where he lived, arriving about half an hour later.

Robb took a look around, too, and spoke with Maguire, and also did not talk to the two homicide investigators, although they knew he was there. Every cop on the scene knew that the bosses had arrived. They all exerted themselves at their tasks with exemplary zeal.

Cooley repeated his story to Robb, using nearly the same words he had used with Maguire and the two homicide detectives. Nash and the patrolmen from the blue-and-white confirmed it in separate conversations with the two bosses. The bosses were not happy. It was late, it was raining, it was cold, and a news helicopter was swooping around above, making it difficult to converse and shining its light in everyone's eyes. Several news vans had also appeared, held back by the roadblock, but obviously sniffing blood. Robb called *his* superior, the borough detective commander, Deputy Chief Inspector Charles T. Gavin, and gave him the short version of what had happened. Gavin did not come himself, but demanded that a full report of the event be ready on his desk first thing that morning and told Robb to make a statement perfectly void of information to the press, and to tell them that a press conference would take place at One Police Plaza that morning, too late to make the morning shows and early enough so that there was a good chance something more newsworthy and gory would transpire before the evening local news. Robb supposed that Gavin would soon be on the horn with the chief of detectives. Good. Everyone should be pulled from the cozy covers by this abortion.

Robb returned his attention to it. It is a gigantic annoyance to the New York Police Department whenever one of its officers fires a gun in the line of duty. Cops say that the mass of paperwork generated by a police shooting weighs as much as the weapon that fired the shot. That annoyance becomes actual pain when the shot fired intersects any human flesh at all, except perhaps when the cop doing the shooting is obviously preventing a vicious, saliva-dripping felon from making off with a charming little girl, or similar. When the target dies, as here, and when the target is black and the shooter white, also as here, the pain reaches bone-cancer levels.

When they had finished speaking with the principals involved, Captain Robb pulled Lieutenant Maguire into the backseat of his car and asked, "What do you think?"

Maguire said, "Cooley's a good cop. Nash is very solid."

Robb sighed and said carefully, "I know that, Bob. I meant what about this piece of shit we got here, how are we going to play it?"

"Cooley said the perp charged him with the car. Deadly force. He acted to save his life and Nash's."

"That's the story we're going to go with?"

Maguire, like his immediate boss, was a comer in the department and understood the unspoken footnotes that hung from Robb's question. It is difficult to make captain before age fifty, as Robb had, without being able to speak and understand a language that none but other initiates can comprehend. Maguire confidently expected to make captain, too, within the next couple of years, and he was similarly fluent. Wanting another moment to think about it, he deflected with, "Have you called his old man yet?"

"No, I wanted to check the situation out myself and get our ducks in a row. Who's the stiff, by the way?" Robb was not pressing the question, yet.

"Lowlife. Not a citizen," said Maguire. "Got a nice sheet for grand theft and receiving stolen."

"Violence?"

"No, sir, unfortunately not. And the minority thing, of course."

"Yeah. That's the bitch of it. But Nash is solid behind this?"

"Nash will hold up," said Maguire. "Like I said." A pause. "What I think, sir, is that we should let the system work here. We'll do the normal administrative in the department, take their testimony, the four of them, which will all be consistent, like we just heard out there. Chase of a stolen vehicle, perpetrator's attempt to ram pursuit vehicle, credible risk to officer's life, not to mention potential for harm to innocent drivers, fucking guy roaring the wrong way down the road. Officer fired, killing perpetrator. A righteous shooting, end of story. No deep probing, no reason to believe there was anything funny. Cooley's record is clean as a whistle. Never any paper on him, brutality or whatever. Racism? Hell, his partner's black. So we're fine there."

"There'll be a report," said Robb.

"Yeah, it's a homicide, sir. I would expect the detectives involved to write it up to the best of their ability without fear or favor."

"Just like always."

"Just. And then it's the DA's ball."

"Right. Who caught the homicide, by the way?"

"Steve Amalfi and Oscar Rivera."

Robb consulted the card file in his head that held the names of the hundred-odd detectives who worked in his fief. Nothing popped up, which was good. Had either of the homicide cops been a discipline problem, or a whistle-blower, or under the personal protection of some significant PD rabbi, Robb would have known about it. So he would have a clean, competent report, written by men who could, if it came to that, be burned. Which report no one in the department would read in great detail. There was so much paper passing across the desks of the bosses. The main thing was to ensure that if any shit started flying around behind this, none of it could stick to him or his. He thought he was pretty safe. He could in reasonable conscience convey to Deputy Chief Inspector Gavin the results of his preliminary investigation: a clean shooting—fleeing felon, credible threat—not *another* case of a half a dozen heavily armed white morons blowing forty or so holes in a crippled Negro deacon or an old Hispanic lady or a mentally retarded, minority twelve-year-old.

Let the system work; good advice. The system would work and bring forth a result pleasing to the department and to the decent middle-class majority for whom it labored. That was mainly what the system was for, in Robb's opinion. And he would call former chief inspector Ray Cooley and tell him that his younger son had killed a perp, but that the preliminary investigation was finding the shooting clean. And he would discreetly check on Amalfi and Rivera, too, to make absolutely sure they were solid, that they would also let the system work.

The system now cranked into gear. The deceased was brought to the morgue at Bellevue, there to be probed by the medical examiner, whose duty it is to determine the manner and cause of death. The New York medical examiner is one of the best forensic medical shops in the nation, but even the best shops have difficulty attracting qualified personnel. Cutting up corpses is not what attracts most students to medicine, and most graduates of American med schools do not care to labor for civil service pay. The office was therefore populated largely by foreign born and trained, among whom, now wielding his knife through the chest of Cisco Lomax, was Osman Mochtar. Dr. Mochtar was from Afghanistan. He had escaped with his family during the Russian war and made his way to Libya, where he had obtained a scholarship to study at Garyounis

University in Benghazi. He had been in the United States, in New York, for nearly five years. He thought cutting up corpses was a great job; you did not have to speak English to them, nor did they ever lay upon you unbearable insult, as was the case on the one occasion when he had sought work with patients at a public hospital. He was not a diplomate of the American Board of Forensic Medicine.

Dr. Mochtar extracted eight bullets from the body of Cisco Lomax and traced the course of two more. He determined that the cause of death was massive trauma to the brain from a bullet that had entered five centimeters posterior to the right zygomati arch, pierced the temporal bone, traversed an upward course, and exited through the anterior, left frontal bone. Even without this coup de grâce, the subject, he concluded, was unlikely to have survived long. His seventh cervical vertebra had been shattered by a bullet that had torn through the spinal cord and exited from the right ventral surface of the neck, and there were two wounds in the left arm and six in the torso, the latter doing massive damage to the lungs and other internal organs. Dr. Mochtar dropped the last of these torso bullets into a kidney dish and handed it to the detective standing there. Detective Rivera bagged them in individual bags, sealed the bags, signed his initials and badge number over the seals, and had Mochtar sign them, too.

"So, tell me, Doc," said Detective Rivera, "you traced the path of these bullets, right?"

"Oh, yes. These and two others that I have not got here. They exit to outside, you know?"

"Uh-huh. And they came from the front, the back, what?"

"Oh, definitely all from back, *posterior* as we say. And perhaps, you see, a little to the side in these cases." The body was facedown. He indicated a wire sticking out of the skull wound, and another emerging from a black hole slightly to the left of the posterior midline of the neck. "The others are all directly from the rearward, except the shoulder wound, here at the left side. But this one to the skull is from the right, a fatal wound, do you see?"

"Right, got it."

Rivera left. Dr. Mochtar and a diener turned the body over, and Dr. Mochtar began to stitch up the corpse. The man had run from the police and had, most properly, been shot down. Dr. Mochtar did not think that a corpse shot in the back by police was worthy of much comment. Certainly he did not bring it to the attention of his superiors.

Some short time after the completion of the homicide detectives' report, at eight-forty the following morning, and its delivery up the chain of command, the police department notified the district attorney's office that a police officer had killed someone. The part of the DA where the phone rings in such cases is called the special investigations bureau. It is located on the seventh floor of an ugly Depression-era building at 100 Centre Street. The criminal courts are here, and the DA's office, and the Tombs, which is what New York calls its jail. Normal homicides go directly to the homicide bureau. On the sixth floor, homicide is staffed with several dozen ADAs who believe that they are the best in the business at bringing killers to justice. Whether or not they are, it is undeniable that they work daily with the police force, and of necessity form close relationships with homicide detectives, and so when a police officer is the killer, homicide does not get the case. Instead, it goes to the seventh floor, where the people in special investigations never work with the cops at all, if they can help it. If they can't, special investigations has its own little police force, made up largely of retired police. Its chief target is official corruption, but it is also called in when any arm's-length distance from the NYPD is required, as here.

The person who took this particular call, just after ten, was the chief of the bureau, a man named Lou Catafalco. The bureau chief took the call himself because the caller was Chief Inspector Kevin X. Battle, from the police commissioner's office, which was nearly as high as you can get in the political side of the NYPD and still wear a blue uniform. Battle had a reputation as the man they called in when things became messy. He had served three police commissioners and knew where all the bodies were buried. Catafalco was therefore alert for something interesting, and perhaps a little fetid.

After the usual guy entrée—sports, their respective golf games—Battle ushered in the main event. "Lou, why I called, we had a shooting last night, over on the Henry Hudson. Car chase, stolen vehicle, the actor attempted to ram the detective's car and he was shot. He died at the scene."

"Uh-huh. Okay, where's your guy? I'll send someone over right away."

"He's waiting for you at the Two-oh; but Lou? This is a little bit of a special case here."

Here it is, thought Catafalco. "Oh? Special in what way?"

"The officer involved is Brendan Cooley," said Battle, and paused to let that sink in.

"The poster boy."

"Him. So what we have here is not the kind of officer—and you know and I know that in thirty-nine thousand we're going to get a few of those—the kind that's heavy with his hands, that drinks, that's free with firearms. This is a splendid kid. He's got the police Medal of Valor, as you know, and here in this incident he risked his life to take down a dangerous felon."

"The deceased was a felon?"

"Yeah, a thief, a pro, sheet on him a yard long."

"Minority."

"Yeah, as it happens, but there again, you got a kid who's never had any trouble in that department. Now, Lou, I'm just telling you this as background. Obviously, we'll do our investigation, and you'll do yours independently. What I'm interested in here is doing the minimum damage to Detective Cooley's career. We need to get past this as smooth as we can."

Catafalco asked the obvious question. "How're they playing it?" He meant the press.

"Light. We had good control of the scene, the highway. Nothing in the *News;* the *Times* had a two-incher on A20. One mention on the metro part of the *Today* show. I don't think there's much to worry about on that end. Thug tries to kill cop, gets his, I think that's the story. I figure it to die pretty quick."

"There's the minority thing . . ."

"Yeah, that," said Battle smoothly, "but I'll tell you, Lou, the community will get cranky when it's a bad thing. Hell, *we* get cranky when it's a bad thing. The old lady, the kid with the water pistol shot in the back, the cop was drunk—I'm talking gross violations. This, on the other hand . . . well, your guy will see Cooley and Nash, his partner, who by the way is black, and the witnesses, one of whom is also minority, as a matter of fact, and read the report, you'll come to your own judgment. Steve Amalfi handled the case out of the Two-oh, he'll confirm, of course. All

I'm saying's we'd like the system to work extra smooth on this one, grand jury in and out, so the kid can get back to his life."

Catafalco agreed that this would be a good thing for the kid. After some brief pleasantries, he hung up. He sat and thought for a while, lacing his fingers across his pear of a belly. Catafalco was a tall, heavy, untidy man in his late fifties, with a yellowish complexion and a slick of hair across his domed and freckled pate. He had been bureau chief here for over ten years, and while he had not rooted official corruption out of the isle of Manhattan, neither had he made any major political mistakes nor stepped on any important toes. He understood at some level that he was a placeholder, and that his bureau did not attract sterling talent. Special investigations ran no trials and so did not attract the bright, aggressive, and ambitious from among the new young lawyers who entered the DA each year. These went into the trial bureaus and, after a few years, if they were very good, into homicide. Catafalco was content with the less talented. He told himself that you didn't want flashy people, standouts, in special investigations, not for the slow, dull, but vital work of checking bank accounts and contracts and the mind-rotting task of, say, listening to all the telephone conversations of some suspiciously well-off elevator inspector. He himself was a methodical man, and he liked the slow, steady accumulation of evidentiary particles that, when pasted together, might sink a judge or a welfare clerk. Or a cop. He rose heavily and walked out of his office. Who to send? He heard a door open and a young man appeared in the hallway, a chubby, shortish man with an unfashionable fifties shoe-clerk haircut.

The bureau chief crooked a finger and said, "Flatow, come in here. I got something for you to do."

Back in his office, Catafalco settled into his big maroon leather chair. "You ever work a cop shooting before?"

"A cop got shot?"

"No, George, a cop *shot* someone. A cop *gets* shot, it goes to homicide. A cop shoots someone, kills him, like in this case, we handle it here." Catafalco saw the worry bloom on the youth's face and hastened to calm him. "It's no big deal, this one. A car thief tried to ram a cop car and they took him out. Basically, what you need to do is go down to the Two-oh and interview some people, the cops involved, get their story. Also you'll want to talk to the homicide investigators on the case. They'll be there, too. It's all set up—a boilerplate operation. Get the stories and schedule a grand jury session." Catafalco paused. "You ever present to the grand jury before?"

"Yeah, a couple of times, before they transferred me out of the trial bureau. But I never did a homicide."

"It's not a homicide," said Catafalco quickly, and then, "I mean, technically it is, there's a dead guy, but basically it's a formality in this particular case. The shooting's okay, no question of that. Our job is to process it through the system as clean as we can. In and out, ba-boom! Prep your witnesses, parade them up to the g.j., and get your no bill. You think you can handle that?"

"Sure, I guess." Flatow took a piece of paper out of his pants pocket, smoothed it on his knee, reached for a writing implement, found he had none, began to search again through the same pockets. The bureau chief, sighing inwardly, handed him a Bic. He then gave him the relevant names and a stringent time frame. Four grand juries— two in the morning and two in the afternoon—run continuously in New York County. It would not be hard to slip into one next week and get the whole thing over with.

Four hours later, when Flatow tapped on the door and stuck his head in, Catafalco was just getting ready to leave, for the special investigations bureau typically kept judge's hours, and he had a number of errands to run, including, in just twenty-three minutes, an appointment for a massage.

"You're back already," said the bureau chief. "How did it go?"

"No problems," said Flatow. "The cops' stories were all the same, so we won't have any conflict problems or like that. Cooley, the guy, the shooter, was pretty impressive. He'll be a good witness. He's some kind of hero, too, is what I understand."

"Yeah, he is," said Catafalco shortly. "What about the homicide report?"

"I got a copy. The guy, Amalfi, wasn't that forthcoming. He said anything he had to say was in the report."

"You read it yet?"

"I haven't read it in detail," said Flatow, who had, in fact, hardly looked at it before shoving it into his briefcase. The notion of reading the report *before* interviewing Amalfi and his partner, Oscar Rivera, had not occurred to him. "Basically, captain gave me a summary report that has all the major facts."

"Yeah, that's good; major facts is what we want. The main thing is not to confuse the grand jury with a lot of ifs and maybes. You'll probably want to play down the homicide report itself, concentrate on the testimony. Follow their summary. That should be enough. In fact, why don't you give the homicide report to me; I'll read it and have a copy run off for you."

After Flatow left, Catafalco checked his watch and flipped through the homicide report. It was a good one, complete and detailed, although he did not study the details. He did not have to. If a chief inspector called to tell special investigations that nothing was amiss, then something was very much amiss, indeed. A major favor would be owed the DA's office and him personally should this one slide by as planned. He checked the part of the report that described the dead man. As Battle had said, not a citizen, not a fellow to be much missed. It was unlikely to draw significant heat. Now the only issue remaining was to acquire merit in the eyes of the powers, and to derive some sweet personal juice from the affair. He checked his watch again. He just had time to make the call.

2

LOU CATAFALCO WAS PART OF THE LAST GENERATION OF CATHOLIC NEW
Yorkers to have spent his elementary-school years entirely in the hands
of nuns, and to this he attributed his difficulty in speaking extempore
before a group. He hated any meetings at which he might be called
upon to speak. He feared the slashing ruler still; and of all meetings, he
hated most the one that took place every Wednesday morning in the
office of the chief assistant DA. It was the meeting of all the bureau
chiefs—homicide, narcotics, fraud, rackets, special investigations, complaint, appeals, and the six trial bureaus, which handled the people's
cases in all criminal matters that did not fall under the rubric of the spe-
cialized bureaus. Here the chief assistant DA, the operating boss of the
DA's office, in other words, heard about any problems likely to arise,
and any complaints, and a description of what the particular bureau had
been doing for the past week and would be doing for the week to come.
Simple, routine, but . . .

The chief assistant DA did not much resemble Sister Mary
Angelica (a woman who still made appearances in Catafalco's night-
mares, slashing her eighteen-inch maple measuring device like a cos-
sack's saber), being much taller, six five at least, and with a flat, hard,
vaguely Eastern face. Jewish, too, rather than Irish, like Sister, and the
eyes were gray with yellow flecks, not ice-chip blue. No, it was something about the *look* in the eyes, a look impossible to prevaricate
against, an intelligence impatient with fumfering, with incompetence.
His name was Roger Karp, universally called Butch. Catafalco had

known Butches before, and they were all genial, overweight, happily stupid men. Why did he call himself Butch? To disarm probably. You didn't expect a Butch to embarrass you in public; a Butch told you to forgedaboudit and invited you for a brewski.

The meeting was starting, as it always did, with homicide. Catafalco thought this a little unfair. The position ought to be rotated so that everyone got a chance to be first. Special investigations was always last, except for complaint, which was a bunch of clerks and kids. Favoritism, and homicide always took up the most time. That was because Karp and the homicide bureau chief were buddies from way back. Karp never came down hard on Roland Hrcany, the way he did on some of the others. Catafalco didn't care for Hrcany either. The guy looked like an ape, for one thing, like a pro wrestler—huge shoulders, a jagged Neanderthal face, that white-blond hair, which he probably dyed, hanging down over his collar like some hippie. And he was mean, too. When Karp was on someone, Roland often put the needle in, too, sarcastic, contemptuous . . .

Hrcany finished talking about a case, *People v. Benson.* Karp raised a point about a possible violation of the confrontation clause. Hrcany said it was a *Green* exception. Catafalco tried to recall what *Green* was, as if he ever knew, and gave it up. Some Supreme Court decision. They seemed to enjoy this kind of argument, all the precedents vital to trial work seemed to be in their heads. He couldn't follow much of it himself. Instead he looked at his notes for his turn at show-and-tell. Neighborhood school-board corruption, a hardy perennial. Indictments were almost ready in two cases. A scatter of inspector bribes now in the system and being negotiated. All, he thought, would settle, no trials there. A continuing investigation into the taxi and limousine bureau, clerks taking bribes for licenses. He was fairly sure that would yield a sheaf of indictments. A bad cop in Inwood, Patrolman Martino. And the Cooley case, the Lomax shooting. Just starting on that one, but clearly routine. In and out.

He waited, mind drifting, while the trial bureaus and the other specialty bureaus had their five or ten minutes each. Then Karp nodded to him. He cleared his throat and began. During his presentation several of the chiefs excused themselves and left, pleading more pressing engagements. That was fine with Catafalco, although also unfair. It would be nice to slip out early himself for a change, were he not ever the next to last. As he spoke, Karp made notes in one of those pale green ledgers he used. Catafalco thought it unlikely that the notes were about special investigations. Fine again; he was almost done.

". . . and we're getting full cooperation from the taxi people on this, a lot of good data. We should get at least twenty-one indictments, and I expect the whole thing to wrap up before the first week in April. Finally, a couple of police cases. We have Patrolman Vincent Marino, in that drug-ring business up in Inwood, we'll be bringing an indictment there day after tomorrow, the police are fine with that, a clear-cut bad boy, and Brendan Cooley, a self-defense shooting, no problems foreseen."

Karp raised his eyes and looked directly at Catafalco. "The Cooley? You've investigated this already? I thought it just happened Sunday night."

"Well, yeah, Butch, it was a very straightforward case."

"Really? That would make it unique in the annals of cop shootings." Chuckles around the table.

Catafalco made himself grin, too, and said, "Hey, sometimes it goes easy. We should be thankful and not make trouble for ourselves. The deceased's a known felon, a known thief. The officer involved spotted him in a stolen car and gave chase. A high-speed pursuit then ensued, during which the actor, in his vehicle, attempted to ram the police vehicle. Shots were fired and the man died. Straightforward. I fought the law, and the law won."

Catafalco smiled again with the small joke, but Karp's face was neutral as he asked, "He stopped the high-speed chase and then tried to ram?"

"Something like that. No, not stopped really, sort of slowed and then whipped around on the highway and attempted the ram. He was in one of those giant SUVs, too, a goddamn Jeep Cherokee. You imagine one of those tanks coming toward you? It looks like a clear self-defense to me, Butch."

A couple of long beats while those funny eyes bored into his own. Catafalco felt sweat start popping on his upper lip and forehead. Then, to his relief, Karp nodded sharply once and said, "Fine. Bill, your turn." The complaint bureau chief rattled off some numbers and complained about the toilets down there not working. Karp made a note and said, "Anything else? No? Then thank you, and . . . go forth and do good."

The meeting broke up. Roland Hrcany hung behind, as he often did, to speak a few private words to Karp. The two men were friends, in an oddly rivalrous way, the rivalry existing almost entirely in Hrcany's mind. They had started in the DA on the same day nearly twenty years ago and were among the last survivors of the golden age of the New York DA, when it had been run by the immortal Francis P. Garrahy.

When the last of the chiefs had departed, Roland rolled his eyes, snorted, and said, "Christ, what a putz!"

Karp had no need to ask which putz, although there were several among the ranks of the bureau chiefs, in this age of lead. "Lou does the best he can," said Karp charitably.

"Right, and if you're a clerk boosting postage stamps, the man's all *over* your sorry butt. Meanwhile, the feds get all the real action on official corruption."

"Yeah, that's a shame. I'll tell you what, Roland, since you're so eager, why don't we move *you* over to special investigations? Make a nice change for you. You can go after the mayor."

Hrcany guffawed and held his fingers in the shape of a cross, as if to ward off Dracula.

Karp smiled. "Yeah, right. I rest my case. For whatever reason, this office has never gone after the big boys, even when Garrahy was here. The feds and the state carry the coal on that, and we pick up the bent fire inspectors, which is why we have people like Lou in there. Same with narcotics, same with fraud and rackets. As you know. What did you think of that last case?"

"What, Cooley-Lomax? Why do you ask?"

"I don't know. I didn't like how fast he got through his investigation. When was Lou Catafalco ever known for speed?"

Roland shrugged. "Hey, sometimes it's easy, like he said."

"Uh-huh. You haven't heard any buzz about this one, have you?"

"It's a little early for buzz to circulate. But, if you're uncomfortable about it, you could give the case to me."

This was a mischievous suggestion, and they both knew it. "Come on, Roland, be real."

"Why? Hey, that bozo shouldn't be allowed within five miles of a homicide case, which is what this one is. Why are you rolling your eyes? What—you think I'm in bed with the cops, right?"

"Not in bed, Roland, I would never say that. But the cops are buying you your fourth sidecar and running their hand up your dress."

Roland tried not to laugh, failed, and said good-naturedly, "Fuck you, Karp."

"Thank you, Roland. Hear anything new on the bum slasher?"

"Just the usual scuttlebutt. The cops figure it's one of the homeless, a psycho. Between you and me, it's probably not the department's highest priority. A lot of people think, 'Oh, what a disaster, the bums'll get scared and move out of town.'"

"I hope you're not one of those people."

"*Moi?* Hey, you know me, a soft touch. I gave a dollar to a guy last week. No, wait, I think it was 1988. Why, you think Jack is interested?"

"No, I'm fairly sure he's not. I have a funny prejudice against serial killers, even if they pick people with low incomes. That may be just me, though."

"Oh, I got a great joke reminds me of that. There's these three lesbians on the bum, right? A Jew, an Italian, and a black one. And they're diving in Dumpsters and all, and they find this dead rat . . ."

Karp looked ostentatiously at his watch. "I have another meeting."

"You do? What an *extremely* important man you must be!" said Hrcany, miffed.

"Yeah, I am, and Roland? I'm sure it's a hilarious joke, but let me remind you *yet again . . .*"

"Oh, right, the thought police. For crying out loud, it's only a joke."

"Nothing's only a joke anymore, man. And you have the rep."

"Bullshit! I haven't grabbed anyone's ass in over two weeks."

"Laugh all you want," said Karp wearily, for they had been over this ground many, many times, "but I'd hate to see you crash and burn on this."

Hrcany cocked a hand behind his ear. "Okay, what are the latest rules? Tell me. No sexist jokes, no *honey* or *sweetie* to the secretaries, no pats on the ass . . ."

"No calling Judge Leonora Parkhurst, quote, a fat, dumb cunt, unquote, right out in the fucking hallway in front of Part Forty-nine."

Hrcany reddened. "Who told you that?"

"Everyone, Roland. It's common knowledge."

"Well, she *is* a fat, dumb cunt!"

"No. She is incompetent, a nitwit, a nincompoop, a juridical nonentity, a cretinous, slack-jawed, lazy disgrace to the bench. But she is not a dumb cunt."

"If she was a man, could she be a dumb cunt then?"

Karp sighed. "Get the fuck out of here, Roland."

When Hrcany was gone, Karp stood up, stretched, yawned, and said, "What did you think of that, Murrow?"

From his chair in the corner, shaded by the leafy fronds of a potted palm, Gilbert Murrow, Karp's special assistant, said, "The colloquy with Hrcany? Or the meeting?"

"The meeting, of course," Karp snapped. "The business with Catafalco and Cooley."

"Oh. Well, Catafalco seemed anxious not to draw undue attention to the case. He seemed much more comfortable with the taxi inspectors. Do you suspect hanky-panky there?"

Karp sat down again and looked at the ceiling. He motioned Murrow to emerge from the jungle, and Murrow did. He was a small, neat man in his early twenties, sandy-haired with old-fashioned round, steel-rimmed spectacles on his bland, Protestant American face. He had an oddly Dickensian way of dressing—heavy tweeds, figured waistcoats, shiny high-laced boots, foulard or paisley ties—that Karp found both annoying and comforting by turns. Karp was a traditionalist by instinct and liked Murrow's decorative aspects, and the idea that he, an assistant himself, had an assistant amused him. Murrow was an obscure legacy of someone the DA had owed a favor and, from objecting to the idea of parking this person with him, had come to value the young man. He was efficient, invisible, had a lightning shorthand, and belying his antique mien, knew what there was to know about computers, a subject in which Karp himself remained at pre-Dickensian levels.

"Not hanky-panky as such," said Karp after a moment. "A high-speed chase . . . the boys get their adrenaline pumping, and they catch the guy—it's Rodney King time, they're liable to dance on his head awhile before they're calmed down enough to take him in. Especially if the suspect is from one of our fine minority groups."

"I've always wondered why they did that."

"What, be racists?"

"Oh, no, I take it for granted that they're racists like everyone else in the country. But, you know, they read the papers, they know about video cameras, they know about mass rallies in support of some poor bozo some cops shot twenty holes in for no reason. You would think they would, I don't know, pause? Maybe think, 'Hey, duh, we could maybe get in trouble if we keep shooting this demented old lady'?"

"A demented old lady with a potentially dangerous spoon," said Karp. "Yeah, I ask myself that all the time, Murrow. Most street cops would say that people like you and me aren't qualified to ask it, because we've never faced deadly force or had to use deadly force in response. My wife would be the one to ask that one. On the other hand, it's an outlier problem. Thirty-nine thousand cops, all armed, eight million people, and how many shots get fired in a year? Three hundred? We had a little over two hundred fifty cop shootings last year, twenty dead. On the other hand, that's probably more than there were in all of Europe and Japan combined. We're a violent people and . . ."

Karp paused, for so long as Murrow, who was used to thoughts intruding in this way on the natural flow of his boss's conversation, prompted him, "And . . . ?"

Karp chuckled. "And I have to go to a meeting. Sometime we'll have a longer talk about the role of the police in the criminal justice system."

"Oh, good! Can I invite my friends?"

"Go to your room, Murrow," said Karp, at which point his intercom rang.

"Mr. Solotoff is on the line," said his secretary.

"Shelly Solotoff?"

"He didn't give me his Christian name, sir. Would you like me to inquire?"

"No, it's got to be the guy and there's nothing Christian about him. Look, Flynn, I'm running late. Make my excuses and tell him I'll get back to him." Karp hung up and walked down the short corridor that separated his office from that of the district attorney.

Who was at his desk, in shirtsleeves, playing with a big, unlit claro Bering cigar, and talking with his assistant DA for administration, Norton Fuller. Karp felt a burst of irritation when he saw Fuller, who was sitting in the side chair to the DA's left, where Karp normally sat during a one-on-one. Fuller was a new thing. Previously, Karp and Jack Keegan had met alone after Karp's staff meeting, wherein Karp would tell the DA what he thought the DA needed to know, and the DA would give his orders, many of which Karp would actually carry out. Now, however, Keegan had started to invite Fuller to these meetings. Karp sat down in the other side chair and arranged his face into neutral pleasantness.

"Hello, Jack. Norton." The other two men nodded and continued their conversation, which was about the DA's schedule of political speeches. Karp watched them interact, not paying much attention to the content. Keegan was looking good; politicking seemed to energize him. He was a big man, not as tall as Karp, but more massive, with a red Irish hawk-face and a great mane of silver hair, worn long and swept back. Norton was half his size, the sort of person who in Karp's tough old Brooklyn neighborhood would have been called a *shmendrick:* Woody Allen without the nose or the sense of humor. Karp did not like Fuller very much, but Karp always made an effort to be nice to the man, since it was Karp's own fault that the man was here. Karp hated administrative work, the sign-offs, the endless committee meetings, the columns of figures, and was not shy of complaining about it to Keegan, so that when the DA had brought Fuller in, not as a sort of glorified clerk, but as a grandee nearly as powerful as Karp himself, reasoning (he said) that the operations of the DA were ultimately dependent upon the stuff Fuller had charge of—budgets, personnel, training, scheduling, computer systems, and the like—it seemed ridiculous for Karp to complain. He suspected that Keegan had manipulated him into this situation, a suspicion that had approached certainty when the man Keegan picked as administrative chief was Fuller, a political operative of some reputation in the state. Also Karp's fault; Karp avoided politics to the extent possible and complained bitterly when he had to stand in for Keegan on the rubber-chicken circuit. Now he no longer needed to. Fuller had taken on those tasks. He *liked* rubber chicken and giving speeches in hotel ballrooms. He had a little folding stand that he stood on when he did, so that his head appeared at an acceptable height above the lectern.

Fuller was going through a list of venues Keegan had to appear at. Even Keegan seemed bored. At a break in the spiel, Keegan asked Karp, "You heard the news?"

"About the president?"

"Fuck the president! I mean about McBright. Norton here says he's going to announce today."

"He'll make a fine district attorney," said Karp.

"No, Butch, you're supposed to express horror and predict sheer anarchy and chaos in the streets."

Karp said, "McBright! My God, there'll be sheer anarchy and chaos in the streets. Besides that, do you think he has a chance?"

Fuller answered, "Hell, yeah, he has a chance, the fucker. Historic first black New York DA? The minority vote'll eat it up, and the usual West Side liberal-guilt vote, a lot of that will roll his way, too. I think we got a fucking serious fight here, chief." Fuller had a deep, gravelly voice, remarkable in so small a man. Karp suspected he kept it low through conscious effort. That and the salty language. Being tough was high on Fuller's list of virtues.

"Which means," Fuller continued, "we absolutely have to have the whole goddamn white, ethnic, law-and-order vote, which means we got to have the union endorsements, especially the cops."

"We've always had the union endorsements," said Keegan.

"Right, but McBright's father is a sanitation worker. That's a lot of votes. And there's the Jews, too. This whole fucking Benson thing. You need to come out on that ASAP. In fact, it would be good if you came out with it when McBright announced. Fucking steal some of the bastard's thunder."

Both men now looked at Karp. Keegan asked, "What's going on with Benson, Butch?"

"Roland thinks it's a strong case," said Karp.

"Roland always thinks it's a strong case," said Keegan. "What do *you* think?"

Karp waggled a horizontal hand. "Strong depends on what you're going to do with it. Strong enough to convict? Yeah, I'd say so."

"Remind me."

"Jorell Benson, nineteen, record for strong-arm robbery, did time in Spofford and Rikers. Just after six P.M. in a stairwell of the Bowery subway station on the M line, it's a Friday, last August, he accosts Moishe Fagelman. Fagelman's a diamond merchant. He's going home for the Sabbath. Benson demands his jewels and money, shows a knife.

Fagelman resists and is stabbed. He dies on the platform. Two days later, Benson walks into a shop in the diamond district and tries to sell three stones. The merchant, needless to say, recognizes the stones, calls the cops, and they grab him up. Subsequent search of Benson's room reveals a paper envelope with seven other diamonds. These are identified as belonging to Fagelman. Benson's story is that he found the stones in the subway."

"Well, duh, *I'll* believe it," said Fuller.

Karp ignored this and went on, "No murder weapon was found, and no blood was found on Benson's clothes. The token clerk at the Bowery station, a Mr. Walter Deng, picked Benson out of a lineup as having been through the station at about the time of the murder. On interrogation of Benson's known associates, the police came up with Alicia Wallis, age sixteen, who told the cops, and later testified to the grand jury, that Benson had told her he was going to, quote, get paid off of one of them Hymie diamond guys, unquote, and that he had shown her the proceeds of the robbery on the night thereof. Benson has no significant alibi, admits that he was on the subway at approximately the time of. That's basically the case. The good part, that is."

"What's the bad part?"

"Alicia. At the original Q&A she said she didn't know nothing. Then later, she went to the cops and told her diamond story. Roland wants to call her and cross-examine her as to her conflicting testimonies and let the jury decide when she was telling the truth."

"And you think . . . ?"

"It's a risk. It's allowed under the *Green* decision, as you know, but it's a risk in this case. You got a young girl there, probably show up at the trial in a white dress and Mary Janes—the defense will bring out how she was browbeaten by the cops to implicate her boyfriend, establishing in the jury's mind that maybe the cops did other not so nice stuff to close out a high-profile case with the first likely African-American male. Assuming we get past that, I would predict a conviction on the token clerk's witness and the possession of the stolen goods. Benson, by the way, has an IQ of seventy-two. The question for you, Jack, is do we have enough coal to fire up a death-penalty conviction, and here I'd say we have not."

"That's crazy," blurted Fuller. "He tracked the victim—that's lying in wait. And murder for profit. Two special circumstances. And no mitigation. The fucker's a career criminal. Also, and I can't stress this enough, Jack, the Jewish community is ballistic on this case. And business. The whole diamond trade depends on guys walking around with fucking millions in their pockets, and nobody bothers them. And emotionally, look at the picture—a guy's going home for the Sabbath, and this little piece of shit kills him. I mean, if you're not going to go for fucking death on this one, when *are* you?"

Keegan listened to this rant in silence. He turned to Karp. "Well?"

"I can't help you, boss," said Karp. "I got no experience with death-qualified juries, and we haven't had a likely case since they reinstituted the penalty. You're the only person in this building who's ever won a death-penalty murder case."

Keegan nodded. "Yeah, I guess I am. Twenty-eight years ago, just before they banned it, that was the last one. Before that, I sent four guys to the chair."

"That's a big selling point, too," said Fuller. "In the election. But it won't help if you wimp on this one. Our polls are running three to one to give him the needle."

Karp stared at the man, his eyes widening. "You're taking *polls?*" He looked over at Keegan. "Jack . . . *polls?* To influence your decision on a criminal case?"

Keegan said, "Nah, for crying out loud, it's just part of the campaign. Everybody takes polls, Butch. And, you know, I opposed the death penalty, I spoke against it up in Albany. But now we've got it. We represent the People, and the People, for whatever reason, have concluded that executing murderers is a good thing. And this case, Benson, is *exactly* what the public had in mind when they pushed to change the law, a stranger killing for profit. So Norton's right—if not this, when the hell?"

"Jack, you're the district attorney," said Karp, and got the cigar pointed at him.

"I love when you tell me I'm the district attorney in that tone of voice. You think I'm violating my principles for political expediency?"

"I would never say that, Jack."

"You're thinking it, though. Just tell me one thing: Are you ethically opposed to death under any and all circumstances?"

Karp gave this question some thought. "No. Not under any and all. Probably there are a few, a very few people, your Ted Bundy, your John Wayne Gacy, your Ed Gein, Eichmann, who shouldn't be allowed to breathe the same air as the rest of us. Where the guilt is so manifest that a trial is a formality, and the guy admits it and says he'll gladly do it again. Like that. Maybe. But a semimoron like Benson, who denies it, where we have nothing but circumstantial evidence, a weak eyewitness, no weapon, no forensics? No, then I think not. Life in the can? Yeah. Execution? I'm not comfortable. Obviously, the people I put away for murder, they all did it. The people *you* put away I'm not so sure of."

A frosty smile here. "Funny, that's just how I feel. About your cases, I mean."

"Right. My point being is that we both know about how trials work and how little things throw them one way or the other. It's good enough for the usual kind of case, because in the back of the mind you're thinking, 'I *know* this guy did it beyond a reasonable doubt, but still, if it turns out he didn't, if I missed something, the cops screwed up, then we get off with an apology and compensation.' We kill the guy, though, that's a whole other moral universe. I think I'm pretty good at this work, but I have qualms about my ability to function in that environment. And the state, hell, this *office* is full of prosecutors who got no more business trying a capital case than they do starting for the Yankees."

Karp looked at Fuller as he said this, but Fuller did not pick up the look. Looking down, he was shaking his head from side to side, like a goat searching for a choicer patch of clover.

"No, Butch," Fuller said, "you're not focused on the real problem. The real problem is that Jack stands a good chance of losing the Jewish vote if he gets all squishy about this prick. McBright is a strong death-penalty guy, which is why he's a viable candidate in the first place. I mean a black guy practically has to be if he's going to run for DA in this state. And against McBright, you absolutely have to have that vote, *all* of it. I mean, fuck it, moral scruples and all are fine, but after the election."

Karp closed his ledger and stood. "Terrific! Look, if you're actually going to bring political considerations into this kind of decision, or any prosecutorial decision, then there's no point in me sitting here. You know what I think of shit like that."

"Sit down, Butch," said the DA. After a minute pause, he did so. The DA continued, "And I do know what you think, since you've never been shy about comparing your unsullied purity with my base corruption. In any event, I will come to a decision in re *Benson* on the merits, as I always do. Now, can we move on?"

Karp moved on, summarizing the reports of the various bureau chiefs.

"Oh, some good news," said the DA. "I assume this Marino prosecution is going to go down with no problems?"

"Apparently so. Police Plaza seems to have washed its hands. The guy is a baddie, with a record of petty corruption. Of course, they should have bounced him ten years ago, but who's complaining."

"And Cooley, no problems there?" A long pause. "Butch?"

"A white-on-black cop shooting?" said Karp, pursing his lips in a manner that could have been either judicious or the response to an unpleasant taste. "You're not going to avoid some controversy. Catafalco seems to be moving with uncharacteristic speed."

"That's good," said Fuller. "Speed is good here. We want the thing locked up before we get into serious campaigning. It drags on, McBright is going to make an issue of it. Our position is a simple case of police self-defense. Only one cop with his gun shooting, too, that always plays well. The perp is a known felon. The perp turned his monster truck around, this huge Cherokee SUV, a fucking tank, and charged the police car on a highway. What could Cooley do but shoot? It's a no-brainer."

Karp said, "*Vic*, Norton."

Fuller stared at him. "What?"

"*Vic*. If you're going to use that salty cop talk, technically Lomax is the *victim* here. The *perp* is Cooley. Technically."

"Oh, please," said Fuller, bridling, and then Keegan said, "What I want to know is, Catafalco thinks it's a clean shooting and he expects a no-bill?"

"So he tells me," said Karp, now in a tired voice. It was, he knew, one of his moral failings, to let the exhaustion get to him, to sink into passivity in the presence of people who did not get it, who would never get it, even if he screamed or pounded on desks. He sat back into his chair and observed the other two men through half-closed eyes. Fuller would never get it. Ambition and the hallucination of control had rendered him permanently blind. A man like that should be selling cigarettes at an ad agency or brokering shady bond issues. Keegan was another story. Keegan got it. Keegan had, in fact, taught Karp to get it, years and years ago. Now he got it unreliably, like an old-fashioned radio in a thunderstorm, the message only coming through amid static and howls. Was it mere age, Karp wondered, or the effects of office that eroded the decent man and left the hollow politician, a core of cheap eternal plastic? Or ambition? A term at DA and now he saw higher office as a possibility, maybe follow Tom Dewey into the state house, maybe something beyond even that. Or the times? The dreadful seventies, when public order in New York had nearly collapsed, or the eighties with their twelve hundred murders each year and lesser crimes almost beyond counting, battering the DA's operation into a kind of moral pulp, the natural food of people like Fuller and Catafalco. Now they were in the nineties, hooray, the new gilded age—crime was down, way down, everyone was rich, except the poor, who were suitably cowed now, not at all like the threatening, hostile poor of twenty years ago. The cops ruled the streets again. He wondered why this victory did not taste sweet to him.

Keegan was talking to him, some details about court scheduling, some meetings to set up. Karp wrote in his green ledger, making minimal responses. The meeting ended, and Karp went back to his office.

"How was His Excellency today?" asked Murrow.

"Excellent, as usual," answered Karp, throwing his ledger fairly hard against the side of a steel filing cabinet, which made a loud bass-drum sound in response.

"Uh-oh," said Murrow. "Should I hide, or would you like to take out your frustrations by abusing me and making me cry?"

Karp threw himself down in his chair, kicked it back against the wall hard enough to shiver plaster, and put his feet up on the desk. "It *is* all your fault, Murrow. The corruption of the criminal justice system by politics, the cowardice of its guardians, the worms and vipers creeping in everywhere, the stupidity, the incompetence, the criminal ugliness of this building even, the tackiness of our work environment—all this I lay at your door."

"I'm sorry, sir. I'll try to improve in the future. But aside from that . . . ?"

Karp laughed, not without bitterness. "You know, Murrow, I've been in this business for a long time. I started working for the greatest district attorney of all time, Francis P. Garrahy. This was before the deluge, the whole crime-in-the-streets insanity. He actually expected everyone who worked for him to be decent, honorable, and competent. He actually expected, and I know you'll find this hard to believe, that people who committed crimes should go to jail for the time stipulated in statute, and if they didn't plead guilty to the top count, he would try their ass, and win. Then I worked for a human slime mold named Sanford Bloom. *I* find that hard to believe, but I did, and not only did I work for him, I actually rescued him on a number of occasions from the results of his folly and misfeasance. I quit the office on two occasions, I'm proud to say, and then I came back."

"Why did you?"

"I'm an addict," said Karp. "I need to smell a criminal trial on a regular basis even if I don't do them anymore. I should write 'Stop me before I prosecute again' in lipstick on the men's room mirror. Anyway, eventually I put Bloom in jail. Now we have Jack Keegan, who I have to say is a lot closer to Phil Garrahy than he is to Bloom, but the rot is still there. Politics."

"It's a political office."

"Yeah, right, the people get to decide if the guy's doing a decent job and toss him out if he's not. But you can't decide how you're going to handle a case on the basis of what you think various segments of the population will think about it; then you might as well hang it up. I mean, forget the law and trials and procedures—just haul the defendant up to the top of the courthouse steps and let the mob decide. I really think we're going to condemn this dumb kid to death to keep a segment of the electorate happy."

"Didn't Benson do it?"

Karp sighed. "That's not the fucking point, Murrow. What's happening is that a decent Orthodox Jew with six kids was murdered in the subway and we got a black kid up for it, and we can probably wangle a conviction. What we don't do all the time is execute people like that. It was one of the things that distinguished the great state of New York from places where I personally couldn't stand to live for a long weekend, like Texas and Florida. No more, apparently. And then there's Lomax."

"The cop shooting."

"Right. Here's the first installment of that lecture I threatened you with, the police in the criminal justice system. Okay, first off, we know they do stupid cop tricks. It's part of the game we play with them. A little perjury on the stand, a little illegally seized evidence, the occasional foray into coerced confessions, the very occasional naked frame-up. Every cop wants to be judge, jury, and executioner, if they possible can. It makes their job a lot easier, and especially, it makes them *feel* better. They have a really shitty life. So they do stupid cop tricks, and we catch them at it and throw the cases out, and then they can curse us out for bleeding hearts, civil liberties nuts, which makes them feel good, too. And if we don't catch them, which is a percentage I don't like to think about too much, then they can say, 'Hey, we did our job—*you* guys fucked up.' That makes them feel good, too, *and* superior to a bunch of candy-ass lawyers. So it's a win-win for the cops, which is why they keep doing it."

"You think this shooting is a stupid cop trick?"

"I don't know. On the one hand, there's the incredible-idiocy defense. Is it credible to believe that the NYPD—in the situation they're in now, with the Mollen report, with the exposure of corruption, with these crazy cop shootings, here in the post–Rodney King era—would actually conspire at the highest levels to cover up a bad shooting? I would not buy that at this point in time."

"You think it's not a cover-up?"

"Not as such. I think every ass above captain on this thing has got to be stuck inside a pair of stainless-steel Jockey shorts. No one has ever actually said, 'Hey, let's lie, cheat, and steal and get old Cooley off the hook.' But I do think they want to make it go away. 'Pay no attention to the man behind the curtain, folks.' Like that. And they're depending on us to help them make it disappear, hence the intemperate speed. Hence . . . hmm."

Karp's eyes had gone blank and he was frozen in position; his finger, raised to make a point, stayed erect and directed at the ceiling, as if he were for the moment transformed into a classical statue—Large Jewish Lawyer, Late Hellenistic Period. Murrow did not panic, nor did he call 911 to report a case of narcolepsy. He was used to this tic in his boss. If Karp's mind were a 1950s computer, it would be whirring and clicking and spitting out punched cards.

After a decent interval, Murrow said, "Hence . . . ?"

Returning to the world, Karp said, "Oh, nothing. It just now occurred to me that I never mentioned the kind of vehicle Lomax was driving when I was talking to them in there, and it wasn't mentioned in the press that I could see. But you recall Catafalco mentioned it, the brand name, and so did Norton Fuller just now. A Cherokee. What do you make of that?"

"Catafalco called Fuller and told him about it."

"Yes, speaking of stainless-steel Jockey shorts. Old Lou was covering his ass. Which means he's about to do something that needs some ass-coverage in re Cooley."

Karp glanced at his watch, then got out of his chair and put on his suit jacket.

"You going somewhere?"

"Yes, I intend to get my raincoat on, pick up that bag in the corner over there, call Ed Morris, and have him drive me in a police vehicle to Chelsea Pier, where I will play a vigorous game of basketball with my daughter."

"Speaking of corruption."

"No, actually, the state pays me to think deep thoughts about the criminal justice system, and I think my deepest thoughts when out on the b-ball court."

"A plausible answer," said Murrow.

"I'm glad you think so. When you finish wising off, I want you to sneak around special investigations and find out who's handling it for the grand jury. Do you have any dull, stupid friends?"

"Not that I'd admit to. Why?"

"Because after you find out who it is, you will make at least one. Him. Or her. I want to find out what's going on in Cooley without having to ask anyone."

Murrow vanished into his cubbyhole. Karp was about to leave when he noticed the pink message slip on his desk. He dialed the number. It was picked up on the second ring.

"Hey, Butch."

"Shelly. Long time. I thought you went out West."

"I did. San Diego. But, like the man says, when you're out of town, you're out of town. Long story. Anyway, I'm back. I'm with Fenniman, Bowes."

"Criminal practice?"

"Oh, yeah. Plus a little bribery and manipulation, the usual. Look, let me buy you a lunch, we'll catch up."

An instant's pause, then, "Sure. Sounds good. When?"

"Tomorrow okay? Check your calendar."

"I don't have to. I always eat lunch in. Or out. You remember."

A deep, rumbling laugh came over the line. "Oh, God, yes, the cancer wagons. I'm still digesting a knish from 1973. How about La Pelouse?"

"Ouch! I'm a civil servant."

"I'm buying."

"No, you are not," said Karp pleasantly.

Another laugh. "Looking forward to it, buddy."

Karp put down the phone and thought about why he had for that instant considered putting Shelly Solotoff off with an excuse. "I'll have my secretary set it up" was a good one, and then it wouldn't happen and the other guy wouldn't call again. He didn't exactly dislike Solotoff. He'd known the man for years and years, never actually friends, but not enemies either, rather the sort of uncomfortable relationship that grows up whenever one party seems a lot more interested than the other. No, that wasn't it, although Karp would never have called Solotoff in a similar situation. He wants something, Karp thought. About a case? Hard to believe. A job offer? More likely. But maybe he was just lonely, a guy recently back in town, looking to renew old acquaintances; maybe he felt isolated, beset, friendless. . . . Karp put on his raincoat and picked up his gym bag. Yes, he could understand that.

3

As Karp left the office, his secretary got up from her desk in the tiny cubicle she occupied and ran after him. A small, pale, red-haired young woman from the Republic of Ireland, she spent much of her considerable energy snapping at the heels of her gigantic boss like a terrier at a bull, so that he would show up where he was supposed to show up without, as she put it, *fergettin' his bluidy head.*

"And where are you off to now?"

"Personal time. I'm going to play basketball."

"Basketball?"

"Yes, Flynn. The player attempts to fling a large orange rubber ball through a steel hoop set high above the floor, while other players try to stop him. Or her."

"I know what basketball is, sir. I'm not a complete yokel, you know."

"Of course you're not a yokel, Flynn. When I think of sophisticated women, you come right after Simone Signouret. Now what can I do for you?"

"Yer fergettin' yer mobile." She did not say "again," although she dearly wished to, and held out the device to him.

"D'you see, sir, the *principle* of the t'ing is it's supposed to go *with* you. That's why they made it so *small,* if you take me point."

Karp exhibited one of his famous glowers, jammed the cell phone in his raincoat pocket, and stalked out. He was one of the dwindling minority who thought that the whole point of ditching work was to ditch work and be out of reach for the duration of the ditch. But Flynn had never once allowed him to slip from the office without that goddamn warbling pickle.

An hour and some minutes later he was playing basketball, three-on-three, half-court, twenty-one wins, winners' ball, and not, in fact, thinking great legal thoughts, but rather thinking nothing substantive at all, which was a delicious relief. Karp had at one time been one of the best young basketball players in the country, a high school all-American, and a standout freshman at Cal. In his sophomore year, however, some gigantic people had tromped on his knee in a game, ending any possibility that he would be another Bill Bradley, and turning his competitive instincts toward the law. He now had an artificial left knee, but he could still score a phenomenal percentage of shots from anywhere on the half-court.

If this kid would get out of his face. The kid was a little over five-nine, and lucky if she hit one-twelve on a damp day. She had a peculiar, large-featured face, not pretty nor plain either—remarkable, memorable in a way hard to describe—with close-cropped dark hair, now sweat-welded to her forehead, and looking at him like a hunting python out of odd, slanted eyes the color of Lucky Strike's fine tobacco. She was guarding him just right, too: close enough to block the sort of feeble jumper Karp was up to these days, and far enough back to avoid a hip and a blast past. He himself had taught her to guard like that, and wasn't he sorry now?

Karp caught a movement out of the corner of his eye, faked left, and whipped a pass around his back at a charging teammate, who went in for a score. That made it eighteen all. The two other men on Karp's team were both his age or a little younger, a dentist named Irv and an NYU professor named Doug, both of whom had played some college ball, although not at Karp's level. The three opposing players were their daughters, all of whom could outrun and outjump their old-fart opponents, which advantage the old farts typically negated by skill, guile, brutal use of their heavier bodies, and selective cheating. Today, however, the girls were hot, and the dads were having trouble even staying even. Karp moved around his daughter, took a pass in the paint, dribbled once, pushed off his good leg, and released the ball. To his astonishment, Lucy Karp came out of hyperspace and blocked the shot. Karp leaped in to smother her return shot, but she outstepped him easily and passed to Althea, who, outpacing her own sire, passed to Jessie, who sank an eight-footer.

From there it went downhill (the penny at last having dropped), and the girls kept the game wide and ran the pants off the fathers, who were reduced to howling, fouling, red-faced, sweat-streaming impotence. On the last play of the game, Karp's daughter and Althea executed a pick-and-roll that would not have embarrassed Larry Bird, and Karp, who had seen it coming, raced to the basket to block the shot, found himself a step late, and had to watch Lucy Karp go up like a homing salmon at the falls to sink it for twenty-one and game.

Irv the dentist threw himself on the floor and pounded it with his fists. "That's it!" he cried. "Beat by a bunch of girls! I'm taking the gas. Honey, the insurance and the will are in my desk in the office. Have a nice life!" The girls were dancing around, hooting with glee and giving each other high fives. Doug slapped Karp on the back and leaned against him, in a parody of exhaustion. "Oh, sharper than a serpent's tooth."

"It had to happen," said Karp. "They're getting better and we're getting older."

"Yeah, but so soon? I was hoping for an early pregnancy to intervene."

Irv got up off the floor, pointedly ignoring Jessie's offered hand. "Get away from me, you! And from now on, back to the kitchen! Knit me a sweater!"

After a good deal of similar, they left for the respective locker rooms. In the lobby, showered and breathing easily again, Karp suggested taking the girls out for a bite, to celebrate their first victory.

"Not this time," said Doug. "I have to grade papers. And, believe me, it's going to be all F's. I hate the young."

"That's a fine idea," said Irv. "I got two root canals this afternoon, and if they think they're getting any novocaine, they got another think coming. Let 'em writhe."

Then the girls emerged looking rosy, even Althea, who was rosy in a milk chocolaty way, and the others left, Irv loudly talking about golf from now on, leaving Karp alone with his daughter. Lucy was wearing a nurse's dark wool cloak, a beret, a black wool skirt, black tights, and heavy lace-up, black boots. She carried her school gear and her athletic stuff in a big Swedish army musette bag. As far as Karp knew, his daughter had hardly ever bought clothes that had not been used at least once. This did not jibe with what he had learned from the fathers of similarly aged daughters, but he had long since given up expecting his kid to fit into any common social groove.

"You're not crying, I see," she said.

"I'm a big boy. I can take a whipping. I have to say, you looked pretty good. You're improving."

"Thank you. But I do play just about every day. And we have a good coach at school. Girls' basketball is suddenly big, so they're more serious."

They walked out of the huge Chelsea sports complex and into a blustery day. Rain was still falling in fits, and the wind from the Hudson bit at the face.

"You haven't changed your mind about the team, I guess," said Karp.

"Don't start, Dad."

"Hey, it's your life. But, like you say, girls' ball is big. And you have the skills. And the size. You're probably still growing."

"Bite your tongue!"

"You could get a scholarship."

"Dad, I speak thirty-eight languages. Getting a scholarship is not going to be a problem. Assuming I want to go to college."

"I didn't hear that," said Karp. "All I'm saying is why not give it a try? You can always drop it, if you really hate playing."

"I'm not competitive."

"Oh, really? Gosh, you could've fooled me in there just now."

"That's not the same thing. That's just fun. I like playing the game. I don't like the winning and losing part. Beating the other guys. It makes me sad. And winning—the way people look at you like you're something special, like *they* won something because they're in the same school as you. And the way the parents act at the games . . . it's not for me." She looked up at him. "I'm sorry, really."

She really was sorry, he thought, and he made himself shrug and say, "Ah, forget it, it's no big thing. I'll have to wait for the twins."

"Oh, *there's* competitive. If they can stop fighting each other for five minutes, they'll be a terror on the boards. Although, you know, Giancarlo is probably more like me than he is like Zak. Zak eggs him on, and he goes with it because he can't stand for Zak to be doing something he's not. Which is weird, because twins are supposed to be the same.

Like when they find two of them separated at birth and they both married Mabels and they're both firemen who like to go ice-skating."

"The mystery of genetics."

"Yeah, especially in our family."

Karp declined to pursue that subject, always a vexed one when conversing with his mutant offspring. They waited in the scant shelter of a doorway for his car. Karp watched the traffic flow by and reflected briefly that this was the street up which Cooley had pursued his car thief. No, a little north of here. He wondered whether he should ask Morris to drive him up to the scene, take a look at the ground. He had always done that when he was trying a murder, actually walk the pavements, look in the apartments where human blood had been shed . . . and then he dismissed the idea. It wasn't his case, not his responsibility. That was for the young farts now, he was done with that part of it.

"What's the matter, Dad?"

"Huh? Why? Did I look like something was the matter?"

"Yeah, you looked like you lost your dog."

Karp laughed. "You've inherited your mom's laser vision."

"Your laser vision, too." Lucy squeezed his arm. "You looked sad. It's not *me* again, is it?"

"No, just the usual—work, everyday corruption and stupidity."

"Who's being corrupt and stupid?"

"Everyone but me, of course. No, we got this stupid kid accused of killing a citizen, a subway stabbing. It's a death-penalty case, or Jack's going to make it one. It annoys me, is all."

"Did he do it?"

"I don't know. Probably. Convictable, but not ironclad enough for me to want him dead. This god-awful death-penalty crap screws everything up."

"A good Catholic position. We'll convert you yet."

"You better bring your lunch, girl. Here's Morris with the car. Can I drop you someplace? Home?"

"No, thanks. I have some places to go."

"Like where?" asked the dad.

"Just around," Lucy evaded. "Friends. I might go by the church after."

Karp nodded and got into the car. "See you for dinner. Great game, kid."

She waved as they pulled away from the curb.

"How was the game?" asked Ed Morris.

"We got whipped."

"By girls?"

"A fluke, obviously."

Morris laughed. "Or you're getting old, boss."

"Just drive, Ed," said Karp sourly. He sat back in his seat, banished thoughts of aging bodies, and contemplated his daughter. It was hard to know what to do about Lucy. Karp was not the only one trying to figure her out. There was a whole cottage industry up at Columbia-Presbyterian Medical School studying her brain by means of the most advanced technology, and they seemed to be stumped, too. But they had already determined that Lucy Karp could unerringly reproduce all the sounds the human vocal apparatus was capable of generating, with no apparent effort, had an eidetic memory for grammar and vocabulary, and if exposed to a native speaker, could master any language that had yet been thrown at her in something like seventy-two hours. Of the earth's 6 billion, there appeared to be only one other example of a hyper-linguistic prodigy, a Russian boy. In all history, the phenomenon had appeared less than half a dozen times.

Karp recalled that Mozart had had a major problem with *his* father, and Karp had long since resolved that, despite her gift, Lucy would have as normal a childhood as possible: no going on quiz shows, no exhibition as a freak of any kind. Nor had she, although her childhood had been as far from normal as could be imagined. Which was Marlene's fault. No, don't get into the blaming business. At least Lucy had physically survived her mother's bullet-riddled home life and was now a fine kid, really, although he wished she would have more fun. Clean fun, of course, not the kind he read about in the papers, blow-job clubs at fancy schools. No, safe from that, at least. He thought about the game. Lucy had been wearing a baby sweat suit, as usual, but the other girls had been wearing what Karp continued to think of as underwear, although it was marketed as sports apparel. Jessie had been clad in a cut-down top that left her belly bare and had chosen to cover her loins in what looked like silver paint, thin paint, too, that Lycra or spandex, whatever they called it. Irv seemed not to care that his daughter's butt and sexual organs were per-fectly visible. Come to think of it, wasn't noticing the sexual allure of girls of one's daughter's age a sure sign of incipient senility? One good thing about Lucy, in that regard, she was practically a nun—modest clothing, like today's World War II refugee look, and for school she had concocted a kind of uniform—even though uniforms were no longer required at Sacred Heart—out of thrift-shop scroungings. Not a violet-hair or piercings type, Lucy, and no tattoos either, that he could see, although she could have the entire Book of Revelation illustrated on her somewhere he couldn't see. That would be like Lucy, a secretive kid. Also, from her mother, he himself being as frank as the new day, or so he truly believed.

Like where she was going just now? Not to the malt shoppe with the gang, unfortunately. Good works, probably, with street bums. Which you couldn't call them anymore, Karp knew, having been informed by his daughter with some heat that they were "the unhoused." Fine, he was enough of a bleeding heart to sympathize, but he also knew that the bottom layers of society were particularly rich in predators, not to mention the violently unhinged. *His baby!* Of course, Lucy could take care of herself, not a naïf, her, but still . . . she also got that from her mother, along with the instinct for the hidden life, the peculiar unhealthy interest in the wrong side of society, in violence. No, the violence, that was pure Marlene, not Lucy. Lucy wouldn't hurt a beetle, a girl who would not step on a spider, would probably cuddle up to Son of Sam and try to make him change his ways; Marlene, it would be two in the ear and move on. No, unfair, she was trying. She had given up the crazy shit, the poking guns at men, and worse stuff she used to do in the line of protecting women that he did not want to think about, and now a respectable executive in a growing security firm, a relief, so that all his formidable Jewish worrying energies could concentrate on the girl, didn't want to stifle her though, it was *her* life . . . and the church stuff, he was waiting for her to grow out of that, something completely beyond him, although reportedly on his mother's side a long line of Talmudic scholars, so maybe that was genes, too. Losing a child to vice, that was common. There was one guy he knew, a lawyer, whose daughter was an actual call girl, and the drugs, that wasn't just uptown anymore—but losing a child to virtue, that was harder. What could he say? Don't be so *good?* Girls didn't become nuns anymore, did they? His secret fear.

Maybe she got that from him. He understood that he was known around the courthouse as something of a Boy Scout, not exactly a figure of fun, but not one of the boys either. Was he becoming a prig? Butch Javert? Sea-green incorruptible, like Robespierre? Inhuman? He didn't think so. Like he'd told Murrow, he'd covered up corruption in his day, slid around the strict letter of the law from time to time, in a good cause. It was inevitable, law being a human institution and humans being all crooked timber. So was keeping Jack Keegan in office a good enough cause to justify what Fuller was clearly doing? Karp had to trust his gut on that, and his gut roiled when he thought of putting spin on criminal cases to satisfy political ends. Or maybe that was old-fashioned, too. Was he yesterday's man? A pathetic relic of a better time? Old, getting old . . .

He physically shook his head to clear these thoughts out of it, drawing a sidelong look from Morris. He heard a warbling, which at first he didn't recognize. Something wrong with the car?

"That's for you, Butch," said Morris. Blank look. "Your cell phone."

Karp fished it out, found the right button, and punched it. He listened and said, "I was just thinking about you."

"Yes, that's a new service of MCI," said his wife. "The cell phone reads your mind while it gives you brain cancer. Where are you?"

"On Fourteenth behind a garbage truck, symbol of my day. I just left Lucy at Chelsea Pier."

"Good game?"

"They beat us."

A whoop in his ear. "I love it. The fall of the patriarchy cannot be long delayed. Did she gloat?"

"No. In fact, she was very commiserating, which made me feel worse."

"Poor Butch! I suppose I will have to pump up your ego tonight via my marital obligations."

"Assuming I can still get it up. What's going on?"

"Oh, the usual. I have an appointment with Kelsie Solette this afternoon, which I am not looking forward to, and I have yet another meeting on our filing."

"Kelsie Solette is big-time. Why does she need protection?"

"Oh, they all need protection, largely from themselves. They bust their hump to get to be superstars, and then they discover that seven million people have no other thought than to rip a piece of their garment off. Or their flesh, and then it's boo hoo, Marlene Ciampi can save me.

But, of course, they still have to be seen, which means hanging around clubs in basements with no lighting and one exit, run by the Mob, with the drug supermarket going on in the ladies'." She sighed theatrically. "Meanwhile, everyone down to the stock clerks are going around comparing how much money they're going to be worth when we get this IPO off the ground."

"How much will you be worth? Not that you're not priceless already."

"I haven't a clue. In fact, I think the whole thing is going to fall apart. Internet stocks, yes. I mean that's a feeding frenzy like the tulip mania or the twenties before the crash. But not a security operation, I mean, be serious. It's about as sexy as a sink full of dirty dishes. Unfortunately, Osborne's become a maniac on the subject, and Harry, too, who I always thought had his head screwed on right. What it comes down to at this point is sitting in endless meetings with a lot of little jerks in five-thousand-dollar suits and trying not to drift off. Apparently the next stage is to drag us around to institutional investors to give our spiel and show them that we're not a bunch of thugs with saps and tiny cameras."

"I thought you were."

"Yes, but this is the *new* security. The world is a dangerous place, the rich getting richer, the poor getting ever more pissed off, governments collapsing, and so on and so on, opportunities internationally for a highly disciplined firm, with modern management, blah blah blah. Complete horseshit, but since I'm a good little soldier . . ." Marlene sighed again. "Listen, the reason I called, I'll be late at one of these crap sessions, and I wanted to make sure you'd be home when the boys were delivered from after-school."

"No problem. Now that we conquered crime, there's not a hell of a lot for me to do. Will you be home for dinner?"

"Probably later. Feed the monsters and I'll see you around eight. Is Lucy dining in?"

"I forgot to ask. She wandered off with that look where she doesn't want to say what she's doing. The bums, is my guess."

A good guess. After she left her father, Lucy walked north along Eleventh Avenue, the unfashionable western edge of the Chelsea district. For now, the residents were still largely Puerto Rican, the landlords were too somnolent to smash and condify everything, the bodegas were still bodegas rather than galleries, and the restaurants served *comidas croillas* and not Mediterranean. There were still small remnants here of the New York that was, a fur warehouse, a few small factories, the big rail yards north of Twentieth. These tended to block the yuppie tide, as did the public housing projects and the two mental-health outpatient centers. Lucy should have been heading back to the Upper East Side, where her school was, to make her three- and four-o'clock classes, but she had already decided to cut them. It was something she did more often than formerly. It was a very good school, but it bored her. Her classmates bored her even more, rich girls, lunching on ice cubes to stay razor-thin, talking about clothes and boys.

She had promised to work a shift at the soup kitchen run by Holy Redeemer at Twentieth-ninth and Ninth, but that was not until five, and before she went there she wanted to check on some people who lived in the neighborhood of the rail yards.

The wind was blowing south, driving cold rain with it, and she walked with her head down and the hood of her cloak drawn up over her beret and clutched tight. She was therefore nearly upon the slow-moving, dark figure before she was aware of her, an oversize mobile fireplug, the familiar shape of people who in cold weather habitually wear every piece of clothing they own. It was a woman, pushing a rusting grocery cart piled with the usual plastic bags. She wore a wool cap, with a cheap, flowered, plastic rain kerchief over that and a set of men's overcoats, and a poncho made of a tan garbage bag. Lucy said, "Hey, Elmira."

The woman looked at her suspiciously, as if surprised to hear her name on human lips. Her face was cinnamon-colored and ashy with the chill. She blinked away raindrops, saw who it was, grunted, and said, "Gimme a cigarette."

Lucy, who did not smoke, always carried cigarettes. She offered a Marlboro. The woman took it, stuck it in her nearly toothless mouth, waited for a light like a duchess. Lucy gave her one with a Bic.

Lucy asked, "Are you going up to Holy Redeemer?"

"No, I'm gon' eat in peace today. I got me bread and SPAM. And cheese. I got me a nice piece of cheese today."

"You should get some warm food on a day like today, though. Hot coffee. We're making vegetable soup and biscuits. And salad. And pie."

"What kind of pie?" Suspicious. Greedy.

"I think apple."

The woman pushed her cart along for half a block, puffing the cigarette hard and mumbling to herself. "I might do it. Or I might not."

Lucy doubted Elmira would come. Some of them would not emerge from the isolation they had imposed on themselves for dinner at Le Cirque, much less for a church-kitchen meal. From things others had told her, Lucy knew that Elmira was ashamed of her missing teeth. And she was too disorganized to set up and keep the free dental-clinic appointments she would need to get them fixed. Elmira was low-end homeless, although not the lowest, not by a long way.

"Well, I'll see you, Elmira. Take care." The woman didn't answer. Lucy stretched into her usual aggressive urban pace and quickly left the shuffling woman behind. At Thirtieth Street, Lucy turned west toward the yards. It was a scruffy area: warehouses, garages, anonymous, blank-faced industrial structures, five-story apartments built for workers back when this was the south end of the great freight-handling district of the metropolis. It was one of the last neighborhoods in Manhattan still connected with the physical movement of material things, another world from the real New York, the one that grew rich beyond all imagination off the fabrication of images and the manipulation of data.

Lucy came to a rusted chain-link fence with one end peeled back from its support. She slid through and descended a rough, weedy embankment to a concrete apron overlooking the sunken Metro Transit Authority–Long Island Railroad yards. Graffiti covered every vertical service, some of it elaborately wrought, and with a certain barbaric beauty, a museum of the doomed. There in the shadow of a high, buttressed, gang-tagged retaining wall, she found what she was looking for.

It was a kind of village. The dwellings were constructed with varying degrees of art and skill out of large corrugated cartons, fiberglass, scrap lumber, sheet metal, and the ubiquitous black plastic. There were a dozen or so of these structures, each occupying one of the bays marked off by the tapering buttresses of the wall. At either end of this fancy district (walls, roofs), there were humbler dwellings, sometimes only a plastic tarp covering a shopping cart, or a crude tent. The social center of the village was a fire flaring in an oil drum, silhouetting half a dozen lumpy figures clustered around it. Her foot struck a pebble, making a small sound, and the group stopped its buzz of conversation. Two dogs yelped and growled. Every face turned to look at her, wariness showing in each one. When they saw who it was, they visibly relaxed.

A tall, bearded black man wearing a greasy olive-drab mechanic's jumpsuit hailed, "Hey, Lucy. My girl! What you got for us today? Chicken?"

"Vegetable soup, bread, salad, and pie."

"Pie? Pie is good," said the tall man, who was called Real Ali. "Hey, Benz, you going to get some of that pie?"

"I might," said the woman thus addressed, a large, heavily swaddled woman with a pitted Hispanic complexion. "Lila Sue likes pie. Is there any meat in that soup?"

Lucy said, "No, no meat, but we got a bunch of bones cooking in with it. How's Lila Sue today?"

Mercedes Ortiz, who was never called anything but Benz, stroked the head of the creature leaning comfortably against her padded bosom. Lila Sue was looking at the fire with pleasure, her large, dark eyes reflecting the sparks. She was a pretty girl, as far as features went, elfin, yellowy tan, with a sharply pointed chin and a straight little nose. Lucy thought she was probably in her late teens, although it was hard to tell. No one knew where Benz had picked her up, but they were inseparable.

Another man, dark, thin, spoke up. "Lucy, what we want is a little room service around here. How come you don't deliver, is what I want to know. I'm too beat, to use my feet, to go and eat."

Real Ali said, "Man, you think you still in Vegas."

The other man became animated and started jumping around the fire, shadowboxing. "Yeah, Vegas, that's where I beat Ron Lyle, eleven rounds. Pow! Ka-pow! Okay, first round, he goes, left, left, right to the body. It don't hurt me none, I'm feeling him out. Pow! Left jab . . . pow!"

"Oh, shut the fuck up, Ali!" This from a man standing opposite, wearing a Raiders cap over dreadlocks and a greasy blue parka with stuffing oozing out of it. He had the twitchy moves and fuzzy features of a crankhead. The shadowboxer bounced away from the fire barrel and started dancing around, twirling his fists artistically. "Hey, let's go. You want to go with the greatest? Come on!"

Real Ali walked over and put a big arm over Fake Ali's shoulders. "Take it easy, champ. It's not worth it. Doug ain't in your class."

"Fuckin' nutcase," said Doug Drug under his breath. "Jesus, I got a fuckin' headache about to take my skull off. You got any aspirin there, Lucy?"

Lucy handed him a flat tin of Bayer. He popped it open and tossed half a dozen into his mouth and swallowed them dry. He said, "Think I'll go by Redeemer and get some of that pie."

"Pie," said Lila Sue. "A pie was walking down the street and saw an elephant a flying elephant with silver wings and he said hello Mr. Elephant I want to go to pie heaven will you take me and the elephant says yes I will and then they flew up high high high high high up on top of the clouds and then the elephant said here we are in heaven but first I must have a bite of you, no no said the pie I must have a bite of you because I am a vampire pie—"

"Christ, can't you shut that bitch up!" yelled Doug. "Benz!"

"Shut up yourself, asshole. She ain't doing you no harm. She just telling a story."

"—And all the other vampire pies came out of vampire heaven," Lila Sue continued, "and bit on the elephant and the elephant said oh oh I am all eaten I will change into an angel so he did and the angels came and changed all the vampire pies into flowers but flowers that had wheels and televisions and they rode down the hill until they weren't in heaven anymore and they said let's look for the mother pie . . ."

Doug Drug pulled a filthy rag out of the pocket of his jacket. "Hey, stick this in her mouth, Benz."

"Get fucked," said Benz.

Real Ali said, "Go eat, Doug, or go score one. Your fuckin' personality is deteriorating."

Doug looked across the fire at Desmondo and Ralphie, the two other men in the group, but saw no rush of support. He said, "You going over?"

"Yeah, we'll go over," said Desmondo, and Ralphie nodded in agreement. "I think I heard this story before, anyway." A chuckle of acknowledgment floated around the fire barrel. Every story was different, and every one had the same pointless eloquence. Lucy reflected that of all the people in the little group, Lila Sue and she probably had the most in common, both of them having strange brains. Lila Sue could tell stories by the hour, that being the only part of her intellect that had any real function. She could not dress herself or go a block without getting lost or stepping into traffic and would walk away cheerfully with anyone.

The three men departed, and Lucy moved around the fire to get closer to Real Ali. Lila Sue's story had sunk to a low warble, like a TV on in a distant room. He grinned at her and said, "You looking for your boyfriend?"

She felt her face heat. "He's not my boyfriend."

"You wish he was, though."

"I do not!"

"Uh-huh. Well, he ain't been by today. You probably meet up with him up at the church, cut up some vegetables together."

Lucy ignored this. "How's Canman?"

"Hell, honey, I don't know. He's acting like a spooked cat. He keeps talking about Joe Romero."

"Was he friends with him?"

"Oh, he just knew him from around, you know, from the streets. Joe helped him haul stuff once in a while. He thinks the slasher's after him, gonna do him like he did Joe. He's talking about moving out of the paper house."

"You mean to a shelter?"

Real Ali laughed. "Hell, no. The Canman, he rather get his throat cut than go in a damn shelter. Canman don't like rules and regulations. I'm not particularly fond of them myself, if you want to know. Nah, he was talking about the tunnels."

"I should go talk to him. Is everyone else afraid, too?"

"Not particularly. I figure we're pretty safe here, all of us being together. Someone's up most of the time, and we got the dogs. No, the slasher, he's going to take out people sleeping alone, like Joe, and the guy he did before Christmas, that Chaney character, over by the convention center. Anyway, life on the mean streets." Real Ali laughed. "You ain't afraid of no slasher, are you, Ali?"

Fake Ali did a little shuffle and said, "The greatest ain't afraid of no man or beast."

"I'm going to see him now," said Lucy, and walked down the cracked concrete to a low black structure snuggled into one of the bays. It was made almost entirely of baled newspapers covered with tar and plastic. Its roof was a cone of scrap lumber and lath, tied together tepee fashion, and covered with a wrapping of tar paper, plastic, and foil sheeting from insulation. Smoke emerged from a tin pipe above. It had two windows covered with translucent plastic sheeting and a low door, made of packing-crate slats, plastic, and duct tape. A canvas laundry cart was parked next to it, like a Toyota at a suburban ranch house. Lucy knocked on the door.

"Who?" said a voice after a considerable pause. A dog barked sharply, twice.

"Lucy."

"What?"

"I want to talk. Can I come in?"

Nothing. Lucy pulled back the door and entered. A small yellow mutt trotted up to her, sniffed her, and hopped back up to his master's side. The man was sitting cross-legged on the edge of a bed made out of baled newspaper, with a layer of orange finger-foam on top. A thin white man in his mid-thirties, he had a patchy tan beard and long, unwashed hair. He wore a mixture of military surplus and Vincent de Paul throwouts: OD fatigue pants, a flannel shirt, a gray wool sweater with ragged elbows, Adidas patched with duct tape. It was warm in the room, musty with the smell of dog, unwashed man, wood smoke, wet newspaper, cigarettes, and over all, the sweetish stink of the residues in the hundreds of aluminum cans, which, in bags and cartons, occupied half the volume of the dwelling. Hanging from the low ceiling and stuck in corners were hundreds of beautifully crafted ornaments made from tin cans—flowers, angels, animals, human figures. They jingled faintly in the slow air currents. Tools were lying neatly on a low brick-and-board table, with coils of wire and, more ominously, a large can of Hercules smokeless powder. Canman made booby traps to protect his gear from thieves. No one went into the paper house when Canman was gone from it.

The place was heated by a small stove made out of a washing-machine drum. It had a hood and pipes of scrap sheet metal and was swathed in pink fiberglass insulation and duct tape where it ran through the tepee roof, and a little door cut out of a car door, incorporating a single hinge. Like everything made by Canman, it was simple, elegant, perfectly functional. Light came from fat plumber's candles stuck in elaborate tin-can candlesticks, posed in niches carved into the paper walls. Lucy sat down on the floor, which was thick with industrial-carpet remnants.

"Make yourself at home, why don't you," said the man without looking at her. He was working with a long knife and a pair of pliers on a device he held in his lap.

"What are you doing?" she asked to break the silence.

"What does it look like?"

"You're fixing your can crusher."

"Yeah, and if you knew that, why did you ask?"

"I was making conversation. I was being social."

The man snipped off a piece of wire and glared at her. He mugged looking around the room. "Uh, man's living in a place like this, what makes you think he wants to bullshit with people? Go home!"

"I'm concerned about you."

"Not my problem. Go away!"

"You're feeling better, I guess."

The man picked up his knife and pointed it at her. "Hey, look. I was flat on my back last month, you brought me juice and aspirin, you walked Maggie. I didn't ask you to, and it doesn't mean you own a piece of me either. I don't need your soup. You want for the aspirin and the juice? Take some cans. You want money. Here!" He pulled a few greasy bills out of a pocket and flung them at her. The dog growled.

She did not touch them. "Real Ali says you're running scared."

"He does, huh? Real Ali should mind his own fucking business. This is why I got to fucking get out of this slum. I came here, built my place, it was nice and peaceful, everybody was living down at the station, fucking beggars. Now it's wall-to-wall crazy people. It's like Times fucking Square here."

"It seems a shame to leave here now you've got it fixed up so nice."

"See, that's what you don't understand. I don't need this. I got a knife, a pliers, a snips. I got a hand-baler and a can crusher and my wagon. I could put a place like this together in two days, if I got the paper and the plastic. The stove takes down, but I got a better idea for one, make it out of a muffler and exhaust pipes. A smaller place, someplace quiet, just big enough for one. Build it like an igloo. Get away from these crazies."

"Then why don't you hang out with sane people, have a real life? You're smart. You read." She gestured to a double row of paperbacks sitting in a milk crate. "You can make things, fix things. You're a terrific artist. You could get those can sculptures in a gallery . . ."

"Sane people? Where? Wall Street? The government? Corporations? You think those people are sane? They're nuttier than Fake Ali out there. There's no fucking difference between what you hear on the news and what Lila Sue spits out. You think that's an improvement, being a slave to crazy people, wrecking the planet, turning everything into cash to buy shit they throw away? Don't even know they're crazy. Which is as crazy as you can get. You want me to hang with sane people? Find me three. Two."

"I'm sane."

"Ho! You believe angels talk to you. Jesus rose from the dead."

"What do *you* believe in, John?" she asked mildly.

"Me? This!" He held up his knife. It was a military knife of some kind, shiny and pointed. "I believe this is a knife." He scratched the mutt behind her ear. "I believe this is a dog. I believe life is a pile of shit and the world would be a better place if more people were dead. Especially those pathetic loonies and hypes you hang out with."

He put the can crusher down on the floor and began fumbling through his pockets, his face twitching, cursing under his breath. A baggie of pale tan pills appeared. He grinned and held it out to the girl. "Join me?"

"Maybe later."

A snort, and he ate two of the Percodans, swallowing them dry. "Maybe later," he said derisively. "You know if Jesus was hanging around nowadays, he'd be into everything, hanging around with the lowlife. I thought you were trying to be like him."

"I doubt Jesus would be a doper, John. He was always casting out unclean spirits."

"Yeah? Well, I don't have any of them." He lay back down on his bed and flung an arm across his eyes.

"Actually, you do," she said, but in a low voice. She stood up and retrieved a felt pen from her bag. She wrote her name and phone number on the newspaper wall. "If you're going to leave here, I wish you'd tell Real Ali where you're going. And I left you my number. Call me if you need anything."

"I need you to get lost."

4

THE FROG PERSON WAS EXPLAINING RULE 174 OF THE SECURITIES ACT, AND
Marlene was drawing tiny linked roses on her yellow pad, as she had
done when bored, starting with her days at Holy Family parochial school
in Ozone Park, Queens, and continuing through Sacred Heart, Smith,
Yale Law, and the district attorney's office. Had she kept all of them, she
could have run a garland from New York to San Diego, for she was often
bored, in the way good soldiers are bored between battles. Rule 174 gov-
erned the quiet-period phase of the complex train of events that places
a private company's stock before the public, the so-called initial public
offering, the IPO, which, Marlene believed, is what the nineties had
instead of really good rock and roll.

Marlene was not interested in the quiet period, or any other period
within the purview of the Frog Person, who was the man from the
underwriters, Kohlmann Mohl Hastings. His name was Foster Amory,
and Marlene had uncharitably focused her resentment at the whole
process upon him, for he was the man responsible for Sherpa-ing the
Osborne International IPO up the stormy rock face of infinite wealth.
His eye fell upon her and she shot him a glare that made him look away.
Marlene felt a pang of guilt. It was not his fault that her colleagues had
turned into appalling greed-heads overnight. Or that he really did look
like a frog.

The general purpose of Rule 174, Marlene gathered through the
roses, was to prevent firms about to unleash stock from hyping the stock.
Were it not for this rule, some unscrupulous businesspeople might tell

lies about their firm's prospects or tell things to some people they did not tell to everyone. The Frog Person now paused, and his song was taken up by William Bell, Osborne's general counsel, more of a bird than a frog: a crane or a stork. He had sandy hair, watering blue eyes, and glasses that he had constantly to push back on his long, pointed, red-tipped nose. Marlene called him Ding-dong Bell, although he had never been anything but nice to her and was not notably nuts, except about this IPO, a pathology he shared with everyone else around the table except, apparently, Marlene.

He was going on about Rule 135, which comprises a long list of for-bidden sorts of press statements. Marlene let her mind drift, for she herself would not willingly talk to any journalist, nor did she own any financial secrets. She completed a rose border and idly looked around the table. At its head, Lou Osborne, the CEO, seemed his usual rock-hewn self as he listened very carefully, indeed, to the people who were going to make him a multimillionaire. Osborne was a former Secret Service agent who had taken early retirement a decade or so ago and built this firm into the fastest-growing general-service security and investigations operation in America's fastest-growing business. He had done this largely by picking up smaller firms and integrating their operations into Osborne's own, making limited partners of the owners rather than spending any hard cash. Marlene's firm, an outfit specializ-ing in services to women, had been the first of these. Her former part-ner, Harry Bellow, was now Osborne's VP for investigations. Harry was there next to Osborne, his baggy cop face interested but blank. She caught his eye and received a tiny wink. Harry was not entirely corpo-rate yet; as a former NYPD detective, he did not take suits all that seri-ously, but he was a lot more corporate than Marlene was. Moving along the table, there was Marty Fox, VP security, shaven-headed, with the hard face of one of the better Roman emperors. He was a former FBI agent, an old buddy of the boss's, and he thought Marlene should be working for him, since she also handled security. Marlene did not agree, and since she was a partner, too, and had Harry's vote, he could not force the issue. Then came Deanna Unger, the chief financial offi-cer, about ten years Marlene's junior and the only other woman in Osborne's top management. A cat-faced blonde in an Armani suit, smart, ambitious, she was always reasonably cordial to Marlene, but clearly preferred to play with the boys. Sisterhood had stopped being powerful. Marlene suspected that Unger thought the VIP operation was fluff. Finally, on Marlene's right there was a wiry, small man in his mid-fifties with pale blue eyes and pencil-lead pupils that never seemed to expand. Oleg Sirmenkov was VP for international operations. He had spent most of his professional life running security at Soviet consulates in the United States, and at the embassy in D.C., which was how Osborne had met him. It tickled Osborne to have a former KGB colonel working for him, and it apparently tickled Sirmenkov, too. A man who laughed a lot, and loudly, so that you hardly noticed that the laugh never got all the way to those funny eyes. Next to Harry, Oleg was Marlene's favorite VP.

"Are you as bored as I am?" she asked out of the side of her mouth.

"Not bored in the least, I assure you," replied Sirmenkov sotto voce. "I am fascinated. But I have been to some *very* boring meetings. This is the Kirov by comparison."

Bell was now droning into Section 11, which laid out the liabilities for making false statements or phony claims in the prospectus. The only document that could be given to prospective investors was the prospectus itself. Any documents that Osborne used in the road show had to be taken back, lest they violate Section 5.

Oh, the road show. Marlene was to be one of the stars of the road show. Marlene knew famous people; despite what Deanna might think, Osborne felt Marlene's operation gave the firm some unusual shine. It might not have brought in as much as Harry's corporate investigations, or the security and training stuff that Fox did, but glamour sold, which was why insurance companies hired actors who had played doctors to appear on TV for them.

Bell finished, and the Frog from Kohlmann started on the schedule for the road shows, during which the principals of Osborne would visit big institutional investors and tell them why they should buy stock in a firm of private dicks. There was an actual script for this, and a director the Frog had brought along, a kid who looked about seventeen and the only person in the room besides Marlene and the CFO who had hair more than three-eighths of an inch long, who was now talking about setting up rehearsals. The task was to fake enough sincerity to carry the investors along with the illusion that it was a sure thing that big was better in security, and the whole dangerous-world line of malarkey. Everyone seemed enthusiastic about this but her, like kids talking about putting on a high school play. She wondered why. The lure of show biz? The prospect of immense wealth? Briefly she longed to be part of it, to submerge herself in a group mind for once. But the inner watcher, ever alert, tugged her away, and she looked at them, as from a distance, and felt the exhaustion rise up, although she kept her face pleasantly neutral throughout.

The meeting ended. Marlene grabbed up her doodles and left the conference room without indulging in any of the postconference chitchat normal on such occasions.

Sirmenkov fell into step with her. "What is it, Marlene. Why everyone happy but you? You look like dog died." He paused. "Did dog die?"

"No, dog live," said Marlene, a little miffed at having revealed this much. "Dog in office."

"So why is this frowning? You don't want to get rich as God in heaven?"

"Oh, I don't know, Ollie. I'm just generally pissed off these days. I'm not made for sitting in meetings and telling lies and ordering people around. I need action. Don't you? Don't you want to go and torture a dissident once in a while?"

Sirmenkov looked pained and mimed delicacy. "Please, Marlene, that was another directorate entirely from us. We are being guards only, like yourself."

"So you love all this, right?"

"I confess, I do. I am a late convert to capitalism, you know. I have of convert . . . hm, what is this word . . . *rvrenyeh* . . ." He made an expressive gesture with his hands to his heart, thrusting outward.

"Zeal?"

"Just so, zeal. I love this stuff. I wish very much to be extremely rich."

"And you think that will solve all your problems?"

"Those to do with money, surely." He laughed, showing gold teeth.

"I wonder. You ever see a movie called *The Treasure of the Sierra Madre*?"

"Of course I see, many times. Also I read in school. Is book by B. Traven, socialist hero. Very popular with former regime. Ah, you mean how lust for gold destroys men. Yes, but only stupid men, as in film."

"Right, but I was also thinking about wasted effort. I guess I can't believe that this market is going to get all excited about an IPO from a security company. It's not exactly high-tech."

"But *is,* Marlene! But is—we are extremely high-tech. And we expand into Internet security very fast. Marty will tell you—he has all those boys down there with the long hair and the T-shorts."

"*Shirts.* Still, I think everyone is going nuts over a long shot. Also, suppose it works. I don't know. I spend a lot of my time with very rich people, mostly people who've made their pile off dumb luck and flash. I don't find them a particularly happy bunch. You won't believe this, but a lot of rich people take drugs and drink too much, and screw up their marriages, and are mean to their kids."

He chuckled and rolled his eyes. "Marlene, you break my little heart. Now, believe me, honestly, you only say this because you have American guilt. Is from being rich all your life: you say, 'Oh, money is nothing.' But if you see only poor, poverty, your whole life, the way people, I mean intelligent people, how they live in other countries, filthy flats, cold, rotten clothings, bad food, then you don't think is something wrong with rich. You will see. Somehow, you will learn to like."

"If not, you haf vays, right?"

After the tiniest pause, a booming laugh. "Oh, Marlene, you are amusing woman, I tell you the truth. Seriously, though, you should not worry the IPO will fly. It is good time for it."

"You mean the market?"

"I mean events. Events make market."

"What kind of events? By the way, do you want to get lunch?"

"No, I can't, I have big meeting with Lou and . . . some others. Another time? Tomorrow, maybe?"

"Sure. What kind of events?"

"Events in world. Is dangerous place, like the man said. And how is your charming daughter? We have not seen her so much as before."

"Still charming," said Marlene shortly, somewhat thrown by the abrupt change of subject.

"Good! You should bring her around more often. I enjoy to speak Russian with her. She has for some reason a Petersburg accent. I tell you, that is a remarkable girl. Please say I send regards." Another golden smile and he slipped away down a side corridor.

Marlene went back to her office. This was four times the size of the

one she had occupied as a minor bureau chief in the DA and approxi-
mated the scale and luxury of those given to assistant DAs in television
dramas. It was really the best office in the place next to Lou's, which
caused no little resentment among some of the other VPs. But Osborne
had reasoned that the VIPs who made up Marlene's clientele deserved
nothing less. She had furnished the office in institutional teak, simple
and uncluttered, the *Architectural Digest* effect of which was quite
undone by the clutter that Marlene spread around her—papers, books,
CDs, magazines, clippings, and in the corner, on a dog bed, an immense,
black, wheezing Neapolitan mastiff. There were three windows along
one wall, from which she could look down thirty-two floors to Third
Avenue. On another wall she had hung a big Red Grooms lithograph of
a street scene in lower Manhattan, Lafayette and Spring to be precise,
and a framed length of tan silk, upon which her daughter had cal-
ligraphed a Chinese poem, "Quiet Night Thoughts," by Li Po. Or so she
said. It was supposed to be calming to contemplate. Marlene sat in her
chair and contemplated it—and was not calmed. The other two walls
exhibited material that Marlene would not have hung had she been in
charge, but Lou had insisted, more or less in return for the nice office
and the suppression of any bitching about the dog. This material com-
prised her diplomas, framed photographs of Marlene with famous
clients, and laminated newspaper articles about some of her more legal
exploits—shootings, rescues, notable cases. Most clients thought it was
impressive and a little scary. Marlene thought the wall a souvenir of a
ridiculous and somewhat disgraceful life.

She ordered a tuna sandwich and a Coke and began work. VIP operations had something over 150 clients, scattered around the world,
nearly all people with famous faces and subject to the less attractive
aspects of fame. Several hundred employees were occupied in advising
these people about their security, and in some cases actually guarding
them. Marlene had discovered that the skills she had learned in
parochial school were just those needed in big business: neatness, punc-
tuality, disciplined focus, Christian forbearance, a good memory for
small facts, a pleasant mien, and a willingness to punish transgressions
instantly and nearly without thought. She was good at the work. VIP ran
like a clock. Marlene took no shit at all from the clientele, who seemed
actually to enjoy being mildly abused; Marlene supposed that it was

something of a relief from the interminable adulation that was their ordinary lot.

The morning passed into afternoon. Marlene read reports and project estimates, took and made calls, held meetings. She told her staff about the IPO meeting, as it touched on blabbing, and resisted with some irritation their attempts to wheedle more details out of her. In fact, she didn't have the details, having drawn roses instead of writing them down. There came a moment just before four when she was alone. She told her secretary to hold calls and to order a company car and driver, locked the office door, and opened a closet. She slipped out of her skirt and heels and into a baggy orange coverall that had CIAMPI & SONS PLUMBING printed on the back in square white letters. Over that she donned a yellow slicker with traffic glo-strips on the back. She put her feet into rubber knee boots, tied her hair into a red bandanna, and slapped a white hard hat on her head. From the closet shelf she took a clipboard heavy with greasy forms and a four-cell flashlight.

"I'll be at Kelsie Solette's apartment," she told her secretary.

"Are you going to be in her show?" said the young woman, eyeing the outfit. "I thought that was beads and fringes and piercing."

"No, but after I get done there, I figured I would hang around a construction site and talk trash at guys walking by."

"A lot of body insults, I hope," said the secretary, a plump woman. Marlene walked out, making a disgusting noise with her mouth in reply.

The rock star Kelsie Solette lived in the Daumier, a Fifth Avenue hotel that had recently been turned into condos buyable for something like a million dollars a room. Marlene had the driver drop her off a block away from the entrance, to get some rain on her outfit. She entered through the service entrance on Fifty-eighth and rode the service elevator to the seventeenth floor. No one stopped her or asked what she was doing there. At the door marked 1702, she knocked, waited. The door clicked and opened wide; a pretty young man with long hair, a scruffy beard, ragged jeans, and a black Tainted Patties T-shirt stood in the doorway. Tainted Patties was the name of Ms. Solette's band, Marlene recalled. She waved her clipboard. "Gas company." The young man registered Marlene, assessed her as a nonentity, and turned away, leaving the door open. Marlene entered the apartment and followed the youth into the living room.

It was decorated in the bland but heavy style that newly rich people buy from fashionable decorators: huge, cold, promo paintings, oversize furniture done in expensive fabrics, large, complex Italianate floor lamps, "collector" pieces—a Shaker sideboard, a Louis XIV breakfront in antique white. The living room was dominated by a huge entertainment center consisting of a TV half the size of a highway billboard, a high, black rack of stereo equipment with speakers as tall as a man and thin as a deck of cards. The Tainted Patty sat on a couch in front of the TV and began thumbing the remote.

"Where's Ms. Solette?" Marlene asked.

A jerk of the head. "Bedroom."

"Peter Filson around?"

"Somewhere, I guess. I don't know." Flick. Flick.

Marlene went through a dining room, where the remains of a take-out feast from the previous evening stood congealing on a long mahogany table, and into the kitchen.

There she found a large man fussing with a coffeemaker. He had a low brow, from which arose a profusion of oily black curls that descended aft to his neckline. He had on a black silk shirt, which was open, showing a well-cut bodybuilder's chest and abdomen, black slacks, and black Nike sneakers.

"You Peter Filson?"

"Yo. Hey, you know how to work this thing?"

"You're missing a part. The thing that holds the filter."

"Maid didn't come in today. I don't know what the hell I'm doing here." He abandoned the project. "I'll call out."

"Mr. Filson, do you know who I am?"

The man looked at her dimly. "Power company?"

"I'm Marlene Ciampi." Nothing. "Osborne International? Security? We've been trying to get in touch with you."

Light, though flickering. "Oh! Oh, yeah. Right. Sorry. She wanted you to, you know, check out the system, like because of that guy, and she's been getting more of these letters."

"Uh-huh. Mr. Filson . . ."

"Hey, call me Pete. Listen, can I just call up for coffee? We got in at like five this morning."

"Be my guest, Pete."

After the call Filson said, "So, like, what do you guys do? I mean Kelsie's already got me, so . . ."

"Pete, how do you know who I am?"

"How do I . . . ?"

"Yeah, you're standing here talking to a woman in a jumpsuit and a hard hat who says she's with a big security agency. I haven't shown you any ID. I just walked in here, unannounced. That kid in the living room let me in."

"Yeah, Billy the drummer."

"So I could be anyone."

Filson frowned now. "They're supposed to check everyone downstairs and call up."

"Right, Pete, but they didn't, because I came in through the service entrance. I just pounded on the door there and a janitor let me in." Marlene was starting to sweat a little because the apartment was overheated, and she always found the labor of conversing with extremely stupid people more exhausting than violent exercise. She took off her hard hat and slicker and placed them on a counter along with her clipboard.

After a moment's puzzled frowning, the man said, "Well, yeah, because you got that stuff on. He thought you were from Con Ed or whatever."

Marlene stared at him. "That's great, Pete. Look, is Kelsie up?"

"Yeah, I heard her yelling at the dog. You want to see her?"

"I do." Marlene left the kitchen, and he called after her, "Hey, I ordered you some coffee, too, and like Danish and stuff?"

The bedroom was large and dim and smelled strongly of stale perfume, marijuana, and tobacco. A king-size four-poster bed was on one wall, and in it sat the star, stroking a Lhasa apso dog, smoking, and watching a large-screen television with the sound off. The dog started yapping when Marlene entered.

"Oh, shut the fuck up, Jeepers!" Kelsie Solette cried. The dog, undeterred, wriggled from her arms, dropped off the bed, and prepared to defend her territory. "Who the hell are you?"

Kelsie Solette had a pinched hillbilly face, saved from indistinction by enormous cornflower eyes. The thick mascara of last night smudged her pasty cheeks, and her thin blond hair was arranged in gelled spikes, her trademark look. She sported a dozen or so earrings, a nose ring with a three-carat canary diamond in it, and a row of pearls stuck through her left eyebrow. She was wearing a black T-shirt with iridescent sequins sewn on it in a swirling pattern.

"I'm Marlene Ciampi."

This took a few seconds to register. "Oh, yeah. The security lady. Cool. That's a whacked look. Where'd you get the outfit?"

"From my father. He's a plumber. Look, Ms. Solette—"

"Kelsie."

"—Kelsie, I've just been talking to your bodyguard—"

"Yeah, Pete's great, isn't he?"

"Well, actually, no, not as a bodyguard he isn't. I just walked in here on the strength of dressing like a utility worker. You basically have no security at all. Jimmy Coleman could walk in here anytime and slit your throat."

"He's in jail," said the singer nervously. "Isn't he?"

"Is he? I heard he went to Rikers on a 240.30, agg harassment two. That's an A misdemeanor. When was that? Four months ago? He could be walking any day. He'll be out and he'll be pissed off, unless you think he's forgotten you. And at least we know about *him*. I'm more worried about the ones we don't know about. The letters."

Marlene sat down on the edge of the bed. The dog, which had been yapping continuously, a steady, idiotic, nerve-scraping noise, now decided to bite Marlene on the ankle. She trod delicately on its little paw. It yelped and ran under the bed, and then the two of them had to get under the bed and chivy the creature out and calm it, or actually Kelsie did the calming while Marlene sat and tried to control her irritation.

When quiet had been restored, Marlene said, "Look, Kelsie, your manager called us for a threat assessment. We did the assessment and sent it in. No response. Have you read it?"

"No, man. Petey handles that end."

"Kelsie, I'm sorry, but Petey can just about handle ordering coffee. And maybe he can pick you up and get you through a crowd at a club, and scare off a drunk trying to hit on you. But you're under at least one serious stalking threat, and you need serious protection."

"Oh, shit, man! Pete's been with me since the day."

"Fine, keep him around. My point is you need a pro in here. I could have someone assigned today, write up a plan, staff you up . . ." Marlene stopped. Solette was shaking her head.

"I don't know. You mean like a stranger? Being here all the time?"

"Well, yeah . . ."

"Uh-huh. No, that sucks. This is my home, you know? I don't want people I don't know hanging."

She's worried about the drugs and the sex, thought Marlene. People leaking stuff to the tabloids. "Our people are very well trained and completely confidential," Marlene said primly.

"I mean, if it was you, that would be different." Solette turned on her for the first time the famous smile, which, helped by a growly voice and a good deal of body language, had generated a sheaf of platinum records and a megahit movie.

Marlene's smile in return was unenthusiastic. "Sorry, I don't do that kind of work anymore. You're a couple of years late."

Solette leaned forward on the bed. "You used to, I heard. You shot a bunch of creeps."

"I did. I gave it up."

"Why? I'd love to shoot Coleman."

"You might think that," said Marlene, "but, believe me, girl, it's not like in the movies. At least it wasn't for me. And eventually I screwed up, and a woman got killed. So I hung up the gun." She waited for this to be absorbed and then added, "Meanwhile, what are we going to do about your problem?"

A buzzer sounded in the apartment. Marlene said, "That's your coffee. Or some nut, one."

Solette was chewing her finger. Now she looked about twelve. "Now you got me all freaked. I have to think about this, talk to people . . ."

Marlene made the usual arguments at this point, but she could see that they were not biting into the stubbornness that was often associated with the sort of determination that made stars. At last she rose, pulled a card case from her packet, and left it on the dresser. "No problem. There's my private number. You call me anytime." Marlene extended her hand, and the singer took it in one that was bed-warm and unpleasantly moist at the fingertips. Marlene left then, declining the coffee and Danish offered by the feckless bodyguard, feeling vaguely stupid and wrong-footed. The moronic disguise! What was she doing running security checks? She had a dozen people to do things like that. She suppressed a familiar irritation, familiar to people who do work that they are good at and find profitable, but do not truly love.

After Lucy Karp left the settlement at the rail yards, she walked to Holy Redeemer and helped prepare and serve the evening meal. She did this once or twice a week. Formerly, she did the same service at Old St. Patrick's on Mulberry, but she thought they needed her more at HR. The clients were lower on the food chain than the ones at St. Pat's, many of whom had actual homes. Redeemer picked up most of the people who used to live in Penn Station and who now clung precariously to life in the shrinking zone of nongentrified Chelsea and the grates and doorways of the Midtown West Side.

Or so she told herself. As she prepped, stirred, served, she kept looking around, as if for something forgotten. This meal had netted forty or so people, mostly men, but a few women, now eating at half a dozen trestle tables. Paper tablecloths were on the tables and real dishes and cutlery and napkins and slightly wilted overage flowers. The nuns who ran the place believed that the main function of a soup kitchen was not soup per se, but civilization, something a lot harder for the homeless to obtain on the island of Manhattan than mere food. Lucy believed this, too, and acted the part of hostess, making conversation with the insulted and injured, exhibiting good table manners, and feeling, generally, like a complete fool. No one seemed to notice that she felt utterly unsuited to the work, a fraud. She was, she knew, not nearly as good as people believed her to be, was a wretched thing, in fact, selfish, a hypocrite.

What she really wanted to do, all the time, and exclusively, was study languages. She accepted helping the miserable as an obligation of her faith and envied the nuns who appeared to take positive joy in it. Envy was, of course, a sin; but pride was a worse one, and she knew she drooped with pride; it oozed disgustingly from every pore. Unique in the world, as everyone kept telling her. People at the lab, scientists visiting from all over, from Europe, Asia, astounded scholars, all wanted a chance to peer into her brain, a waiting list a yard long, as for a particle accelerator or a radio telescope; it held, they thought, the secret of language. No wonder it swelled a girl's head. A good thing, too, she was an ugly geek, or she would have become some monster of ego, like a rock star, cut off from God. But, no, the whole *point* was that this muttering, filthy derelict across from her was also unique, just as loved by God. Why couldn't she, even for one instant, pull her mind away from the boil of three dozen languages and the lure of the other three thousand, word and nuance, idiom and tone, and the bottomless mystery of grammar? And there he was.

Lucy felt her face color as it always did, and she was ashamed, as she always was, and turned away to refill a tray of bread from the bin in the kitchen. When she came back to the dining area, he was among the guys, talking it up, spreading light and laughter. She paused by the doorway to spy on him. Tall, nearly six feet, and thin, dressed in his winter costume, a cheap, fake-fleece denim jacket and jeans, and his red muffler and Broncos wool cap. Nothing special to look at, most people would have said—a bony, mobile face, a long nose, pink at the tip from the chill outside, dirty-blond, ear-length hair, and blue-gray eyes that made her want to wet her pants when he looked at her. And looking, she thought, as she always did, stupid, stupid, although that did not keep her from making calculations, seventeen minus twenty-six was . . . so when she was twenty-five, he'd be . . . no, *stupid!*

Lucy had never had a big crush before. She went to a girls' school; she didn't have a social life to speak of, a couple of close friends, all as geeky as she, a social status at school so low that people speaking to her at lunch had to be disinfected by trained technicians before they could speak to anyone else. The people she met up at the lab where she spent the rest of her spare time just wanted to talk about her Wernicke's Area or stem affixes in Old Slavonic.

David Grale. How often had her pen, poised to take down some flaccid fact in chemistry or American history, slid into those lovely characters and outlined them, made them 3-D, shadowed and crosshatched them, adorned them with vines and ivy, placed them in hearts, before she'd ripped the sheets into tiny, tiny pieces, as she quaked with shame! And did it again.

He was talking to a man called Airshaft—so-called because some malformation had placed two symmetrical, squarish dents in his temples—and with Ralphie and Desmondo, from the yards. As she stepped forward and put out the new bread, Ralphie caught sight of her and waved, and then David Grale looked up and smiled and motioned her over.

She smiled back in a controlled, sophisticated way and started to stroll casually over, whereupon a schizo sitting at the table she was passing jerked back his chair, tripping her, and she went headlong onto the floor. She was considering crawling under one of the tables and closing her eyes until everyone left, and later inventing a story about narcolepsy, when she felt a hand on her arm, and it was he helping her to her feet, a concerned look on his face.

"Are you okay?" Grale asked.

"Yeah, fine. My feet are too big." She laughed harshly, blushed crimson. Perfect.

He sat her down with the other men, leaned back in his chair, waved his hand elegantly, and called out, "Marcel? Another round of cognacs, if you please." And to Lucy: "The service here is terrible lately. You should have seen it in the old days. Champagne flowing like water, the glittering crowds, the true sweetness of life . . . all gone."

Lucy said, "Ah, yes, the baroness was saying much the same thing just the other day. The *caille en sarcophage* were overdone. As for the Kool-Aid . . . barely drinkable. And it's so crowded that no one comes here anymore. Sad, really."

"True. Still, the floor show remains amusing." Grale turned in his chair toward the kitchen doorway. "There's an indefinable appeal about a man carrying a bus box that makes you completely forget Fred Astaire. There's nothing in theater quite like it, don't you find?"

"Except two of them carrying a coffee urn."

Desmondo said, "You guys are nuts," and stood up. "I got to go help a guy put stuff out. You coming, Ralphie?"

Ralphie got up, too, rolling his eyes and shaking his head. They dumped their dirty dishes in a big rubber box and left, followed by Airshaft, who left his lying there. The diners drifted out of the hall. Lucy and Grale sat and talked quietly and inconsequentially, making small jokes and allowing many long silences. It was her favorite time in her entire present life that was not connected with linguistics. Then, as usual, Grale said he had to indulge his only vice, looking up in mock fear as he did so, bobbing his head, as if he expected a celestial censure. It was still dripping outside, so they leaned against the wall under the overhang of the basement entrance, looking out onto Twenty-eighth Street. He smoked, and she smoked to keep him company, although it was not a habit, and she did not really enjoy it after the first aromatic flare.

"So what's the language of the week, Lucy?"

"Gaelic."

"Say something in it."

"You're the most wonderful man in the whole world and I lust after you, body and soul, and may God forgive me," said Lucy in Gaelic.

"Wow! What does that mean?"

"If you don't shut the door, the cat will escape and eat the chickens."

He laughed. "And why Gaelic especially?"

"Oh, we're doing this big project with Harvard linguistics, and Berkeley, too. They want to take me sequentially through the whole Indo-European reach, from Ireland to modern India. They think it'll tell them something about linguistic affinities. Like the closer the languages, the shorter the time to learn, and also they'll be studying my brain in the MRI while I do it." She shrugged. "I sort of wanted to get more into African languages, but they're paying, so . . ."

A cloud had passed over his face. "What's wrong?" she asked.

"Oh, sorry—a little distracted. Tell me more about this project."

"No, really . . . what's wrong?"

"Ernie Whalen. I'm starting to get a little concerned about him. Actually a lot concerned."

"Jingles? What's wrong with him?"

"Nothing, as far as I know. It's just that I haven't seen him in three days. He's not in his usual flops, and people don't recall having seen him. Not even Airshaft, and they usually hang with the same group. So . . ."

"You think something might have happened to him?"

Grale flicked away his cigarette, shook his head. "I don't know. It's a dangerous lifestyle. Funny. These guys, our guys—people think they're all the same, but they're just as different from each other as straight people. I mean except for the actual crazies. Desmondo's an entrepreneur. If he were white, and educated, and laid off the crack for a while, he'd be down in the Alley running a dot com."

"Ralphie would be vice president for public relations."

"Right. Real Ali would be a professor of comp lit at NYU," said Grale, laughing.

"What would Canman be? An artist? Or an engineer?"

Grale frowned. "Oh, Canman. You still hanging around with him?"

"I saw him today. He seemed worse than usual. Nasty."

"He's always nasty."

"Not like this. He's scared. I think it's the killer. He's thinking about leaving, going down to the tunnels."

"Is he?" Grale sighed. "Maybe he'll find peace there." A thin smile. "Sometimes it's hard to love them the way I should. I am further from perfection than I would wish."

"Oh, stop it! You do more than anyone else."

"But it's never enough. The poor you have always with you, always, always, always." He lit another cigarette. "Sorry. I'm tired. I just have walked ten miles today. I'm *really* worried about Jingles."

"What, you think . . . ?"

"It's a possibility. This guy, whoever's doing it, he can't, you know, be a stranger, like those kids a couple of years back who were squirting lighter fluid and setting guys on fire. Nobody's seen any strangers around and, believe me, I've asked. I'm starting to think the worst."

"You mean it's one of the guys?"

Grale nodded. "It could be. And it can't be one of the nutcases either. If it were, they'd be walking around with blood all over them, holding the knife and talking to the Martians. No, this bastard is smart, and well-organized, with a grudge against the world and a place to hide. And he gets around, too. There's been one in Chelsea, one up in Clinton, and one under the old highway near the West Village. You're shaking your head, but you got to admit it's a possibility."

"It can't be Canman," said Lucy vehemently. She thought of the man in the paper house that afternoon, the look of fear and rage on his face, the long, shining, sharp blade in his hands.

"I know it's hard to believe someone you like would do horrible stuff like that," said Grale, "but I mean, face facts. You said yourself he was nervous. Maybe that's why."

She was about to protest, but as she looked in his face, she saw he had that look on, what she secretly called his St. Francis face: guileless, kind, humorous, utterly sweet. Irresistible.

"What should we do?" she blurted instead. "Not the cops . . ."

"No, of course not. I'll go find him and talk to him."

He doesn't like you, Lucy thought, but said only, "What if he goes into the tunnels?"

"Oh, that's okay," said Grale easily. "I know the tunnels. I have lots of pals in the tunnels. And look, don't worry. I can't believe he's the one either. But maybe he's scared because he saw something. I'll find out."

5

As he had promised, Karp was waiting on the corner of Grand and Crosby at four-thirty when the bus from St. Joe's pulled up and disgorged his twin sons. He spotted them, they spotted him, and there was that little jolt of love, mixed on this occasion with irritation, which he consciously suppressed. He waved and grinned.

The Karps had never gone in for stupid twin games, such as identical dressing, but their twins had taken differentiation to an extreme. Isaac, called Zak, the elder by two minutes, had already, at eight years, turned into something of a roughneck, hot-tempered, an athlete, and the self-appointed protector of his gentler brother from all save himself. Giancarlo, called Zik (a name he had borne in the days when they were two indistinguishable lumps) only by his brother, was an artist, a musician, and a diplomat of sunny disposition.

"Yo, Daddy," called Giancarlo happily. "Where's Mom?"

"At work."

"Can we get pizza?"

"Of course," said Karp. "How was school?"

"Okay, except Zak got in a fight."

"Shut up, Zik!' yelled Zak, and stalked away up Grand Street. He had the hood of his parka pulled up, and he was walking hunched like a old monk to keep it covering his face. Karp took a couple of steps, grabbed his son by the shoulder, and tipped the hood back, revealing a magnificent shiner.

"You're such a rat, Zik," snarled the malefactor.

"Oh, what were you going to say?" Giancarlo responded. "You walked into a doorknob? You know the school's going to call."

This was true, and it would not be the first time. The kid got into fights. The parent-advice columns were unanimous that this was not a good thing. Karp himself had not been much of a fighter beyond the usual school-yard scuffles and arguments around games. He was now at something of a loss. As he recalled, his own father had never been involved in any disciplining of Karp and his brothers. And certainly he had never met a school bus. Raising the kids was Mom's job. Karp had on this occasion been obliged to cancel a late meeting, one of those affairs that he had arranged and which would take a week and any number of personal calls to reschedule. Marlene did not have to cancel any of *her* meetings. Marlene was making more money than he did now, by a little. Was that the reason? But he had the more significant career, they both agreed about that, so why wasn't he getting cut some slack there? He loved his family, but still . . . And did he, in fact, have a career? He wasn't DA. He wasn't going to be DA. A couple of years ago he had been DA in all but name, but now there was Norton Fuller snapping at his heels. Fuller was nearly ten years younger and unencumbered by wife and three. Norton was at his desk right this minute, or maneuvering or conniving or cranking out paper, and would be in there long after dark, just as Karp used to. Norton wasn't halfway down the dreaded mommy-track, sitting in a gritty Original Ray's settling an argument about pizza toppings. Down in Karp's subbasement, the Wounded Patriarchy shook off its uneasy sleep and rattled its chains. If you had married someone *normal,* the beast whispered, someone *regular,* you wouldn't have this problem. No one else has this problem. You would have *normal* children . . .

Karp took several long, shuddering breaths, as he had learned to do before foul shots, and whipped the beast back into silence—for the moment.

"So, Zak, you going to tell me what happened?" Karp asked when the pie had been delivered and served out.

"Nothing happened. Derek Rafferty got in my face."

"It was my fault, Daddy," said Giancarlo. "Derek pushed me down and Zak came over. He wasn't even playing with us, and he told Derek not to do it, and Derek socked him, and he socked Derek. Twice. And his nose bled all over. It was like *ER.*"

"Why did Derek push you?"

"Oh, well, we had these tubes? Like paper tubes from Christmas paper, and we were playing samurais with them, bopping each other and yelling 'euuuahggh!' like they do, and talking pretend Japanese and making karate sounds, and I said some real Japanese, like Lucy taught, and Derek said it wasn't real, and I said it was, and my sister could speak Japanese perfectly, and he said I was like BSing, and we yelled and then he made his eyes, you know, slanty with his fingers, and he said 'Karp's sister is a Jap, Karp's sister is a Jap.' And I put my tube down, and I said if he was going to be a racist and insult my family, he could bite it, and he called me a faggot and I walked away, and he came up behind me and pushed me down. And then Zak came over."

"*He's* the faggot," added Zak.

"Let's not use language like that, Zak," said Karp, eyeing the crowded restaurant for flapping ears.

"Well, he *is!*"

"Really. Do you happen to know what the word means?"

A brief look was exchanged between the brothers, a microburst of raw information. Karp simply *knew* that whatever science might say, these two particular little people communicated telepathically. Giggles first, the pair growing and feeding on each other, then helpless laughter, Coke squirting through nostrils.

"Homosexual," Zak got out at length. The boys were leaning against one another in the booth, shaking and blowing bubbles.

"And what's a homosexual, hm?" Karp asked.

Giancarlo said, "It's a boy"—giggle giggle giggle—"who likes . . . *dolls and dresses* and stuff."

"I see. And do you have any evidence that this Rafferty likes dolls and dresses? And stuff?"

"He does, but it's secret," said Giancarlo, sitting up, with the crazy art-light agleam in his eyes. "He has this secret room, like in his house, that he built into his closet, and he goes in there at night, after dinner, and there are shelves and shelves full of dolls and dollhouses, and he goes in there and takes off his regular clothes and puts on a pink dress and white tights and those little shiny shoes with buckles and a curly blond wig and plays with his dolls, and he has a Quake demo going on his computer so his family won't know. One day his little sister finds out because so many of her dolls are missing; she sneaks into his room and finds out his secret, and he realizes he will have to kill her . . ."

More hilarity, and it went on in this vein for the rest of the pizza, with Zak adding particularly gory edits from the side. When the narrative had descended into irretrievable silliness, Karp said, "I appreciate that you want to stick up for your brother, but I think from now on you should let Giancarlo fight his own battles."

"He can't fight," Zak said.

"I can, too," said the other disdainfully. "I just don't *choose* to."

"You have to fight sometimes," said Zak.

"Yeah, but not about brain-dead dumb stuff. Did you fight a lot when you were in school, Daddy?"

"Oh, I guess the usual amount. Some kid shoves you, so you shove back, and you're rolling around on the street. But I wasn't a menace to society like some people I know."

"He means you," said Giancarlo.

"I *know*, dummy!"

"Idiot!"

"Faggot!"

After a barely perceptible instant they both burst into laughter. Karp picked up the last slice and thought, there's too much Marlene in the mix there. He could almost see those sensible, solid, simple Karp genes fighting what had to be a losing battle. Of *course* his twins would turn out to be like no twins he had ever heard of, unique probably, like his sad and unique little girl. He sighed around the pepperoni and resigned himself yet again to love that passeth mere understanding.

"How're the boys?" asked the mother, when she ambled in at seven-thirty. Father and daughter were on a disreputable red velvet couch, watching television.

"They're killing monsters in their room," said Karp, looking up. "I was going to put them down after this movie, but now Mommy can do it."

She ducked out and returned five minutes later, changed into faded jeans and a cotton sweater, holding a generous tumbler of red wine in her hand.

"Working late again, dear?" Karp asked sweetly. "Or is it *him?*"

"Oh, *him!* I'm glad you think I have any time for dalliance. Actually,

it was a woman. What are you watching? Oh, the end of *The Graduate*."
Marlene slid into a slot on the couch next to Karp. "Yes, indeed, the dear,
dead sixties. Are you sure Lucy should be watching this?"

"She hates it," said Karp.

"Well, yeah," said the girl. "I can't believe people liked this
garbage. It's practically a commercial for stalking. I mean the girl finds
out he's having sex with her *mother* and tells him to get lost, and he
keeps coming around, and then he breaks into the church and inter-
rupts the ceremony, and what? *She goes away with him?* Give me a
break!"

"It's romance, dear," said Marlene, although had she been entirely
honest with herself, she would have agreed that the film made her feel a
little creepy, too.

"Oh, right! Would *you* go out with him if he'd slept with your
mother?"

"Well, actually, Dustin and Mom dated for a while, but I don't think
they ever went all the way, so I really can't judge. How was school?"

"Mercifully brief. I ditched class after I played ball with Dad."

Marlene made a gesture of despair. "Oh, terrific. Fifteen grand a
year!"

"I'll pay you back every penny."

Karp said, "That's not the point, as you well know. You're supposed
to go to school. You're a kid. If you're having trouble, tell us and we'll try
to fix it."

"Nothing's wrong. It's just boring."

"School is *supposed* to be boring," said Marlene. "That's why they
call it school."

Karp gave his wife a sharp look. "Thank you, dear. That was helpful.
Seriously, Luce . . ."

"Seriously? Seriously, I hate it. I hate the kids. I mean, like I have a lot
in common with a bunch of girls who worry about their nails and what
clubs they're going to bust into, and what kind of sex they're having with
whom, and who eat ice cubes for lunch to stay thin. I have no friends.
People go out of their way to dis me in the hall. The teachers hate me . . ."

"That's not true."

"It is. They want kiss-butts or girls who are terrifically rich and polite
even if they're totally stupid."

"Oh, I think you're exaggerating, but nevertheless . . ."

Lucy let out a sharp breath and nodded. "Right. You're right. I'll try not to ditch too much anymore. But . . . you know, sometimes the whole thing . . . I just need a break."

Karp knew very well, actually. He patted Lucy's hand and said, "Okay. Sure."

Marlene asked, "So where were you all day? You look like you just got in."

"Out. Around. I served at Redeemer's for the dinner. And then I was with David the rest of the time."

"Oh, David again? When are we going to get a look at this guy?"

Lucy shrugged. "He's real busy."

"I'm sure. Meanwhile, I'm having some serious problems with you spending so much time with him, especially when you're supposed to be in school. I think you should cut down."

"Why? You'd be in heaven if I were *dating* all the time. Then it would be fine. You wouldn't care *what* I did if it was with some rich dork from Collegiate or St. X's."

"One, I would care, and that's insulting. And, two, the point is this guy is what, twenty-eight, twenty-nine?"

"He's not that old."

"Okay, but he's a grown man. And despite your talents, you're only seventeen. You've got no business spending all your time with a drifter ten years older than you who you don't know anything about."

"He's not a drifter. He's a Catholic aid worker. He lives in the Catholic Worker hostel. He's been to all the bad places. He was in Bosnia. He was in Sudan and Burundi. He's just recuperating here so he can go off to some other god-awful place."

"So he says. People can say anything about their past."

To avert the detonation he could feel approaching, Karp said lightly, "Where I would draw the line is if he had L-O-V-E and H-A-T-E tattooed on the backs of his fingers. And of course, if he wasn't a Yanks fan . . ."

Both of the females ignored this. Marlene said, "And all this homeless business. Okay, you want to go to a church basement and prepare a meal, that's one thing. But wandering into God knows what alley with all kinds of deranged people at all hours—I think that's completely out of line for someone your age. I mean I've been concerned, but I haven't said anything until now, and if you're starting to cut school to do it, well, I'm sorry. I think it's starting to be perverse. You have to stop."

Lucy shot to her feet. "I'm not going to listen to this . . . *wu zhi ji tan!* How can you call yourself a Catholic?"

"Oh, excuse me? I'm going to be told how to practice my religion now?"

"Girls, girls . . ." said Karp.

Lucy stalked off, muttering in foreign tongues. It was a peculiarity of hers that she never used bad language in English, although she could, and often did, scorch paint in any number of others.

Slam!

"Well, dear, you handled that well," said Karp after a short interval.

"She wants to kill me. She won't be satisfied until she's dancing the fandango on my grave."

"She loves you so much she can't see straight," said Karp. Marlene started to say something but stopped and instead finished her glass of wine. Karp muted the television, and they sat for some time in the flickering dark. The film ended and people sold stuff at them, silently mugging the virtues of shining things, and then the news came on.

"Unmute it," said Marlene. They watched the lead story. Richard Perry, a wealthy former congressman from New Jersey, had been kidnapped along with his party of six by unknown persons somewhere in the Balkans, where he had been engaged in a humanitarian mission. They showed some film of Perry posing with a famous photographer and a famous writer, a woman long dedicated to lost causes, in front of a white Land Rover on a muddy mountain road. Then the grave faces of the news team, male and female, the male one giving out that no group had claimed credit for the outrage, that the president, a close friend, had expressed shock. Then the human side—Perry's wife and two young children ducking in the glare of TV lights outside their New York apartment, while a mob shoved little boxes and boom mikes at them.

"Shit!" said Marlene. "Oh, shut it off!"

Karp did. "It's a dangerous place."

"Yeah, but, not to be self-centered, he's also a client of ours. I think we're providing security for that trip. Oleg must be throwing up. Christ, they'll probably delay this goddamn IPO now, and we'll have to go through the whole thing again from scratch."

"Well, now that you're in such a good mood," Karp said, "I should tell you that Zak got into another fight today."

"Oh, for the love of Christ! Is he okay?"

"A shiner. I spoke to him sternly. He was protecting Giancarlo, which I thought was at least mildly exculpatory, but I suggested to him that a quick trigger for violence was not a successful life strategy in the long run."

"Is that a sly dig, my sweet?"

"Not at all, my angel," replied Karp with a straight face. "You're a responsible corporate executive and a model of civility. Who was the woman, by the way?"

"What woman?"

"The one who kept you from the bosom of your family until the middle of the night."

"Oh, *that* one. It was Sybil Marshak, as a matter of fact."

"No kidding? What did she want?"

"She . . ." But at that moment the boys arrived and swarmed their mother, full of the news, questions, arguments, stupid riddles, and small-boy presence, demanding and tender. She dispensed maternal being for half an hour and then rousted them off to bath and bed, at which time they both regressed five years, as they usually did, and she indulged herself in the hidden romance, her chief joy nowadays, truth to tell, and all the sweeter for the knowledge that it would not last much longer. She stroked, she talked, she read from the current favorite (*The Hobbit),* she answered the questions that baffled the great thinkers, about death, heaven, God, and kissed them good-night, whispering into their ears her secret name for each, which, she thought, they had not ever shared, not even with each other.

By the time she was through, Karp was in bed. She undressed and climbed in with him.

"You were saying?"

"Was I? Oh, right: Sybil Marshak. You know who she is, obviously."

"Runs the West Side Dems."

"Yeah. The last person I expected to see. You ever meet her?"

"Just to handshake, and to receive compliments on my extraordinary physical beauty. Jack and she are fairly close. It's hard to get on a state ticket under the D. column without Sybil. What did she want?"

"She says she's being stalked."

"Stalked, huh? Those damn Republicans!"

"Hot flashes, more likely."

"It's not legit?"

"I don't know yet, but it doesn't look like a serious case. There's no specific guy involved, just feelings, doors slamming in the parking garage, phone calls that hang up, seeing the same person on the street at the same time every day. No letters, no recordings, no physical evidence at all . . ."

"What, she's nuts?"

"I wouldn't go that far. If you rub my back, I'll be your friend for life. . . . Oh, thank you. Great." After silence interrupted by sighs of pleasure, talking into the pillow. "Anyway we get people in there a lot, in VIP, mostly women, I'm sorry to say, but some men, too. Famous, right? Rich. They're not supposed to *have* any problems. But actually they're under a lot of stress. Okay, they got the pills, they got the therapist, they got the sex and the toys. But still there's this panic—'Oh, am I worthy, oh, will I lose it all?' And eventually it comes out. They go agoraphobic, or they can't fly in planes anymore, or they get all compulsive. Sometimes it comes out in paranoia, which is what I think we got here."

"So what did you tell her?"

"I said we'd watch her for a couple of days, a week, see if anything jumped out. I also advised her to get rid of her gun."

"Sybil Marshak packs heat?"

"Unfortunately, yes. Got a license and everything, which is no surprise: she could get a city license to do pedophilia in public. I tried to convey to her the downsides of firearms, accidents and so forth, but she's a hardhead. She really thinks someone's after her. She insisted I take care of her personally."

"Which you refused."

"Which I accepted. It struck me today that if I don't get out of the office once in a while, I am going to go batshit."

"No guns, right?"

"Oh, put a cork in it! No, all's I'm going to do is watch her back for a day or so, with a light team, see if I see any characters hanging around her I don't like. I'll put a trace on her phone, too, talk to her building—the usual. Min Dykstra can run the place perfectly well for a couple of days, I mean the bureaucratic stuff, and it'll make Lou happy. He likes me to mingle with the great and near great."

"Speaking of greatness, when is this stock thing coming off?"

"Oh, I don't want to talk about it!" Marlene groaned. "In fact, technically, I'm not *allowed* to talk about any of it. Ha! I love when the law demands behavior I would do anyway. Virtue without pain." Some silence here.

"Is that still my back you're rubbing?" she asked with a small gasp.

"Not technically, no."

The following morning, whatever good mood Karp had brought to the day from the high jinks of the previous night was dissipated by the news Murrow brought.

"He can't be serious," said Karp.

"Apparently he is. The grand jury is scheduled for tomorrow. My new friend Flatow intends to waltz in there, call Cooley, call Nash, call the guy from the ME, and that's it. No homicide investigators."

"Did you ask him why?"

"In a roundabout way. He said Catafalco told him that it would be a waste of time because it would just confirm the testimony of the two officers."

"Oh, Christ! Did you get the report?"

"No, Flatow just had the precis from headquarters. Apparently he handed it over to Catafalco and hasn't seen it since."

"And he didn't think it was important enough to ask for?"

"Um, not really. George is a follow-orders kind of guy. A stamp collector, by the way. He has a nearly complete set of British Empire Trinidad and Tobago." Murrow vamped extreme ennui. "Tell me I don't have to keep hanging out with him."

"If you didn't want to be bored shitless, you shouldn't have become a lawyer."

"I'm sorry—everything I know I learned from TV. Who are you calling?"

"Catafalco," said Karp, punching a speed-dial button. He waited. Murrow heard: "Butch Karp. Is Lou in? . . . Yes, I would. . . . Lou? . . . Yeah, fine. Look, Lou, on that Cooley thing, do you think you could shoot the homicide report on that over to me? . . . Because I want to read it, Lou. . . . Uh-huh. . . . *Fuller* is handling it? What does that mean, Fuller is handling it? . . . Uh-huh. Yeah, I see. Okay, Lou, right. I understand. . . . Uh-huh. Right, talk to you later." Slam of the phone. "Fuck!"

"Uh-oh," said Murrow.

"Uh-oh is right." Karp knitted his hands behind his head and leaned back in his tall judge's chair. After a minute or so of silence, during which his assistant could practically see the gears whirling behind his eyes, Karp said, "Murrow, this is an interesting situation. My colleague Mr. Fuller has informed one of our fine bureau chiefs that all matters to do with the appearance of Detective Cooley before the grand jury are to be referred to him and to no one else. The question I put to you is, what is my play in response?"

Murrow waited a beat to see whether this was a rhetorical question. Karp's gaze told him it was not. He answered, "Well, in the first place, it's a big incursion on your authority. You're chief for operations, he's chief for admin. This is clearly part of an operation, so—"

"But is it? Public relations comes under admin. Cooley's is a case that might have a major impact on the office's public image. And the DA's political future. Not a bright line, at least not to Fuller."

"Then you should go to the DA, grab up Fuller, and duke it out."

"Okay, but think how that would play. I go in there whining that Catafalco's keeping the homicide report to himself because Fuller told him to. Fuller smiles his rat smile and says, 'Oh, Butch, I didn't mean *you*. Of course, *you* can read it. I just didn't want to read about it in the papers until the legal process is complete. I mean, grand jury proceedings are supposed to be secret, aren't they? I'm trying to control copies,' and so on and so forth. So I look like a turf-covering whiner, and I wasted the DA's time, one; and, two, suppose I do look at the homicide report and I say, 'Whoa, this is a fishy shooting.' What happens then?"

"You pull the case off the schedule until we figure out how to handle it."

"Uh-huh, but that lands us back in the DA's office again. Now we have to look at the DA's motivation."

"Which is . . . ?"

"Ah, now you have me. What is, in fact, going on in the tortured soul of Jack Keegan? Here we have a confident and talented public figure, a man who aspires to greatness. Unfortunately, he spent his formative years under the influence of a man who was undeniably great, and who had what was basically a very simple soul. Francis P. Garrahy just knew what was right and just did it. He wasn't perfect, of course; maybe sometimes he wasn't even right. But when he *did* decide that something was right, he had absolutely no doubt about what to do. Jack isn't like that. He lives in a world that's a lot more complex than the one Garrahy lived in, and it worries him. And he's ambitious in a way that Garrahy never was. Garrahy thought that just being the best district attorney in the history of the world was a pretty good deal. Jack wants to sit on the Supreme Court someday, and it colors his every decision. Be warned, Murrow: if you want a pure heart, eschew ambition."

"Like you?"

"We're not talking about me, though," said Karp a little sharply. "So . . . Jack is serving two masters—his sense of decency that he learned at Phil Garrahy's knee, and the demon ambition. As we're in an election year, the demon has got a lot more power, which is why Norton Fuller is being jacked up to his present influence. Jack wants to think that because he's got me in there, the great traditions of the office are being maintained, and meanwhile Fuller will handle the dirty jobs, with Jack sort of not knowing what's going on."

"You think Mr. Keegan is in on this business with Cooley?"

"Good question. He's in but not in. Fuller would never throw his weight around with Catafalco like he's doing unless he thought he had backing from Jack. But Jack hasn't actually told him to do anything. He doesn't need to. Fuller's skill is knowing when Jack needs faintly stinky stuff done on his behalf *without* having to be told. Okay, now let's say I go in there and say, 'Jack, this grand jury case is fucked—the shooting stinks.' Fuller then says, 'That's a matter of opinion, Jack, but what's sure as God's green apples is that if we come down hard on Cooley, we will lose the police unions, and the election.' Jack turns his noble head and looks at me. Now, what's my play?"

"I have no idea."

"Then listen and be enlightened. I have two alternatives. One, I can let Fuller roll me, which would mean he could roll me at will in the future, which means that my usefulness to Jack and this office would be at an end. Or I could say, 'Jack, if you do this, I will resign in protest, go to the press, make a stink.' In which case, I'm out of a job I can do better than anyone else on the horizon, and which Jack and the office badly needs. So for me, and for what I still pretend are the higher values of the New York DA, it's lose-lose. This was a conclusion also arrived at by the nuclear powers. I have the H-bomb, but I don't use it. It gives me status and leverage, but not control. And therefore . . . ?"

"And therefore you will avoid such a confrontation."

Karp grinned. "Very good, Murrow. We'll make a conspirator of you yet."

"My boyhood dream. Meanwhile, what do we do?"

"Oh, I'll think of something. But before I get any further into it, I need to get my hands on that report. Make it happen."

Sybil Marshak lived in the Wyoming, a famous pile of rococo white limestone on Central Park West in the Eighties. Marlene picked up the surveillance a little after four, having spent the day flashing false smiles at a covey of investment bankers, literally on Wall Street. The Osborne agent was Wayne Segovia, a sharp, dark, wiry man with a neat spade beard. When Marlene walked up to his car, he was smoking a cigarillo and doing crossword puzzles in a pulp crossword magazine.

"What's a five-letter word meaning 'black,' starts with an *s*?" he asked when she slipped into the car, an anonymous gray Honda. On the front seat was a big Nikon with a Polaroid back and a 500mm lens on it.

"Try *sable*," said Marlene. "Anything doing?"

"Just snapping citizens." He indicated an envelope full of Polaroid photos on the dashboard. "So far nothing stands out. I was hoping for a guy with long hair and fangs carrying a 'Death to Marshak' sign, but no."

"She go out?"

"Once. Hopped a cab to a hair salon on Sixty-third and Madison, got a rinse and set. I would've gone with a lighter color, bring out her eyes a little."

"We'll put that in the report. Anything interesting?"

"Not that I could see. But this is a damn stupid way to check for stalkers."

"Yeah, it is, but humor me for a couple of days. Anything on the phone?"

A black electronic device was on the backseat, with a coiled lead that ran into a plug in Segovia's ear. "Just the usual. She gets a lot of calls. Makes a lot, too. If I was her, I wouldn't be so casual about using a cordless to make them, considering the kind of political stuff she's into."

"I could mention that, too. Most people don't realize how easy it is to steal off a cordless." Marlene popped the door. "I think I'll go up and talk to the building staff."

She did so. The doorman on duty said he had noticed nothing, heard nothing about any stalker. He assured Marlene that no one could get into the building without being checked out. Every visitor had to be announced. It was a good building. Marlene thought it was a good building and, like all buildings, was about as secure as Central Park if anyone really wanted to get in. Kelsie Solette's building was a good building, too. She did not say that, however, but went into the bowels of the basement to interview the janitorial staff and the super, who also assured her of the goodness, etc.

When she emerged into daylight again, she found that Wayne was standing outside the car waving wildly. She trotted across Central Park West.

"What's up?"

"She's in her car, heading south."

They both jumped into the Honda, and Wayne screeched into a U-turn.

"Why the car? Why not a cab?"

"Maybe she wants to park and neck," he said. "Maybe she's going out of town. There she is, the Lexus."

By running a light at Seventy-seventh, Wayne had slid into convenient trailing range of the black Lexus. They followed it down to Broadway and Fifty-fifth, where the car hung a right and disappeared into an underground parking garage.

They pulled into a loading zone across the street. A building was being renovated two doors down. The sound of riveters and metal bashing made it hard to converse. "What now?" shouted Wayne.

"Use our highly trained mental powers to intuit where she's going and whether anyone there is plotting to harass her."

Wayne chuckled. "Ah, boss, I wish I had you along every day. Meanwhile, what's a Siberian river, two letters?"

"Ob," she replied as her phone warbled. She thumbed it, announced herself, stuck a finger in the other ear, listened.

"Doesn't fit," said Wayne. "I think it ends with *k.*"

"Agh!" Marlene cried.

"Ag? Nah, no good. I said it ends with . . ." He stopped because she was talking rapidly into the phone, snapping out directions to someone, promising to arrive at a place.

She thumbed off the phone and thrust it back into her bag, cursing softly.

"What's up, chief?"

"Oh, nothing—my daughter is involved in a murder again." She met his eyes, gaped, made a shrill sound edged with hysteria. "Not a sentence we hear much, do we? Especially the 'again' part."

"She's not . . . ?"

"Oh, no, nothing like that. She hangs around with a class of people who tend to get their throats ripped out more than your average taxpayer, and apparently it was her turn to find one today. I should go."

"You want me to drive you?"

"No, I'll hop a cab. I might have to scream my head off a little while, and I don't want to embarrass myself in front of the staff."

With that she got out of the car and was just about to cross the driveway of an underground garage when a squeal of tires and the roar of a powerful engine made her hesitate. She saw the Lexus race up the ramp. It was moving so fast it actually flew for a part of a second when it crossed the drainage depression at the ramp entrance, then crashed down heavily on its springs. It missed her by a foot, and she had barely a glimpse of Sybil Marshak's pale face as the car hung a screeching left and accelerated down the street.

Marlene went back to the car. "What the hell was that all about?"

"A sale at Bloomingdale's?" offered Wayne Segovia.

"Follow her, wise guy. Call me on the cell when you get to where she's going."

The Honda zoomed away. Marlene paused and stared for a moment into the entrance to the garage. What had frightened Marshak so much that she had driven her car without really looking into a New

York street, a maneuver that nine times out of ten would have resulted in a crash? It was only the construction vehicles parked to the east that had slowed the traffic enough to make the rapid exit and turn possible. Something real or a phantom of the mind? Marlene turned and walked back toward Broadway, a cab, and her daughter. One crazy person at a time was her thought.

La Pelouse, Karp knew, was one of the remarkably many places in the city where lunch cost in the neighborhood of a hundred dollars without tips or drinks. It was on Sixty-fifth off Lexington, a frosted-glass window with the name in gold script on it, and a shiny black door under a stubby black awning. He had never been there, since he was an old-fashioned boy and thought a hundred dollars was still real money, an amount that if you lost it on the street would make you cranky all week.

Inside, past the tiny entrance lobby and the funereal maître d', was a plain, dove-gray room with white trim, lit by white plaster sconces, in which eighteen tables sat like altars, and a long banquette occupied the left wall. Every table was occupied. As he followed the maître d', Karp noted the famous faces—big-time movie stars, a network anchor—and thought that, among the more anonymous diners, nearly every name would be associated with some profitable large enterprise. Shelly Solotoff was sitting at a banquette, with a cell phone pressed to his ear. When he spotted Karp, he smiled, waved, moved the phone to his other hand, extended his right for a shake without rising, cupped the mouthpiece, said, "Butch—long time! Want a drink? I'll be done in a sec."

Karp sat and studied the man as he talked. A big man, not as tall as Karp but heavier, a lot heavier than he had been when the two of them had worked at the DA. His hair was dark, medium long, with an attractive whitening at the sides. It had the perfection that expensive barbering and skillful hair-weaving provided. The face was tan, as if he had just come in from the yacht. He looked good, in the manner of male models. Karp checked out the eyes and jowls for signs of plastic surgery and thought he detected that slight Ken-doll stiffening of the underlying muscles. Solotoff caught him looking and gave a little wink. His eyes were large, knowing, and bright brown. His suit was made of a kind of shimmery gray stuff that Karp knew was Italian and expensive, and which Karp would not have worn to a masked ball. The tie was metallic bronze, over a stiff-collared shirt of white silk with little monograms on the French cuffs. Patek Philippe watch, cuff links . . . yes, he could have guessed, tiny gold scales set into onyx.

Solotoff shifted the phone again. "No, no, Charlie, no jail time *at all,*" he was saying now. "The deal sucks. . . . Right. . . . No, they can't use that evidence, Charlie. . . . No, trust me on this. . . . Yeah, I'll call him after lunch. I got to go, Charlie. . . . Right. Okay, I'll be in touch."

Solotoff smiled and shook his head as he switched off the phone. "My local counsel. Case in Connecticut. The usual, preppy selling E to his buddies. Bad search, but Charlie, the guy's a nervous Nellie. You know who the father is?"

Karp admitted he did not, and Solotoff told him the name of a former U.S. senator.

"That what you do now, Shelly? Dumb rich kid dope cases?"

"Pays the rent. How about you? Still stocking the jails with dumb poor kids?"

Karp shrugged, put on a social smile. "I didn't write the law."

"An unworthy cop-out. Unworthy of you, I mean. Typical of the average DA."

A waiter appeared, bearing menus a yard long. Solotoff waved his away. "Jules, just tell Cyril to make me one of his truffle omelettes. He knows what I like. And an avocado salad and a bottle of Vichy."

Karp opened the menu briefly, folded it, and handed it back to the waiter. "I'll have a corned beef on rye and a kasha knish. And an orange soda."

The waiter goggled for an instant, looked nervously at Solotoff, then donned a condescending smile at m'sieu's little drollery. Karp said, "Tell Cyril to make me another one, easy on the truffles. And the rest the same, too."

The man wafted away.

"Wow," said Solotoff, "a long time. What is it, fifteen years?"

"About that. You're looking good. Wealth suits you."

"You know, I think it does. I'm amazed, frankly, that you're still there. I heard that you left for downtown a while ago. And you went back?"

"Jack asked me to do homicide, and I went for it."

"But then you got blown out of the job. Some race thing?"

"Yeah. A long story. People were carrying signs, 'Ku Klux Karp.' It was just one of those New York things. Jack hid me in staff for a while, and now I'm chief assistant."

Solotoff was shaking his head. "Unbelievable! How can you stand it with all those lames up there?"

"Not all that lame. Roland's still there. You remember Roland? I'd put him up against anyone in the country in a courtroom, on a homicide."

"Oh, right, Roland! The blond beast. That's the exception that proves the rule. Is he still pinching secretaries on the ass?"

"Not that he lets me see. We have policies about that now."

"Yeah, I almost forgot the goddamn bureaucracy. And the corruption."

"You going to offer me a job? Or are you just trying to make me feel bad?"

Solotoff laughed, an odd croaking sound without much volume. "A job? Hey, in a New York minute. Just say the word."

"I don't think so."

"Why not? Really."

Shrug. Karp was growing bored with this line. "I guess I just like public service." Lame.

The other man sprang to it. "Oh, please! Public service is for kids. It's postgraduate school—you learn how the system works, how the judges like things, get a little trial practice. But staying in it? It's strictly for losers, man. It's white-collar sanitation work. You clear the darkies off the street so the quality doesn't have to look at them. I mean it's a joke."

"Not necessarily. Laugh if you want to, and I know you want to, but at the end of the day the system's all we have between anarchy and the police state."

A contemptuous snort. "Yeah, that's a Francis P. Garrahy line. I remember it well, the old fraud. Christ! Someone as smart and competent as you—it's like meeting a grown man who still collects baseball cards and plays flip with them."

"Phil Garrahy was a number of things," said Karp, feeling the edge creep into his voice, "but fraud wasn't one of them."

"Oh, give me a break! Mr. Fucking DA! He was in office as long as

Brezhnev and just as sharp there at the end, and even when he had his game, the Mafia controlled half a dozen major industries, all the unions, and Tammany Hall. Corruption was absolutely endemic in practically every city bureau, and virtually every cop in the city was on the pad, during which time Garrahy's greatest achievement was nailing the quiz show scandals."

"We'll have to agree to disagree on that, Shelly."

"What, it's not true? Plus the guy caught the biggest fucking break any DA ever caught—all the years he was in there crime rates were at the lowest in centuries. Which might have been helped by the fact that the cops were running a reign of terror in the less desirable parts of town. You ever notice how you never see a black face in those Times Square photographs from the forties and fifties? Fifth Avenue? Central Park? That's why. Nightstick justice, aided and abetted by you guys back then. Totally corrupt, and based on wholesale police perjury. And don't think it's not still going on."

"I said we'd have to agree to disagree on that," Karp repeated in a tone that did not invite rejoinder. Solotoff locked eyes with him for a long moment, and Karp saw something in them that he could not identify—not fear exactly, but . . . something dark and complex. Then it was gone, and Solotoff laughed again. "Jesus, I had you going there for a while. Still the old grouch . . . good old Butch! Ah, here's our food."

They ate, and the conversation turned small. Sports, political anecdote, the antics of judges, movies, family. Solotoff was on his third wife, a cosmetics-empire heiress, and trophies of the hunt. Solotoff had the big condo on Park, the place in Quogue, membership in the best of the clubs that took Jews. He did most of the talking, he having the best toys. Boasting, sure, but maybe a tone of desperation there underneath? Karp wondered why this fellow was trying to sell a half-stranger his life in this way, or why he was trying to crap on Karp's. But he had determined to get through the wretched meal with good grace and covered adequately his lapses of attention. He found his mind drifting toward the Cooley case, running along in a parallel track that allowed him to utter the required grunts of appreciation, ask the appropriate questions. An idea rose, gelled—a plan, risky but feasible.

They finished. Karp declined the dessert and watched Solotoff line his arteries with crème brûleé. Solotoff made a call on his cell, and when they got to the street, a pearl-gray Lincoln was just gliding up to the curb.

Solotoff shook Karp's hand vigorously and said, "Hey, I was serious a while ago. I hate like hell to see a smart guy like you fucking wasting his time." He lowered his voice "The DA's no place for a *yiddisheh kop, bubeleh,* and you know it. Let the goyim take out the garbage! See you around, pal."

Not if I see you first, thought Karp, but he smiled politely until the car door closed. By the time his own ride showed up, the plan was fairly complete. This is why I'm still at the DA, asshole, was the thought he threw after the retreating limo.

6

AT THE SEVENTEENTH PRECINCT, THE DESK DIRECTED MARLENE TO A detective second grade named Fred Paradisio, whom she found in a typical detective-squad bay of the type that has been described so often that it is as familiar as a suburban bathroom. It smelled of burnt coffee and sadness, and the mingled low-end aftershaves of its inhabitants. Paradisio was a barrel of a man with oily, thinning black locks, and a head disconcertingly wider at the jaw than at the top. He had large, friendly eyes that lied, "Hey, I'm just a slob like you, you can trust me, pal." Marlene identified herself and asked to see her daughter.

"Sure, Mrs. Ciampi," said the detective, "but if we could, I'd like to talk to you a bit first. You want some coffee or a soft drink?"

"I want to see my daughter."

"In a second." He pointed. "Have a chair."

Marlene bobbed her head and sat.

Paradisio settled himself in his swiveler and opened a notebook. "Okay, the situation here is that at two forty-six P.M. today 911 logged a call from your daughter saying that she had found a dead body in a makeshift shelter on a service walkway above the MTA rail yards. She was told to wait for the police. At two fifty-seven, a patrol vehicle arrived at Eleventh and Thirtieth, and the officers descended to the scene described by your daughter. This was a shelter made of newspapers baled together and waterproofed. Apparently there's a kind of homeless hangout under there."

"Yes, I know," said Marlene impatiently.

"Oh, yeah? You're down there a lot, communing with the home-less?"

"No, but she is."

"You mean you let her run down with those people? She's not like a runaway?"

"No, she is not. Detective, what's the point of this? I'd like to see my daughter now."

"Just a second, let me just get through this." He peered again at the notebook. "The officers at the scene entered the newspaper structure and found a black male later determined to be Jerome Watkins, and he was determined to be deceased at the scene. They called it in, and me and my partner proceeded there. We are ruling it a homicide right now, subject to further investigation. We rousted all the other derelicts in the area and found your daughter in a packing-crate structure occupied by a black male named Ali Rashid Kalifa, aka Moses Belton. Belton has a record: armed robbery, assault, larceny. Served a couple of jolts upstate back in the eighties. Did you know about this? Your daughter hanging around with that type of person?"

"Yes."

"You approve of this?"

"Detective, are you investigating my fitness as a parent?"

"Uh-uh, no, what I'm trying—"

"Then get to the point, finish whatever you *are* doing, and let me see my daughter!"

Paradisio looked hurt, in a studied way. "Fine. Your daughter actu-ally found the body. According to this Ali, or Belton, she went and made the call, cool as anything, and then lost it. Ali or Belton said he was com-forting her when we got there. She looked like she'd been crying, as a matter of fact. Okay, let me get to the point here . . ."

"Thank you."

"The structure where the body was found was occupied by a man named John Carey Williams, aka Canman. Williams is a two-fer man. He buys aluminum cans from other homeless and crushes them and trans-ports them to the recycle center. Apparently this person is some kind of special friend of your daughter. We would really like to talk to him."

"You like him for the bum slasher?"

Paradisio's genial-slob persona nearly cracked beneath this unex-

pected remark, but he coughed and recovered. "Gosh, I didn't say anything about the bum slasher. I didn't even say that Watkins was slashed
at all."

"But he was, or you wouldn't be going through this act with me.
What is this, vic number four? Even if he's just taking out lowlifes, you
still got a serial killer on your hands. You think Lucy saw something, or
knows something about this Canman."

"Let's say she hasn't been forthcoming."

"If you would just let me *speak* to her, Detective, I'll let you know
whether she knows anything or not. Or do I have to go all lawyerly on
you now?"

Paradisio did not want lawyerly. Marlene was led to an interview
room, in which she found her daughter with an American-history text
and a notebook open in front of her, calmly doing her homework.

"Well, homework!" said Marlene. "We should get you in jail more
often."

To Marlene's surprise, the girl rose and embraced her and said, "Oh,
I'm so sorry! I mean about yesterday . . . I keep losing my temper at you.
I don't know what gets into me. Demonic forces." Lucy laughed uncon-
vincingly. Marlene held her away and looked her over. She was wearing
her usual uniform: a black sweater over a white shirt, a black wool skirt,
black tights, and some kind of surplus combat boots. There was no color
in her face and her eyes looked bruised.

"You're forgiven. You're a model of filial deportment compared to
the way I acted at your age. Listen, we got us a little problem here."

"I didn't do anything." Wary.

"I know you didn't, but they think for some reason you're withhold-
ing information, and you can't do that. Recall that you're still on proba-
tion from that stunt you pulled last year. You do not want the police cross
with you. Sit down and tell me what happened."

Lucy slumped in her chair and closed her book with a bang. She took
a deep breath and began. "Okay. After school I went to Holy Redeemer
looking for David. He wasn't there, so I scouted around the neighborhood, you know, the homeless hangouts, and then I went down to the
yards. I talked to Real Ali—"

"Excuse me, this is Moses Belton?"

"I don't know about that. I've always called him Ali, or Ali Rashid.

I'm teaching him a little Arabic. He's a Muslim, the regular kind. Anyway, no one else was around, so I looked in Canman's paper house. There was someone on the bed there, and at first I thought it was Canman. He was all covered up with blankets. But then I realized that his dog wasn't there. And I went over and touched him, and I saw that it was Fake Ali. We call him . . . I mean, we *called* him that because he really thought he was the fighter. He was pretty crazy, but harmless, really a very sweet person, except if he thought you were George Foreman. Anyway, I saw he was dead. And . . . I sort of lost it then—I ran back to Ali's and told him, and he calmed me down, and I walked up the block and found a pay phone and called the cops. That's it."

Marlene sighed heavily in the silence after this. "You really have the life, don't you, baby?"

The girl looked away from this sympathy and piled her books into the old musette bag she used. "Yeah. Could we go now?"

"Not quite. The detective out there thinks there's something you're not telling. About this guy Canman. John Carey Williams. He's a friend of yours?"

"Just one of the guys."

"Lucy, darling, now is not the time to be evasive."

Lucy bowed her head and froze. Marlene waited a minute. She could hear her daughter's breath go in and out. Then Lucy said, "I guess I saw him. When I came out of the paper house. He was on the access walk, maybe a hundred yards away, and I saw Maggie. His dog. I yelled at him, but he turned away and ran. I'm sorry. I should have told the cops, but . . ."

"He's a friend of yours. I understand. You know, the cops are starting to like him for the slasher. What do you think?"

"I don't know, Mom!" The tears started to leak. "I don't know *any-thing* anymore. Now, could we *please* go home?"

"You've read this already?" asked Karp, indicating the homicide report on the Lomax shooting. It had arrived four days after he had asked for it, the day the case, assuming all the players could be rounded up, would actually be presented to the grand jury, having been resched-uled from the previous Friday.

"Yeah," said his special assistant.

"What do you think?"

Murrow gathered his thoughts. "I don't know, chief. A couple of cars sliding around on the wet road, bullets flying everywhere . . . I mean, who knows what really happened? The report says the evidence is not inconsistent with the testimony of the officers involved."

"Yeah, but that's like saying the Warren Report is not inconsistent with the evidence they decided to gather and use." Karp tapped the folder on his desk. "There's something funny in this thing. No, two things funny. You know what they are?"

"No, and I'll bet you're going to tell me."

"No, you tell me." Karp opened the folder, splaying out the crime-scene photographs over his desk. "What's wrong with this picture?"

Murrow leafed through them. They were of the Cherokee and the surrounding road, and the unmarked police vehicle. The Cherokee was full of bullet holes, and its left fender and headlamp were smashed. The police unmarked was similarly damaged, with a severe crumpling of the left front and side. That much was clear; the pictures of the road and the side barriers, with chalk marks and tape measures, were more obscure.

"Well, there was a glancing head-on crash of some kind," Murrow ventured. "That confirms the cops' story at least. Lots of bullet holes in the Jeep. You can see where the slugs went through the rear seat. But wait a second . . ." He shuffled through the eight-by-ten glossies. "The windshield has three holes in it. That seems to confirm the police story. I guess I'm stumped on the fishy part."

Karp smiled. "The autopsy, Murrow! Holes in the windshield, but no holes in the front of the vic. Lomax was killed from behind. But I doubt if your pal Flatow is intending to bring that out to the grand jury. The guy had ten bullet wounds in him, with eight bullets recovered. Of those, seven were from Cooley's gun, one from Nash's. Nash must have shot the man after the cars stopped moving because he was driving during the chase and didn't have his gun out. Cooley was shooting from outside the car, too. But, of course, it's impossible to distinguish the shots he took then from the ones he fired during the chase. Like you say, cars whirling around, night, a confused situation. Lomax could have been bouncing around in there, and just by chance all the bullets ended up in his rear."

"Pretty unlikely, don't you think?"

"Very. But we don't build cases on unlikely, especially not with the Blue Wall holding solid. In any case, that's what the grand jury will hear." Karp collected the photographs, stacked them neatly, and returned them to the report folder. "Well, what else is new? A cop does a bad shooting and skates." He seemed lost in thought. Murrow waited a decent interval and asked, "What was the other thing? You said two things were fishy."

"Oh, right. The other thing is we got two experienced cops sitting on a street in the middle of the night waiting for a major collar to go down. They're waiting for a gun dealer, they're going to grab a bunch of automatic weapons—a pretty big deal. Then this car drives by. The officers state that they recognized the vehicle as stolen from a radio report and pursued it, which led to the chase in question and all the shooting."

"That's fishy?"

"Murrow, it's the fishiest thing about this goddamn case. It makes no sense at all. Let's say they made it as hot. Let's say the car belonged to, I don't know, the mayor's favorite aunt. Is it credible to you that they would have left their assigned position in a gun bust they'd been working on for weeks to go chase it? And if they chased it, does it make sense that they would have tried so hard to stop it with gunfire, in clear violation of police department regulations? I mean, where was the win in it for them? Even if they caught the guy, even if the chase didn't result in someone running into a car full of nuns, they were still headed for a gigantic chewing out. You assholes left your post for what? A stolen car? Give me a break! So what was it?"

"They were overtaken by a sudden insane animus against car thieves?"

"Maybe," said Karp, laughing, "but then they would have used the old sudden-insane-animus defense. No, really—it's the key to the whole thing. A fishy shooting is always a pain in the butt, even if it's a lot clearer than this one; you get a cop up there, he says he was in fear of his life, it's hard to prove even manslaughter beyond a reasonable doubt, never mind depraved-indifference murder, unless maybe he put ten bullets into an unarmed old lady in a nightgown in broad daylight in front of a bunch of Shriners. Here you got darkness and danger, you got a known felon in commission of a felony, you got a motor vehicle, deadly weapon in use—typically, that would be a gimme for the cops, and, you know, I wouldn't have even looked at it probably, if it wasn't so obvious that they were trying to sneak something through. On the other hand, if what we're looking at here is a *personal* thing, if Cooley and Nash weren't just pursuing a random hot car, if the reason they were so weirdly anxious for a crappy stolen-car collar was because they *knew* Mr. Lomax . . ."

"Then you have the element of intent," Murrow finished.

"Just right, Murrow: the element of intent. So—*did* they, in fact, know the man? If this was a normal investigation, we would get the cops to find out whether the two defendants had any contact with the victim, and what that relationship was. But since the defendants are cops, we can't, or we can't right now."

"Because of the . . . um?" Murrow gestured vaguely in the direction of the DA's office across the hall.

"Yes, because of the um. If I still had Clay Fulton here, it would be a different story, but they kicked him upstairs to Police Plaza, and if I went to that yo-yo who's running the DA squad now, the news of the request would be in Fuller's hands and up on the twelfth floor of One PP practically before I put the phone down. However, I have a plan."

"May one know it?"

"Not just now. Meanwhile"—here Karp looked at his watch—"you might wander by and see if the grand jury has taken up this case yet. It'll do you good to see corrupt practices taking place before your very eyes."

"Okay, but why don't I stand up and in a voice of doom cry out, 'Cooley! Cooley, you knew the victim! Cooley, you murderer!' Then if he turned white and fainted, we would know he was guilty."

"Good plan, Murrow. Let's use that as a fallback if mine doesn't work. Now, scram."

When Murrow was gone, Karp hit a speed-dial button. One of the secrets of the modern age is that every important person in the world has a private number, known only to a select few. Karp had one of these, and he knew a bunch of others, such as this one, mostly people in New York's criminal-justice and forensic establishments. Karp's mind did not often dwell on Judaica, but he liked the image of the Nine Just Men for whose sake Ha-Olam does not destroy the wicked world, and while he did not puff himself up so much as to consider himself personally one of these, he imagined that all of the Just would have each other's private numbers.

After a few rings, a throaty bass voice said, "Yeah, Fulton."

"Clay, it's Butch."

The voice turned softer, and they chatted about family, sports, the local scene. Fulton was one of Karp's oldest friends, one of the first black college graduates to serve in the NYPD and a mentor from Karp's earliest days at the DA. He had been head of the DA squad and had functioned almost as Karp's private police force until being promoted to inspector and kicked upstairs, where the bosses could keep a closer eye on him.

"They keeping you busy up there?" Karp asked.

"Oh, you know—it's paperwork mostly. They found out I could spell. Surprised the shit out of them, I think, me being a colored fellow and all. Strategic planning they call it."

"What's the strategic plan?"

"Frisk as many niggers as possible is the main one."

"Is it working?"

"Hey, crime rate's down. Of course, it's down just as much in cities where they don't do shit like that, but that don't cut much ice up here on the twelfth floor. How's by you?"

"Not that great, actually. I need to talk to you about stuff, but not over the phone. Lunch?"

"Sure, where at?"

"How about Lemongrass on Varick?"

Pause. "Isn't that a vegetarian place?"

"Uh-huh. It smells of carrots and no cop would be caught dead eating there. See you in a bit."

It did smell of carrots, and purity, and contained several elegant, slow-moving young waitpersons, who seemed by their expressions to be suffering directly from mankind's abuse of the planet. Lucy ate here all the time, which was how Karp had learned of the place. Both men had a meatless, cheeseless, taste-free dish of quasi-lasagna and filled up on the bread, which was surprisingly good.

"This better be worth a set of ribs at Jack's," grumbled Fulton when the waitress had tripped off. Fulton was a big, dark brown man in his late fifties with a brush mustache and a balding dome of a head. He had an elegant gray suit on, and silver cuff links with gold detective badges on them. His expression, disarmingly genial at most times, was now a little wary.

"You got it, a whole cow, if you want. Push that crap aside and take a look at this." Karp handed a manila folder across the table.

Fulton opened it, saw what it was, and shot a hard stare across the small table.

"What's going on, Butch?"

"That's what I need to know. Read the whole thing, especially including the autopsy. Take your time."

Fulton did so, reading silently, spreading the pictures out over almost the whole of the table, including those that were quite out of place in a vegetarian restaurant. When he was done, he shoved the papers and photographs back into the folder and handed it back to Karp.

"So?" Fulton said.

"So what do you think?"

"About what? This Lomax? He fought the law and the law won."

"Come on, Clay."

"Oh, don't you give me that 'Come on, Clay.' Let me ask you something—do you know Ray Cooley?"

"More or less. Not personally. He was borough chief of detectives. Retired a couple of years ago. What's he got to do with it?"

"I'll tell you what, Stretch. There is probably not a senior cop in this city in the last twenty-five years who was more respected than Ray Cooley. When the Mollen Commission shit hit the fan, they got Ray Cooley to clean out the Manhattan houses that were dirty because everybody knew he was clean as a whistle, and that he was a cop's cop and wouldn't sacrifice the little guys to protect the big ones. And he didn't. And he *was* decent, especially compared to the usual gang of Paddies they got running the department—I'm talking about racism here. Never a hint. Now, Ray had two sons, both of them cops. Brian, the oldest, got himself shot. He was working undercover out of the Two-eight, talking out there one night to a CI he had, over on Fourteenth east, and somebody drove by and popped a bunch of caps. They were trying to get the snitch, but they got Brian instead. He pushed the snitch down and tried to return fire, but they got him. The younger son, that's the fella you have in that file; got the Medal of Valor two years ago. You know what he did?"

"No, I don't, but—"

"Listen! A hostage situation. A guy holed up on the fifth floor, stoned out of his gourd, he's got his girlfriend and two little kids, and a pistol. The girlfriend's mother runs out of the place, calls the cops. These are black people, by the way. Brendan Cooley happens to be in the neighborhood. I think he was working the Three-oh then, before he went over to anticrime. So him and his partner answer the squeal. Okay, you know a hostage situation, you got your protocols, your regs. Call for the specialists, the negotiating team, the snipers, the helmets, the SWATs. Brendan goes in there, and he decides this guy isn't going to wait for that, he's going to pop in the next two minutes. So what does he do? He stands in the doorway, he throws down his weapon, he takes off the vest he put on, he even rips open his shirt, and he goes, 'Hey, you want to shoot someone, shoot me! Go ahead, shoot. But, for Christ's sake, let the woman and the kids go!' For some reason—I don't know, God was having a slow day, maybe He decides to tweak this fuck-head's brain the right way—and he goes with it. He lets the kids go, the girlfriend. By the time they roll up the heavy artillery, Brendan's got the guy's piece and they're sitting on the bed together, the guy's crying his eyes out on Brendan's T-shirt. What do you think of that?"

"Sounds like something of a cowboy, Brendan."

"That's what you derive from that story?"

"Yeah, speaking as a cowboy myself. How come they didn't ding him for not going by the book?"

"Oh, they chewed him, all right. But the press got ahold of it, and it was too much for them, especially given that the usual story is white cop blasts black guy. Here the white guy saved three, maybe four, uptown-type folks."

"And what's the moral of all this, Clay? That he saved four so he gets to cap one for free?"

Fulton waved a finger in Karp's face, a finger like the barrel of a .38. "Hey! Don't be a jerk! The moral is, number one, Brendan Cooley is a good cop, and not just with white people, and two, the status of Ray Cooley in the department is such that his son, his *one remaining son,* is about as untouchable as anyone has ever been in the department. He could be dealing smack out of a whorehouse across from City Hall and he'd never see a courtroom. You may not like it, but there it is. If you think the job is going to go after him because he shot a mutt like Cisco Lomax, in a halfway plausible self-defense situation, you are nuts."

Karp had been breaking a lump of bread into small pieces and lining them up neatly in front of his plate, as if to shield him from what he was hearing. He said, "Look, we know each other for what? Getting to be twenty years now. You know I'm not a cop-baiter. If you recall, some years ago a rogue detective was doing assassinations to order for a dope king, and you found out about it, and he snatched you up and tortured you to find out what you knew and if you had told anyone yet. And when that trio of thugs you used to run out of the Thirty-second Precinct broke you loose, you arranged for them to whack him."

"That would be hard to prove."

"I don't *have* to prove it," Karp snapped, and in a milder tone said, "I'm talking to an old and trusted friend here. With whom I am unfailingly honest. To resume, these guys also took care of any witnesses to that particular cop's felonies, all justifiable shoots, of course, and you covered up the guy's evil empire, and he got an inspector's funeral, and his widow got the pension. This was in the interest of protecting the rep of the department and maybe also the rep of the bad detective, who happened to be black and was also a pretty good guy before he jumped into the shit. And, if you recall, I sat down for all of that. Hey, I know it's rough justice."

"What's your point here, Butch?"

"That I know how the game is played, which I shouldn't even have to demonstrate to you. But since you've gotten so puffy now you're a boss, I thought I would anyway. But I also know there are lines, and you know that as well as I do. We don't do frames, that's one line. We kick out cases that don't pass the laugh test. We like it when the guy who actually did the crime is the one the cops bring in, not just a guy who did some similar crimes and they want to get his ass off the street. And, especially, while I'd like the line here to be pushed back in the direction of a little less tendency to violence, I believe we still draw the line at assassination."

"What are you talking 'assassination'? Where the hell did that come from?"

Karp tapped the report. "From here. Look, I have no question it's a bad shooting. But you know and I know that I would never ever be able to make that case, not against that copy anyway, for reasons you've just eloquently laid out for me. And you know that if I spent energy worrying about evil shit that went down on the island of Manhattan where I *don't* have a decent case, I wouldn't have the strength to take a good piss. But this one worries me. I want to know why two perfectly rational, competent cops took off on a high-speed chase, with guns blazing, to rescue some dentist's sport utility vehicle from a car thief. Hah! I can see by your face that it worries you, too. You saw the same goddamn thing I did when I read that report."

"Bullshit!"

"I know you too long, Clay."

Fulton slammed the table, drawing looks. It was not a table-slamming sort of place. In a controlled hiss, veins bulging on his forehead, he said, "Well, what exactly do you expect me to do about it, pal? Call in the snakes on Ray Cooley's kid?"

"Of course not. Start an IAD beef on this guy and the snakes would be falling all over themselves, deep-sixing unpleasant evidence. It'd be son of Warren Commission. But it should be pretty easy to find out if that really was a chase of a stolen vehicle, if it was reported and sent out, if Cooley reported himself in pursuit. You're the guy who has all those crime pattern reports. And if it was that, well . . . all you got to do is tell me it was just a boyish outburst, a mistake in judgment. They were bored, say, middle of the night, a hot car goes by, they figure on a quick collar just to pass the time. But the guy runs, and it gets out of hand, the adrenaline shoots up, the bullets fly . . . Honestly, hell, I'd love a story like that. Just bring me that story and you'll never hear anything more about it from me. It's not like I got nothing better to do."

"And say it's not that story?"

"If it's not . . . ah, shit . . . well, then, I'll have to decide how to go forward with it, depending on the available evidence and the nature of the case, just like I always do. But in any case you're out of it. Your name'll never come up."

"It better not, Stretch. I don't intend to spend the rest of my time on the job running a motor pool out on the ass end of Staten Island." Fulton stood up abruptly, threw some bills on the table, and walked out. Karp caught up with him on the sidewalk, under the restaurant's pink and pale green awning.

"You hate me now, right?"

"Ah, fuck, I don't know," said Fulton, a disgusted look on his face. "The old days when we were working together and I didn't give a rat's ass about what the bosses thought, I would've gone into this with you, no problem. Now we got a crew up there in the Plaza, they're falling all over each other to show they're not a bunch of Paddy racist motherfuckers, they got to have some more black faces up on the top floors. I mean I know I'm good, but I'd be kidding myself if I pretended that wasn't a part of it. Meanwhile, I *am* there, and I can do a lot of good, not just for myself—shit, you know I'm not into that crap—but for the job, and providing a little counterbalance for boss types who think that walking while black is a major felony. But the downside is, now I *am* a boss, I have to think like one, and even though it pisses me off to see how I slipped into that thinking, there it is. I bought it, now I have to pay for it." Fulton smiled bleakly and shook Karp's hand as his official car drew to the curb. "You keep me honest, Stretch. But not *too* honest, hear?"

"Deal," said Karp, and then as an aside, "You almost might want to have a talk with the partner, Nash."

"Why would I want to do that? Because he's black?"

"No, but what you said, about doing some good, about counterbalance. You always kept pretty good track of rising black detectives. There could be trouble for him, if I'm right. I mean if I'm right, he told a couple of fibs there to cover his partner. Do you know him?"

"As a matter of fact, I do: one of my boys, as you guessed. A good guy, wife and kids, a solid cop. There is no way, I mean *no* way, I'm going to involve him in this crap."

"Not even a friendly heads-up?"

"Nothing, because this conversation never took place."

"But you will look at those calls?"

"Yeah. Give me a couple of days. I'll call you," said Fulton out the rear window, and the car drove off.

Murrow reported back to Karp late in the day. "Well?" asked Karp. He was comfortably seated with a pile of case files on his lap, feet up on the desk.

"As expected. No indictment, smooth as silk. Cooley and Nash are back in harness as we speak." Karp just nodded and returned to his reading. "What are you going to do, boss?"

"What *can* I do? The wheels have ground, and the ham sandwich has not been indicted. Did you see this? Shawn Cisco Lomax's epitaph. An inch and a half on page A20 of the newspaper of record."

Murrow picked up the tiny clipping and saw it was from the one-column digest of regional news that the *Times* ran daily on one of its back pages. He read, "Police Shoot Car Thief on Henry Hudson Highway. Police officers in pursuit of a car thief opened fire when the fugitive turned the SUV he was driving around on the northbound West Side Highway and attempted to ram the unmarked police vehicle pursuing him. Shawn Lomax, 23, of 312 W. 127th Street, was pronounced dead at the scene. Police sources said that Mr. Lomax had a long criminal record. The two police officers involved were not injured." Murrow put the clipping down on the desk. "Gosh, it's in the papers, so it must be true." Karp ignored the remark and kept reading. Murrow, usually sensitive to his boss's moods, ignored the snub. He was oddly reluctant to leave, without . . . without what? Some assurance that the good guys were going to win? He was very young.

"Did you hear the latest? They found another dead street person."

This time Karp looked up. "Where?"

"In a midtown parking garage. What does that make this month, six?"

"The same MO?"

"No, this one was shot, apparently. It could still be the same guy."

"I doubt that very much. Murderers tend to be creatures of habit, and crazy murderers even more so. I wonder . . ." Karp shut down the emerging thought.

"Wonder what?"

"Nothing, Murrow, don't you have something to do?"

"Go talk to your daughter," said Marlene when Karp got home that evening. He was happy to see her by the stove stirring, which always gave him a shameful atavistic thrill. He was taken aback, however, by her tone.

"What happened?"

"You heard about the new homeless killing?"

"What, that shooting midtown? Oh, shit! Don't tell me she was involved in that one, too?"

"No, surprisingly, but she knew the guy. She's broken up about it, plus I told her if she kept hanging around those people, I was going to pack her off to live with Patsy in Santa Barbara. Unfortunately, they don't allow us to lock them up in convents anymore."

"A hollow threat, surely?"

"No, I was serious. She has to learn to listen, dammit!"

Karp let this go by. "Where are the boys?"

"I said they could stay at Matt Fleming's until later. I'll pick them up. I have to go out anyway." She lifted the cover on a pot of potatoes and turned down the heat. "By the way, the famous David is coming to dinner tonight."

"She invited him?"

"No, it was me." Marlene gave an extra stir, more vigorous than the stew really needed, and shook off the wooden spoon on the edge of the pot, like a rim-shot in Vegas. "Another crime against my name. He seemed perfectly reasonable about it, though. Maybe he can talk some sense into her. She absolutely *can't* go hanging out in dark alleys with bums until they catch this bastard."

Karp changed out of his lawyer costume and into jeans and a worn sweatshirt. He announced himself at Lucy's door and received a grumbled admittance. Once inside, he made that quick, near-furtive inspection familiar to all parents of teenagers, a forbidden window on the secret life. As usual, the room was neat as a nun's cell, a little too neat, to Karp's thinking, betokening a compulsive mind, perhaps unhealthily so. The room contained a simple box spring and mattress, a Door Store desk and swivel chair, a Tabriz carpet of some value on the floor, and on two of the walls modular birch bookshelves stretched from the floor to the ceiling, solid with books, almost all of them dictionaries and works in languages Karp couldn't read. Over the bed hung a large polychrome crucifix in the Spanish style, dripping blood drops and radiating agony, that always gave Karp the willies when he saw it. The wall over the desk was corked, and on it were pinned pictures and documents of various kinds, all secured with four pushpins at the corners and lined up square: family photos (numerous), school awards (few), Polaroid snaps of pals (fewer), a reproduction of a painting of Cardinal Mezzofanti, the Pete Rose of language, who could translate 114, and one of Francis E. Sommer, the DiMaggio, who was fluent in 94. Raised above these was an oval photocopy of Simone Weil, which disturbed Karp nearly as much as the vivid crucifix. All Karp knew about Weil was that she was a French Jew who, having escaped the Nazis, starved herself to death in sympathy with concentration camp victims, which in Karp's view was not the sort of role model appropriate for a seventeen-year-old. His gaze shifted quickly to the center of the cork and the large world map, which showed with pins how the kid was gaining on the language superstars. There seemed to be more every time Karp looked, pushing forty by rough count. The competition with Weil, if any, was not apparent to the paternal eye, which noted again the absence of rock stars, kittens, Garfields, or other normal teenage-girl stuff.

The abnormal was at her desk. Her head, round, shorn, and vulnerable, was drooping like a spent blossom on her long, thin neck as she wrote in a notebook. From the cassette machine on the desk came the voice of a man speaking a language curiously like English, but incomprehensible to Karp.

"What's that?" he asked.

She switched it off and swiveled around to face him. "Dutch. The text on the list. It's easy."

"Say something in it."

"Ik weet dat je het niet goed vindt, maar ik doe het touch."

"Which means?"

"'I know you don't think it's right, but I'll do it anyway.'"

"That seems to be your motto." Karp sat on the bed. "What're we going to do about this, Luce? You're driving her nuts."

"She's driving *me* nuts. My gosh, if she wanted me to be a nice, regular little kid, she should have paid some attention a little earlier."

"She just wants you to be safe and happy."

"No, what it is, she's guilty that she neglected me while she ran around protecting women with firearms, and, *mamma mia,* look how I turned out. It's an embarrassment." She flung back in the chair, making it squeak. "And then she goes and . . . oh, God! I can't believe she called him, like I was a little kid and she was making sure he wasn't a molester. I'll die!"

"No dramatics, please," said Karp. Then they heard the elevator arrive, which they both decided to ignore. "Look, at the risk of being overly rational, this is the situation you're in, and so my advice is make the best of it for the couple of years you have left at home. Everyone has a cross to bear, so to speak. Like you all say, offer it up."

Lucy glared at him, then sighed, closed her eyes briefly. "Okay, I'll try. You're right. It's just . . . I was really upset is all. I tend to lose it when my friends get killed."

"You knew this guy well?"

"Oh, yeah, as well as any of them let you know them. Desmondo

Ramsey. Early twenties, got into the crack business as a teenager, went to jail, tried to live at home but . . . he comes . . . he *came* from a respectable family, by the way, over in Newark. Three sisters, all college grads, mother runs a dry cleaner's. Anyway, he couldn't stand the pressure, his family guilting him out all the time, so he split and came to the city. Hustled things—not stealing, I mean street trade, hauling stuff for street merchants, like a lot of them do, laying stuff out, holding good sidewalks for them. That was his big ambition, to have a table. He was a good salesman, too, friendly, a nice smile. Once in a while one of his merchants would give him something to sell, a pen set or a watch or a radio. He read books, too, you know, not a dummy at all. We used to talk about stuff, Malcolm and Fanon, and the Church. And business stuff, like how to succeed, stuff like that." She sighed. "And now he's dead, someone just shot him down like a dog."

"It's a rough life," said Karp.

"Yes, I know. They're out there getting murdered, and my social role is to be protected and sheltered in the upper-middle-class cocoon, according to her, get good grades, have respectable middle-class friends, go to a good college, shop, chatter . . ."

"Lucy, when I rank sheltered middle-class girls, you are not in the top ten, I hate to tell you. You're not probably in the top million. I mean you've *done* your lower-depths adventure already, you've been shot at and kidnapped, and God knows what else. Don't you think it's time for a rest, maybe catch your breath a little?"

"No, I don't." Lucy sprang to her feet, a false and cheerful look on her face. "I should help set the table, shouldn't I?"

7

"ACTUALLY, IT WENT A LOT BETTER THAN I EXPECTED," SAID KARP. "A LOT better, for example, than this bagel." He was in a rear booth at Sam's, near the courthouse. Sam's was an antiquated joint of the type that used to be called a luncheonette in New York. It was dark and cozy, and the red leatherette of its booths was nearly black with age, except where patched with Mystik tape, and the air therein was dense with the scents of coffee, toast, bacon, and the extra something that once made all places smell exactly the same. He was having breakfast with his old pal, V. T. Newbury. Newbury worked in Washington now, for Treasury, doing something fairly cryptic about big-time money laundering. He had worked for Karp for over fifteen years at the DA, and whenever he was in town arresting distinguished bankers, he arranged to spend some time with Karp. Karp prized V.T.'s judgment, although not necessarily in reference to the doughy oval.

"What's wrong with it?" asked Newbury. He was a small, ridiculously handsome man with the chisel-cut features of a twenties cigarette-ad drawing. A scion of venerable New York wealth, he had nothing whatever in common with Karp, except deep mutual affection and a mordant sense of humor about the criminal justice system.

"It's not a bagel. It's white bread in a doughnut shape. An abomination. It's like . . . like . . ."

"Ladies no longer wearing gloves out of doors. Yes, the decline of a once great tradition. My commiserations. Tell me more about this fellow. Did you like him?"

"Well, sort of, as much as I could like someone with whom my daughter spends every available moment and who is ten years older than she is. He seemed pretty decent, and everyone was on their best behavior. Got a scruffy beard, dresses down-market, but clean. Well-spoken. He's from upstate somewhere. I guess he's the kind of guy, a woman sees him and wants to fatten him up or something. That kind of appeal. He's a Franciscan."

"A priest?"

"No, what they call a Tertiary, like a lay order. I didn't know they had them. He lives in a Catholic Worker hostel on the Lower East Side. According to him, he's been in some rough places. That was what we mainly talked about, Bosnia, Sudan. He's dying to get back there, if you can believe it. Like I said, everyone was being their charming selves, even Marlene. Their charming Catholic selves. Many references to the Holy Spirit.

"You felt left out.

"I did, a little. Off-base. I mean if your kid is hanging out with a bum, that's one thing. You can give him the bum's rush. If she's hanging out with . . . I don't know . . . a saint practically, what can you say? Be a little more evil, honey?"

"You're thinking maybe this guy is taking advantage of her?"

"What, sexually? Lucy?" Karp let his jaw drop. "You know, that's the one thing that never occurred to me. Never entered my mind."

"The dad is always the last to know."

"Uh-uh, that's not the worry with Lucy, especially not with this guy. The worry is we'll get a postcard from the Congo some day: 'Dear Mom and Dad, taking care of lepers in the middle of a guerrilla war here. Don't worry.'" Karp laughed. "Go have children! Now I know."

"I wish I could give you some advice," said V.T., "but, as you know, Anabel and I have not been blessed. I was always threatened with military school, myself."

"Not an option," said Karp, "although Marlene gets on a tear sometimes she's going to ship her out of town if she doesn't get her school act together." He pushed his half-eaten pseudo-bagel aside and signaled the waitress for more coffee. Newbury took the moment to examine his friend more closely. Not a happy man, he thought, and not because of his daughter either. The skin of his face had the stretched and sallow look that, experience taught, indicated tension and frustration. His smiles seemed forced, as if having to push up through a membrane of suffering.

"How's work?" Newbury asked in a casual tone.

"Oh, the usual. Putting asses in jail."

"Not. Really, what's wrong?"

"You got time for this?"

"Oh, a long story?"

"Semilong," said Karp, and plunged into the Cooley affair, and the situation with the election, and the execrable Norton Fuller, and what Karp proposed to do about it. At the end Karp asked, "So . . . what do you think?"

"I think you have a serious problem. Has Clay called you back yet?"

"Not yet, no."

"An interesting moral situation. Both of you want to stay in jobs where you think you can still do some good, and where the alternatives, like letting yet another incompetent bozo take your place, seem even worse. But you might have to ignore some bad stuff to keep in there, and then you have to ask, where do you draw the line? The old Schindler's list business, the good Germans . . ."

"That's hardly a fair comparison," said Karp. "Whatever happens, no one is sending me to Dachau."

"No, when you leave the DA, you'll be sentenced to private practice and the chance of enormous wealth, and this will keep you out of heaven. Some people, maybe including Lucy, would say that by comparison a jolt in Dachau is a day at the beach."

"You're not being very helpful," said Karp a little grumpily.

"No, and that's because this is the four hundred and twelfth time we've had this conversation, or a similar one. You're an essentially honest and decent man working at the top levels of a system that's essentially dishonest and indecent. You have authority enough to acquire responsibility, but not enough to change things much for the better. So your choices are, also for the four hundred and twelfth time, either, one, quit and earn an honest living; two, get off the pot and run for DA or political office, where you can put on your silver armor and fight the good fight with no holds barred; or, three, do a couple of ass-kissing favors for some pols and get appointed to the bench, where you can make the kind of law you want until senility takes hold, and even beyond. But this continual angst around a DA who doesn't want to play by your rules has not made you happy, is not making you happy, and will not make you happy in the future. Granted, Keegan is in a different moral universe from Bloom, but he's obviously still not pure enough for you, and so, until the second coming of Francis P. Garrahy, you're always going to be harassed by political types like Fuller. It's part of the system."

"I *know* it's the system, V.T. I wasn't asking for a review of my entire life, I was soliciting your advice as to how to carry out a sneak."

"Me being a sneaky guy? Thank you. Okay, here's my advice. It's a good plan as far as it goes. But if you're fighting a political battle, you're going to have to get your hands dirty in politics. You have to manipulate your boss into a position where it's less worse for him to do what you want him to do than what Fuller wants him to do."

"Oh, crap! If I do that, I'm as bad as Fuller!"

"Yes, and if you don't, you'll lose, so why bother in the first place? Sorry, pal, you asked me, and that's the way I see it." Newbury drained his coffee cup and looked at his watch. "I'd love to share some moral agony with you, but I'm due across the street to terrorize a clutch of certified public accountants. Is that the correct noun of venery? A *slick* of accountants? A *cheat?* Whatever." He shook Karp's hand warmly. "Love to the family. And, Butch? Lighten up . . . it's not like it was real life."

Karp watched his friend walk down Baxter Street and felt a stab of envy, not a very familiar stab, and more irritating for that. He did not, of course, envy Newbury's wealth or family or status. What he wished he had was his light heart, his ability to accept the world as he found it, its infinite absurdities amusing, its injustices bearable, its corruptions a given, like the changes in season, without becoming nastily cynical or corrupt himself. As he walked back to the office, he tried unsuccessfully to wriggle out from under the opinions V.T. had laid out, and it must have shown on his face because those of his staff he encountered gave him serious nods in greeting, and the few smiles that dawned as he passed were stillborn. And that was another thing, which he hardly dared admit. He was lonely. Unlike the lost age when he had started at the DA, when a lawyer commonly spent a whole career in public prosecution, the present was an era of flux. Except for Roland Hrcany, and

Keegan himself, everyone Karp had started with was gone. Keegan could not be a friend, of course, and as for Hrcany—as Roland himself often remarked, when you had a Hungarian for a friend, you didn't need any enemies. Karp stifled the self-pity, however, like the good stoic he was and stood nobly with his hand out in front of his secretary's desk while she slapped a short stack of early phone messages into his hand. "And Himself would like to see you when it's convenient."

"Himself, eh? What did His Excellency want?"

"He did not vouchsafe to me, Mr. Karp. But Mary said it was important . . . about a murder, she said. Mr. Hrcany is in there now. And the other one."

Which was Fuller. Fuller, inevitably, was the sort of little toad who puffed himself up by oppressing staff and was widely resented. This he took as a token of his effectiveness in administration.

Karp went into his private office and flipped through the pink squares. Only one was of immediate interest. He pushed the button.

"You found out something," he said when Clay Fulton picked up.

"Yeah. That incident we were discussing."

"Why did the chicken cross the road?"

"That one. I'm in the information business, so it was not unusual for me to ask for all the stolen-car reports put out on the evening in question and their time of transmission. Guess what I found out?"

"That the chicken crossed the road before the car in question was reported stolen," said Karp confidently.

"You got it."

"Which means that he crossed the road for some other reason, which means that he was pursuing the driver and not the car."

"I would say that's a reasonable assumption," said Fulton after a brief pause.

"What're we going to do?"

"You know, all in all, I think St. John's is going to whip Duke. A good big guy is going to take a good small guy every time."

"Not if the small guy is very fast and very sneaky."

"Nice talking to you, Stretch. If you take my meaning."

After he hung up, Karp had this thought: I'm becoming a pain in the ass to my friends. After taking some moments to recover from the irritation and anger this revelation occasioned, he grabbed one of his ledgers and walked to Keegan's office, remembering at the last moment to bring his face back to neutral. The DA was at the head of his conference table, flanked by Fuller and Hrcany. He looked pale, and there was a pinched expression on his face that Karp did not recall seeing there before. Fear? They all looked up when Karp entered and took the chair at the foot.

"What's up?" he asked, to which Keegan glowered, Roland rolled eyes upward, and Fuller said, "We have a problem."

"It's not a *problem,* Norton," Hrcany replied. "We call them cases. Somebody shoots somebody else, we investigate and come to a conclusion, and then we indict or don't indict the shooter."

This was Fuller's turn to roll his eyes.

Karp looked directly at Keegan. "Jack, what's going on?"

Keegan said, "A little while ago, I got a call from Shelly Solotoff. You remember Shelly, Butch?"

"Yeah, I had lunch with him last week."

"He's representing Sybil Marshak. Apparently, one day last week she shot a mugger in a garage midtown and fled the scene. She called Solotoff this morning, and he called me. We are now deciding how to handle this mess."

"What mess?" asked Karp disingenuously. "Roland just pointed out we have a procedure here. Why don't we follow it?"

"Oh, please!" snapped Fuller. "It's absurd to pretend Sybil Marshak is the same as some drugged-up kid with a gun."

"She's no kid," said Roland. "You got that right, Norton."

"But she had a gun," said Karp. "Drugs we don't know. Did Shelly say anything about drugs?"

"Very funny," said Fuller sourly. "But the press is going to be all over us in a very short time, and we need to get our ducks in a row. Obviously, we can stall for a little bit, feed them some junk about the continuing investigation, and no comment until the results are in, but afterward . . . I mean she is absolutely fucking key to the campaign. I mean she controls something over thirty percent of the typical primary vote in Manhattan—"

"And?" Karp interrupted.

Fuller was taken aback. "Well . . . clearly, we have to ensure that . . . ah . . ." He hung up, fumfering.

"Yeah, it's hard to come right out and say it," Karp observed. "Because putting the screws to some poor schmuck for political reasons, that's business as usual. But easing off on someone for political reasons is a crime, isn't it?"

"Who said anything about easing off?" Fuller protested. "I never used any such language."

Karp ignored this, and turned to Hrcany. "We have some facts, I presume."

"Yeah, I talked to Jim Raney, at Midtown South. The vic is a homeless named Ramsey, Desmondo. A short sheet for dope possession and trespass. Nothing but jail time. No violence, no weapons charges. The body was found in a garage on Fifty-fifth off Broadway, dead a couple of hours when they found it. Anonymous call. Well, it being a homeless, they figured it for another one off that serial killer and shifted it to the task force that's running that thing, a detective Paradisio over at the One-seven, and it rattled around there for a while, until they decided it wasn't the same guy after all, and Ed Rastenberg, Paradisio's partner, shot it back to Midtown. So it's a little stale by now, but Raney goes into it, the usual, known associates, any enemies, and so forth. A blank. Okay, this is a bum, so we're not burning overtime here, but, to his credit, Raney persists, and he gets the idea of checking the cars in the garage where it took place. Turns out there's a video camera at the entrance that picks up the license plates pretty good, and he runs the plates of everyone whose car was in the garage at the time of or thereabouts. Not an easy job, but they did it. And they get a list of names and start calling, just fishing, really, did anyone see this guy, anything peculiar. Marshak was one of the ones got called."

Hrcany paused there, significantly.

"This was yesterday?" Karp asked.

"Yeah, and this morning she calls her lawyer and comes in. Doesn't look so good for Sybil. Leaving the scene. Lying low. Only gets a conscience when the cops are nosing around. Naughty, naughty Sybil, and her such a big liberal. Her story is she was in shock, post–traumatic stress, and she's very sorry."

"Raney interviewed her?" Karp asked.

"Yeah, with her attorney present, so he didn't get a hell of a lot. He says she says Ramsey came at her with a knife, and she plugged him. Calls it in to 911 later without giving a name, which checks out. But"— Hrcany paused significantly—"there was no knife recovered at the scene. There was a watch, though, a Lady Rolex, gold, in the vic's pocket."

"Marshak's watch," said Fuller. "That proves it. He ripped her off and she—"

"No," said Hrcany, grinning, "not Marshak's. She doesn't know anything about any watch. She said it was a knife he was flashing. But right now: knife, no; watch, yes."

"Witnesses?" asked Karp.

"As a matter of fact," Hrcany replied, "Marshak said she thought she did see another man hanging out in the background while Ramsey allegedly assaulted her. Another black guy; she said she'd recognize him again. The cops are looking, but"— he waved his hand dismissively— "basically, what we have here is woman shoots and kills unarmed man, and we have only her word that he threatened her. I think we can maintain man deuce, plus leaving the scene."

"Manslaughter two?" cried Fuller in outrage. "Are you crazy! Sybil Marshak? Christ, the woman'll be a hero to every woman who ever got accosted in a parking garage. And her word—hell, if you can't trust a woman like that, who the hell *can* you trust?"

Karp and Hrcany looked at each other. Hrcany's eyes almost vanished beneath their upper lids. The DA was examining the tip of his unlit cigar, as if the solution had been written there in tiny letters by a remarkably prescient Nicaraguan.

Hrcany said, "Okay, Norton, we'll let her off with a warning, and not only that, we'll sponsor a law. Any rich white bitch with a gun gets to kill one poor black guy and no hard feelings. Or maybe we should make it two, or three."

"Oh, get real, Roland!" Fuller snarled. "Why the hell shouldn't we take her word for it? It's not like she knew the guy, that she had something to gain from shooting him. What, you think she was a crazed racist? Marshak? The woman marched in Selma, for crying out loud! She's the biggest ACLU bleeding heart in the city. She had to be in legitimate fear of her life, or she never would've done it. I mean, if you can't see that . . ."

Karp noticed that Fuller got white when angry, while Hrcany got red, and wondered idly whether this meant anything about their characters. Hrcany was just beginning a sarcastic rant to the effect that people accused of crimes often took liberties with the truth, when Karp said, almost to himself, "She probably *was* in fear of her life. She thought she was being stalked."

They all stared at him. "How do you know that?" the DA asked.

"She was a client of my wife's. Or, no, I think she just came in for a consult. Marlene trailed around after her for a couple of days, but couldn't spot anyone. That doesn't mean she wasn't being followed by someone."

"See! There you are," crowed Fuller.

"Not really," said Karp coldly. "It just means she was spooked. It doesn't necessarily have anything to do with the shooting we have here. Look, this is a premature discussion. I don't know why we're here. Clearly, there's a prima facie case against Ms. Marshak on the evidence as it now stands. We should charge her, as Roland suggests, with manslaughter second and see what develops. The police may find the witness, and depending on what he says, and whether we believe him or not, we can reconsider the charges, up or down." He looked at the DA. "Or am I wrong, Jack? Are we really starting to throw naked political influence into the balance when we assess charges?"

Keegan held his gaze for what seemed a long time before he looked away, and then there was a quick, barely perceptible glance at Fuller. The DA said, "No, of course not. We'll charge her and see what happens with the witness, if any. It's early days yet on this."

The meeting dispersed, although Keegan motioned Fuller to stay behind to talk press and politics.

Karp motioned Hrcany to step into his office. "What do you think?"

"Of all that?" Hrcany gestured in the direction of the DA's office. "Pure politics. I think Jack's running scared on this election, and the little scumbag is feeding off it. We haven't had a serious contested election for DA in I don't know how long, and now we do. McBright is waving the figures for how we charge people on account of their race, heavier the blacker, and how we never go after bad cops or corrupt landlords or the kind of respectable people who make a good living off the misery of the downtrodden, et cetera. It's a pile of shit, we know that, but we also have an electorate that's more swayed by that kind of thing than it used to be. If McBright really gets the vote out uptown, Jack's in trouble. Let's say he holds on to the unions, the cops and all, and he loses the beautiful mosaic—then the white guilty-liberal vote is the swing, and now we got a leader of that vote up for homicide. I think it's rich." He laughed unpleasantly.

"I mean, do you think Jack or Fuller is going to . . . I don't know, screw up this case in some way to win the election?"

"Not to win the election, no. But Jack's not worried only about the election or, mainly, to tell the truth. I don't know if even little Norton understands that. Did you see him? He's scared shitless about his federal judgeship. He sees it flying away with old Sybil because if she goes down for this and the party thinks Jack didn't pull every wire he could to get her off, he'll never get sponsored, unless he moves to North Dakota and starts a new life under an assumed name. Sybil's got strings to every politician in the state."

"And this cuts no ice with you," said Karp dully. Roland's attitude always tended to annoy him a little, and now it annoyed him a lot. Although Roland had supported the outcome Karp sought, a pursuit of the case without fear or favor, it was clear that the man had a personal issue with the accused.

"No ice at all, buddy. Oh, I'm going to love nailing that hypocritical bitch. It will give me an enormous amount of pleasure to put her fat ass in jail for a long time."

"Assuming she's guilty."

"Yeah, right," said Hrcany dismissively. "Actually, I'd like it better if Marshak was the bum slasher, but this'll have to do."

"So you're saying that Marshak was not officially a client of ours," said Lou Osborne.

"Not officially," said Marlene. They were in Osborne's office, an expensive area that yielded nothing in modernity to Captain Picard's office on the starship *Enterprise*—the expected glass and chrome, and the smooth and snaky molded wooden desk and cabinets, and chairs like clever steel-and-fabric traps. Osborne had to be content with non-imaginary technology though, and he had a lot of it—a computer workstation behind his desk on an AnthroCart, and two large-screen monitors set into a bookcase that lined one wall. One of these had a stock market feed on it, and the other had CNN running silently. The other walls, those that weren't windows, contained Osborne's photos-with-the-famous collection and various awards and testimonials, and a large, bland abstract oil.

To Osborne's questioning look, she responded, "Someone comes in and says they're being stalked, the first thing we do is find out if there's any solid evidence for it. Otherwise we're running a therapy shop, not a security operation. Even VIPs are nuts sometimes, hard as that is to believe."

"But there was a real stalker with Marshak, wasn't there?" He poked his chin at the TV screen. "They're saying that's why she had the gun, she was in fear of her life."

"That may well be, but, in fact, no one we saw followed her into that garage. We were there. In fact, Marshak almost ran me over getting away. Now, I'm not saying she wasn't so spooked that some bum walks up to her to ask her the time and she plugs him in a panic. I actually told her to get rid of that gun."

"And you're a witness. You're going to have to testify against her, that you saw her there at the time of the shooting. And they'll say she came to you expressing fear and you told her to, in effect, see a psychiatrist. Jesus Christ! That's why we *have* a VIP department in the first place. A prominent woman walks in here, I don't care if she says she's being chased by Martians, you put someone with her!"

He stared at her briefly, that cold Secret Service–Marine Corps stare, and then his eyes flicked up to the TV screen.

She decided not to get mad. "Lou, relax—you know this isn't about me, or about Sybil Marshak. I take it there's no news about Perry or his people?"

"Not a word. Oleg flew out there the minute we heard, of course, and he's off in the mountains with a crew he put together. God knows he's got enough contacts out East there, but . . . they don't even know if it's political, Serbs or Albanians, or just a gang of freelancers."

"Assuming there's much difference. Have you thought about delaying the offering?"

At this, Osborne tossed a glance at the stock market screen, where he had hoped to see his own stock floating ever upward the day after tomorrow. "I've been on the phone with the underwriters all morning. They're panicking. If we don't go out on schedule, it'll be a signal to the market that we don't have our shit together. It'll be years if ever before we can float another one." Again the glance at the screen. "It's like voodoo; once you have the curse, it's hard to get clean again. What about that singer?"

"Kelsie? A problem, too. But we're covering her at the depth she needs without involving her people. We got a man in the building, twenty-four/seven, and we follow her when she's out. She knows about that, but not about the inside guy."

"And this Coleman? The stalker?"

"He's out and we're looking for him, but . . . it's not like we're the cops. I got Wayne on it."

"Fine, fine . . . but, Marlene?" Here he shrugged into his inspiring-boss persona. It was a little frayed just now, but she had to applaud the effort. "Let's make an extra effort to ensure that no one newsworthy gets into trouble this week? Please?"

"I'll try. And don't worry too much about the IPO. I'm sure it'll be fine. Fastest-growing business in the U.S., la-di-da."

A thin smile. "Lap of the gods, right. Aren't you spending the money already? Everyone else is, including my wife and kids. What have we got you down for—one point two million shares."

"Yeah, just like Harry. At three cents a share, what does that come to? A whole year's worth of Big Macs."

"No, Marlene, that's not the way it works. Your strike price is set at six and a half. We're planning to offer at eight, which means that you don't make any money at all unless . . ." He stopped, because his vice president for special security had her eyes crossed and her fingers in her ears and was going wah-wah-wah.

"Well, I'm glad someone around here's still happy," said Osborne.

Lucy Karp was lying on her back inside a narrow metal tube full of clanging noise. In her ears were air-powered earphones, like the ones that serve out dull music to passengers in flight, and there was a similarly designed microphone in front of her mouth. Through the headset a man was speaking phrases in German and then repeating them in English. Lucy repeated the German phrases and answered the question asked. It was simplified language, the kind native speakers use with children and foreigners (What is your name? My name is Lucy. How old are you? I am seventeen. That is a table. That is a chair). Over the next few days, she would be introduced to the elements of grammar, a vocabulary of about sixteen hundred words, and a raft of idiomatic expressions. At the end of the week she expected that she would be indistinguishable, except for a certain poverty of expression, from a native speaker of that language. As she spoke the words and acquired the language and perfected her pronunciation, the magnetic-resonance-imaging machine was recording the flow of blood to different areas of her brain. Pictures of this would later be printed out in brilliant false colors and distributed to scientists around the world, who would argue interminably about what, if anything, the patterns meant.

The session ended. Lucy slid from the maw of the device and replaced the metal articles she had removed, a gold cross and several sacred medals, and a couple of enamel pinks from a junk shop, and her belt. She spent a few minutes exchanging pleasantries with the technicians in charge of the MRI machines and with Kurt the German, then went in to see Dr. Shadkin, who ran the lab and who had seduced her, with an astute combination of money and friendship, into becoming an experimental subject.

"Lucy! How did it go?" said Shadkin when Lucy rapped on the doorframe. He was rotund, bespectacled, bush-bearded, with thick, ear-length hair parted in the middle. He looked more like a medieval innkeeper than one of the world's great lights on the acquisition of language by the human brain. Lucy answered, "Squeak, squeak-a, squeak squeak."

"No kidding? Would you like a food pellet? A sip of water? Access to sexual intercourse?"

Lucy smiled. Shadkin was the only one of the scientists she had met who still treated her like a regular kid. The others all acted as if they regretted the silly ethical laws that prevented the vivisection of teenagers. No, unfair; but they did seem to look right through her, or maybe that was only, as Shadkin maintained, the general lack of social skills among scientists, especially, oddly enough, social scientists.

"Not right now, thanks. Make any great discoveries today?"

Shadkin looked sourly at his monitor, on which was an outline of a brain pieced with blotches of blue, yellow, and red. "Progress is slow, but don't tell the NSF. The variations that seem to appear in your brain are real, but they don't seem significant enough to explain what you do. And then there's this damn delay. You use the noodle and then comes the blood. What we really need are recordings at the neuronal level. You wouldn't reconsider having the top of your head sliced off?"

"Squeak-a *squeak squeak!*"

"Just kidding, ha-ha. Meanwhile, the linguistic geographers are pretty excited about the Indo-European project, though. Are you having fun with it?"

"It's just a job, Doc," said Lucy morosely, but seeing the look of concern that appeared on his face, added, "No, I take that back. I kind of like the idea that languages evolved, and I wonder why. Why do they always diverge and never converge? Why don't they ever improve, like everything else? Surely, by now there should be a language in which everything thinkable could be said without ambiguity."

"I thought that was French."

She laughed. "Yeah, right. Anyway, it is kind of interesting, except . . ." She let out a sigh. "I'm tired."

"I guess you are. Look, kiddo, you need a break, take some time off. Let the big-domes wait for their data."

"Maybe."

"Hey, I'm not kidding." He tapped the monitor with a knuckle. "See this blue smear? Excessive seriousness. You need to loosen up. Go a little crazy. I say this as your personal physician."

"Okay, Doc. I'll try, in my pathetically serious way. I shall buy a box of Cracker Jacks and, perhaps, if I feel up to it, ride the carousel."

She waved and left, before she had to absorb any more well-meaning advice. The subway was filling up. A ragged black man on crutches got on at Seventy-second Street and sang "Swing Low, Sweet Chariot" as he shuffled through the car. Lucy put a wad of dollar bills in his cup as he went by. All the other passengers pretended not to see this, although several shot her dirty looks. She pulled out a German dictionary and memorized *Bleibe* through *Boden* for the rest of the trip to Thirty-fourth Street.

At Holy Redeemer, people were starting to gather for the five-o'clock mass. She sat in the rearmost pew, pulled out a kneeler, and got down, but her mind was too restless for common prayer. She did not, in any case, wish to pray. In the recent past, the spirit would have come to her, unbidden, filling her with uncanny joy, and she had imagined, despite all she had read, that this would be a constant thing, like her talent with languages, but it proved not to be so. Treats for beginners, one of the saints had called it, and like the spoiled baby she was, Lucy wanted

more. The notion of actually doing spiritual work dismayed her: Was
God yet another struggle like *math*? Oh, far, far harder than quadratic
equations, as she knew in her bones. The worst was that she suspected
that her mother had gone through the same crisis at about the same
age—there had been hints enough—and had blown a big raspberry at
deep religion and had gone off on her merry way, doing exactly what she
pleased, while punching her card every week in the good old thoughtless
devotional Catholic way. Lucy had no intention of going that route, no
intention, but intention was not, apparently, good enough. Her mind
wandered, as did her gaze, and she spotted David Grale in a side chapel.
He was lighting candles, five of them, and then he sank down before an
image of the Virgin and appeared deep in prayer. She watched him,
examining as best she could in the dim light the curl of his hair and the
tender, exposed nape of his neck as he bowed his head. She discovered
her mind filling up brimful with what they used to call impulse thoughts;
she became disgusted with herself entirely and stalked out.

Lucy sat on the steps, hunched under her cloak in the late-afternoon
chill. In her bag were scattered packs of the cigarettes she gave away,
and she found some Marlboros, twitched one out, and smoked it, without much pleasure, to get back at her body via that small pollution. She
watched people: old Latinas in black, people from the varied races of
Asia, mostly poor, a few old white Catholics in shabby, unfashionable
clothes—the small daily mass crowd, the pathetic remnants of her
mother's church.

He came out and sat next to her. They sat in silence for a while, for
which she was grateful. He always had this calming effect on her, stilling
the boil of language in her head.

Then he asked, "Anything wrong?"

"No!" instinctively; then, "Yes. I find that the world is not perfect."

"Then the world must be changed." He laughed. She laughed, too.
The line was from Pasolini's *The Hawks and the Sparrows*, St. Francis's
comeback to the friars sent to preach the Gospel to the birds. The hawks
still killed the sparrows; what can we do? cried the friars, it is the way of
the world. *Then the world must be changed.* David had a tape of it, and
they had watched it together in a church basement.

"I'm going over to the yards. I heard someone say they saw Canman
today. I thought I'd check it out."

"I'll come with you."

They walked over. She made amusing conversation, with mimicry. She was, of course, a perfect mimic. Sometimes when he laughed, he clutched her around the shoulder, and she felt blood flush into her face, and not just her face either.

They went through the fence and down the rutted, trash-strewn path to the walkway. There they heard the sounds: shouts and a shrill keening. Lila Sue.

David broke into a run and Lucy followed him, her bag slamming against her hip, her cloak flying behind. When they got to the settlement, they found Real Ali attempting to get between Doug Drug and Benz, who were apparently trying to kill each other. They were in the center of a circle made up of inhabitants, watching the fight with fear on their faces, or avidity or insanity, depending on the twists of their particular psyches. Benz clutched a forty-ounce beer bottle with the bottom smashed off; Doug held a long chunk of dark pallet wood like a ball bat. Someone had kicked the fire barrel over. Smoke and sparks and cinders filled the air, the red glow from the fire lighting the faces of the combatants from below: Doug's dark skin like a furnace coal, his eyes red-lit, Benz's big teeth glittering demonically, the large black warts on her sweaty face throwing little moving shadows. The two fighters, the man and the woman, shouted curses at one another, not very imaginatively but with feeling and much spit. Ali was dancing between them, arms out, palms flattened, making soothing noises, "Come on, man, you don't wanna hurt nobody"; but they did. Lila Sue stood off to one side, in front of the hut she shared with Benz, howling, seemingly without taking a breath, her knuckles screwed into her eye sockets like spark plugs.

Grale moved instantly to stand before Doug and started to talk in his sweet voice, the meaningless, calming nonsense spoken to mad dogs or crazies. The poised stick wavered. Benz screamed and tried a dash around Ali. She was a great heavy sack of a woman, swaddled like *l'homme Michelin* in many layers, and she drove him backward several steps. Doug swung his stake at David. The blow whistled by his ear and landed on his shoulder. He staggered almost to his knees. Still, he did not try to protect himself. He spread his arms outward, martyrlike, offering himself.

"Hit me again, Doug!" he cried. "Does that make you feel better? Go ahead, hit me!"

Without knowing exactly how she had come by it, Lucy found she had a piece of fractured concrete in her hand, about the size of a softball, with a protruding sharp edge, and she found herself running toward Doug, around the struggling Ali and Benz, toward his blind side.

"Lucy! No!" David shouted. What she heard, though, was only the breath rushing through her mouth and the drum of her mother's blood in her ears. She wound up like an outfielder and slugged the man as hard as she could behind his ear, and when he went down, she was kneeling on his chest with the rock raised high above her head for the death blow when David swept her into his arms and smothered with his body the demon she had somehow become.

"What, um, what happened?" Candlelight on faces, David's and Ali's. She looked around. They were in Ali's hovel of cardboard, pallet wood, and plastic, familiar ground, but something was wrong. She was lying on his mattress, and there should have been a table with the Qur'an on it, and a straight chair and the neatly stacked orange crates that held Ali's paperback library. But everything had been smashed and broken and pushed into piles. "Did he hit me?"

"No, girl," said Ali, "you hit *him.* Like to busted his head."

A shock of fear. She looked at David, who had an awful red scrape down one side of his neck. "I didn't hurt him, did I?"

Ali said, "Nah, he got a hard head, Doug."

She rubbed her face. "God! This is weird—I can't remember hitting him. I remember the fight, Doug and Benz and you trying to break it up, you and David, and then Doug hit David. I thought he was going to kill you. And then I . . ." She shook her head energetically. "No, it's . . . wait a second . . . now it's coming back. I had a rock. I hit him in the head with a rock."

"Yes, you did," said David gently. "That was a different Lucy than the one we usually see around church." She felt herself blushing and was glad of the dark.

Ali chuckled and said, "Good thing, too. The boy *needed* a rock upside his head. Fool been smoking sherms all morning. I *hate* that angel dust."

"Was that what the fight was about?" Lucy asked.

"Nah, I don't know *what* in hell that was about. I think Benz thought he was messing with Lila Sue. You know how she gets."

"I calmed her down," said David. "She's really a very loving person." He sighed. "I guess if we were going to get all social worky, we would try to find someplace for that girl, but somehow I can't bring myself to do it. They make each other so happy." He looked around and seemed to see the wreckage for the first time.

"What happened in here? Not Doug?"

"Nah, the damn cops," said Ali. He started picking up items, examining them for damage, and tossing those few that failed to meet his generous standards of usefulness out the door.

"Cops?" asked Lucy. "Cops can't do that. They can't even come in here without a warrant."

Ali laughed and said, "Uh-uh, sugar, warrant's for when they bust into a home. Me being a homeless man, I don't *have* no home, so I guess they don't need no warrant."

"I don't think that's true, but anyway, they had no right to break up your stuff. Why did they do it?"

Ali set an orange crate on end and placed a couple of books carefully on its shelf. "Well, you know they don't need no reason, but these particular cops that did it was looking for Canman. I told them I didn't know where he was staying. They said, I mean the white one, they said I do know, I was his running buddy, and he starts pushing me around, like they do, and I go, 'Officer, only thing I *know* is there is no God but God, and Mohammed is the messenger of God.' And my own name. Everything else is speculation, and did they want me to speculate. And I told them that if they wanted to know every damn thing I knew about Canman, they should go talk to the other cop who came around last night. That's when the white guy went nuts and started busting up my stuff. The black fella, he wasn't too enthusiastic about it, I could tell, but I guess he had to back up his partner's play."

David started to help Ali pick up, but the older man waved him away, saying he had his own way of doing things, and he didn't want anything good to be mistakenly tossed out. He set up his rickety table, and after wiping off and kissing his Qur'an, he placed it in the center. "The funny thing was I did see Canman this morning, early, just after I done my morning prayers. I'm always the first one up around here anyway. He was skulking around the paper house with his dog, just like a dog his own self, to look at him. I asked him was he coming back to live here, and he snarled at me, just like a damn dog. Pulled a knife on me, too. Boy was scared, I tell you that."

"Of what?" asked Lucy. "Of the cops?"

"Maybe. The first cop kind of hinted that they had him in their sights for the slasher since Fake Ali got it. That would scare me. But, look, that Canman, he been scared for a long time, scared of stuff that go way past the cops. Stuff nobody but him can see. A sad cat, that Canman."

David asked, "Ali, do you think he's the one?"

"He could be. He got enough hate in his soul to cut people up. But it's not like I got any what you call evidence for it?"

"Where do you think he is?"

Ali gave David a long apprising look and answered, "Well, like I told them all, I don't know, which is God's honest truth. But if *I* was going to look for Canman, which I am not, I guess I'd start under Penn. I hung out there five, seven years, back before they cleaned us all out of there, before they cleaned us out and all. And when I *got* there, he'd *been* there longer than any of us. Not that there ain't some been there longer than him. Some people been down there so long they ain't hardly people anymore. Live on rats and garbage." Ali lowered his voice. "And other stuff. Human flesh. Someone goes down a station at three in the morning and never comes back up. What they say, anyway. I guess he's gone back under. No cops down there."

"But there are," said David. "There are regular patrols. I've been on some of them."

"Uh-huh, son," said Ali, stooping to pick up a broken chair. He shifted it in his big hands, trying to see how it could be fitted together again. "I mean *under. Under* under. Them tunnels is *deep.* Nobody down there but the rats and the mole people."

Lucy and David left a little while later. When they were back on the street, Lucy turned to him and said, "I'm sorry."

"Sorry? About what?"

"You know . . . losing it. Getting violent. It never happened to me before. I feel sick."

He stopped walking, faced her, and put both hands on her shoulders. "Stop it! You do this all the time. Stop eating at yourself! You did something wrong, but you did it for good reasons."

"Why should that make a difference?"

"It does. The intent of the act counts. You didn't do it out of some secret pleasure or to go along with what someone else was doing, or out of fear. You thought Doug was going to hurt me, and you acted without thought. It was a failure of attention." He grinned at her. "That seems to be your particular fault, if you don't mind me saying so."

After a moment, she smiled back. "*Mea maxima culpa.* I guess I was upset because, well, I was thinking of my mother and how I would rather not turn out the way she has, and when I do things like . . . oh, just things in general that remind me, *yin shui si yuan,* it drives me up the wall."

"Your mother seems very nice," he said diplomatically.

"In her saner moments," she snapped, and then sighed. "Oh, she *is* very nice. She's a great woman, and I admire the hell out of her, but I don't want to *be* her. We drive each other crazy. I guess all kids do."

"I wouldn't know. I never had a family." Then, to cover her embarrassment, he added quickly, "What was that thing you said? Was it Chinese?"

"Oh, yeah, a four-character idiom. It's a habit I picked up when I was living a lot with this family, the Chens. Chinese speakers are always slipping them into their speech, practically without thinking, like we do with 'anyway' and 'whatever' and 'like.' It means 'When you drink water, think of the source.' Anyway"—they both laughed—"what are we going to do about Canman?"

"I don't know. Finding him would be a good start."

"Down in the tunnels."

"I guess, if that's where he is. You're dying to come, aren't you?"

She nodded. "Do you think the mole people really live on human flesh?"

"I have no idea. But people do, if they're desperate enough. In the Sudan, where I was, there were famines all the time. In the camps you would see some people eating meat, sheep they said, but you never saw any sheep around." They were at a light, the evening traffic rushing up by Tenth Avenue. He looked out at the river of steel, and she saw that his face had lost the brightness that ordinarily shone from it, replaced by the sort of expression they put up on crucifixes in rural Spain. "But God for-gives all," he said. And then suddenly the brightness turned on again, like the light that just then turned from red to green. "Even you, Lucy, you horrible old sinner. Even me, if you can believe it."

"But you're good," she blurted out.

A ghostly smile. "Only God is good, kid. Me? Oh, me, you have no idea."

8

THE NEXT MORNING LUCY AND HER FATHER, TYPICALLY THE TWO EARLIEST risers in the household, sat companionably at breakfast, Karp whipping through the *Times,* ignoring the travails of nations, including his own, focusing on the scant crime news and sports. Here a little basketball discussion, March Madness, they were nearly down to the Final Four, when she asked abruptly, "Daddy, the police need a warrant to come into somebody's house, don't they?"

"Ordinarily, yes, unless in hot pursuit of a suspected felon," Karp replied, reading on.

"What if it's not a regular house or apartment? Like if it's a little shack where a homeless person is living?"

Karp dropped the paper shield. "Hm. That would depend. If a guy's sitting on a park bench or sleeping in a doorway, no—it's a public place. In the home, the governing rule is from *Payton v. New York*—you need a warrant except in exigent circumstances. The question then is, what's a home? A homeless shelter is a home under *Payton;* a cave on government property is not. But there was a case a couple of years back where the cops rousted a guy out of a tent he'd set up in Central Park, and the courts threw out the search. Kind of a nice decision, too; the judge said something to the effect that a place of usual repair at night was a home under the law, regardless of its lack of ordinary amenities."

"So if cops like came into someone's shack that they built, and busted up all his stuff, that would be against the law."

"Well, destroying property without good probable cause is always against the law, warrant or no warrant. An exception would be, for example, if they have reason to suspect there's drugs hidden in the bodywork of a car, they could tear it apart. This is an actual situation?"

"Yeah. A guy I know who lives down by the yards was raided the other day. They roughed him up and smashed all his things. They were looking for the slasher, but Ali didn't know anything."

"They arrested him?"

"No."

"Interesting. He get the name of the cops? Badge numbers?"

"No. They were detectives, I think. Plainclothes. They were looking for this man, they call him Canman, who had the place where I found Fake Ali's body. And Ali—I mean Real Ali—he already told another detective what he knew, which was nothing. He's black—Ali is—and, you know, you think, 'Oh, it's more cop racism,' but one of the two cops was black, so I guess it couldn't be that. But why would they send two different cops to talk to the same person?"

"Oh, some screwup," said Karp. "Tell your friend to report the abuse anyway."

"They won't really do anything, will they?"

"Probably not, but it adds to the record. The type of cop who racks up a sheet of persistent abuse, sooner or later he's going to do something they can't ignore, and at that point, if he's got fifty complaints against him, the bosses will maybe toss him out on his ear. If not, they might let it slide or defend him."

"That sucks."

"What else is new?" Karp agreed, but as he took up his paper again, he was thinking. Detectives harassing the homeless; okay, it happened, they were hot on a trail, sometimes they did not bother with the niceties. A pair of detectives, one white, one black, not exactly common in the NYPD, and they weren't the team primarily responsible for the slasher murders. That was Paradisio and Rastenberg, a pair of lilies. It could have been some other players from that team, but Karp doubted it. Why? No reason, except that little tingle that told him he was right. The rail yards were right in their stomping grounds, too. Had Cooley and Nash been assigned to the slasher team? Unlikely, and even if so, why would they cover the same ground that other cops already had? Preventing just that, conserving resources, was the whole point of a police task force. Again, the notion that Cooley was pursuing something personal, as with Lomax. Now Detective Cooley wanted this Canman character, but for what? Karp's eye paused at an article on the New York page: "Marshak Assailant Had Violent Juvenile Record." Oh, the *Times*! Now they've decided he was an assailant, not a victim, which went well with the statement of a "source" at the DA that they had not settled on the precise nature of the charges pending further investigation, although second-degree manslaughter could not be ruled out. There was no evidence that Ms. Marshak (the actual assailant here) had been attacked. Police sought a possible witness. Karp wondered who the source was. Roland, probably. More significant was the unnamed source who had sent Ramsey's juvenile records to the reporter, C. Melville Bateson. A great name for a *Times* reporter—solid, like the pillars of a public building. Ramsey, it seemed, had done six months in Spofford for armed robbery at age seventeen. Juvenile records were supposed to be sealed, and their revelation at an adult trial was prohibited by law. They were easy enough to obtain, however, if you made the effort, and you wanted to blacken the character of a victim, and you were inside the system; like, for example, Norton Fuller.

As he mused on this, Lucy interrupted his thoughts. "It's so unjust. Can't you do *anything?*"

Karp put the paper down again. "Technically, yes; practically, not much. It would come down to the word of two police officers against that of a homeless man. No case, even if your guy's telling the absolute truth. It's an imperfect system."

"The *system!*" Contemptuously. "Everyone blames the system, but the system's made up of people, all of them doing bad things a lot of the time. How do you stand it?"

Karp often wondered the same thing, and now he thought, uncomfortably, of his conversation with Solotoff. Sighing heavily, he replied, "It's not easy, kid. It is just that it's better than the obvious alternatives. Letting crime flourish, for example. Arbitrary violence, for example, which is a lot more feel-good than the law. Look at how popular those movies about the Mob and rogue cops are. The law can't touch the villain, so the hero whacks him out. End of story. But in real life . . . ? You know, your mom was into that for a long time, in real life. Did *you* like it?"

The girl sniffed. "Oh, I guess not. But can't you do *anything?*"
"Oh, yeah," said Karp, smiling. "I'll think of something."

Lucy walked out the door, fully intending to go to school. But as she strode down Lafayette to the Lex station, the events of the past days bore her down. She could not remove from her mind the moment when she had touched Fake Ali's shoulder, and his body had slid backward, and the wound in his throat had gaped open like an obscene grin. And the fight with Doug, and what the cops had done to the harmless, decent Real Ali. The world was full of death, sin, and depravity, a choking fog. The thought of sitting in a bright classroom full of silly girls, concentrating on the glories of literature or the course of American history, nauseated her, as did the fact that she had been cutting classes fairly regularly and was hopelessly behind, had failed or would fail all her midterms, and owed in the next two weeks term papers in both French lit and American history that she had not started to think about. At the subway station, therefore, she found her body moving as if controlled by an outside force, away from the Lexington line and through the crowded tunnels to the uptown N train. She toed the yellow line, close to the edge, and stood there as the train came in, the scream of the wheels and the roar of air and engine obliterating thought for a grateful instant. Maybe a crazy person would push her and that would be it, but none did, and she let herself be jostled into the car by the crowd, exhausted and ashamed of these thoughts. She found a seat and gave it up immediately to an old man with a cane. She got the usual embarrassed smile from him, and the usual scowls or confused looks from the able-bodied in their seats. The faces around her seemed gargoylish, oozing sin, selfishness, cruelty. And was she different? Hardly. She would have committed murder, too, had she not been stopped by David.

Rising panic, a foul taste in her mouth, sweat cold on her forehead. The bodies pressed against her as the train swayed. She couldn't bear it. The train stopped, and she squirmed out. Thirty-fourth Street. She stood on the platform, frozen in the moving mob. I'm losing my mind, she thought, this isn't happening to me. The train pulled out. She heard music, a saxophone. She turned. A black man in a skullcap and a long, dirty raincoat was playing "Autumn Leaves," a sweet, rich sound, amplified by the concrete vault of the subway. Across the tracks, on the downtown side, she saw a Chinese man kneel and open a violin case and begin to play the same song, in harmony, a spontaneous duet.

She listened, rapt, until the end of the song, then dropped a dollar into the horn man's case and found that she could move again. One of the little city miracles. She left the subway with a lighter heart and went off to find David Grale. At Holy Redeemer, she found that he had been by the kitchen earlier and had gone off with the bike. This was a grocery man's rig with a big hamper over the front wheel, which was used to bring supplies and food to people too debilitated or ornery to come in for services. One of the layworkers said that David was planning to cruise the yards. Lucy walked west and found the bike where she expected, leaning against a torn chain-link fence. She descended to the homeless village, where she found David and Benz half-dragging, half-carrying what looked like an enormous duffel bag, which, from the sound it made, must have been full of scrap metal. Lila Sue danced around them, flapping her hands in agitation. As Lucy came closer, she saw that it was not a duffel bag, but a man.

"It's a balloon man, he fell from the upstairs tracks in the sky," said Lila Sue helpfully. Lucy's heart sank.

"Hi, Lucy," said David. "Can you give us a hand here?"

"Oh, no, not another one!" she wailed.

"No, just old Jingles," said Grale. "We found him down on the tracks. He's comatose."

"He's comatose and his other toes are frozen," said Lila. "It was too cold on the tracks in the sky, and the pain came through at once, puff puff, said the rain train. Let me tell you my story, Lucy."

"Not right now, Lila," said Lucy. She grabbed one of Jingles's arms, Benz grabbed the other, and David heaved up the bottom half. Jingles, a person of complex ethnicity, was dressed in the usual multiple layers, the top one of which was an army field jacket of extraordinary filthiness. It was covered, as were the equally foul trousers, with dozens of small metal objects—pop tops, squashed cans, gears, fragments of automobiles thrown from street crashes, broken tools, parts from a TV, pieces of a toaster—necessary to keep the CIA from tracking him by means of the beacon they had implanted in his body. These accessories gave him his street name. As she carried, Lucy tried not to think about the grime under her hands, or the smell, a compound of wine stink, unwashed human, and something sharp, sweet, and chemical. Hideous, but one was not supposed to mind those things in the service of the afflicted. She tried (and failed) to imagine St. Catherine licking the sores of the lepers and for inspiration looked back at David, who gave her his angelic grin and said, "He sure stinks, doesn't he? Wine and huffing glue, the famous death-wish cocktail. If Benz hadn't've found him, he would've puked up and strangled in the vomit. And what a loss to the world that would be."

"The boss of the world likes me," said Lila Sue. "I bring her flowers and balloon pickles, and you know what?"

"What, honey?" said David. They were at the incline now, and David was supporting most of the dead weight.

"She has every color, even green and purple chocolate! Now I have a different story."

"Later, Lila Sue," Benz grunted as they lay Jingles down at the top of the slope. As they did so, the man jerked violently, and his face turned slaty blue while appalling noises issued from his mouth. Benz shrieked.

"Christ, he's choking," David cried. "Lucy! Benz! Flip him over. Pry his mouth open. Do it!"

They heaved Jingles over, slipping on the littered ground. David straddled the man, locked his hands under Jingles's midriff, and heaved several times. Cringing, Lucy pried open Jingles's clenched jaws and was rewarded by a spasmodic series of coughs and a gush of foul-smelling yellow fluid all over her hands.

Jingles coughed some more, shook, pissed on himself, and settled again into oblivious slumber, snoring. Lucy held her hands out in front of her like a zombie.

David laughed. "You should see your face, Lucy."

"Oh, shut up! What am I supposed to do now?"

He put an arm around her shoulder. "It's all part of the saint biz, kid. You'll get used to it. Or you won't. Meanwhile, I can only baptize you with water."

He led her across the street and down an alley, where they found a standpipe and faucet without a handle. He took one from his jacket pocket and turned on the water. She washed her hands and dabbed with a handkerchief at the splatters on her skirt and stockings. She sank once more into shame.

"What are we going to do with Jingles?"

"Oh, I'll get him over to the VA. They'll keep him for a week until he dries out and then toss him back. And in a couple of weeks, if he doesn't get hit by a car or fall asleep on the tracks, I'll have to do it again. The poor ye have always with you. And the stupid, and the miserable, and the hopelessly damaged."

"Why do you do it then?"

"Why? It's my calling. And I don't have many other skills." He shut off the water, pocketed the handle. "Not like you, for example. Why do *you* do it? And why aren't you in school?"

She shrugged. "I don't know. It just seems like the right thing to do, helping people. The middle-class life, you know, school and having stuff, and buying stuff . . . it gives me the willies sometimes. I want all of that"—she gestured widely, taking in the armies of the destitute of New York—"to go away. I want things to be different. So people like Jingles and Benz and Ali can have real lives. How much would it cost? And this city has so much money, it makes me sick, and it's the poor old Church that has to take up the slack, people like you . . ." She stopped, embarrassed again. "I mean, it can't go on, can it?"

"Oh, yeah. You'd be surprised what people can take and how long horrible things can go on. Meanwhile"—he jabbed a thumb in the direction they had come from—"this is paradise. Jingles's life would be pure heaven to two-thirds of the people on the planet. We have to believe in ultimate mercy, you know."

"Ultimate mercy? You mean grace?"

"I mean death." He had for just a second that look on his face, the stranger she sometimes saw there, and then the lovely smile was back, and he said, "I tell you what—lend me your fancy cell phone, and I'll get old Mr. J. picked up, and then I'll run you across on my bike and we'll distribute charity for a while, and then we'll have lunch. I can tell you need cheering up, my little saintlet. Let's see if we can't generate a few moments of joy."

Thinking of something, Karp called for Murrow and told him what to do. Murrow wrote it down with his small golden pencil in the little leather-bound notebook he always carried.

"Is that legal?" he asked.

"Barely. It's also one of the large number of barely legal things you would not like known that you've done."

"Check. Are you going to the big press conference?"

"I might drop by. I might stand in the back and sob because my words aren't being taken down by newsies to decorate the Bloomingdale's ads."

"Yes, it's sad. I assume this conference is to respond to McBright's speech. What did you think of it?"

Karp picked a thin sheaf of paper from his cluttered desk and flipped through it casually. "An impassioned cry for justice. Unfortunate for Marshak that Desmondo Ramsey had a photogenic, middle-class, grieving family. Basically a decent kid with a few problems, not unlike yourself, Murrow. My daughter knew him slightly, as a matter of fact. Did you catch the reference in the *Times* to his juvie record?"

"Yeah. Character assassination of the victim. He was in on a stickup as a kid, so, therefore, okay to blast him. But what you asked me to do . . . that's on another case."

"Yes, it is, but you notice McBright mentions Lomax, too, and also our old pal Jorell Benson, accused killer of a politically significant group member. The picture he's painting is of a DA's office that skews justice according to skin color and politics. A black guy gets shot, they give the white fellow that shot him a pass, just like they're getting ready to give Sybil a pass. A black guy is accused of killing a white, they put him up for the death penalty." Karp thumbed through the transcript pages. "Here's a good part: 'That beautiful lady Justice has a blindfold on. And the job of district attorney demands that her blindfold be tight across her eyes, so that skin color and class and how much money or political influence you have and whether you're homeless or not doesn't matter. But Jack Keegan has tugged that blindfold down so far you can't call it Justice anymore. Another one of those little tugs, Jack, and we might as well call her Ms. Lynch.' Pretty powerful stuff."

"But untrue," said Murrow in a tone tinged with hope.

Karp gave him a hard look, then smiled and tossed the transcript down. "Of course, untrue. And also somewhat true. In fact, Justice is unequal. It's the case that almost everyone on death row in this country got there by killing white people. It's the case that most black defendants are poor and are defended by public defenders with no resources and less than adequate time to prepare cases. It's the case that the cops and us tend to pay more attention when a lowlife kills a citizen, black or white, than when a lowlife kills another lowlife, and it's a fact that a really high proportion of mutts in this town are black or Hispanic. It's the case that the system *depends* on those inequities, because if every accused felon we got in here could afford to mount a case like Sybil Marshak is going to mount, we would have to expand the courts and prosecutorial systems a hundredfold. But I also think that the inequities are the result of class and poverty. It used to be Irish, Jews, and Italians—now it's blacks and Hispanics. There's no specific racism involved here like there was in the Jim Crow South. Out on the street, with cops, it might be different, but not here. Okay, I'll give you that if Benson had killed his cousin the crack dealer, we would not even be thinking about seeking death. On the other hand, given the vic, I think Roland would come down just as hard on Benson if Benson was a nice Jewish boy." Karp grimaced. "Hell, *harder* probably, and his instinct is to cream Marshak, too. So, in that sense, McBright is demagoguing. There's no . . ." Karp moved his hands, searched for a phrase.

"Element of intent?"

"Exactly, Murrow," Karp agreed, after a brief pause to determine whether the kid was cracking wise again. "The element of intent. We're corrupt, but not vile. I don't know about you, but it keeps me going. Now, scram and do that stuff. Let me know how it goes."

Murrow went off, and Karp had to restrain his impulse to call him back, to forget the whole thing. He screwed around with minor stuff all morning, wrote a set of blistering memos to ADAs whose case preparation was not up to his standards, had a couple of brief meetings, spent a good deal of time resisting the temptation to make himself feel more useful by creating work for others. In fact, much of what he used to do had been taken over by Fuller. It was all the administrative stuff he disliked doing, but had recently found that it was just this stuff that had allowed him to get anything important done. It turned out that a threat to delay a load of new furniture was a greater goad to right action than a lawsuit that might cost the state millions or throw some poor sucker unjustly into prison. Fuller had those threats in *his* pocket now, and Karp, as a result, found himself a lot less potent bureaucrat. The good side of this was that it gave him much more time to poke around the office, visiting courtrooms and making a nuisance of himself to the sloppy and unprepared. He also had time to drop by press conferences.

This was a big one: the area outside the elevator bank on the eighth floor was jammed with TV crews and print reporters and lit with the glare of many lamps. Karp went to the back of the room. A little group of ADAs was back there already. Karp knew a few of them, all ridiculously young-looking. He traded a few wisecracks with Dave Pincus, a homicide guy, and chatted briefly with a few others whose faces he did not immediately know, a thin dark woman in her first few months at homicide, named Meghan Lacy, and a slim, bespectacled blond guy in a good blue suit, Peter something, whose job Karp could not immediately place. He recalled that he used to pride himself on knowing all the more senior ADAs, those who had been there more than a year or so, but it seemed that faces had lost their bite on his consciousness, or maybe it was just that these young, unformed faces had too little bite, like the interchangeable ones who populate TV sitcoms. Or maybe it was the mental decrepitude of age.

Karp was tall enough to see over the heads of the crowd, and he had a good view when Keegan emerged from the DA suite with Fuller and Hrcany in tow. All the TV lights went on now, and the three of them all got that bleached look, like earthlings being levitated on a light beam to a flying saucer. Keegan stepped up to the thrusting mikes and read a short statement. He said that his office had always followed the law without fear or favor, that it would continue to do so, despite claims to the contrary from irresponsible political opponents intent on increasing racial tension to their own selfish advantage. It was not his usual policy to comment on cases before charges were filed. In view of the substantial public interest in a number of current cases, he thought it responsible to make an exception. He introduced Roland as homicide bureau chief and then prepared to take questions.

The journalists shouted all at once; this was not the White House. Keegan restored some order and picked up a question about Marshak. No, charges had not been decided upon. The investigation was ongoing. The DA was not aware of who had leaked Ramsey's juvenile record. It was not this office. He deplored it and said it would have no effect on the charges brought, if any. No, no charge had been ruled out. Murder? No, no indication that such a charge was justified at present. No, nothing was ruled out.

Peter, who was standing close to Karp, murmured, "Headline: 'DA Considering Murder Charge for Marshak.'"

Karp smiled and replied, "Subhead: 'I'm No Racist Nazi, DA Claims.'"

"It's a shame he has to do this," said Peter. "The election, I guess."

"You guess right. It's still a no-win for him."

The press had exhausted Marshak. Now they turned to Benson. Was the DA going for the death penalty? With such a weak case? It wasn't weak, said the DA, and turned to Roland, who stepped forward and gave a rundown on the strengths of *Benson,* referencing a bunch of other cases where the DA had convicted on the same sort of evidence. They had an eyewitness; they had the loot. Would they be asking for death if the victim hadn't been a Hasidic Jew? That had nothing to do with it, said Roland, straight-faced. Karp knew in his deepest heart that making such a cynically false statement in public was as entirely beyond him as winning the New York marathon and wondered briefly whether this was a defect or a virtue in a public official. So much for Benson. Karp saw a thin brown arm go up. She said her name, he didn't catch it. But he caught the name of her paper.

"Mr. Hrcany," she said. "You seem to be taking your time investigating the murder of a black man shot by Ms. Marshak, and yet the shooting of Shawn Lomax was whipped through the grand jury in record time, despite a number of unexplained details about the shooting and the behavior of the police officers involved, Brendan Cooley and Willie Nash. Could you explain why that happened?"

The volume in the room went up two notches. Cooley's was a familiar name to city beat reporters. Roland was clearly taken aback by the question. He made the mistake of glancing at Keegan, which would look terrific on tape—a sneaky subordinate checking the coming lie with his boss. Then he rolled his great shoulders, squared his jaw, and said, "I have no idea what you're talking about, Miss Umm. Although I'm not intimately familiar with that case, I understand that the officers involved shot Mr. Lomax to defend their lives. The . . . Mr. Lomax tried to ram their car with the stolen car he was driving."

"Did he? Well, could you tell us then why all the bullets that struck him came from the back? He was shot ten times in the back, Mr. Hrcany. How could he be shot ten times in the back while he was allegedly driving head-on toward the police in their car?"

Uproar, actual baying. Roland's face became immobile, its faint smile fixed like a slug in formalin. "I have no information as to, in reference to, the details of the case. The grand jury obviously has made a decision not to indict . . . to consider this a justified shooting, and . . ."

"Did the grand jury see this autopsy report? Did the district attorney tell the grand jurors that Shawn Lomax was shot in the back ten times?" She had a carrying, mellow, cultivated voice, unexcited, each syllable evenly stressed, like an elementary-school teacher asking Johnny whether he had done his homework.

Karp saw the warning front of red appear on Roland's cheeks and sent an urgent thought message: *Just say we'll look into it, be gracious, and get the hell out of there!* But no; Hrcany was an iceberg in the courtroom, absolutely unflappable, but he was not in one now, and he was being embarrassed in front of his boss and Fuller. By a woman. By a black woman.

He said, "This is not the place to split hairs about what the grand jury did or did not see, *miss!* Grand jury testimony is secret by law—I don't know where you got hold of that information . . ."

"I have a copy of the police report."

"Which I'm sure you're not authorized to have. Can we move on?"

Roland pointed to a man. But, of course, the man wanted to know the same thing the woman wanted to know. Blood in the water. Was the DA running a cover-up? If the report was correct, would the DA reindict? Would the police report be generally released? Was Cooley getting a special deal? All the sorts of questions that weren't meant to obtain answers as much as to make public officials look like prevaricating saps on television. Roland's voice grew harsher, until he was practically screaming answers at the reporters. Karp saw Keegan grip Roland's arm and speak into his ear. The DA stepped forward, promised a full investigation of the Lomax affair, and closed the conference. He attempted a dignified exit toward the DA suite door, but he and Roland and Fuller were mobbed by shouting reporters. A couple of cops from the DA squad moved forward to try to clear a lane to the door, but there were too many people, and the TV cameramen, seeing actual conflict, were drawn forward by blood lust. The boom mikes swayed over the press like the pikes of the villagers attacking Frankenstein's lab. Karp thought to himself, why not? And, signaling Peter Whoever and Dave Pincus to follow him, they surged like icebreakers into the throng, using their hips and elbows with abandon.

No one, it turned out, was injured, except in their dignity. Karp managed to shoehorn Roland into an elevator, along with Peter, Pincus, a couple of other ADAs, including Meghan, and a lone cop. Roland's face was brick red by now, and the negative aspects of his personality were in full spate. The elevators in the DA wing are notoriously slow, and during the descent from eight to six Roland had ample time to vent, and he did so in the most vile and obscene terms, concentrating upon the sex of his tormentor and her race, too. Karp was silent during this outburst, not from shock, for he understood something of the demonic forces rolling free beneath the conscious surface of Hrcany's mind, but because he honestly thought that, failing some verbal release, apoplexy was a real possibility. When the car stopped, Meghan Lacy rushed out as if to escape a contagion. Her face was bleached of color.

"You want to talk about this, Roland?" Karp offered, but this was rejected with a snarl as the man stalked away to his office. Karp went back to his own room, feeling traitorous and low. He twiddled a pencil and otherwise wasted public funds. He stared out a dirty window. He thought about touring courtrooms, which generally got his blood pumping, but just now he lacked the energy. A little tap at the door. He grunted assent, and Meghan Lacy came in. Her face looked damp, as if she had been crying and had splashed water on it. Her large, dark eyes were pinkly puffy. She came right to the point.

"I want a transfer. I don't want to work for that man anymore."

"A little extreme, don't you think? He just had a bad day."

She sniffed. "If you had a bad day, would you spew out sexist, racist crap like that?"

"No, but I'm not a tormented Hungarian genius like Roland Hrcany." Karp said it lightly, but she did not smile. She was one of the ones who came to prosecution out of a desire to make the world tidy, to mete out punishment with a fair hand, to work for justice. That type tended to become chronically angry when they finally realized that this was not what public prosecution was all about.

"And what Bateson was saying? Is it true?"

"Was that Bateson? C. Melville? Of the *Times*?"

She nodded.

"True? I guess partly. She obviously had the police report. Like the DA said, we'll look into it. About transferring, why don't you think about it for a while? You're a good prosecutor. You should stay in homicide."

"Not while he's there. I've noticed it a lot before this, you know. With women. Sly digs, snickers with the boys. Okay, that's like par for the course, right? He never actually, you know, did anything actionable. As for just now: God knows, I hear a lot of ripe language, but this was"—she cast about for words to describe it, failed, settled on—"over the line."

Karp cleared his throat. This was not the first of this sort of conversation he'd had with sharp, young female attorneys in re Roland.

"Look, Meghan—Roland has a problem with women, and with African-Americans, true, but in almost twenty years of working with him, I've never known it to affect his substantive judgment on the job. He has a problem with women because when he was ten, his family was escaping from Hungary during the revolt there when a big Russian bullet went through his mother's head and splashed her brains all over him. I think he just froze up then, some way, in the understanding and tenderness department, and he never got around to unfreezing. I hate psychologizing anyone, but I'd say that Roland finds it hard to trust anyone female. Given that, the fact that he's never, as far as I know, blocked any woman from advancement is significant. And, as you point out, he keeps sex out of the office—no pinching, no hustling. Okay, that's one thing. Then he came to America, where he started in a school in Brownsville that was eighty percent black kids, and he was a skinny white kid with a funny name, who talked funny English. It was not pleasant, and it went on for a long, long time, which is why he made himself into the moose he now is. Is he a racist? I can only say he's kept that out of his work here, too." Karp spread his hands. "They say to understand all is to forgive all. Meanwhile, he's a great prosecutor, and you can learn a lot working for him."

She looked sulky, as the self-righteous often do when called upon to forgive. "A lot of people have had hard lives. That doesn't excuse it."

"No, I guess not." Karp took in a big breath, let it out. "Do you intend to take action, as having been damaged under the equal opportunity laws?"

Her mouth opened, but she thought again and shook her head. "No. I don't need that on my record. The boys don't like it, unless the guy's run his hand up your dress and promised you a fucking pay raise if you let him touch it. He'll dig his own grave, eventually." She got up and left.

All afternoon Karp waited for a call from Keegan, to meet, to strate-
gize the catastrophe, but none came. Apparently, on this issue he was out
of the loop. Maybe Jack didn't trust him anymore. That made them even.

He went home early, not as early as a judge, but early for him. He was
surprised to find Marlene there before him, on the old couch in front of
the TV, remote in her hand, flipping between NBC, ABC, and CNN.

He hung up his raincoat and sat down next to her. She offered a
cheek, and he kissed it. "Where is everyone?" he asked.

"The boys are in their room playing with matches. I paged Lucy, but
she hasn't called back yet."

Karp looked at the screen. There was an inset still photograph of a
familiar face: Richard Perry, in happier days. The rest of the screen was
taken up with a shot of a road, at night, in some town, damp from rain,
tatty, trash-strewn, not America. In the background, groups of soldiers
were standing around a few vehicles, drab Humvees and Land Rovers
painted white, the kind of Balkan scene that had over the past decade
become as familiar to television audiences as Letterman's grin. In the
foreground, an earnest young woman in a rain parka was talking at them.

"Perry's dead?" asked Karp.

"No, he's alive. They got him out."

"No kidding! Who, the army?"

"No, Osborne. Shh! Watch this!"

The scene changed—a taped segment, obviously recorded earlier—
it was daylight there in the Balkan village. Several tan Toyota SUVs
pulled up to what seemed to be the same soldiers. A door opened and
out stepped a tough-looking man in a black jumpsuit. He turned around
to open a back door, and Karp saw that OSBORNE INTL. was written in
white across his back. Then Richard Perry stepped out of the Toyota,
and all the soldiers applauded. Cut to Perry, a close-up; he was
unshaven, looking wan and exhausted, saying that it was good to be alive
and that he couldn't thank enough the team that had extracted him from
captivity. More tough guys in black jumpsuits got out and grinned at the
cameras. The announcer came back on and gave a brief description of
where Perry and his party were now—en route to a hospital in
Germany—and then back to the anchorperson with a split-screen, and
Lou Osborne was there, in his office, talking about how great it all was
and how Osborne never gave up on its clients.

"How did Osborne get them out?" Karp asked.

"Oleg did it, him and a bunch of ex-Soviet antiterrorist hard guys he has on retainer. It was the Serbs who snatched Perry, apparently, a splinter group, pissed off about Kosovo. The news broke just as I came in with the boys. Lou called me and told me to turn on the tube. I've been riveted ever since."

"I didn't know Osborne could do that—run rescue missions."

"Oh, Oleg has a pretty free hand in that area. Drag enough dollars through those places and rats come out of the woodwork. Lou, of course, is ecstatic."

"It's a good thing. Hard to lose someone like that."

"Oh, not about Perry as such. It's the IPO. It goes out tomorrow under the best possible conditions."

"So you'll be rich," said Karp neutrally.

"I guess. Rich enough to afford to eat at Paoletti's tonight. Why don't you grab up the monsters and I'll smear some makeup over my raddled face. My treat."

"What about Lucy?"

"I'll leave a note. But she doesn't eat anyway."

The next day, a Thursday, the last one in March, Karp saw that Shawn Lomax had finally made it into history in the Newspaper of Record, front page above the fold. There was a picture of Mrs. Martha Lomax, the mother, standing with the usual liberal dignitaries in front of a church. McBright was right next to her, holding an arm. The story was bylined C. Melville Bateson. It had never occurred to Karp that C. Melville was a black woman when he had told Murrow to fax the *Times* city desk, anonymously, the police report on the Lomax shooting. Maybe that was racism and sexism in him, too, but it didn't matter at this point. For twenty years Karp had been married to his idea of public law, trying to build something fine, or at least to keep the memory of something fine alive, against the slow water-drip erosion of stupidity and moral rot. And now he was down in it, too. Ten, even five years ago, it would never have occurred to him to leak a document to the press, and now he had done it, in a good cause, naturally, but wasn't that what they all said? It was like the first adultery. The first time you talk yourself into thinking it's true love, and before you know it, you're taking stone-faced whores to hot-sheet hotels. He thought yet again about what V.T. had said. Karp was stuck between unsavory choices. He was not going to somehow convert Jack Keegan into the man Garrahy was, the man he *needed* to work for, and for some reason he did not have it in him to turn into Garrahy himself. And maybe Solotoff had been right—maybe *Garrahy* wasn't even Garrahy. So he had thrown a bomb. He was a fanatic, after all, everyone said so, and that's what fanatics do. He tossed the paper away, as disgusted with himself as he had ever been.

But it got worse. On arriving at the courthouse he was summoned to the DA's office. Keegan was at his desk, flanked by Fuller. The DA's face was dark with anger. Fuller's bore its usual bland look, but it seemed to Karp to be a little too self-contained, as if the man were holding back an expression more pleased, even triumphant. Through his mind there flashed the thought that they'd found out about the homicide report, and that this was curtains. He sat down, opened his ledger, and asked, "What's up?"

"Wait," said Keegan in a dead voice. Karp noticed that the tip of Keegan's prop cigar was crushed as if he had pounded it on the table. A tape recorder was on his desk, and his fingers danced close to it, as if eager to mash PLAY. Hrcany walked in. Whatever the problem was, Hrcany clearly did not know about it. He was his ordinary cocky self. He pulled a chair away from the conference table and sat.

"Somebody die?" he asked.

"Listen to this!" snapped the DA, and started the tape.

It was scratchy and muffled, but the words were perfectly clear, as was the identity of the speaker. The screaming voice was silent at last, and Keegan stopped the tape.

"Where in hell did you get that?" Hrcany demanded.

"It came up through the mail room in an interoffice pouch, with a note saying copies had been sent to the networks and the papers. How could you have been so *stupid*, Roland? On top of what's been going on,"—Keegan flung up his hands in disgust—"it's a total disaster."

"Hey, I lost my temper in a goddamn elevator, with no one but staff around. Is that a crime now?"

"He still doesn't get it," said Fuller.

Hrcany sprang to his feet. "Oh, go fuck yourself, you mealymouthed little putz!"

"Sit down, Roland, goddammit!" After a frightening pause, when for an instant it seemed to Karp that Roland would not, that he would spring across the intervening distance and tear Fuller to pieces, the man slumped back into his chair.

"I'd like to know who the fuck recorded that tape," Hrcany snarled. "There were six people in that elevator car—me, Butch, Pincus, a cop named Bradley, Meghan Lacy, and another assistant . . . Christ, I bet it was Lacy, that little bitch!"

"It wasn't Lacy," said Karp tiredly. "Lacy came to me later to complain about it. I talked her out of writing you up."

"So who was it? You?" The glitter of paranoia flicked on in Hrcany's blue eyes.

"Of course it wasn't me, Roland, and I hardly think it was Dave Pincus. Did you know the other guy . . . Peter something?"

"No, I thought you did."

"Right, and I thought he was a pal of Dave's or Meghan's from the office. He was wearing a lawyer suit, and he had the top edge of a plastic ID card showing in his breast pocket. A ringer."

"What? You think I was set up?"

"I don't know. The guy might've just hung around hoping to pick up something rich. It was pretty confused, as you recall. He must've had a mini-recorder in his pocket and turned it on when you started your rant."

"Listen to me, now!" the DA broke in, rapping hard on his desk. "I don't give a rat's ass how it happened. It happened, Roland, and it's on you. And I don't want to hear any horseshit about what's a crime and what's free speech. We've had cabinet officers dismissed in this country for telling a dirty joke. People have had their political careers wrecked for a chance remark, and let me tell you, buster, what's on that tape is no chance remark. It's sick! I have had twelve phone calls from the press this morning, asking me what action I'm going to take. I've put them off because I wanted to talk to you first."

Karp watched the DA's face form itself into a mash of righteous hypocrisy. "Look, Roland, I want you to know this isn't about the election or politics. It's simply unacceptable behavior, I mean the indication of attitudes that we simply cannot tolerate in a public organization like this. I think you need help, and I suggest you find some. And I think we should make this painful situation as brief as we possibly can, so . . . let's make it immediate, as of close of business today."

"You're *firing* me?" Hrcany was stunned. He turned and looked at Karp openmouthed, as if to say, this is some kind of joke, right?

"Is this really necessary, Jack?" Karp offered. "A leave of absence . . ."

"Dammit, Butch, I canned *you* for a lot less. I was able to hide you for a while—what you did, it could've been an accident. You got no history in that area, unlike Roland unfortunately, and people forget. But not this."

Roland was staring at Keegan. From where he sat, Karp could see a vein bulging dangerously in the man's temple. "You're *firing* me? After eighteen years? For this shit?"

"You can resign," said Keegan in a dull voice.

"Fucking right I resign, and fuck the bunch of you!"

Hrcany got up and stalked out of the room, slamming the door behind him.

There was a silence, which Karp broke by saying, "I can't believe this. I can't believe you're doing this."

"I have no choice. There's going to be a firestorm tonight and tomorrow . . . you saw the way the press is . . ."

Karp wasn't listening. "This whole thing sucks. It stinks of political expediency."

"Oh?" Keegan's voice rose. "The last time I checked, this was a political office, and let me tell you something, boyo: when *you* do the shitwork, and *you* kiss the fannies necessary to run for a political office, then *you* can pontificate to me about what the hell is necessary to run one." Keegan had turned dark pink in the face and was now jabbing in Karp's direction with his damaged cigar.

"You want my resignation, too, Jack? You can have it."

"Oh, pipe down! Don't get more noble on me than I can stomach! I don't want your resignation. I want you to take up where Roland left off, clean out this mess."

"Mess?" Karp goggled.

"Yeah, dammit! This mess in homicide. Benson, Marshak, the cop killing, what's-his-name, this Lomax thing, the bum slasher. It's wrecking us. I need you to fix it."

"What, you want me to take over *homicide?*"

"Right, homicide."

"You're making me bureau chief?"

Was that a little cloud that passed over the big pink face? Karp could usually read the DA pretty well, and he thought the man was burning a little too much coal in the sincerity engine. Karp snapped a quick look at Fuller. Fuller met his gaze levelly, but could not help showing a little tightness around the eyes, a lick of the lips, like a lizard practicing a go at a beetle. They were up to something. Karp felt his belly hollow out. There was no trust here. Had there ever been any? It didn't matter.

Keegan said, "Not officially. You can pick anyone you want as deputy, let him deal with the routine stuff. I want you to handle the high-profile cases. Get us out of this right, and we'll see about making it permanent." The DA brought a big politician's grin up from his collection of smiles. "Hell, it's what you always wanted, getting back there. You know you've been mooning after it like a damn kid in a toy store for the last five years. It used to drive Roland crazy."

Which was true, and so it took a good deal of resolve for Karp to say, "I need to think about it. For starters, I need to talk to my wife."

He went back to his office and sat for a while, feeling faintly nauseated. He had thought that by this time he had become utterly void of personal ambition, and it shocked him badly to find that it was not true. He wanted homicide badly, and the knowledge that Keegan knew that and was using the promise of a permanent appointment thereto as a manipulative tool did not entirely still his lust for the job. They wanted to keep him on the reservation until after the election, to saddle him with the political messes they had made, after which . . . who knew? The irony, of course, was that this leak had made the mess far worse, although building political pressure had been an essential part of his plan. But he had not expected this turn, he had really not expected Roland to ruin himself and leave Karp with the great soggy tar baby of homicide. He had imagined that he could stand off more, a gray eminence on staff, skillfully tweaking the system. Staff people did it all the time, leaking and lying—it was practically in the job description. But if he took homicide now, he'd be right in the center of it, having to fix what he himself had broken, with the prize he shamefully lusted for dangling from the hands of the DA and his nasty little . . .

Karp picked up the phone and pushed the speed button for Marlene's private line. It rang a long time before someone, not Marlene, picked it up, a man in fact, whose voice was loud and seemed slurred. There were peculiar noises in the background, thumping music, many voices, punctuated by shouts and whistles. The man said that it was crazy in there, but he'd try to find her. A clunk as the receiver was tossed down.

Shortly, he heard his wife's voice.

"What's going on? It sounds like a party."

"It *is* a party. We started drinking champoo this morning. You should come over and drink some. You could see distinguished corporate security personnel dancing on the desks in various states of undress. There is someone's tie hanging from my desk lamp. I expect panties to follow."

"This is about Perry?"

"Oh, Perry! Foo on Perry! He is rescued. We is rescued by his rescue. Perry is old news. The IPO went off today. Opened at eight, went to sixty and a quarter, and is hovering at fifty-five and a half. Fifty-five and a half. Fifty fucking five. And a half."

"Is that good or bad for the Jews?" Karp asked. She was clearly drunk, and he felt vexed about it because what he needed now was the calm, sensible, no-bullshit Marlene to succor him and support him and say, sure, take a job that involves no home life to speak of and eighteen-hour days, and I will pick up the emotional slack for you, darling . . .

"Oh, definitely good, especially those married to Osborne principals who have one point two million options at eight. Listen, Butchie, we're all going out to eat and carouse the night away. Could you do the boys and all?"

"Sure," in a flat voice.

"You're so mahvelous. Lovie love. See you later. Bye."

Karp put down the phone. Into his mind floated an aphorism his mother had often used—the worst thing in life is not getting your heart's desire; the second worst thing is getting it. He had missed her, really missed her ever since he was a child and cancer had closed her eyes for the last time, but he felt an unbearable pang of loss just now, the kind that makes you want to wail "Maaaaaa!"

The next thing that floated up unbidden was a bit of wondrous math: 1.2 million at 55 equals beaucoup, beaucoup buckerooskis. His mind skidded away from it. A ridiculous figure anyway, not real money even, some kind of accounting game. And too bad it had happened today, because he really wanted to talk this through with Marlene. Or did he? Hell, she got to do what she wanted, staying out however long the job took. Why couldn't he? Karp was not at all prone to self-pitying resentment, but he was not immune to it either. He felt a space opening between himself and the woman, and maybe part of what was prying it open was the fantasy money. Into that space rushed thoughts about being back at homicide, about having a real job again, the one job he was born to do. He walked the few steps to Keegan's office and told the DA that, yeah, he'd do it. If it could be fixed, he would fix it.

9

THE NEXT WEEK OR SO PASSED IN SOMETHING OF A DAZE FOR MARLENE. Everyone in the office down to the secretaries had gone a little batty. They had set up a television set in the coffee room tuned to a business channel, and there was always a little knot of people around it, cheering and groaning with the movement of OSBN on the Nasdaq. People were not used to having their net worth rise or fall by several thousand dollars in an afternoon, not to speak of the few in the company for whom the daily wiggle was measured in millions.

Of all Marlene's colleagues, none had embraced the new situation with more simple delight than Oleg Sirmenkov.

"What do you think of Boxter by Porsche, Marlene?" he asked her one morning. "Is good car, yes?" He sat on the edge of her desk and flipped his new gold Dunhill on and off.

"A good car, yes. Get a red one. Is what we call a pussy car, Oleg."

He looked dismayed. "What? Is not strong enough the engine, you mean?"

"No, it means beautiful, young girls will come over to you when you drive it, and ignore that you are old and decrepit, and wish for a ride."

"Am not so old and decrepit yet. I can still go to the field with youngsters."

"As in Kosovo."

"Exactly so. And a good thing. Maybe we would not be rich as we are now if Perry and his friends are dead."

"True enough. It was really amazing how you knew just how to find them. I can't get over it."

Sirmenkov shrugged modestly. "We were lucky. Plus, good preparation, good contacts, good operatives." He laughed. "Unlimited bribery as well. But, now, tell me, what are you going to buy? You have so much more than I do, is crime."

"I haven't bought anything. I thought you had to wait six months before selling any stock."

"What? They don't tell you? No, of course, they tell—you was right there next to me."

"I guess I wasn't listening."

"You are so foolish sometime, Marlene, I do not believe you. Is margin account. Margin! See the little man, Mr. Amory. He has set up accounts for all of us."

Indeed, as Marlene discovered via a call and a brief visit, Osborne had arranged for the broker to provide margin accounts secured with stock. Marlene went out at midday, cabbed downtown, had a nice chat with the Toad, who explained that a bank would lend Marlene spending money on the value of her stock. Typically, stock value rose more quickly than interest, so the loan could be financed by selling off small blocks from time to time. What if the stock declined? Marlene wanted to know, and was met with an expression of pity, as for someone worrying whether the earth would ever collide with the moon. Thus assured, she was handed off to Ms. Lipopo, at the private department of Manhattan Trust, and introduced to the pleasures of high-end private banking. No little glass cubicle, exposed to the gaze of the peasantry waiting for tellers; instead, a dark-paneled office, with Edwardian touches and a Kirghiz on the floor. Marlene wondered if they had extruded Ms. Lipopo especially for her, she looked so new and shiny, a slim, golden, thirtyish person of jumbled ethnic antecedents, precisely suitable for personally banking a one-eyed, burnt-out liberal matron. If, Marlene mused, Marlene had been an Irish brickie who had hit the lottery, would that Ms. Lipopo have had a beer gut and a skein of dirty jokes?

The young woman caused Marlene to sign a large number of forms (which, though a lawyer herself, she read only negligently, for who could not trust Ms. Lipopo?) and served coffee and petits fours on fine porcelain. After the signings, Ms. L. turned to her computer terminal, elegant fingers poised. "How much would you want to start with? The limit is fifty percent of market value, but you may want to set up with a lesser amount just for immediate use. Ten percent?"

"That sounds right," said Marlene from Queens, suppressing the "duh."

"At today's prices, let's say five-five." Ms. Lipopo smiled, showing white teeth and lovely pink gums. Everyone was being *so* nice to Marlene recently. Could it be the money?

"Five-five meaning . . . ?"

"Five point five million." Another charming smile. Ms. Lipopo loved her work.

"Oh, well, yeah, just for my immediate needs," said Marlene, a fine sweat popping out on forehead and upper lip. Shortly thereafter, she left with a nice checkbook bound in genuine black morocco, a little portfolio (ditto) containing a sheaf of forms and densely printed publications, and a credit/debit card of a peculiar dull metallic-gray color, which was apparently the loveliest and most prestigious color a credit card could ever be. No toaster, no mug with the bank logo, but you couldn't have everything, she thought. Or, thinking again, in my case you could, me now being so rich that . . . the metaphor machine stumbled here. More cold sweat. This was stupid. It's only money. Okay, a lot of money, but still . . .

She passed a bank, an ATM lobby. Drawn by a mysterious force, like an earthling under the control of body snatchers, she found herself bellying up to the device, slipping the new card into the slot. My immediate needs, she thought, and punched in five hundred. The little door whined, and there were twenty-five twenties, actual money. She snatched up the wad and looked around, as if she were ripping someone off.

This was nuts. She hailed a cab on Broadway, and on the ride uptown she tried to think of anything but the money, which was like the old saw about not thinking about a purple rhinoceros and, besides, she had never been much good at controlling her thoughts. Not a mental-discipline type, her, not like her daughter, apparently, or her husband, which was where the daughter must have picked it up, along with her other Karp-like characteristics, such as a tendency to be judgmental, a little self-righteous maybe, a bit hard on old Mom or wifey, as the case might be. Which might change with the new money, might it not? Money was supposed to grease the wheels, make things easier. Why people wanted it, right? Why they killed and whored for it, or killed themselves. Don't think about it, then. Clear the decks. Think about . . . what? Husband and family. What husband? Never around anymore, and when around difficult, irritable. Doesn't talk about work like he used to, a bad sign, he's worried about something, keeping something stashed deep away, what could it be? Another woman? Butch? Of course, the wife is always the last to know. Plus, he goes into this crazy job situation without a prior consult, violation of prime marital directive, not good. Lucy also never home, consorting with that guy, good-looking enough, thin and wiry, beautiful blue eyes: like mother, like daughter, in that respect. Sex? Ridic! But probably be good for her . . . no, what am I thinking? Guy's nearly thirty, she's a baby, practically, although the stories you hear about private-school girls nowadays, blow jobs galore at the junior prom. Still, time for the kid to drop that religious stuff, get on with real life, like I did, and look at me—one eye and fifty-five million bucks, ha! She'll probably want me to give it to the poor, or the Church. Maybe I will, some, just to show her I really am generous. Butch is a miser, but I'm not. He hasn't said a word about the IPO either, not even "Good for you, girl"; like he doesn't want to think about it. Or maybe I'll endow a chair at Smith, which is the only way my daughter is going to get in there. The Marlene Ciampi Professorship for the Study of Religious Hysteria in Language Geniuses. Or I could get away. They'd all be better off. Buy an island. Buy a town in Italy. Take the boys. No, not Zak, Zak needs a man, ninety-two pounds in his socks and most of that testosterone. Would Giancarlo come? Maybe. We could have a warped relationship. He could collect porcelains and incunabula and look after his crazy mother. Eccentric. Poor are crazy, rich eccentric. I could have a string of horses, but I hate horses. Cars. I love cars. A Ferrari for starters. And dogs. Hundreds of dogs, vast kennels, yes, the dog lady growing old in her palazzo with hundreds of dogs . . . No! *Don't think about the money!* Money would change things, not *really* change. I'm the same as I was before. We all are.

The cell phone buzzed just then, and she answered it, relieved to be out of the coils of racing thought. It was Wayne Segovia.

"Marlene? I'm down at the Daumier. It could be we got a situation here."

"The Daumier?" She was still a little narcotized by mammon.

"Yeah, Kelsie Solette's place. I got a call from Donny Walker. He thinks he spotted Jimmy Coleman cruising the street. Saw him a couple of times. What do you think?"

"Stay there, I'll come by." She checked outside. "I'm at Third and Forty-sixth. I should be there in ten minutes."

She gave the cabbie the new address. Donny Walker was a kid they had put on the staff of Kelsie Solette's building, in the reasonable expectation that a short jolt in Rikers was not going to dissuade the stalker Jimmy Coleman from his heartfelt vow to make Solette his own or, failing that, kill her and himself. People like Coleman represented the most difficult challenge in the celebrity-protection business. The law couldn't touch them beyond petty sentences for harassment, which typically only solidified their determination. The only way around this was to nail the guy on a major felony, without endangering the client at the same time. That, or shoot him, one; but Marlene didn't do that anymore. She felt her brain slide into a different mode as adrenaline cleared the stupid monologues from her mind like a stiff breeze blowing through a smoked-up kitchen. Ah, action!

It had taken Karp the better part of a week to get his homicide chops back. Roland had vanished without a word to anyone—no farewell party, no parting gift from the loyal staff. Karp had called once and left a message on the machine at Roland's place, and so far no reply. He was secretly relieved. He was also relieved to find that Roland had run a fairly tight ship. The people were reasonably competent, the records were in order. The ship was somewhat tighter than Karp would have liked. Roland was the kind of administrator who kept everything flowing through his fingers and ruled by yelling, which meant that the staff tended to keep mistakes to themselves and hesitated to seek guidance. Karp made no major changes in procedures, but met individually with each of the thirty-odd staff members, assured them of his continuing confidence, received a rundown on their caseloads, made some gentle suggestions, and in general attempted to suggest to them that he was not one to bite their heads off if they goofed. Which they would. Tony Harris was Roland's deputy, which was good; Karp had known Harris from his first day on the job, had trained him, and trusted him. He made it clear that Harris would handle the day-to-day running of the bureau, while

Karp focused on the big-ticket items, Benson and Marshak. And Lomax, but Karp did not mention that to Harris.

The homicide bureau chief's office was a little smaller than the one he'd occupied up on the eighth floor, and more crowded, with a desk at one end, a glass-topped conference table in the middle, a worn and cracked green leather couch along one wall, and the rest so occupied by bookcases and filing cabinets that a normal person had to navigate by walking sideways. The paint was yellowing and dirty, as were the windows. No young law school graduate going private would have tolerated such conditions for a minute, but Karp and his colleagues in the courthouse were used to it, and to the notion that public officials were obliged by their choice of profession and its critical importance to the commonwealth to work in squalor.

Two people were sitting on the couch at the moment. One was Terrell Collins, a tall, caramel-colored, crop-headed man wearing horn-rims, a gray suit, and glistening Florsheims. The other was a broad-shouldered young woman wearing an olive suit with a white silk T-shirt beneath it. She had bold *indio* features and a mass of thick black hair: Mimi Vasquez. Both Vasquez and Collins shared some history with Karp, and as a result of it were slightly nervous with him, or rather expectantly concerned. Collins had second-seated Karp on a notorious trial, the same one whose loss had lost Karp his original job as homicide bureau chief. Vasquez had prosecuted a teenaged infanticidal mom a couple of years back, in which Karp had involved himself in a way that, while serving Karp's idea of justice, had cut Vasquez out of the real action. Both of these people had no doubts about Karp's basic integrity or competence, but they both considered that working closely with him could, under the right conditions, be like accepting a copilot's berth on a kamikaze bomber.

"I suppose you're wondering why I asked you here," said Karp in a mock-portentous voice. They both laughed. "Your mission, should you choose to accept it, is to get the DA out of the jam he has gotten himself in because of this goddamn election, and by so doing serve justice, God, the people, and our precious American way of life. Whaddya say, kids?"

"Will it take long?" asked Collins innocently. "I have a dentist's appointment."

Vasquez said, "That was incredibly inspiring, Butch. I want to say that I'm behind you all the way, or until it becomes personally inconvenient."

"Gosh, you guys!" said Karp. "I'm deeply touched. Let me pause and wipe away the tears." He clapped his hands smartly. "All right! We have two cases, both politically hot. Whichever way they go, they are each going to piss off an important constituency that the DA needs to get elected. The DA told me to fix them, and I intend to fix them. I have a suspicion that what the DA means by fix, whether or not he knows it himself, has to do with figuring out what the maximum political advantage is and then crafting our cases to make that happen. But this is not what I intend to do." He paused to let that sink in.

"My own feeling," he resumed, "is that the DA is mistaken, and that skewing cases in this way is a disastrous strategy because the office of DA is different from a general political office. The mayor and the governor have to balance competing goods, and if the goods they support have more beneficiaries than the goods they don't support, then they stay elected, and if not, not. But that's their job, that's what they're for. But we don't have competing goods, or anyway we shouldn't. We have the law; we have procedure; we have skill and judgment. We know what a good case looks like. And so I propose that the best politics is to just go by what's carved in stone on the outside of the building: 'Every place is safe to him who lives in justice—be just and fear not.'"

They stared at him. After a short pause, Collins asked, "Are you serious?"

"Damn right I am."

Vasquez said, "Um, Butch, that's very idealistic, but . . ."

"No! It's not idealistic. In this case, it's pragmatic as hell. Look, Vasquez, as soon as we start thinking directly about political consequences, we get lost in a tangle we can't get out of, which is not the case in plain-vanilla politics. The side that loses the election might feel sorry for itself, it might have to pay more taxes or get less services, but it doesn't feel *betrayed*. If the losers were actually right about policy, sooner or later things will get worse and they'll win the next time out. Rah-rah, democracy in action. But here, if we screw around with a prosecution, it *is* a betrayal, and people will see that, and they won't forgive Jack Keegan for it, and all the political influence in the world won't save him. I'm not sure he realizes that, but I do, and that's how we're going to proceed in both these matters."

"Shit, man," said Collins, "we have to be *honest* now?"

"I'm game," said Vasquez. "It'll be a refreshing change. What do you want us to do?"

Karp could see that she wasn't letting herself believe him, but at least she was peeping over the wall of cynicism all these young attorneys erected after a few months on the job. He smiled encouragingly. "Good. You have Marshak. Raney's the cop on it, a very bright guy, inclined to be helpful. Go see him, get involved. I know they don't like us hanging close to them, and usually we don't have the time, but we're going to free you both up of everything else you have for the duration of these two cases. Push him to find the other guy, if any. Check out the vic. Talk to the people he hung with. We want to try to reconstruct his last day. Most important, did he pack a knife, did anyone ever see him with a knife? And the watch. Where did it come from, where did a homeless guy get a high-end Rolex watch? There's a story there; find out what it was. On the Marshak end, what was she doing in that garage? You need to talk to my wife on that. And my daughter."

"What?"

"Yeah, the accused was a client, or almost a client, of my wife's. She thought she was being stalked. In any case, it happens that Marlene was at the vicinity of the crime at or near the time of. She saw Marshak make her getaway. Also, people who knew her in the weeks before it went down, what was her general behavior, her morale? Most important—did she know the victim, any connection whatsoever? Raney will help you out."

"You said your daughter?"

"Oh, yeah. Lucy helps run a soup kitchen down in Chelsea. Ramsey was one of the regulars. She can give you background on him and his homies. Along with that, see his family, get a sense of what the guy was like. Details, Vasquez, it's all details. Bring 'em in, the more the better." She nodded, scribbled on a yellow pad. He pointed a big finger at her. "Every day on this, okay?"

"Got it." She seemed a little brighter now, energized. "I have an appearance in ten minutes."

"Okay, go. See Tony about getting out from under everything else. See you tomorrow."

Karp turned to Collins. "You—you have a much harder problem because you have a case that's supposedly made already. Basically, I want you to remake it."

"Remake it," said Collins neutrally.

"Yeah. Let's face it, Jack is going to ask for death on this one, absent any serious flaw in the case. Everybody is out for this kid's blood. The crime is tailor-made to appeal to everyone's New York violence fantasies. Black criminal kills respectable white family man in the subway for money. We are bound and determined to kill the guy who did it."

"It's the law."

Karp nodded impatiently. "Yeah, I know it's the law. And I know we can probably convict him. That's not the point. Unlike the chief justice of the Supreme Court, I happen to still believe that actual innocence is an exculpatory fact. I need you to convince *me* that Jorell Benson stabbed Moishe Fagelman to death on the M line, *me,* not a bunch of retirees and high school graduates who want to get home to their families."

"I don't get it. What is it about the case that you find unconvincing?"

"A bunch of stuff. Benson was a strong-arm mugger, a chain snatcher, a knock-down-women-and-take-their-bags artist. Why did he decide to go with a knife? And, by the way, where's the knife? Two, it's a big jump from petty mugging to hitting a diamond merchant. He had to know the guy was carrying diamonds, and what he was carrying them in. It was, you'll recall, a little leather pouch. The perp took only that. Benson is a sixth-grade dropout with a seventy-two IQ. Is it credible that he could put a hit like that together and then not know that every diamond merchant in the city would be looking for just those stones, and then come waltzing into some booth in the diamond district and try to sell them? Three, our eyewitness, Walter Deng, ID's Benson from inside his token booth as the man who supposedly ran by on his way out. I'll stick you in a token booth, and I'll run by, and I guarantee you won't be able to tell me from Joe Pesci."

"Deng picked him out of a lineup."

"Right, which means he picked one out of six. Sorry, but I don't feel comfortable killing Mr. Benson for rolling snake eyes. Finally"—Karp took a deep breath—"finally, Terrell, the guy has an alibi. He was home with his mother, his sister, and her two kids when the crime went down. They were watching a basketball game."

Collins shrugged. "Relatives lie to protect their families."

"Uh-huh, but did these? Let me ask you a question? You have any brothers or sisters?"

"One of each. Why?"

"I have two brothers. If one of them was accused of committing a violent murder for gain, and he came to me and said, 'Tell a lie, give me an alibi,' I wouldn't. Would you?"

Collins thought for a moment. "Maybe I would."

"Oh, bullshit! Perjure yourself, put everything you've worked for at risk? Because your brother wanted a little extra cash and killed someone to get it? Come on!"

"Okay, I take your point. I'll go over the case. But the cops . . . Jesus, they're going to hate me for this."

This was Roland's influence, thought Karp, his one great flaw as a prosecutor, his desire to stay palsy with the cops. "Fuck 'em, then," Karp snarled. "They're *supposed* to hate you. You want cops to love you, join the Police Athletic League."

They discussed some reporting details, and then Collins rose to go. Karp made a restraining gesture. "One other thing. You know Lucius McBright, don't you?"

Collins's face took on a suspicious cast. "Why would you think that?"

"Because you're politically active, and ambitious, and live in his district, and attend the same church where he's a deacon."

A nervous smile. "You've been following me around?"

"No, your address and church affiliation are in your personnel records. I'm a trained investigator, remember?"

Collins laughed, relieving some of the tension. "I guess. As a matter of fact, I do know him. Not well, but we've talked some. Why?"

"I want to meet him."

"Call his office. He's a public official."

"I don't mean that way. I want to converse with him informally. If you could set it up, I'd consider it a personal favor."

Collins nodded. "Sure. I'll see what I can do." He left. Toward the end of the day, he called Karp and said, "The man said, come to church this Sunday."

"Church, huh? No problem; thanks, Terrell. He'll find me?"

"Oh, yeah." Collins laughed. "You'll be easy to spot."

• • •

Wayne Segovia was waiting in his car, a tan Nissan this time, parked in a bus zone on Fifth, across the street and a few dozen yards uptown from the entrance to the Daumier. Donny Walker, a muscular, young black man, was in the backseat, dressed in a brown handyman's coverall with the building name and DON embroidered in the breast. Marlene got into the passenger seat.

"What's up, guys?"

"I spotted him when I was taking out some junk from the service entrance," said Walker. "He cruised by up Fifty-eighth, real slow and turned onto Fifth. I stayed where I was, and then he came by again, same thing. A Honda, light blue, New York plates."

"You're sure it was him?"

"Absolutely. Glasses, the blond hair, no chin. He was driving real slow, so I got a good look."

"Okay. You get his plates?"

Walker spoke a number, and Marlene wrote it down. "I'll call this in to the cops. He's in violation, coming this close to her building. I can get him revoked. Good work, Donny."

The man grinned. "If they snatch him up, can I drop this janitor act?"

"You could be a doorman," said Segovia.

"Really? Gosh, my boyhood dream. A uniform with gold on it! Marlene, tell me I'm not dreaming!"

"The fact is, we need to get you closer to that stupid woman than a doorman," said Marlene. "I should take another run at her now that old Jimmy's started coming close. She might be more inclined to listen." Marlene smiled at Walker. "Can you be a rock musician? For Tainted Patties you just need the three chords and some attitude."

"I'd rather hump ash cans," said Walker.

Marlene called the complaint in to the Nineteenth Precinct, and they all waited, talking companionably. Shop talk at first, idiots I have guarded, the freakiness of celebrity and its discontents. The talk grew more personal. Segovia passed around a pack of snapshots of his family, a pretty wife and a fourteen-month-old, a rottweiler he was training. Marlene liked this. She enjoyed the company of her troops more than she did that of the Osborne executives with whom she spent most of her time. The troops were very much of a type, these men and the few women in the trade, physical creatures, impatient with routine, bright but without much academic talent, rebellious under bureaucratic controls. The part of her that had never really integrated with the dutiful and brilliant student, the dutiful and loving mom, blossomed among them.

A pause in the conversation. Marlene checked her watch. It was taking them a damned long time to respond. Walker said, "I should go back and watch the service entrance."

"Yeah, go. We'll wait here for the cops," Marlene agreed.

Walker left the car and loped through the traffic, disappearing around the corner.

"A good guy," said Segovia. "He's tickled about the stock. He wants to buy a boat when we can sell it." He shook his head. "It's amazing. I never thought I'd be hanging on the damn stock ticker. Every time I come home, Stella says, 'Hey, we hit fifty-eight and three-quarters today,' or whatever." He looked at her, grinned. "Hell, if I'm happy with twelve hundred shares, you must be out of your head."

Marlene did not want to discuss the money, however. "You going to get a boat, too?"

"Me? Uh-uh. Stella's got that earmarked for the college fund. How high do you think . . ." He stopped, stiffened, stared across the street. "Oh, shit! There he is."

Marlene followed his gaze. Through the moving cars she could make out a short man in a red jacket and baseball hat. It was the familiar livery of a large Madison Avenue florist, and naturally the man was carrying a long white box wrapped in red ribbon. The man had the hat pulled down low, but she saw the eyeglasses and the familiar profile. Jimmy Coleman. He was carrying his flower box in a peculiar manner, narrow end against his chest, left hand high, right hand low and hidden underneath. A thought flashed through her mind: people don't carry flower boxes that way; that's the way they carry rifles.

Segovia popped his door. "I'm going to nail the little fucker," he said, and was out of the car and dodging across the street before Marlene could say a word of warning. Without thinking, she snatched up her bag and followed him. She had to wait for a couple of trucks to go by, and while they passed and she bounced on her toes in frustration, she heard the first shot.

Holding up her hand, she crossed in front of a cab, made a car slam on its brakes and honk furiously. When she got clear of the roadway, she saw the doorman lying in a heap at the entrance to the Daumier with a dark stain spreading on the back of his maroon uniform coat. She ran into the lobby just in time to see Coleman shoot Wayne Segovia through the chest and disappear into the mail room.

Marlene knelt beside Segovia, who was gasping and expelling bits of bloody froth. She yanked off his tie, popped open his shirt. In the right side of his hairless, tan chest was a red-black hole just southeast of the nipple. Hideous, bloody foam was drooling from it, and every labored breath produced a raw plumbing noise. Osborne had insisted that everyone who worked in the field take a serious first-aid course every year, and so Marlene knew immediately that this was a sucking chest wound and that she had to get something to patch it or Wayne would die of anoxia in a few minutes. Something airtight, waterproof . . . She upended her bag and studied the jingling heap that fell out onto the floor. Lipsticks, compact, wallet, date-minder, cell phone, pack of tissues with one remaining, a folded sheaf of twenties. She shoved the twenties inside the tissue package, held it to the wound, hard. The sucking noise diminished. She yanked off Wayne's tie, ran it under his body, and bound the expensive dressing into place. Then she called 911 again and demanded an ambulance for two or more, reported the shots fired, and briefly described an incipient hostage situation. Nine one one wanted to chat some more, but she cut them off.

"Hang in there, Wayne," she said. "The cops and the ambos'll be here real soon. I'm going after him."

She rose. He grunted something, waved weakly at his left chest.

"Oh, right," she said, and removed Segovia's pistol, a serviceable Beretta nine, from its shoulder rig. Then she headed for the elevator.

When she got to seventeen, the small lobby was empty, but the door to 1702 hung ominously open. Inside the door was the hapless Pete, lying in a blood pool of unlikely extent, a surprised expression on his dead face. The flower box, with its red ribbon, lay discarded beside the body. Coleman certainly didn't need it anymore.

Marlene ran directly to the hallway that led to Kelsie Solette's bedroom. Another body lay on its side, half out of one of the bedroom doors, a woman, blonde, spiked hair. Marlene's heart froze. She knelt. No, not the client, someone else, a girlfriend of the band's, a groupie. Marlene checked the bedroom. A man lay half-sitting against the bed, his head lolling, his T-shirt black with blood.

Marlene moved on, holding the pistol in front of her. She had not touched a weapon in over two years, except for the firing practice Osborne demanded. She had stopped carrying. She had sworn an oath that she never would again. She nudged the door to the master bedroom open with her foot. There was the bed, and she could hear the frightened yips of Kelsie's dog, but muffled as through a door. The room was L-shaped, she recalled; a little corridor led to a dressing table and, beyond that, to the private bathroom.

She paused at the corner of the L and looked around it cautiously. He was sitting there, at the little dressing table, with his rifle across his knees, talking in what sounded like a reasonable voice to the closed bathroom door. Marlene examined the weapon. Some kind of cheap military-surplus job, a Mauser bolt-action with a box magazine, the stock and barrel cut down to about eighteen inches, and wrapped roughly with silver duct tape. A deadly piece of shit, she thought, like its owner.

Who was toying with the cosmetics spread in messy array across the table. As he talked, he occasionally lifted an item to his face and sniffed. He was in paradise, along with his beloved, surrounded by her intimate life and her scents. "Kelsie, I *love* you. Don't you understand that? I'm the only one in the world who really loves you." From behind the door, nothing but yapping.

Marlene said, "Jimmy, put the gun down on the floor."

He turned his head. She saw that his glasses were fixed with Scotch tape at the temples. He licked his lips.

"Jimmy, real slow now, grab it by the barrel with your left hand and lay it on the floor. Come on, it's over now."

She could see it working in his eyes before it happened. He stood, whirled, fired a shot through the bathroom door, and Marlene shot him neatly through the right shoulder. He staggered, went down on one knee, still clutching the weapon. He rested the sawn-off butt on the floor. Marlene heard the bolt work, heard the tinkle of the spent round. She rushed forward. His back was toward her, but she could see what he was doing.

"Jimmy, please put it down, *please*—" she cried, stepping closer, bracing herself to kick the stock of the rifle.

Coleman called out, "I love you, Kelsie!" He had the muzzle under his chin, and when he pulled the trigger, it blew his blood and brains all over Marlene.

Lucy Karp handed the priest, Mike Dugan, a Phillips screwdriver. An associate pastor at Old St. Patrick's on Mulberry Street, he was lying on his back with his hands deep in the entrails of a beat-up Champion UH-100 commercial dishwasher someone had donated to the parish kitchen. St. Pat's was Lucy's regular church, although she had not been by as often in recent months and had switched her volunteer work entirely to Holy Redeemer. A pang of guilt here. Father Dugan had been her main man in the religion area ever since her first communion, and she did not want him to feel abandoned. Or so she imagined. In truth, she was feeling abandoned herself.

Dugan slid out from behind the monster and grinned at her. An odd bird, this one. He was a Jesuit, had been on the staff of the vicar-general in Rome, and then had fallen, badly, no one knew why, ending up as a second fiddle in a pokey New York parish. Brilliant and mysterious, which is why the mother doted on him, and the daughter, too. He had a broad, lumpy Irish face, a shock of black hair, and blue eyes of the kind called penetrating, although they only penetrated on rare occasions. Mostly they skipped over the surface of life with an amused and kindly look, as now.

"I think we got it, kid," he said, standing, stretching, groaning theatrically. "Be a priest, Michael, me dear mother said to me, be a priest and you won't be breaking yer back like yer father and grandfather before ye. And look at me now!"

"Oh, the shame of it, Faather," replied Lucy, falling in with the shtick. "And all for a dishwasher."

"Yes. In the old days, the Church didn't need dishwashers. We had nuns!"

"So ye did, and they were happy to do it, the good sisters. Oh, the holy Church is in a sorry way, Faather."

The priest put his finger to his cheek and applied an impish expression. "Well, we have to see if the blessed thing works, and to do that we need some soiled dishes, do we not? And how do we soil dishes? Why, by eating off them, that's how."

"Ah, Faather, 'twas not for nothing that you read Aquinas for years and years."

The priest walked over to the refrigerator and peered in. "Ah, Mrs. Camillo has left one of her famous chocolate cakes, the lovely woman!"

"Isn't that for the poor, Faather?"

"The poor ye have always with you," said the priest with a dark look. "And we have milk, too."

"Would you be wantin' yer wee drop now, Faather? I wouldn't mind."

"I'll wee drop you on your head, girl. Get us some plates and glasses."

They ate at the table, cake set out on plates, with glasses of milk.

"Ah, this is the fat life, isn't it?" said Dugan, smacking his lips. "Free cake, and no man to say us nay. Sometimes I sympathize with old Luther. We're corrupt to the bone."

The cake was too rich for Lucy's taste, but she ate every crumb, to be companionable. They loaded the dirty stuff into the Champion and threw the switch. The machine gurgled and whirred into life, and Dugan cheered, hugging Lucy.

"Well, now, hasn't this been the grandest day since the cardinal archbishop slipped on a dog turd getting out of his limousine?" Dugan turned to her and looked into her face. The penetration flicked on. "And where have you been hiding yourself, Lucy? We've missed you."

"Oh, going to and fro on the earth," she said lightly. "Mostly around Holy Redeemer, the soup kitchen. Doing some stuff with the homeless."

"Well, good for you." A pause. He smiled. "That's where David Grale works out of, isn't it?"

She swallowed and willed the blush to stay off her cheeks. "I guess. I mean, yes, it is."

Dugan stared at the vibrating dishwasher. "An interesting young man. I understand he's been in some bad places."

"Yes."

"Very romantic, those bad places."

"What do you mean?"

"Oh, just that it can become something of a habit. I knew young priests like that in Salvador."

"You were in Salvador? During the war?"

"Yes, I was," he said in a tone that did not encourage curiosity. "Tell me, does he talk about his experiences?"

"No, not really. I mean stuff comes out. I mean we were talking about the mole people, in the tunnels, and someone said they, like, eat human flesh, and he told me about seeing people doing that in Sudan. But he doesn't, like, *discourse* on it."

Dugan closed his eyes briefly and sighed. "No, he wouldn't. Does he go down in the tunnels?"

"Sometimes, I think. We're looking for someone we know, who might be in trouble."

"This has to do with the poor creature who's murdering the homeless?"

"Yes, the slasher."

"You think this friend of yours might *be* the slasher." It wasn't a question.

"I don't think so, but the cops are looking for him on it." She dropped her eyes. The penetration intensified.

"And you're simply dying to go down the tunnels with David, aren't you, amid the putative cannibals, to search out a mass murderer and bring him back to God?"

"It's not like that!" Turning sulky. "And he's not a mass murderer. He's just a confused and scared guy."

"Your mother is worried about you, you know that?"

"Yes. But what do you want me to do, stop my life? She's always worried about me, and ninety percent of it is guilt. She thinks I'm going to turn out crazy and violent, like she is."

"She's reformed, you know."

"Hah! Anyway, I can take care of myself. She knows that perfectly well. She imagines I'm *in love* or something, and I'm going to do something crazy and stupid."

"And are you?"

This was her cue to stamp out in a huff, covering her retreat with blasts of denial, but she did not. She did not have to. Dugan was not her parent.

"Oh, not in the way she thinks. He's not interested, and he's too old and all, but I do have feelings. I mean literally." She blushed again and laughed. "You know, thump-a-thump, gasp, tremble. It's embarrassing."

"I bet it is. And . . . ?"

"And nothing. I just suffer. But I think it's connected in some way to, you know . . ."

"Your sense of spiritual abandonment?" he asked. She nodded dolefully.

"You don't have ordinary connections? With boys your own age? Dating?"

"Oh, please! For starters, look at me! I'm easily distinguishable from Britney Spears, and so, you know, it's not like I have to set up a velvet rope to keep the crowds back. Second, guys my age, they're not interested in the kind of stuff I am. I could hang out with the nerdy crowd, but the truth of it is I'm not really a nerd, either. At least I can *talk* to David." She sighed dramatically. "Maybe I should just sign up with the Ursulines and put myself out of my misery."

"You have no true vocation," he said evenly. "It would be something like a fraud, wouldn't it?"

She slumped. "I guess. I guess there's no place for me at all, except lying down in an MRI machine. Maybe I should just let them extract my brain for scientific study. At least then I'd be halfway useful."

Dugan held his hands in front of her face, brought the thumb and index finger of each hand together and made tiny reciprocal motions with them. "You know what this is? The world's smallest violin playing 'My Heart Cries for You.'" He knuckled her on the top of her head.

"Ow! Oh, Faather, don't hit me agin! I'll be good and niver will I go behind the pigsty with Kevin O'Flaherty anymore."

"Seriously, you lunkhead! You are deeply loved, marvelously good, gorgeously talented, and obscenely rich. You should be as happy as God in France."

"The same could be said about Simone Weil."

"Oh, would you forget her for two minutes! You're not Simone Weil, who is also, incidentally, a good argument for some measure of orthodoxy. Listen to me: You were not made to run through tunnels after wretched people with the likes of David Grale. The gift you have, which you acknowledge is from God, is simply too great to risk in that way. And it's grossly irresponsible for David to tempt you to do so. And don't give me that stubborn look! Look, you know that St. Teresa, at age eight, went off down a road with her brother to find some Moors and get her head chopped off so she could be a martyr. Do you think it would've been a good thing if she'd succeeded?"

No answer. Lucy was doing the teenage clam.

"And anyway," he added, struggling to control a temper that had often been his undoing, "Grale is not all he seems."

That got her attention. "What do you mean by that?"

"I mean everybody in a St. Francis suit isn't St. Francis. There's a darkness in him that touches on unbalance. Don't tell me you haven't observed it? Or do the glands interfere with your judgment?"

"There's nothing wrong with him!" she snarled with a violence that surprised her.

But not him. He sighed and put his arm around her shoulder. She stiffened, but did not shake it off.

"Okay, we'll drop it. Just promise me you'll be careful."

"Sure."

"And if you're really interested in tunnel lore, I can put you with someone who knows them pretty well. Did you ever meet Jacob Lutz?"

"I don't think so. Who is he, a cop?"

"No, a dweller; a cannibal, too, for all I know. They call him Spare Parts."

"You know *Spare Parts?*"

"I do. He comes by occasionally to talk. We play chess, too."

"Gosh, he's like the king of the tunnels. I only saw him once, from a distance. What's he like?"

"A troubled soul; like you, like me," said the priest. "In mortal form he's very large and stinks to high heaven, much like some of the early saints, I suppose. I'll set something up. We'll have tea."

10

In the aftermath, Marlene learned the difference between working private and being part of a billion-dollar security empire when there were bloody corpses to figure out. The police, for one thing, were a good deal nicer to her than formerly, first, because there was not a boss cop in the city who did not dream of a fat postcareer position with a firm like Osborne International, and second, Osborne itself swarmed the area with lawyers and other helpful people. Ms. Solette, scratchless physically, destroyed emotionally, was spirited away to an undisclosed location, with her dog. Marlene was allowed to change her blood-soaked clothes and take a shower right there at the crime scene, although not in the bullet-holed bathroom. Min Dykstra, her assistant, arrived with a change of clothes and clean undies, and a willingness to provide a broad crying surface on either of her shoulders, if desired.

It was not desired. Marlene's first (and nearly sole) interaction with her was an inquiry about Segovia. Answer: in critical condition but still alive. The other four victims were dead, but this toll seemed to have little effect on Marlene, who drifted off to one of the three other bathrooms. She then spent a long time in the shower, so long a time that Dykstra, normally as unflappable a young woman as could be found, kept checking her watch and fingering her cell phone and listening at the bathroom door. Was Marlene having a nervous breakdown in there?

She was not. She was washing her hair. Marlene had a mop of heavy, thick, curly black hair, worn neck length and cleverly cut so that it would cast a shadow over the false eye. But now there were things in it. Tiny bits of skull and scalp with wispy blond hair still clinging that fell to the bath-tub floor, as well as little gobbets of matter looking like pink-gray earth-worms, parts of the organ in which James Coleman had recently main-tained his sorry existence. She nudged one of these toward the drain hole with her toe, which immediately prompted the long-anticipated retch session. This, too, went on for longer than expected.

Dykstra heard the water stop at least, and shortly afterward the sound of a hair dryer. Her heart swelled with relief, for she believed that deranged people do not use hair dryers. She had, however, only worked briefly for Marlene Ciampi.

Who emerged, looking scrubbed and wholesome, except around the eyes, smelling of expensive soap and the best shampoo, and dressed in baggy khaki trousers and a black cotton sweater. She sat through a straightforward interview with a police detective, and then she was whisked away, quite passively, by Dykstra and a covey of hefty VIP-section Osborniks, down the service elevator, out the back way, and into a waiting limo. The press, of course, was in full cry, the com-bination of celebrity and violence being without question the most desirable of all news stories. But Marlene's troops were skilled at pen-etrating and evading their wolf packs.

Shortly after they departed the scene, in a black van with smoked windows, a cell phone rang. Dykstra answered and said, "It's your husband."

Marlene stared for a few seconds at the instrument extended to her as if she were unaware of its function, then took it, listened, and said, "Yes, I'm fine. . . . Really. . . . No, I didn't kill him. He killed himself. . . . Yes. . . . Yes. . . . No, I have to go back to the office and write up my report. . . . No, it can't. . . . Yes, I'll see you tonight." All this was delivered with the affect of a recorded announcement. Dykstra and the other people in the limo cast covert glances of admiration at their leader: after something like that, to be so cool! No one said much during the rest of the trip.

Karp put the Solette affair, and his wife's part in it, out of his mind for the rest of the day. He was good at this putting away, from long prac-tice, for if he had gone into uxorious conniptions every time his darling had diced with death, he would not have had enough emotional resources left to run a hot dog stand. Besides, he also knew from experience that Marlene detoxified best when left alone. She would need him eventually, but not just yet. He paged his daughter, leaving a message to call immediately, and called the twins' school and said that he would be picking them up himself. Thus, he put into action the Karp Family Post–Traumatic Stress Coping Mechanism, a regrettably well-oiled machine, and hoped for the best.

A knock at the door and in came Murrow, looking forlorn, a special assistant with no one special to assist. As acting bureau chief, Karp did not rate a special assistant, and Fuller, who had immediately moved into Karp's old office, had no use for him. Technically, Murrow was an ADA, but one with little experience. He had been reassigned to criminal courts, but no one knew quite what to do with him at this point.

"How are you getting on, Murrow?" Karp greeted him. "Working hard?"

"They have me in the complaint room. I'm thinking of bailing out, actually."

"Yes, I can understand that. Being an assistant DA is harder than being a special assistant lounging on velvet cushions and reading spicy novels the day long, as was your wont."

"Yes, I'll miss that," Murrow said, smiling faintly. "And the imported chocolates. The fact is, while I enjoyed working with you, I don't like regular ADA work . . . I don't think it's my cup of tea."

"No, but neither is it anyone else's. I think you're spoiled."

"Quite possibly. I feel sort of squishy and rotten. In any case, I thought I'd drop by to say thank you and farewell."

"Not so fast. Listen, if I were to get you up here temporarily, how would that be?"

"Homicide?" Murrow looked pale.

"Not as such. But I have various things going on where I'll need some help. Technically ADA work, but not routine at all."

Karp made some calls, called in some favors, and the thing was done. Murrow went off happy to get, as he said, his toothbrush and teddy bear. Karp called Vasquez, but got the recorded message from the cell phone company. He intended to stick Murrow as second seat to Vasquez on the Marshak thing, a fairly outrageous act, but he was feeling outrageous lately, cut off by the toxic situation from his usual careful habits. It would work, though: Murrow was tenacious and bright, and maybe the case wouldn't come to trial at all. The kid could get his feet wet without too much harm done.

The phone rang, the private number, and he snatched it up. It was not, however, one of his family or the DA or one of a small group of close associates. It was Shelly Solotoff.

"I hear you got fired again," said Solotoff.

"It was Roland who got fired, or resigned. I'm just helping Jack out here."

A low chuckle, not pleasant. "Poor Roland! All his bile displayed in the press. I was glad to see that Jack didn't even make a pretense at defending him. I mean why be loyal or anything when the feminists are on your ass?" The ironic smoothness of Solotoff's voice was tempered by crackle and the sound of traffic. A cell phone.

"What can I do for you today, Shelly?" asked Karp, nor did he keep the distaste from his voice.

"You're handling the Ramsey shooting, I take it."

"Mimi Vasquez is, but she's reporting to me for now. Why?"

"Because earlier today Ralphie Paxton called me."

"Him being . . . ?"

"How soon they forget! Ralphie is, or was, Desmondo Ramsey's friend, adviser, and running buddy. Our witness. He saw the whole event. And he picked up the knife."

"The knife."

"Yeah! The knife Ramsey was going to stick into my client."

"Uh-huh. Where is this person now?"

"Sitting right next to me. We're on our way to the precinct to make a statement."

"We? Are you representing Mr. Paxton, too?"

"I'm advising him. I don't think he needs representation, as such."

"Really? I thought leaving the scene of a crime in which you were a participant was against the law."

Solotoff laughed. "Oh, well, if you decide to charge him with crap like that, maybe I'll take him on pro bono. Sorry to deprive you guys of your great white defendant, but I assume I can tell Sybil that no charges will be filed."

"That would be a premature assumption at this time. Let's talk to Mr. Paxton first and then we'll see."

Solotoff did not respond to this. Shelly often did not respond to things he did not want to hear, Karp recalled. He sounded high, excited, as if he had pulled off some coup. He wanted to chat, but Karp did not want to chat with him. After he hung up, Karp rang Vasquez again and got her this time.

"Where are you?"

"With Raney at Midtown South. What's up?"

Karp explained. Vasquez said, "Crap! Well, that's that. She seems to be off the hook if this guy holds up."

"Not so fast. I want you to grill old Ralphie, slow fire, lots of basting. Make sure he really saw something. If you have to, take him down to the garage, draw chalk lines. Obviously, full forensics on the knife. Get a picture of it, pass it around to his homies, see if anyone ever saw him flash it."

"Got it. I take it you think Ralphie showing up just now is a little too convenient?"

"A little. Especially with Solotoff involved."

"He's shady?"

"I don't know. He has something going on, an extra agenda." With me, Karp thought, but didn't say. "Oh, and another thing. We need to know about the watch."

A pause. "I'm sorry? What does the watch—"

"Oh, come on, Vasquez! The guy is holding a Rolex worth five, six grand retail. Why is he trying to mug a woman in a parking garage? Where does a street guy get a thing like that? Even on Park Avenue they don't throw gold Rolexes away in the trash. It doesn't fit, and I hate it when stuff doesn't fit. One more thing: I'm giving you Murrow as your second, assuming we go forward with Marshak."

"Mookie?"

"Yes, Mookie. And, yes, he looks like a preppie dweeb, but, in fact, he's incredibly smart, energetic, and you can abuse him to your heart's content. He'll bounce back like an inflatable doll."

Vasquez grumblingly agreed and conceded also that the watch was peculiar, but did not sound particularly anxious to throw energy into the question.

After she was off the line, Karp diddled around for an hour or so, then called for a car, drove to St. Joseph's, picked up the twins, and came back to the office. There they were made much of by secretaries and staff, given copy paper and colored markers, and diverted much government property to private use in contravention of the laws of New York. It was a rare treat for both of them; Zak hung around the cops, who were always passing through, eyeing their gear and striking up remarkable firearms conversations; Giancarlo drew pictures of rockets, ray guns, and aliens. Lucy called back on the page, and he told her to come by the office, which she did shortly thereafter.

"How's Mom?" she asked.

"She says she's okay. We'll see. Let's be extraspecial kind tonight, okay?"

"I thought she wasn't carrying guns anymore."

"It wasn't her gun, and she apparently saved the life of one of her people and also her client. It must have been a tough choice." He looked her over, suppressing like a good dad his desire that she look more like the schoolgirls he saw on the street instead of like a postwar refugee.

"You look tired," he said solicitously. "Where've you been?"

"At the church, with Father Mike. Daddy . . . ?"

"Mn?"

"Did you ever have two really good friends that both like you, but who didn't like each other?"

"I've had that experience."

"What do you do? It's horrible!"

"You can't do anything, honey. Keep 'em apart and hope for the best. These are friends at school?"

"No, it's Mike. He thinks David is, I don't know, strange or something. He really kind of flared up about it, which is not like him . . . I mean about other people. He flames me all the time."

"Well, he *is* strange," said Karp, and got one of the famous Ciampi-women black looks. "I meant most people don't live like St. Francis and go off to dangerous places to help refugees or whatever. What do you think Mike was getting at? That the guy was a phony?"

"No, not really. I think Mike screwed up himself, with the Church, I mean, so he's always on the lookout for people who think they know more than the Church does about religion."

"Really? He seems to be fairly liberal with your mom's antics."

"Oh, Mom's just a common criminal. It's okay to be charitable to those." She fell silent, thinking: Mike Dugan thinks I lust after David is what it is, and that I'm going to get myself in trouble. And I *do* lust after him, but it's stupid schoolgirl lust, and I'm in no great danger from it; pathetic, really. Still, Mike should know that, so . . . what if it's something else? Something he knows, or senses? He's so damn smart, Father Mike, I can't believe he's behaving like some Irish parish priest like we joke about, but for real. So what could it be? And as she mused in this way, she recalled the odd things she had noticed about Grale and ignored or excused. That remark about why God lets them live. About the slasher being an instrument of mercy. Those scary blank moments when he suddenly wasn't there. She felt a chill and shuddered. Her father noticed and asked what was wrong, and she said nothing, but it wasn't nothing.

The phone rang. Giancarlo struck like a snake and snatched it up. "Mr. Karp's office," he said; then, handing over the instrument, "It's for you, Daddy."

"I should hope so," said Karp. It was Vasquez.

"Was that a secretary?"

"My kid. What's up?"

"I did Paxton. If he's making it up, he's real good. I took him through it half a dozen times, from every angle I could think of. Raney did him, too. Basically, he says they were cooping in the garage. They have like a route in that area, they dive in trash cans for high-end magazines, and also they pick over things that people leave out on the streets. There's a little blind corner in that garage they use to stash stuff."

"There's no guard?"

"Hey, it's the low-end economy. They slip the poor guy a tax-free twenty and no questions asked. They're merchants. Anyway, they were there, checking over their finds, and Ramsey spots a woman walking by, going over to a Lexus. He was high, Paxton says, wine, and he'd smoked some dust. And he says, 'Look at that rich white bitch. We should take her off.'"

"Sorry, Ramsey or Paxton says this?"

"Ramsey does. And he pulls out his knife and accosts the woman, Marshak as it turns out, and she pulls a gun. Paxton didn't see the gun, but he hears the shot and sees Ramsey go down. Marshak gets in the car and books. He goes over to Ramsey, and he sees he's gone. She got him right through the pump, by the way, according to the autopsy, one shot right on the money. He grabs up the knife and takes off. That's his story."

"And how did Paxton come to contact Solotoff? A sudden spasm of civic responsibility?"

"No, Solotoff had the various homeless hangouts and shelters plastered with handbills. If you know anything about this crime, come see me: reward, five grand for useful information."

"That's a nice reward. A reward like that can powerfully stimulate the imagination. Did you suggest to him that he was making up the whole thing to get the cash?"

"Of course, and I outlined to him the penalties for perjury and assured him that if we did find him perjurious, we would go after him to the full extent, et cetera, but he sticks to his story. Ramsey attacked with a knife, was slain in self-defense."

"What's the knife look like?"

"Oh, the knife is good, too. Solotoff brought it in in a plastic bag. Cheapo six-inch hunting knife, a Taiwan product. It's got prints on it. Obviously, forensics has it while we speak, but a good assumption would be that some of the prints are Ramsey's. It doesn't look that great for the good guys, boss."

"No." He paused. "And the watch?"

"Zilch on the watch. He never saw the watch, never knew Ramsey had it. He affected surprise and outrage when I told him that Ramsey had died with a gold Rolex in hand. He was pissed off because they were supposed to split everything down the middle. Ramsey was holding out on him. He says."

"Yeah. So he wants us to believe that a street merchant with no recent record of violence, and with a six-thousand-dollar watch in his pocket, which he doesn't tell his partner about, and which we have no idea where he got it, all of a sudden decides to mug this woman and gets killed with a knife in his hand, after which his partner takes the murder weapon and keeps it safe until prompted to come forward by a reward."

"The mugging is explained by the dope. The knife being taken is explained by panic."

"Oh, please!"

He heard her sigh over the line. "Hey, what can I tell you? That's his story. Raney thinks it's bullshit, too. So . . . what do you want me to do now?"

"Not sure. Need to think about this some more, but I can't right now."

He replaced the phone. Lucy looked inquiringly at him. "You were talking about Desmondo and Ralphie, Desmondo's murder and all, weren't you?"

"Yeah. Ralphie came in and told his story. He said Ramsey was doped up and attacked Ms. Marshak with a knife, and she shot him."

"Do you believe him? Ralphie?"

"I don't think so, but he's sticking pretty hard to the story. What do you think? You knew both of them, didn't you?"

"I guess. I thought I did. But you never know about people. I always thought Des was pretty straight-up. He drank wine and smoked a little, but he wasn't a dealer."

"My guy says Ralphie says Ramsey was dusted when he went after this woman."

Lucy shook her head. "No way. Des didn't do hard drugs that I ever saw or heard about. Ralphie might've. Ralphie was sort of a slimeball, and the two of them were, you know, the way a kind of straight-up guy will let a slimer hang out with him because he's sort of half-sorry for them and also because it like makes him feel good to have a follower? That was them."

The twins came in then, ravenous and sugar-stoked, having consumed all the candy in the secretary's little disk, and demanded junk food for their supper. Karp obliged, being an old junk-food glutton himself. Lucy feigned enthusiastic agreement, although, like her mother, she found American fast food faintly nauseating. Unteenlike, she found herself unexpectedly solicitous of her family's grosser tastes, peace being at a premium this particular evening. Karp accepted this pose unawares, and Lucy reflected upon the ease with which we can fool people who love us.

They went to the McDonald's on Canal. Lucy nibbled one of their waxy salads while the men pigged out on meat and cheese. She amused them by translating the Chinese characters for the food. A hamburger was *han wu mei guo,* or "harmonious American thing"; a sandwich was *san ming zhi,* or "three bright managing," a good name, Lucy pointed out, because not only did it sound right, but it adverted to the brilliance of the food's design, enabling the eater to handle two breads and a filling at once.

Thus sated, the four made their way home in a good mood, much skipping about among the crowded, scented streets of Chinatown, capped by a breathless run up the five short flights to the loft. Karp thought he knew what he would find there: Marlene soaking in the hot tub, a couple of empties scattered around, the smell of wine and rose petals. He would hold her, she would cling to him and wail. He had done it all before, and while it was not his favorite part of the relationship, it was one he knew pretty well and accepted.

But this was not what he found. Marlene was dressed in pajamas made of heavy black-figured silk and a soft-looking tan robe, neither of which he recalled seeing before. She was watching television and sipping cognac. Lucy took one look at her mother and retreated to her room. The twins did their usual scramble and competition to tell her the news of the day, but she seemed impatient with them, snappish. She indicated by a number of signs that she did not wish to play just now, and Karp took the hint and diverted the boys to their own room, where, God knew, there was enough stuff to keep them busy for a decade.

He changed and came back to the living room. A commercial for a car company was on, but Marlene seemed to be watching it raptly, as if it were a complex metaphor for the ultimate secrets of existence. Karp observed his wife for a while as he sat next to her. Except that she took a sip of cognac at regular intervals, she could have been a waxwork.

"How are you?" he said tentatively. His eye went, against his will, to the cognac bottle, which was about a third gone.

"Fine."

"How did it go with the . . ."

"The shooting. That went fine. Lou was very understanding and complimentary. He said to take off as much time as I needed."

"That's good. You could use a break."

"We closed at sixty-one and one-quarter today," she said in the same dull voice.

"That's good."

"Yes, it's good for business when we save a client with lots of bloodshed all around. Did you know that Oleg killed twelve people getting Richard Perry out in Kosovo? I only killed four. Still, a six-point rise on the day isn't bad."

"You didn't kill anyone. It wasn't your fault."

"Yes, that's what Lou said. He said it about fifty times. He kept watching the stock tape on the TV screen while he was telling me it wasn't my fault." She took a gulp of her drink and splashed some more into the snifter. She fingered the material of her robe.

"I picked this up on the way home. I was thinking about getting someone to drive me back to the Volvo, and then I thought, hey, I don't need to do that. So I called a limo service and came home in a white Caddy with smoked windows. Did you know people stare at you when you're in a car like that, trying to see who's in it? And I had him stop off at Bendel's and I bought this outfit. This is pashmina. It cost twenty-five hundred. The pj's were seven-fifty."

Karp didn't know what to say. A strange, tight feeling was in his chest.

She said, "I want to go away, take a trip. Paris, we'll rent an apartment, or we could get a place in Tuscany." She turned to face him for the first time, a weird light in her eye, and grabbed his arm. "Let's go, Butch! Let's shitcan the whole mess and go!"

"You're kidding, right?"

"No, I was never more serious."

"Marlene, what're you talking—I have a job, you have a job, we have kids, they're in school. We can't just take off."

She dropped his arm and turned back to the television, which was playing a generic sitcom. The canned laughter was like some insect burrowing into his brain.

"Fine. I'll go myself."

"Marlene? What's wrong? Why are you acting like someone you're not?"

She shrugged. "I'm rich. Very rich. Very rich and very drunk, and the very rich and very drunk are very different from you and me."

"Oh, horseshit, Marlene! You're not rich. You have a bunch of stock options that you can't sell for six months."

"Untrue. I have a bank account with five and a half million in it, plus a credit card that they never send you a bill on, you buy what you want and Ms. Lipopo takes care of it. Five and a half million, less what I spent on what I'm wearing, less the five hundred bucks I jammed into Wayne's sucking chest wound, but I'll probably get that back."

"You *borrowed* against the stock?" said Karp, horrified.

"Yep. That's how it's done, buster."

"Oh, Christ! What if the stock goes down? What do you do then?"

"It doesn't go down. It only goes up." She made a little swoop with the glass in her hand to demonstrate the difference in the two directions. Cognac splashed on the pashmina robe, but she didn't seem to notice.

He stood up, glared at her, and turned to walk away, and she said, "And if it starts to go down even a teeny bit, we'll shoot a few more people. Then it'll go up up up again until it hits the sky."

The next morning Marlene awoke to pain and nausea and a gap in her memory where living, breathing neurons used to be. She groaned and opened her eye. In her field of vision was the nightstand on her side of the bed. On the nightstand was a light, a couple of magazines and paperback novels, and an empty bottle of Hennessy. Empty. That was impossible. The bottle was one of those Lou had given out to the troops when the IPO went through, and she had opened it just last night because she needed a drink after. After what? She rolled over, carefully, and checked out the other side of the bed. The pillow was undented, the sheets and blanket and bedspread undisturbed. Butch had not slept here last night. Uh-oh. Now she noticed that she was dressed in an unfamiliar robe and heavy silk pajamas, both smelling unpleasantly of stale cognac, and she noticed also a faint and nauseating odor coming from somewhere below. The dog? She licked her dry lips and managed a weak whistle. Thump thump and a whine at the door. Holding her head so that it would not fall off, she swung her legs out of bed and took a couple of tottering steps, whereupon her bare foot landed in a generous pool of vomit. Uh-oh again. She flung off her clothes and staggered into the bathroom, where she ate four aspirins and got into the shower, first hot and then, for punishment, ice-cold for as long as she could stand it.

The previous day's and evening's events now started to arrive at the conscious layers of her brain, like static-ridden communications from a war zone. Coleman; Wayne; Lou Osborne; the $3,000 lounging ensemble; the fight with Butch. That one was hard to remember. Did she throw things? Did she follow him around the house clutching a bottle of booze and shrieking? Impossible; obviously some of those false memories you heard so much about. She should call him and find out what had happened, apologize if required. Or maybe later, after she had cleaned up this mess.

She dressed in painter's overalls and an old pink T-shirt, scrubbed what needed to be scrubbed, and some things that didn't, such as the kitchen, including the stove and the refrigerator. Marlene considered herself something of a slob compared to her mother and her married, stay-at-home older sister, but she was actually fairly neat, and she had a husband who cleaned up after himself and a daughter who was practically an obsessive. She now demonstrated where her daughter got it from. Polishing the refrigerator racks with tiny pieces of steel wool. By noon she was done, and dissatisfied. Clean enough, but there was something wrong, displeasing, a little tacky? That couch, for example. The bedroom furniture. Some of it was actual junk from when she had been a struggling single, and the rest was over ten years old.

Suddenly she was restless. She had to get out. She walked the dog, then called the limo service. What to wear? She had nothing to wear. A rampage through her closet. *Aiiii!* She must have been insane to have gone out in public in these rags. What was she thinking? Living in a crumbling loft in Chinatown? In *Chinatown?* You couldn't even say it was SoHo with a straight face. She was shoving clothes into plastic trash bags when the buzzer rang. The dog looked up expectantly and fawned. Marlene ignored this, and the creature slumped away to its lair under the kitchen table. She threw on her coat, grabbed her bag, and was off.

The driver was a short, tan man named Patel. He seemed glad to see her as he opened the door. She told Patel to take her to Bloomingdale's.

"So we are going shopping today, madame?" asked Patel.

"Yes, shopping, just a couple of things."

Marlene ordinarily was not much of a shopper. She had little time for it, and she harbored a secret contempt for women who spent a lot of time buying stuff, or talking about buying stuff. Marlene had been a poor girl at a rich high school, rescued from shame by the school uniform, and after school hours by defiance. She had adopted the garb of the tough-Italian-neighborhood semislut, which had the additional virtue of being cheap. She had gone to college and graduate school during an era when nearly everyone wore boho rags, and afterward there was another kind of uniform: severe suits by day, retro-thrift-shop finds at other times. Marlene did not care much about clothes. Or so she imagined.

But she had developed the habit, over many years, of buying a little something for herself when blue, a habit certainly as widespread and as unacknowledged as, say, masturbation, and upon which retail battens. Usually it would be a small thing: perfume, cosmetics, a scarf, underwear. Something semisecret at any rate. And so she gravitated to the lingerie department of Bloomie's and found herself in front of a table displaying La Perla sets. Marlene had, in fact, one of these already and had suffered or enjoyed that mixed pang of guilt and luxurious pleasure that paying a hundred bucks for a bra and panties provides for some usually prudent women. She touched the flimsies, held them up admiringly. They were silk satin in coral, eggplant, aqua, with lacy panels of contrasting colors. She picked up one, two, couldn't decide between them, or maybe that one . . . that was nice, too. She let out a giggle. Oh, the hell with it, she thought, and bought one of each color, ten in all. The saleswoman took the magic card and gave Marlene a look she did not recall ever receiving from a saleswoman before.

She wandered now through the designer floor. The thought occurred: I can buy anything I want. Anything. Any. Thing. She tested this novel notion by picking up an ivory Ellen Tracy suit ($700), which fit, but which was wearable in no remotely probable social situation in her immediate plans, and then down on the main floor again, where she dropped $200 on Lancôme lipsticks and moisturizers, although her skin felt moist enough, somewhat sweaty, in fact.

Out on the sidewalk she waited until Patel cruised by with his pearl-gray Caddie, one of the numerous chauffeured cars that circled Bloomie's like schooling fish. Patel stashed the loot in the trunk, and Marlene got a smile from a package-encumbered, knockout blonde in a leopard coat. A knowing smile from one of the Sisterhood of Spend to another. Marlene got into the car and said, "Ralph Lauren on Madison."

Ralph sold her a fitted patent-leather motorcycle jacket in navy, and she got the same look from the salesclerk when she flashed the card. This purchase marked the first time Marlene had ever bought a garment without looking at the price tag. After that, down the avenue: Chanel for a couple of suits, Manolo's for half a dozen pairs of handmade stiletto mules and several slingbacks, Celine's for a pair of caramel glove-leather jeans and a long-sleeved, red silk T-shirt encrusted with tiny Swarovski crystals. Here she did glance at the price tag, out of scientific curiosity, and found it cost an even grand, plus tax. I just paid a thousand dollars for a T-shirt, said a voice in her head. More giggling in front of the mirror. The crystals flashed hypnotically as she posed. She wore the pants and the T-shirt out of the store. They made her old leather trench, until lately the most expensive item she had ever bought for herself, look like a burlap sack. In the car she said out loud, "This is crazy. I am nuts."

"Madame?" said Patel.

"Nothing," said the client. "Go to Gucci's."

Gucci's provided loose-fitting faux-snakeskin pants and a dress of the same ($2,300) plus a real crocodile bag with a silver chain, a steal at $8,000 and change. They drove to Dolce & Gabbana. Crystals were apparently the thing at D&G. They had crystal *bras*. Marlene bought one. Then she bought a black silk, see-through, chiffon shirt with gold cuff links to go over it, and an embroidered silk suit *avec* gold embroidery and crystals to go over that, and more shoes to round out the outfit, mink-trimmed pumps, the whole bill around $15,000. She had stopped sweating by now. People with the special dull gray card apparently did not need to sweat, and she hadn't eaten since breakfast, but for some reason food did not attract her. The sun had sunk low now, people were leaving work. On Madison the cabs were multiplying like guppies, but the lovely stores were still gaping for more nourishment.

Oblivion is the goal of all addiction: the boozer's blackout, the junkie's nod, the speed freak's mindless motion. Marlene had not known that shopping could cause the same effect, but then she had never shopped for eight and a half straight hours. She was dead to the world as she stood in front of a full-length mirror at D&G, looking at a stranger wearing a white, floor-length silk jacket completely covered with tiny crystals and weighing ten pounds. She definitely remembered buying that, for $78,000. Somewhat later, after a vague interval, they kicked her out of Barneys because they wished to close the store. She could see that they were reluctant to do so because she was clearly buying out the place. A few moments later, she sat in the backseat of the limo, surrounded by charcoal gray Barneys shopping bags and boxes, and recalled that she had a husband and family. She directed Patel to head home and rummaged in her bag. Her cell phone was off, she found, which was a shocker because she never turned her cell phone off. She had a little bag from Cartier's in her hand. Another shocker because she could not exactly recall stopping by that famous store. A number of gift-wrapped items were in it. Apparently she had bought gifts for her husband and her entire family. Watches? Probably. She had a gold Baume et Mercier on her wrist that had not been there when she'd started out that morning. She looked through the Barneys bags with some curiosity. She found a brown leather fleece-lined coat; a couple of de la Renta dresses, a multicolored Fendi lizard bag, yet another crocodile purse, this one by Bulgari, and a white Valentino couture suit. She felt numb, as if the great dentist of capitalism had shot her whole body full of novocaine. She was starving, too. No wonder; eight o'clock and she hadn't eaten for twelve hours. At the corner of Third and Thirtieth she directed Patel to a cancer wagon, where she bought a kielbasa with mustard and a can of Coke. They drove on, she munching ravenously, and at the first pothole she squirted mustard all over her $1,000 T-shirt and Coke on her $1,800 faux-snake slacks. Somehow it didn't matter. She could go out again tomorrow and get more. But the accident made her less numb, which was no good. She spotted a liquor store, dashed out, and came back with a quart bottle of Hennessy. Just a taste to wash that sticky, greasy film out of her mouth. There was a little bar in the limo, so she was able to make herself a civilized drinkee. And another around Eighteenth Street. And a third at Broome and Lafayette. She drank slowly, like a lady, and arranged all the charge slips in a neat bundle. Just for fun, she added up the totals with the tiny flat calculator stuck to her new checkbook: it came to $150,921.35. She looked at the number, which for some reason was expressed in a numerical system she did not understand, and put the device away and gulped down the rest of her drink, not like a lady at all.

Numb returned, and so she felt pretty good when she burst into her loft with Patel burdened like a brown burro under her purchases, confronting her startled family, reeling slightly, glittering with crystal, dabbed with grease, stinko.

Karp looked at her and thought, who are you, and what have you done with my wife?

11

THE CHOIR MEMBERS AT ZION BAPTIST WERE DRESSED IN BLOOD-RED ROBES
with white collars, and they were singing "I'm Glad Salvation Is Free."
Karp sat in a rear pew, not sharing the gladness at all, about as moved
by the music and fervor as one of the square pillars that held up the
vault of the roof. Karp had a tin ear and no faith in anything but the law
and, on good days, love. For most of his life he had placed religious
leaders in the same class as people who sold damp lots in Florida over
the phone. This opinion had been modified somewhat by his daughter,
whom he loved dearly, and who was devout and no fool, so there might
be something in it after all, although not for him personally. His daughter said that there was a God gene—some people had it and others did
not. His wife, according to his daughter, did not, although she went to
church regularly. Or had.

Karp had not had much to do with his wife since she got rich.
Marlene had always had, he supposed, a few loose toys in the attic, and
at times in their twenty-year relationship she'd done things that had
made him angry, such as risking her life and risking the lives of the kids;
shooting people; skirting the law; breaking the law; grabbing the law,
throwing it to the ground, and stomping all over it while laughing . . . but
these had all been Marlenesque excesses, arising from the woman's
peculiar sense of justice. He could understand it, even where he did not
approve. This business with the money though . . .

He checked his watch discreetly. McBright had probably wanted to
make a point by dragging him through this, but, if so, Karp had gotten it

in the first half hour. He looked around at the flock. Everyone was beautifully dressed, the men in suits, the women in bright dresses that seemed to include more than the usual amount of cloth, the children brightly decorated like Easter eggs. Capes and shawls were fashionable here, and nearly every woman was wearing a hat. The only people not so attired were a small group of European and Japanese tourists crammed into one section of the balcony, observing the primitive but fascinating religious rites of the Americans. Time passed; now a soloist, backed by organ and choir, was well into "Take My Hand, Precious Lord." Karp sighed and shifted in his seat and looked at his watch again. It was still the old, beat-up gold Hamilton he had worn since law school. The Rolex Oyster with diamonds she had bought him—the kind of thing only a dope dealer or his father would wear—remained in the drawer. Lucy didn't wear hers either, and Karp rather suspected she had hocked it to fund some charitable enterprise.

The choir stopped singing, and the pastor rose to stand behind the podium. Many clergymen in New York bear the title of reverend, of course, but when people said "the Reverend" in a certain tone, they meant this particular one. He was massive, cocoa-colored, broad of brow, heavy of jaw, bristly of mustache, and wavy of hair, and he had a great, deep, growling voice. His theme this morning was youth, African-American youth in particular. These youth were in trouble: babies having babies, drugs, gangs, gangster music, no jobs, no religion. Why had this situation come about? The Reverend didn't say outright. He cast broad hints, though. There were forces that did not want African-American people to advance, and these forces were in cowardly fashion targeting black children. But, he declared ringingly, we can fight racism. (Cries of approval.) We can fight prejudice. (Again.) But when the forces of so-called law and order, the representatives of privilege, start *murdering* our young men with impunity, that's different. (Angry shouts of agreement.) And he went on to describe one version of the death of Desmondo Ramsey, in which Ramsey had innocently approached a wealthy white woman, and she had shot him down just like those Alabama sheriffs used to, and the authorities were just going to give her a pass on it. Is that right? (No, no!) He touched on Benson, railroaded for a crime he didn't commit because they had a rich Jew killed and they needed a black boy to throw to the wolves. (Angry cries.) Then there were these homeless getting killed in their sleep—all black men or Hispanic men. The police said there was no racial angle. No racial angle? Stand on your head, anyone who believes that. (Laughter, calls of "Tell it!" and "Right on!")

Then, somewhat to Karp's surprise, the Reverend took up the tale of Cisco Lomax. Cisco, he said, was a local child. His mother was right here today. Cisco was not an angel. He had a record. White men had poisoned him with their dope. He had stolen and been punished for it. But he had a woman and children he was caring for, unlike so many others. He was getting his life turned around. And he was shot down like a dog on the highway, by a white cop who didn't even get a slap on the wrist. Is that justice? They said he tried to run down the cop with his car, and they had to shoot him. They had to shoot him ten times, *ten times! In the back!*

Here Karp, who had been allowing the sermon to glide past him until now, snapped to attention. As the Reverend ran through the changes on this bit of fact, in the skillful, ironic manner for which he was known, with the congregation following him heartily with the traditional responses, Karp had little trouble figuring out who had leaked it, for it had to be a leak. As far as he knew, only a limited number of people knew the location and number of Lomax's wounds. The autopsy details had, significantly, not been presented to the grand jury. Interesting, and almost as interesting, come to think of it, was that depiction of the Ramsey-Marshak confrontation, and the detail about the watch. An even smaller number of people knew about the watch. Karp found that since he had become a leaker himself, he was much more interested in fellow leakers, and in whether they were malign scumbags like Fuller or good guys doing bad things out of necessity, like him. He hoped.

The Reverend finished his sermon with a roaring peroration, during which no one in the cavernous place could have entertained any doubts that African-Americans were in a bad way; that the white power structure liked it like that; that they were virtually lynching black kids again; that we were not going to sit down for stuff like that; and that with the help of Jesus, the eternal judge, we would see justice done in the end.

There was more music after that. Karp expressed the body language of boredom and got a number of not-terribly-Christian looks from his neighbors. When the service concluded, he lounged by a pillar and let the crowds flow past him. Someone touched his elbow. He turned and found he was looking into the face of Lucius McBright. They shook hands. McBright had a powerful grip, powerful enough that he did not have to show it off. Karp recalled that the man had been, of all things, a boxer in his youth, and a Golden Gloves contender, or maybe an actual champion, he couldn't recall which.

"You have a car?" McBright asked.

"No, I came by cab."

"Up to Harlem? Lucky man. Come on, we can go in my car, we'll get us some breakfast."

Karp followed him out of the church, McBright stopping to chat with the Reverend at the doorway. He introduced Karp, who got a formal nod and no offer to shake hands. McBright was about Karp's age and had put on some pounds since his light-heavyweight days, but he was still an impressive-looking man, five inches shorter than Karp but broader across the shoulders. He wore round, rimless glasses and a short, natural haircut and had on a beautifully tailored, navy, pin-striped, double-breasted suit. His color was coffee with two creams, and his eyes were a surprising shade of hazel.

McBright drove a silver Chrysler Concord Lxi. They got in and drove up St. Nicholas. A sunny day, blue sky, little fleecy clouds showing above the apartment houses, God's golden Sunday light over battered Harlem.

"Like the sermon?"

"I thought it was inspiring," said Karp. "The Reverend is a great public speaker."

"I'll tell him you said so. It'll make his day."

"And besides the inspiration, I was also impressed by the information. He revealed a number of things that are not generally known."

"The Reverend has a lot of friends," said McBright in a tone that closed the discussion, and he shifted the conversation to Collins, whom they both agreed was a fine young man, and then to basketball, and they talked about the teams in the Final Four for the rest of the drive.

At 145th Street they parked and walked a short distance to a large restaurant. Called Suellen's, it was clearly the place to go after church for Harlem's gratin. Karp spotted a congressman, a university chancellor, and a major narcotics dealer, although not at the same table. McBright

was obviously well known in the place, and they were seated immediately, but it took them a while to get to their seats, as McBright stopped
along the way to chat with the occupants of several tables. Karp was the
invisible man here, which was rather the point, he thought. He didn't
feel as uncomfortable as McBright probably thought he was feeling,
having spent many hours of his youthful athletic career in milieus in
which he was the only, or nearly the only, whitey.

They sat; a venerable waiter brought coffee and a basket of sweet
rolls. McBright pointed to these. "Don't start on them. They sold those
on the street, fools forget all about crack cocaine." He took one. Karp
did, too, and they were indeed marvelous, as was the coffee.

McBright sat back, chewing, and made a gesture with his hand.
"Your meeting, boss."

Karp had the feeling of setting out on one of those rope bridges in
action movies. This meeting seemed like the worst idea he had ever had,
and it had a lot of competition in that league. But thinking this made him
laugh, and he admitted it to McBright. "Yeah, well, this seemed like a
great idea when I thought it up, but now . . .? The thing is, Jack Keegan
doesn't know I'm doing this, and if he did, he would fire me, without
hesitation. He would regard it as a betrayal."

"Isn't it? Maybe you think I'm going to win, and you're currying
favor."

"Obviously, you don't really think that, and Collins doesn't think
that, or neither of you would have participated in this meeting. But if
we're going to probe each other's sincerity, we might as well just eat
sweet rolls and talk basketball." A little eye-wrestling here, ending with
a wry grin from McBright. Karp continued, "I read that speech you gave
at the Urban League. I thought it was a good speech. I thought you were
right on principle and wrong on the DA. We don't have a racial bias that
I've been able to see. It's not part of the culture."

"Yes, well, we disagree on that. Was that your point?"

"No, my point is that injecting the race question into a DA campaign
is the wrong thing to do. Even if it helps you win, it's still the wrong thing
to do because you will win upon a basis that will make it difficult or
impossible to run the office. The power of a DA is just different from the
power of a mayor or a governor. You introduce ethnic politics into it,
you're going to call for an equal but opposite response from Jack, and

there are plenty of people happy to encourage him to do that. And then you have something real ugly. I don't want to see that."

McBright was looking at him incredulously, a bemused smile on his lips. "You're *advising* me on my campaign?"

"I'm giving you my take on what's going to happen."

McBright laughed. "I can't believe this. Nobody is that naive."

"Actually, I am. I'm a total loss when it comes to politics. I'm always doing the wrong thing. When I was a kid just starting out in the DA, we had Phil Garrahy in there, and when I knew him, he was old and sick, and he was undecided on whether he wanted to run again. Keegan was homicide chief then, and he thought he had a lock on the job, if Garrahy declined, and I took it upon myself to convince Mr. Garrahy that he should run, and he did, and won, and he died seven months later, and the governor appointed a complete asshole into the job. That was my first foray into electoral politics, and this is my second. Just so you know I have a track record."

A chuckle this time. McBright seemed genuinely amused. "Okay, I take your point. I'll consider it."

The waiter hovered. McBright asked, "You want to order?" and Karp said, "I'm fine with coffee and rolls. I'm not a breakfast guy."

"I am." McBright ordered steak and eggs with grits, then the waiter glided off. "So, was that it?"

"No. I also wanted to say that we have three major cases with racial overtones, Benson, Lomax, and Marshak. In my opinion, all three of them are flawed."

"I rest my case."

"No, because *I* am on them, and I will fix them. Now, I am not going to insult your intelligence by claiming that if the three gentlemen of color in question had been solid citizens, they would be in just as much trouble, or dead. They were not solid, they all had some kind of sheet on them, plus Ramsey was homeless, and cops are lazy. Show them something that quacks and waddles and they'll say it's a duck, never mind if it's the right duck. If you want to get into an argument about why black kids get introduced into the criminal justice system at about nine times the rate that white kids do, then fine, but leave the DA out of it. That's not the first, or even the fifth, place you should look, and the proof of it is me sitting right here."

"And you're a big racist."

"That's right, I'm a big racist. Everyone else in the office is way to the left of me."

"Since they got rid of Hrcany, anyway."

"Roland wasn't much of a racist, if by racist you mean someone who does bad things to people because they're the wrong color. I never saw him do that, and I worked with him for nearly twenty years. I'll give you that he had a mouth on him, and when he had something nasty to say, which was often, he touched on all the characteristics of the target, including the unmentionable ones. I talked to him about it a million times, but it didn't penetrate. But you could also say that the Reverend Jackson was a racist because he once said that when he heard footsteps behind him at night and he turned around and he saw it was a white guy, he felt a rush of relief."

"And was ashamed of it, don't forget that part. Well, we could chat about race relations and who's the biggest bigot all day, but why don't we just turn to the last page? Why should I believe you? I mean you *are* from the enemy camp."

Karp sighed in frustration. "Oh, for crying out loud, McBright! I know, and you must know that I know, that young Collins has been leaking you everything that's been going on in the DA since day one, and you've been leaking tidbits to the Reverend for amplification. You have to know I'm telling the truth, unless Collins is making stuff up, and I kind of doubt that. As far as loyalty goes, I'm not a camp guy. Ask Collins. I'm loyal to Jack in the sense that I'm not about to betray any confidences or weaknesses of his to you or anyone else, but my primary, no my *only*, loyalty is to the office and what it's supposed to stand for, my idea of it. Let's say I'm loyal to the better angels of Jack Keegan's nature, and not to other kinds."

McBright shook his head. "You're a piece of work, Karp. Don't put any of that shit on your job application."

"I don't need the work, man," said Karp sourly. "I have a rich wife."

Who at that moment was emerging from a nasty dream, in which haughty, black-clad store clerks wearing maroon lip-gloss insisted on removing her daughter's clothing in the main aisle of Calvin Klein, explaining that she was not creditworthy and refusing to look at any of

Marlene's own credit cards. It's all right, Mom, said the dream daughter, you can't pay for this with money.

Marlene sat bolt upright in bed, her stomach churning, and shook her head violently. Which was a mistake. Something in her head had come loose and was bouncing around in there, causing terminal damage, or so it felt.

That's it, she thought, absolutely no more drinking. Hard liquor, a known poison, what could I have been thinking? No more. Wine only from now on. She got out of bed, did the bathroom, shuffled into the kitchen in her gorgeous robe, now a little rumpled and stained, for she spent a good deal more time in it than she had in any previous robe. The great mass of the Sunday *Times* lay strewn on the big kitchen table. Observing it, she concluded, after a small pause, that it was Sunday and she had missed church. Since the house was empty, she further concluded that her daughter had dressed and fed the boys and led them off to St. Pat's, thus demonstrating *yet again* her moral superiority over her mom. They must have walked.

Her husband was not at home either. The dog was at home, and now he came wagging in, looking particularly lugubrious, to rest his massive head on her knee, the better to stain her pashmina anew with his copious slobber. She patted him absently and then, yielding to a pang of yet another addiction, she rose, loaded up the Gaggia, made herself a double shot of espresso, and burnt a couple of pieces of toast umber. The coffee and the charcoal would absorb the poisons, she calculated, and she swallowed four Advil in case that didn't work. She sat again and waited for the dizziness to cease. The dog made his three circles and collapsed at her feet, sighing.

"I am not having blackouts," she said to the dog conversationally. "Honestly, Sweets, I recall everything that occurred last night. We went to the opera. I bought a season because I always promised myself that if I got rich I would, and I did, and I took Butch because I bought him four season tickets at Yankee Stadium, and it's only fair. I remember he was acting peculiar, like distant. I wore the crystal coat and the Molinari sequined silk with the sleeves. It was *Turandot*, the opera, I remember that all right. With Casolla, Larin, and Frittoli. Butch fell asleep, which I guess is par, and this woman came up to me in the intermission . . . Binky? Bootie? And I said I didn't remember her from this speech I gave once at the Coalition Against Violence, which I didn't, but I said I did, and she invited us to a party over on the East Side, Seventy-something off Park, and we went and . . ." She stopped. The dog sighed again.

"No, wait a second, Sweets," she said and started again. "We went to this party, a big town house, and there was a bar, of course, and I think I was drinking champagne, which was fine because, really, you can't get very drunk on champers. It's only wine. But then later . . . we went someplace else, a saloon, and I was drinking brandy Alexanders, which, they're practically a dessert, not really drinking, and . . . no, I didn't get thrown out for throwing a drink . . ." An image popped into her mind, looking up, the tops of buildings whirling around, and the whitish night sky you get on a cloudy night in the city, as if she was looking up at it from the ground. The coat!

She leaped up and ran into the bedroom, threw open the closet. There was the coat, hanging there, and she saw a big streak of city gutter grease down the back of it and hundreds of tiny crystals torn off the hem. How awful, she thought, but only vaguely. The emotion did not bite deep. For some reason she was not attached to this costly possession. In truth, she was hardly attached to anything much anymore. She shrugged and closed the closet and went back to her coffee. What she really wanted, actually, was some Irish coffee with lots of whipped cream, and so she made a pot of drip with the espresso grind and whipped up a bowl of cream, pausing to admire the cleanliness and order of her refrigerator. A little man now had the food order and took care of all that, and a number of other little men and women now took care of other things: cleaning, the children, the dog, transporting physical objects to and fro. Ms. Lipopo at the bank apparently knew, or knew people who knew, an apparently limitless supply of people who made life in the city a delight of ease and comfort for those with enough money. Which had, of course, formerly included Marlene, but not now. There were even people who shopped for you, should you be blessed with funds and not with taste, but Marlene didn't have any of those because she liked shopping now, loved it, in fact: it was what she did, although she would have to get back to the office sometime. Yes, after she'd had a rest, everyone said she deserved one. She made the Irish coffee in one of the big ceramic mugs because, with those little whiskey-sour glasses that restaurants served the drink in, you hardly had time to taste it before it was gone. She filled the mug halfway with powerful coffee, poured in a lot of John Jameson, and dolloped out the whipped cream. A little shaved chocolate on the top. Perfect.

As was the next one. She sat in front of the TV and drank it, sipping slowly, inhaling the lovely fumes of Irish and coffee and cream. She surfed through the cable fare until she found *Life Styles of the Rich and Famous* and watched that for a while and entertained the idea that she herself was now rich and famous. She could have one of those houses, too. It would take so much time to fill one of them with art and furniture, and when you were done, you could do it all over again, as the woman who was being profiled obviously liked doing. Using up time had recently become extremely important to her. Odd, because she could recall never having enough time. Marlene watched avidly and on the first commercial break made herself another Irish coffee, omitting the whipped cream this time. Terrible for the arteries, that whipped cream! Then she watched a quiz show, then the shopping channel, keeping the Irish coffee flowing, although, to be honest, there was really no point in making more coffee—why jangle the nerves? So she just sloshed the Jameson into the mug. Life was good, she thought, good and getting better. She called the dog over, who licked up various spills and washed her face with his tongue. "Yes, *you* still love me, don't you?" she crooned. "Don't you? Yes, you do. Unlike some people."

Meanwhile, deep below where this Nouveau Marlene lived, down one of those damp stone staircases that exist in even the best-ordered minds, through dripping, dark, torchlit passageways, past spiked and barred gates, in a little low cell full of rustling vermin, True Marlene sat and wept. She knew she deserved this punishment, she was not complaining. People had died, people had suffered because of her stupidity, sloppiness, pride, and arrogance. Her vicious, sick lust for violence. Oh, she had evaded it for a long time, but it had finally caught up with her, more than a hot bath and a little drinking and a nice fuck could cure, far more. Those corpses in the Daumier, Wayne blowing bubbles through his nipple, that final fountain of blood and brains, arcing up, splattering off the ceiling, falling like a rain from hell on her head. Where it belonged. Get over it, say the people who haven't been there, even Butch hadn't been there. Get over it, easy for him to say. Lucy had been there, a little, but Lucy had God talking to her, Lucy was not available.

God didn't talk to Marlene anymore, and she was damned if she was going to beg. She would be damned. *Post–traumatic shock* was the approved phrase nowadays, a curiously sterile, medicalized bit of nonsense. *She's had a shock.* Stupid! Not a *shock;* a shock was when you touch a hot wire—some sparks, some pain, and that was it—not like this, this erosion of the human, this imprisonment. She wept because she missed Butch, and her babies, and the brave boys and girls who guarded the stinking rich, and the life of the little pleasures of frugality, and action, too, the rush of it, and the intense, barbaric pleasure of seeing the bad guys in the dust. At some level, she still hoped for release, that the prince would come and rescue her from the dungeon. Or the princess. But herself, right now, she could do nothing.

"Why do you do that?" Grale asked.

"What?"

"That little pause when you go out a door. When I'm behind you, like just now, I have to watch myself so I don't step on you."

The doorway in question was the entrance to a convenience store on Tenth off Forty-third. It was owned by a pair of Dominican brothers named Santomas, and you could buy there the usual things convenience stores sold in that neighborhood—overpriced groceries, doubtful fruit, beer, sweet wines, lottery tickets—and you could also get at this particular one a wide variety of illicit pharmaceuticals, other than heroin and crack. The Santomas boys, decent fellows, drew the line at those, although they would cheerfully sell you Dilaudid, Percodan, Benzedrine, Darvon, Dexedrine, and Fiorinal, besides ecstasy and LSD. They considered themselves discount ethical pharmacists, like Dart, but without the bothersome paperwork. Lucy and Grale were not there to buy, but to inquire about Canman, a regular customer there for setups, a cocktail of uppers and downers he favored. But the boys knew nothing, having not seen the Canman in several weeks, but they expressed their concern.

They were well away from that door when Lucy answered, "A habit. Something Tran taught me." A nervous laugh. "You know, checking for snipers in the street, people following. I was an impressionable child."

"This Vietcong guy you're always telling me about?"

"Ex-Vietcong. He was a Southerner. He spent twenty years fighting the French and us, and when the war was over, the Communists threw him in jail and tortured him. For a long time he was really my best friend. I mean among grown-ups."

"Gosh, should I be jealous?"

She blushed. "Are you a grown-up?" she asked lightly, but he seemed to take the question seriously. "I'm not sure," he said. "I think there's something childlike about a certain kind of religious personality, a lightness of spirit that you get in very secure and happy children. Sometimes you see it in the faces of old priests and nuns. Unlined faces, a sort of light comes out of them. You've seen that." She had. "Anyway, I think I'm that type, although with me it might be shallowness. Unlike you."

"What type am I?"

"The suffering type. We only come in the two flavors, Good Friday and Easter." He grinned at her. "You poor girl. You seem to be suffering more than usual lately."

"Oh, I'm all right," she began, and then laughed, a sound tinted more than a little with hysteria. "My life is coming unglued, is all. I'm getting kicked out of school, and I don't seem to be able to care about it. My mother . . . we came home from church today, me and my little brothers, and Mom was laid out on the couch, a classic scene, a bottle of booze in her fist, vomit. I got her stirred and she wanted to go shopping, she wanted to buy us stuff. I had to talk her out of calling her car and staggering out, and she screamed at me, which I don't mind, because she's always screaming at me about something, I mean lately. I sort of muscled her into bed and hung around until my dad got home."

"Yeah, drunks are the worst. My mom was one, too."

"She's not a drunk," Lucy snapped, and then sighed. "At least I don't think so. I mean she never was before, but they say the family is the last to cop. My father seems to be pretending that nothing's wrong, but you can see it's really tearing him up. And even besides that, he's worried about something, at work. He's in some kind of trouble, I don't know what. And I'm not helping, I know that. But I just don't feel very charitable. I want to run away from everything, school, the family, church . . . just disappear into the languages . . ."

And more in this vein, Lucy was building up to revealing some of her real secrets, stuff she hadn't ever told anyone. She was trying to trust him now, and it was an act of will, not unconsciousness, as it had been before,

before she'd talked to the priest. They were walking slowly south on Tenth, heading toward Penn Station and the homeless congeries in its environs, in the hope that they would meet someone who had seen Canman recently, when Lucy suddenly realized that she had lost her audience. She felt a pang of intense embarrassment. I'm boring him, was her thought, oh, God, how stupid, laying all this shit on him . . . but he said, "There he is."

David pointed across the street, and she looked and saw the Canman, unmistakable, the billow of dirty-tanish rattails, the pale blob of the face against the black plastic bag he carried on one shoulder, the long army overcoat, the loping stride. He was heading north on Tenth on the other side of the avenue. They both froze, like hunters just spotting deer across a naked autumn wood, but he was deerlike, too, casting his eyes back and forth, occasionally snapping a glance over his free shoulder, and he spotted them through the sparse Sunday traffic. He turned and headed back the other way, trotting, his cans making clanging music. Grale dashed into the street, crying, "Hey, John! Canman! Wait up!" Lucy started to follow, but had to step back in deference to a honking cab. She heard the squeal of tires behind her and a full chorus of horns. A black sedan zoomed out from a parking space across from the Santomas bodega, cut heedless across six lanes, and shrieked to a stop in front of the fleeing Canman. Both front doors sprang open at once, and two men leaped out. Canman instantly reversed course, streaking north again, his overcoat flapping, pursued by the two men, the one in the lead white, the other black. Canman dodged around a truck, and as he did, he dumped the bag of cans. The white man stepped on one of them, skidded, fell. His partner sidestepped around him and chased Canman, who was now running full tilt up Tenth, in the roadway. The traffic slowed as drivers stopped to gape, and this gave Lucy a chance to cut across the road, and so she was able to see Grale standing in Canman's path, his arms out as if offering a hug. Maybe he really did want to hug the fleeing man, but what he got was a stiff-arm to the chest that knocked him back against a parked car. He rebounded just in time to trip up the black man pursuing, and they both went down in a sprawl. Lucy ran over to Grale, who was bleeding from a scraped chin, but before she could get to him, something slammed into her back, and she went facedown into the asphalt.

It knocked the wind out of her, and for a full minute she could think of nothing but drawing breath. When she was able to stagger to her feet, she saw that the black man had a handful of David's hair and one arm up behind his back in a hammerlock. He pounded David's face a couple of times against the hood of a car and then snapped handcuffs on his wrists. So they were cops. She stuffed a tissue against her bleeding nose and plucked at the man's sleeve.

"What are you doing?" she demanded. "He didn't do anything."

The man whirled around, his face set in a snarl, but when he saw her, he did a double take and said, "Police business, miss. Move along now!"

"But he didn't *do* anything!"

"Interfering with an officer, miss. I said move along!" He finished cuffing Grale and marched him back to the black sedan, with Lucy worrying at his heels. The cop tossed Grale into the backseat of the car, which Lucy now saw was an unmarked police vehicle. She tried to stick her head into the doorway of the car, but the cop grabbed her roughly and threw her back. He slammed the car door, and they were just standing there arguing when the other man came trotting up. His face was red, and his pale hair stuck sweat-soaked to his forehead. Lucy found it hard to look at his face, so ferocious was the expression of frustrated rage. Although taken feature by feature it was a handsome face, now it was peculiarly distorted, the eyes retreating into slits, the brow bulging over them, the teeth bared, the jaw muscles knotted. He almost seemed to have a muzzle.

"I fucking lost him," he said to the black cop. "I lost him!" He struck the trunk of the car with his fist, full strength, dimpling the metal but doing no apparent injury to his hand. He paced rapidly back and forth, fists clenching and releasing, while his partner waited calmly, like a lion trainer giving some beast the time to come around.

"Fucking guy is like smoke," said the white cop, and then he shook his head, "or maybe I'm losing it." He laughed, took a few deep breaths, and looked into the car.

"What's this?"

"Guy who tripped me. Looked like he knew the suspect."

"Well, of course, he knows him," said Lucy angrily. "We're church workers, we're both volunteers out of Holy Redeemer. We were trying to find Canman, and we did find him, and then you showed up and chased him away."

"Who're you?" asked the white cop. His face, while still blotched, had once again become the face of a human.

"My name is Lucy Karp. And that's David Grale in there. He's a Franciscan, for God's sake." Lucy saw the black cop whisper something into his partner's ear.

"You know where this Canman character hangs out?" the white cop asked her. "Where he's hiding?"

"Of course not. If we knew where he was, we wouldn't have been walking all over the city looking for him."

The white cop nodded. "Okay, sure, but you could see where we might've made an honest mistake. We've been staked out by that bodega for two days. The guy finally shows up, and you queer the collar. You got to expect we're going to react a little." He turned to his partner and made a gesture, and the black cop pulled Grale out of the car and took off the cuffs. He had a bib of blood down the front of his shirt, and his face was bruised and red-splattered.

"Are you okay, David?" she asked.

He smiled his dreamy smile and said, "I'm fine. Denied my martyrdom yet again."

Lucy turned angrily to confront the white cop and saw that he was staring at her.

"You're the kid who found his last victim, aren't you?" he asked.

"I found a victim, but I doubt very much that it was his."

"You do, huh? On what basis, can I ask?"

"I know him. He's weird, but he's not a killer."

"Really? You've got a lot of experience with killers?"

"Yes, as a matter of fact, I do. More than you have, probably."

She could see the anger start up again in the cop's face, and then vanish, like a small cloud that blocks the sun for an instant. He grinned wryly. "No kidding? But, unfortunately, we can't just take your word for it. The thing is, if your guy is innocent, his best move is to come forward, talk to us, and if he's solid on the facts and the evidence, then he can walk away, and God bless. The way it is now, we got fifty cops running around looking for a serial killer, and he's in the cross hairs. He could get hurt, which would be a shame. Assuming he's not the slasher. Also, you see him again, either of you, you better get on the phone and call the cops." He pointed a finger. "I mean it. Meanwhile, I'm sorry you got in the way of a pursuit, and you ought to get your accidental injuries looked at. You want us to call an ambulance?"

"No, but I want your names and shield numbers," said Lucy.

Again that little black cloud across his face. Then he grinned broadly and said, "Don't push your luck, girlie."

Without another word, both of them got into their car and drove off.

12

"GOOD GOD!" SAID KARP. "WHAT HAPPENED!"

His daughter had tried to slip-slide into the loft that evening, but the dad was lying in wait for her, wanting to discuss earlier events, and grasped her by both shoulders while he checked out her face. It had been washed in a rest room, but the cheekbone and temple flashed a blossoming red-violet bruise, and the firm little chin had road burns.

"Nothing," said Lucy. "I tripped and fell."

"Please! You look like you've been six rounds with Sonny Liston. What happened?"

And he chivied her into the kitchen and made her some tea and listened while she told him the story.

"I think they must have been the same guys that roughed up Real Ali. The white guy . . . he was really scary."

"Cooley," said Karp. "The other one is Nash."

"How did you . . . ? Oh, right, you said you'd check them out."

"I didn't have to. I've had my eye on them for a while."

"Really? How come?"

Karp contemplated his daughter and considered the events she had just described and this question. He was not one for bringing the office home, but from time to time he would discuss a case with his wife, especially when she had some peripheral connection with it. But Marlene was now . . . somewhere else, and Lucy had, in fact, become involved in this one, and he was under no illusions about her innocence when it came to acts of blood. So he said, "How come is that Brendan Cooley killed a man named Lomax last month. He said he spotted Lomax in a stolen car, pursued him onto the Hudson Parkway, and shot him when Lomax tried to ram his car. The black cop you saw, Willie Nash, was there, too, driving. Our guys set a record for running the case through the grand jury, at which time it was not brought out at all the bullets that killed Lomax came from behind. I also found out that the car wasn't reported stolen until after Lomax was dead." He paused and was not disappointed when the penny instantly dropped.

"So they were chasing Lomax, not a stolen car. Why?"

"Ah, that's the big question, which actually I seem to be the only one who wants to know." And he went on to explain Brendan Cooley's unique status in the NYPD.

"So they let him go after he shot this guy, and now he's going after the slasher?"

"They did let him off, but as far as I know, he's not assigned to the slasher team. That's Detective Paradisio's guys—you remember him? And Cooley's not one of them. So . . ."

"So he wants Canman for something else," said Lucy, and Karp saw her face light up in a way so reminiscent of her mother that it brought a stinging to his eyes. "What could it be?" she asked, and supplied the answer. "Obviously, he's running some kind of racket. Lomax was in with him, and he whacked him, and Canman was . . ." She stopped, and her brow knitted. "No, that's not right. Canman wasn't in any racket. Unless . . ."

"What?"

"Well, he had this cart, like a laundry cart, and he used to push it around town collecting cans and other stuff, like from trash piles in the rich neighborhoods. He would sell the stuff to the sidewalk vendors and keep the metals for the recyclers. And people knew him, street people, and like rip-off artists, not real bad guys, just like people who had pipe or aluminum scrap."

"Thieves, you mean."

"I guess. I guess at that level the line between thieves and scavengers is pretty thin. And he'd buy their stuff and put it in the cart and haul it to the recycler. That was his business. So he could have had some contact with stuff that was worse than he usually went in for. I know he used to go by Second and Twelfth sometimes."

"I see," said Karp, not really surprised that his darling was familiar with the city's big nightly thieves' market. "What kind of guy are we talk-ing about here?"

"Canman? He's smart, but he keeps it hidden, mostly. He wasn't always a street person. Back in the life—that's what he calls it, 'back in the life'—he was pretty well-off, I guess, a family, a suit type. I think he was an engineer of some kind. He can make anything out of anything. And then . . . it's hard to say. The only time he ever talked about his life was when he got sick and I was taking care of him."

"Oh? When was this?"

Lucy realized that she had let a secret slip, thought of a covering lie, and then declined to use it. It didn't make sense anymore, especially now that they were sharing confidences. She bobbed her head and had the grace to blush. "Yeah, well, I told you guys I was staying over with friends, to study. This was this past winter. Basically, he just went crazy. He was angry all the time and got into fights at work, and starting weird projects, and he lost his job, and his wife had him committed, and they shot him full of drugs and kicked him out, like they do nowadays, and his wife divorced him, and he ended up on the street. He takes pills. He says he knows enough to medicate himself. He's still angry, but he can func-tion okay. I mean he makes real money. He keeps it in a mail-drop box."

"What's he angry about?"

"The same stuff that gets everyone angry: hypocrisy, unfairness, stu-pidity, the way things don't work, the bad guys winning all the time, injustice. Most people, they just see all that and they say 'What's on TV?' or 'Let's get high,' or have sex or whatever, but some people don't, and some of them go crazy behind it. They can't turn away, and they don't believe in God, so they have no place to go but the street."

"This is your theory of homelessness?"

"Oh, no. Most of them are nuts or dopers or drunks," she said cheer-fully. "God bless them. But some, like Canman, and Real Ali, and maybe David, they're seekers. Saints in training or failed saints, you could say."

"Is Canman the slasher?"

A shadow passed over her face, and she took a moment before answering. "He could be. I know he always carried a knife. I heard he cut a guy once who was trying to rip him off. And he makes bombs, booby traps, really to protect his stuff. I mean it's the street. But I can't believe it, not really." She laughed. "Actually, he looks *too* good for it. It's probably someone nobody would ever suspect." Again, he saw that shadow cross her face.

"That's not how it works in real life, though," said Karp. "In real life, the guy who looks like he did it usually did do it. It looks to me like Detective Cooley chased Lomax and executed him because of some prior relationship that your Canman knows about. And, unfortunately, Canman is in the crosshairs as the slasher just now, which means if Cooley found him, he could just take him out, and all anybody'd do about it is give him another medal."

"Provided the slashings stopped."

"Yeah, but that'd be too late for Canman. I wish someone could get word to him, to get him to surface."

"We're working on that," said Lucy. "He doesn't trust the cops."

"Who does? And what makes it a problem is this damn election. Jack's gone batty on the subject—don't rile the police, don't rile the Jews, don't rile the West Side Democrats, and so we're throwing cases right and left. It's like Italy or Guatemala down there."

She patted his arm. "Poor Daddy! There's nothing you can do?"

"You already asked me that. I have a nasty plan."

"Oh, no! I thought you were the only one in the family without nasty plans."

"Not anymore, obviously. There's still Giancarlo; he's pretty clean as far's I know."

"This is why you've been walking around with that long face lately?"

"Partly."

"And Mom. What are we going to do about her?"

Karp got up and put the cups in the sink. "Watchful waiting. I'm hoping she'll snap out of it, like she has before."

"She needs to go into detox."

"Thank you for the medical opinion. I tell you what, why don't you let me worry about your mother, and you worry about staying in school. I think they're serious this time. You flunk these midterms coming up, and you're toast."

"Don't nag, Dad! I know this."

"Well . . . ?"

"I'll try," she lied.

• • •

"I'm unhappy with this," said Karp, frowning. "This is not what I wanted. And what about the watch?"

He said this to Mimi Vasquez and Gilbert Murrow. Murrow looked uncomfortable, and faintly embarrassed. Vasquez was angry. Her face was flushed and pouty. "You keep saying that, what about the watch, but it's got no goddamn *connection* with the Marshak case. In fact, there *is* no Marshak case, as I just got finished telling you. We've interviewed over twenty of Ramsey's known associates. We asked them about the knife. Answers: don't know; yeah, he had one, but different; yeah, he had that one, if you say so and twenty bucks. Did he do angel dust? Yeah, all the time; no, never; yeah, if you say so and twenty bucks."

"He didn't use," said Karp.

"Why, because your daughter says so? Paxton, who was a known intimate of the victim in this case, swears he used it all the time and got crazy and violent behind it. I would say he makes a more compelling witness than your daughter, who, if I can say so, tends to cast a more forgiving light over these characters than I do, or than a jury will, and I don't even mention the fact that it takes me an hour to wash the stink out of my hair. Nobody we talked to ever saw him with the watch, except for the three guys who said he stole it from them and could they get it back. There is no, repeat, *no* known association between Marshak and either Ramsey or Paxton. Paxton sticks to his story about the knife and the attack like it was attached to his left testicle. And, yeah, it's Ramsey's prints on it. Bottom line? It's a dead end."

Karp seemed to ignore her tone and frustration and asked, "What did you say she was doing in the building?"

"Her insurance guy has his offices there. She was going to do some business with him and then drive out to her place upstate. That's why she had her car. Perfectly innocent. She drove in there, did her business, returned to her car, he jumped her with the knife, she pulled her gun, shot him, panicked, got back in the car, and booked. End of story, an urban tragedy."

"Or so we're being led to believe."

Vasquez banged her hand on the arm of her chair. "Jesus! Those are the facts, damn it! There is no case against her on those facts." Her voice had risen to a shout. Karp stared at her, saying nothing. "Why are you *obsessing* about this goddamn case?"

"Because of the watch."

"Oh, will you please shut up about the watch already! Who cares how he got the watch!"

"I care, and I'm the bureau chief, and don't tell me to shut up in my own office, Ms. Vasquez."

They stared at each other. No contest: Karp had the hardest stare in the building. Vasquez dropped her eyes.

"I'm very sorry, *Mr. Karp.* I'm sorry you're not satisfied with my work." She seemed about to burst into tears. Karp was not feeling that great himself. He had nurtured Vasquez almost from her first day in the office because he thought she was a good prosecutor, and because she reminded him of his wife as she once was, a handsome, scrappy, humorous, tough ethnic girl from a tough part of town. Also contributing to his discomfort: he had thought she liked him and had liked that. In fact, she had been in love with him for years, hopelessly and silently (not unusual among a certain stratum of female attorneys around the place), a kind of office joke that everyone knew about except Karp, which made it funnier. Karp felt hurt and betrayed: Why couldn't she see the point? Vasquez felt abused: Why was he torturing her with this craziness?

At this point, into the strained silence entered the ever tactful Murrow, reading out of his tiny notebook. "Lady Rolex, chronometer, fourteen-K gold with diamond bezel and gold expansion band, serial number zero one seven eight five zero nine two, reading one oh six when logged in, reported stolen from NPK Bonded Warehouse at JFK last August, along with a bunch of other stuff, mainly watches, optics, and perfume. The cop I spoke with, a Lieutenant Robert Maguire, says they suspect that whoever did the theft is fencing the stuff out through a ring run by Augustine Albert Firmo, but have been unable to nail down a case. Firmo seems wise to the usual stings." Murrow looked up from the notebook. "Does that help?"

"I don't know," said Karp. "Is there a connection between Marshak and Firmo? Between Ramsey or Paxton and him?"

Murrow said, "Between a big-time fence and a street guy? Why would there be? Street guys usually sell *fake* Rolexes."

Vasquez shoved her notes roughly into a cardboard folder. "This is ridiculous. What does it *matter?* You think Sybil Marshak ordered a hot Rolex and killed Ramsey because she didn't like the way it looked on her wrist? You might as well look at their horoscopes."

"Calm down, Vasquez," said Karp.

"No!" She stood up, bristling. "I don't understand any of this. Christ, Butch, it's you who's always saying don't speculate, stick with the facts, can you make a case or not, and if not, forget it. And there's no case here, and you're speculating like crazy, like you're on some kind of vendetta against this woman. Or against her lawyer. I don't want any part of it. It's weird and it's . . . sick."

"Thank you, Mimi," said Karp stiffly. "I'll tell Tony you're back on the chart. Just leave your notes with Murrow." She stared at him for a couple of long seconds, then turned on her heel and left.

Karp leaned back in his chair and locked his hands behind his head. "Take a lesson from that, Murrow," he said wearily. "The key to this job is skillful management of people."

"You had her in the palm of your hand. It was masterful."

"Yeah, right. Yet another friend down the toilet. You think I'm crazy, too, don't you?"

"Not as such. But I also see her point. I'm also thinking, what if it wasn't *his* watch? That would cut into your objection about his motivation for his run at Marshak."

"Wasn't his watch? Whose watch was it then?"

"He could've been holding it for someone, transporting it. Maybe someone the cops had their eye on, who didn't want to get caught with it on him. Say this guy uses street people to mule stuff around. Ramsey was something of a hustler. He could've done favors like that for a commission."

"Yeah." Swiveling in his chair, Karp turned his attention to the window, where a greasy rain was falling. Something was nagging at his mind, a connection he ought to be making, something about street people and thieves, but he wasn't making it. And there was something else, too, a name. He thought hard, but couldn't come up with it. It was like that a lot lately, as if part of his mind was locked up with some complex problem, leaving free about as much processing power as a pocket calculator deployed. He was making mistakes, not seeing stuff, screwing up with people. And he knew very well what the drain was. He felt Murrow's eyes on him, the pressure of his waiting. He swiveled back. "When was the watch logged in as evidence?"

Murrow consulted his papers. "The twenty-eighth at six-eighteen P.M. Why?"

"Oh, no reason, really. It showed the wrong time though. Look, Murrow, I got to give this some more thought. You're right, that's a good idea, maybe he was a mule. Okay, let's let Marshak hang for a while. Go and find this Maguire again, ask him to give you a list of Firmo's known associates. Maybe that'll jog something."

Murrow nodded and wrote a note, looking doubtful. The intercom buzzed. Murrow left and Collins came in.

"I want to thank you," said Karp when the young man had seated himself. "I had an interesting conversation with McBright on Sunday."

"He's a smart guy."

"He is, and remarkably well-informed about what's going on in this office. Remarkably."

Karp paused to let that sink in. He was not going to confront Collins about the leakage just yet, but he wanted him to be in no doubt that Karp knew what was going on. And a leak could be convenient, to disseminate both truth and things not necessarily true but which it might be convenient to have known. "In any case, we had a frank exchange of views about some racially tinged cases. Of which Benson is one. I take it you've seen the alibi witnesses, so-called?"

Collins opened a notebook. "Yes, I did. Yolanda Benson, forty-one, and Darcy Benson, nineteen, mother and sister. These are decent people, by the way. The mom's a teacher's aide, the sister's a student at Fashion. The father's an electrician, divorced a long time, but he comes by and helps out. I took the original Q&A and went through the questions again. This was in their home on West One Hundred Thirty-third Street. According to them, on the evening of, Jorell came in just after five because he wanted to watch the Holy Cross–Syracuse game on TV. Jorell is apparently a big college-ball fan, and he had a bet down. He had Syracuse and five points."

"They remembered this?"

"Yes, adamantly. They said it was a close game, and Jorell was jumping off the couch and yelling at the TV. They were eating dinner in front of the TV, and Jorell was so excited he hardly ate anything, and they were having barbecue pork chops, apparently a favorite of his. Anyway, Syracuse won by seven, and Jorell was pumped. He said he was going out to collect his bet and left around seven, returning after midnight. The murder went down at a little past six, so that's a stone alibi, if you believe them."

"And do you?"

"Wait, there's more. I reinterviewed Alicia Wallis, the girlfriend. Sixteen, but going on thirty. She says that on the afternoon prior to the killing Jorell told her he was going to hit a, quote, Jew diamond guy, unquote, that evening on the subway, that he had the knife and everything. Afterwards, he came to her mother's apartment, around seven, all excited and showed her the diamonds and asked her to keep them for him. Which she did. Two days later, Jorell came back, picked up some of the stones, and tried to sell them in the district and got caught. The cops visited her, and she first lied for him, and then she says she got scared because the guy had been killed, and she wasn't about to mess with no murder charge, and she told all. Now, back to the sister. The sister says that Alicia Wallis is a lying little street tramp, and she, Darcy, has been trying to get her brother to dump her for months. Darcy says that Alicia's been balling Oscar Simms since forever, and everyone in the 'hood knows it except for her dumb-ass brother, and if you want to know who stabbed that guy, you could do worse than look at old Oscar."

"And did you look?"

"Oh, yeah. It turns out that the police had looked, too. Oscar's an alumnus of Greenhaven, three years for armed robbery and two other arrests for robbery, dropped to larceny and time served in jail. Oscar has an alibi, too, supplied by a couple of homies, Duane Morgan and Tyrone Apger, also with sheets on them. A pretty tough crew, by the way, with a history of going after the black hats."

Karp voiced a couple of dramatic chords.

"You got it. They were watching a kung fu movie at the Academy, which is downtown, not too far from the murder scene."

"What kung fu movie?" asked Karp.

"Funny you should ask, because Oscar doesn't recall. 'All those movies be the same, man.' No knife on Oscar either, or any physical evidence, but my sense, after talking to Thornberry, the detective who closed, is that the cops didn't look all that hard after they had Benson. Benson looked good to go. The stones, Deng's eyewitness, and Alicia's story—three strikes and he's out."

"We got Deng to look at Oscar?"

"In a six-pack photo, against Benson and four dummies. He picked Benson."

"Wait a second—*after* he had already ID'd Benson live?"

"How did you guess?" said Collins. "Naturally, he focused on the guy he'd already identified. So, basically, if we look at it from the defense's point of view, which you're always lecturing us we should do, the case sits on the possession of part of the loot, a totally fucked ID process, and the testimony of a teenaged accessory after the fact who's screwing the guy who probably did it."

"How does Benson explain the loot?"

"Oh, you'll love this. He says he did it as a favor to Alicia. She told him she found them in a trash can, and she didn't think they were worth much, but could he maybe find out for her. Jorell is not the brightest bulb in the chandelier."

"Can we refocus on Oscar?"

"Maybe over Pat Thornberry's dead body. I'm telling you, the cops are not going to be helpful on this without a big circle jerk involving the eighth floor here and the twelfth floor over at One PP. Also, assuming we have the cops lined up, what do we have on him? No physical evidence, his homies are standing up right now, Alicia is solid for the time being."

"The time being . . ." mused Karp.

Collins nodded. "Yeah, my thoughts exactly. If he's really the guy on this, then Oscar needs to keep Alicia and his pals real happy indefinitely, and Oscar did not strike me as a fellow with the kind of self-control and long-term view that would make that work."

"You're probably right. Sooner or later one of these people is going to want a favor from us, and if someone asks the right questions, the whole thing will come unglued."

"So what do we do?"

"Interesting question, especially now. I think I'll ask the district attorney. He likes to keep decisions like this in his own hands. Meanwhile, good work. I'll probably be working for you if McBright gets in there."

"A racist remark, I believe," said Collins.

"See? My horrible reputation is well deserved."

Collins laughed and made his exit.

Karp got a chance to present these findings to the DA earlier than he had anticipated, for shortly after Collins left he got a peremptory call from Keegan, personally, telling him to get in there right away. He walked up the two flights.

Keegan was there with Fuller, which stifled the tiny hope that Karp always kept alive that Jack would return to his real, or noncandidate, persona and that they could then discuss the legal affairs of the office like menches, as they used to. Karp nodded to both of them and sat down.

"What's this I hear about you sending someone to screw up the Benson case?" demanded Keegan without preamble.

"I wouldn't say screwing up. I would say familiarizing myself with a top-priority case that I'm going to have to prosecute one of these days. And it's a good thing I did, Jack, because there's a lot more to Benson than meets the eye."

"The only thing I want to know is, can you convict?"

"Oh, I think so. I think we could probably blow away the usual inexperienced, overworked court-assigned defense attorney we'd probably get on the case. We do it all the time, as you know. Whether we can blow away the capital-defense-unit lawyers, who are in a completely different class, is another story."

"What do you mean?" asked Keegan, frowning.

"Well, if we were in Texas, they'd be loading the needle right now. Benson's a dumb-ass fall guy of the appropriate race, mentality, and background, like they kill in those states every other week. They give the D to a fat-ass crony who sleeps during the trial, and the kid goes down for it. But we are not in Texas, which you can tell because of the tall buildings and the lack of cowshit on the streets." And he proceeded to tell Keegan what Collins had learned and what Karp made of it.

"My prediction," he concluded, "is that if you go for capital murder in this case, you will lose. Those capital-case people are good. They will tear up little Alicia on the stand. Her connection to Oscar and his merry crew will emerge. Benson's mother and his sister will look like solid gold next to little Alicia. He will walk, and you will look like a fool for bringing a case that weak."

Fuller said, "It's not a weak case. We have the diamonds."

Karp rounded on him. "Norton, we're talking legal strategy here, and with all due respect, you don't know dick about legal strategy, but if we need advice on how many paper clips we're going to need or how it will play in the polls, I'm sure you'll have something valuable to contribute." Norton went pale. Karp turned his attention back to Keegan. "Jack, that's my honest opinion. What we have on Benson won't bear the weight of a capital case, not in the state of New York. And we can't start on Simms because we got no entrée into it while these people are sticking to their stories. Sorry, but there it is."

The DA calculated silently, his face pursing and knotting in the segments appropriate to devious thought. His head started to move from side to side with increasing vigor until it became a full negative shake. "Uh-uh, we have to stick with it. And we should announce that we're going to seek it as soon as possible. Will this guy plead out to life without the possibility, do you think?"

"If you threaten the death penalty? I doubt it. He says he didn't do it. He's been saying he didn't do it since the cops grabbed him up, and he's been consistent throughout, and the cops were not gentle with him, as I understand it. And when the hotshots on the capital-defense team get to him and take a hard look at our case, I very much doubt that they will advise him to seek a plea of any kind. Because they can win."

"But not until after November," said Fuller. "Am I allowed to say that, Butch?"

Karp ignored the gibe. Keegan nodded, said, "Okay. We go with death for now. I'll announce it tomorrow."

"Well, I won't even mention that it's wrong since that seems to cut no ice around here anymore, but we got a situation where one of these phony stories could break down anytime. I mean before the election. What do you do then? Then you're the guy who wanted to put an innocent man to death on a weak case for political reasons."

"Oh, you're the political adviser, too, now?" asked Fuller nastily. "Something you know dick about, if I may say so."

Keegan waved a hand as if dispersing a stench. "I'll take that chance. Now, what about Marshak, speaking of weak cases? Or no case, as I understand it."

"We're still looking at it."

"What's to look at?" said Keegan. "It looks like simple self-defense. An urban tragedy. Let's move on this, get the grand jury to clear her, and get this out of my craw."

Karp made some noises that could be interpreted as agreement, or maybe not, at which Keegan threw him a sharp look but did not press the point. *An urban tragedy,* the words Vasquez had used. Karp did not believe much in that kind of coincidence. He recalled how Fuller had used Catafalco's language in the Cooley case, which had confirmed that Catafalco was leaking to Fuller, and now the DA was using Vasquez's phrase. Vasquez was off the reservation, too.

The meeting broke up. Karp drifted back to his office, feeling as alone and isolated as he had ever felt in his life. Clearly the resources of the office were compromised, at least for his purposes. It was therefore time to move into phase two of the plan. He was sitting at his desk, tapping his teeth with a pencil, and thinking about how to accomplish this when the phone rang: Flynn reminding him that he had an appointment in half an hour uptown at Sacred Heart. Karp resisted snarling back that he remembered, for he had not. A good, even a devoted, father, Karp had little experience with kids in trouble, and it irked him, and he took full responsibility. He himself had been a perfect forties and fifties kid, doing homework, obeying teachers and coaches, never causing his parents a moment's worry. Or so he imagined.

The appointment was with the headmistress, Catharine Royal, RSCJ, an actual nun, to discuss his daughter's future at the school. Marlene was to be there, too, and this prospect worried him more than having to discuss his daughter with a nun, which was getting up there on the worry-intensity scale. On the ride up to Ninety-first and Fifth, he calmed his mind by refusing to think about the problem at all, thinking about lists of things he had to do to ravel the few golden threads of truth from the great knot of political lies that Keegan and Fuller had made of the DA's office. That was still worth doing, he thought. And also, if he didn't think of that, if he considered what was happening to his family, he would not be able to function at all.

Lucy was waiting in the hallway outside the headmistress's office. It was class-changing time, and the hallway was full of lively girls in pretty clothes, in dance costumes, in athletic gear. On none of the fresh young faces was the look of bleak despair he saw on Lucy's.

"What's up, kiddo?"

A shrug. "Midterms are back."

"The bad news first."

"It's all bad news. I flunked everything."

"Everything? French? Not *French?* English?"

"Everything. I cut classes. I didn't hand in stuff." She looked down the hall. "Mom isn't coming?" She sounded hopeful.

"Yeah, she's coming from home." He checked his watch. "Let's go get this done."

Sister Catharine Royal was a heavy woman with a shiny face fringed by short gray hair. Behind large, gogglelike spectacles her blue eyes were concerned, but kind. They sat, and the headmistress went over Lucy's record. Sacred Heart, she said, was not for everyone. It was a rigorous academic environment, and although it also stressed community service, in which Lucy was, of course, exemplary, a certain standard of performance was required, which standards Lucy had not even begun to meet this term. There were alternatives; the school did not give up easily. Stress affected different people differently, and sometimes the most talented students were just the ones who failed to cope. Karp listened and nodded. That was what he felt, too. They were not considering expulsion, yet. But maybe some time off, a chance for tutoring . . .

Then the door opened and Marlene came in. Stumbled in. You could smell her from the doorway. She was wearing a long, fleece-lined leather coat over a translucent shirt studded with crystals, misbuttoned, and with one tail hanging out of her skirt. She staggered to a chair and plopped her alligator bag on the headmistress's desk.

There was a brief, shocked silence. Sister Royal put on a forbearing look, uttered a brief welcome, and started to repeat a version of what she had just told Karp. She had hardly begun, however, when Marlene interrupted. "Look, Sister, let's get down to business. 'Cause let's face it, this is a business you're running here, am I right? A business. You're in business, I'm in business, so let's talk business. I went to school here myself, right? I was a scholarship girl, in the little uniform, you had nuns here then, not like now, 'Yes, Sister,' 'No, Sister,' all that stuff, and chapel. So what I want to say is we want the kid here in school. I mean what else is she going to do all day? Hang out with the bums? I mean *I* hung out with bums, too, but they were a different kind of bums, because she's not what you could call socially developed, and that's important—social development. Of course, she doesn't shoot people, not that I learned that here, don't get me wrong. She comes from a good home. A good home. I'm her mother, um, so I know. I mean, you're not a mother, let's face it. What we really want . . . let's talk a figure. I got plenty. I mean, what do they say, money talks, bullshit walks." And here Marlene let out a hideous cackle and swayed in her chair.

The headmistress shot a glance at Karp and said, "Mrs. Karp, perhaps it would be better if we met at a later time . . ."

"Please, Sister," said Marlene, "it's Mizzzz Ciampi. Not Mrs. Karp. Mrs. Karp is deceased. Mrs. Karp was a wonderful woman, far, far more wonderful than me. Or I. Is that right? She produced my husband, who is a perfect person, as you can see, but my daughter is unfortunately not as perfect, which is why we are doing whatever we are doing. So what are we talking here? You need a new gym? Whatever . . ." Marlene popped open her bag, spilling stuff all over the desk—keys, cards, crumbled wads of high-denomination currency, and a flat pint of Hennessy. It clunked loudly and spun on the polished wood, the focus of all eyes. Marlene grabbed her checkbook and waved it, the pages flapping in Sister Catharine's face like a slaughtered chicken.

At that point, Lucy sprang to her feet, uttered a phrase in a language no one in the room understood but whose tone was unmistakable, and dashed from the room. Karp shot up, stuck Marlene's purse under one arm, hauled his wife from her chair and stuck her solidly against his opposite hip, and said, "I'm sorry. I'll be in touch," to the headmistress and frog-marched Marlene out of the office and out of the building, she protesting loudly and drunkenly all the way.

On the street, he had a little break because Marlene had to lean against a tree on Ninety-first and be sick, noisily and at some length. Karp dashed out to the avenue and tried to spot his daughter, but she was gone. The dead low points of his life came floating by his inner eye, as they will at such times: the moment he had realized that he was too crippled to play big-time ball; the night his first wife had ditched him; the time his second and present wife had been kidnapped; the time that same wife had been kidnapped again, with his daughter; and now. This one was right up there, a competitor in a tough league.

13

A METROLINER WAS LEAVING FOR NEW ENGLAND TWENTY-TWO MINUTES AFTER
Lucy arrived at Penn Station, and she took it, paying cash on board for
her ticket. The train was crowded, filled with suits tapping laptops and
exurban matrons with shopping bags reading paperback novels about
shopping. Lucy found a window seat and rested her head against the
cool, dusty glass as the train pulled out of the station. Another train was
waiting stationary across the platform, and she experienced the common
illusion: for an instant she could not tell which train was moving, and this
made her think of the science class she had just flunked, and of where
she was fleeing—to her best friend, Mary Ma, at the Massachusetts
Institute of Technology in Cambridge. Mary was as prodigious in math
and physics as Lucy was in languages and had left for MIT in what would
have been her junior year in high school. Mary had once used the anal-
ogy of the moving trains to explain the theory of relativity to her idiot
friend, and thinking of this, Lucy felt tears start in her eyes. Which she
suppressed. The train moved into the tunnel, gathering speed. Now she
only saw her reflection, ghostly, transparent, and closed her eyes.

In her head, racing thoughts. Lucy knew enough about spiritual
practice to understand that she should exercise some control over these
because they were agents that helped to convert mere sadness into par-
alyzing depression and neurosis, but she found herself too tired to make
the effort. It was the sort of emptying exhaustion and dryness that allows
intelligent people the world over to sit passively in front of televisions
watching moronic pap. So Lucy watched the movie in her mind. She

would go to Cambridge and start a new life and live in a house with Mary Ma and never have to go to school again. She would make her own money, which would not be difficult for her. She knew people at Harvard, for whom she could be a lab rat; alternatively, she could walk into any international firm or agency and get a job as a simultaneous translator. No problems there. Mary would be delighted to see her. It was just what any hardworking math superstar needed, a neurotic idiot-savant, religious-nut roommate. Mary would, of course, have made her own friends, geeks who spoke in equations, not Cantonese, and how would Lucy fit in there, she who often stumbled on what was seven times eight? Of course, Mary loved her, but just because you loved someone, you didn't necessarily want to have them in your lap. David, same thing, he didn't want her in his lap either, not that he loved her, far from it. Tolerated maybe. She had such a good heart, though, Mary, and Lucy had really done so much for her in the past, wetback that she was. It really wasn't too much to ask, just a place to hang out while she got her life together. But what if she was cold, frightened, rejecting? Mary had that Chinese thing about family.

Lucy opened her eyes. Still darkness, and her ghostly face. The tunnel went on for a long time. She looked around the train, at her fellow passengers. Next to her sat a suburban matron with nicely done blond hair and careful makeup. She was wearing a tan raincoat and a tweed skirt and reading *Cosmo*. The rack above her was stuffed with shopping bags. She played with her pearls as she read about (Lucy peeked) famous people's descriptions of their best orgasms. Lucy wondered briefly if this woman had any children and what their lives were like, and wondered also if a monster was living inside her, as there was in Lucy's own mother. As there was in most people, she imagined.

She shifted in her seat. The car seemed warmer, more odorous: electricity, oil, damp wool, the perfume of the suburban matron, a heavy tropical scent, like frangipani or mimosa. The light, too, seemed dimmer, more orangy now. Lucy looked at her watch, her cheap watch. It seemed to have stopped. Or maybe time had. Her head throbbed. Her chest felt constricted. Hell must be like this, she thought, a train in an endless tunnel, its cars full of the damned working on laptops and reading magazines about orgasms of other people. She would never get off this train not in her head, not in Boston either. Mary would look at her as at a stranger, a feeble smile, embarrassed introductions to people who did not screw up, who had normal parents, who were normal geniuses, who were not stupid freaks. Stupid freaks. Stupid freak.

Stupidfreakstupidfreakstupidstupidfreakfreakfreakyfreak, the train said. I don't care, an interior voice said over the sound of the rails, I don't care, fuck them, I'll show them, they'll be sorry they treated me like that, I don't need them, I can do it by myself, fuck them all . . . and the rest of the usual horseshit of adolescent neuroticism, too tedious almost to mention. Here Lucy was fortunate, in that she had been exposed to at least the beginnings of spiritual training, and as the demonic voices built up to a consuming racket, she began, almost instinctively, to pray, and as instinctively chose the simplest prayer in the book, nothing fancy, asking for nothing but mercy, a one-liner. And not silently either, so that the woman next to her said, "Excuse me?"

Lucy stared at her, her lips still moving. "I'm praying," she said, and ignoring the shocked expression on the woman's face, resumed that exercise: head forward, swaying slightly back and forth, in the manner of some of her paternal ancestors, forcing everything out of her mind but the prayer. Her breathing deepened. The crazy voices shrank in volume. The train burst out of the tunnel and rushed along the top of Manhattan and over the high rail bridge to the Bronx. The sky was full of bruised purple clouds; the sun was descending over the Palisades and, as they crossed the bridge, it shot out great shafts of topaz light, gilding the filthy waters of the Hudson and Harlem.

Lucy was aware of a change at her side. The matron was gone, and in her place sat an elderly woman in a black nun's habit and a soft white cloak. Her face was dark and passionate, and little fires flickered in her deep-set eyes. Her mouth was full and sensual and pursed into an amused twist. When she spoke, her voice was deep and melodious. Her Spanish had a thick Castilian lisp.

"And what do you think you are doing, little girl?"

"Where have you been?" Lucy blurted.

"I am always in the same place, thank God. Where have *you* been is what needs discussion. That, and where you are going."

And they did discuss it as the train swung east toward the gathering darkness and the fancy towns of exurbia: New Rochelle, Mamaroneck, Greenwich. Lucy had enjoyed an intimate relationship with St. Teresa of

Avila since the age of ten, when her mother had given her, for some strange reason of her own, *The Interior Castle*. At first Lucy had imagined that everyone had a private saint, as she had imagined (briefly) that everyone could speak any language they heard after minimal effort. When she had found that both of these assumptions were false, she had kept mum about the former gift, feeling that she had already attracted enough attention and trouble with the latter. Mike Dugan knew about it, but being the sort of priest he was, he kept quiet too. The apparitions happened on their own schedule, sometimes twice a month, sometimes not for many months. It had been over a year just now.

The discussion grew heated. Teresa, of course, had many saintly virtues, but forbearance toward recalcitrant and impetuous girls was not one of them, as she had amply shown during her life on earth. She did not believe such young girls ought to be traipsing around the countryside. Lucy was needed at home. Her duty lay there, and besides, she had received her precious talent from God, and God would in His own time tell her what use she should put it to.

"You did enough traipsing around," Lucy retorted.

"Yes, when directed to by heaven, and very often to my great disadvantage and suffering. Are you being directed? No, you are running away. From your mother's pain, from your failure, from your feelings about this wretched young man. Go back, I tell you, and do your duty!"

"I can't! It's too much."

"God often makes life difficult for His friends."

"Then it's no wonder that He has so few friends!"

The saint's lip creased slightly, and her heavy eyebrows rose. "I said that."

"I know," said Lucy, and then another voice said, "Miss? Miss, are you okay?"

A conductor was leaning over her. The suburban matron was gone, or no—there she was, in the aisle, behind the conductor, looking nervous. The conductor, a pie-faced man with watery blue eyes magnified by wire-rimmed spectacles, looked nervous, too. Lucy recalled that talking to people who weren't there on trains had before this been a prelude to a murderous fusillade. She said, "I'm fine."

"You were talking to . . . ah . . . yourself, miss."

"I was having a religious experience," she replied with dignity. "I am not a danger to myself or others."

Everyone in the nearby rows was staring, craning their necks around to gape, the magazines and laptops abandoned. Lucy blushed. Now that the aura of the experience had passed, she was back in the world of social embarrassment. The conductor turned to the matron and, after a brief consultation, moved the woman and her many packages to a seat in the NO PRAYING section. People were still staring, and some of the ones sitting too close to the lunatic got up and moved to another car. The train was slowing down, gliding into a station. Without further thought, Lucy jumped out of the seat and fled the train. She looked around and discovered that she was in Bridgeport.

She knew someone in Bridgeport. In fact, it was probably a sign. Not Boston, Bridgeport. No, *definitely* a sign, she thought, and trudged out of the station. She asked directions and walked some distance until she came to Main Street, a tatty zone of the old downtown: pawnshops, saloons, cheap clothing and furniture stores. And oriental restaurants and groceries. She found a blue sign that said PHO BAC, in white lettering, and she went into the door beneath it, past windows clouded with steam. Odors of anise and cilantro, and of the fermented fish sauce called *nuoc mam,* and boiling rice. She went through the dining room and past a door that bore a metallic sign: PRIVATE.

Behind it, a small room containing a ratty couch, a round table in the center, some chairs. Four oriental men dressed in black clothes sat at the table playing cards. They looked up, bemused, when she entered. They were in their twenties, their thirties, all with thin, hard faces, three of them pockmarked, one, the oldest, smoothly handsome. His name was Freddy Phat, and he was a gangster. They were all gangsters there. He stared at her, his fine brows knotting.

"Freddy, it's Lucy. I'm here to see Uncle Tran." She spoke Vietnamese, with a fancy Saigon accent.

A smile. "Little Lucy! He didn't say you were coming."

"He didn't know. Where is he?'"

"Out. Doing business. How are you?"

"I've been better." Suddenly she felt weak. She went to the couch and threw herself down on it. The cooking smells from the kitchen reminded her she had not eaten since early morning. She closed her eyes.

"Hey, you're sure you're okay?" asked Freddy nervously. Freddy

Phat had no particular liking for white girls, but this particular one was the most important white girl in the whole world.

"I'm okay. I think I must be hungry."

He grinned. "You came to the right place then." He laughed, and the other thugs laughed, too, hiding their bad teeth with their hands.

She was spooning hot *pho* into her mouth when a thin, middle-aged Vietnamese man walked in from the street. He wore a short, black leather coat and a white broadcloth shirt buttoned to the collar and a white silk scarf. On his head was a plastic-covered rain hat with the brim turned up all around. An unprepossessing figure, oriental anonymous, like a waiter or a clerk, until you studied the eyes. Tran Do Vinh was his name. Tran had been a minor official in the South Vietnamese government's finance ministry who had tried to escape by sea in 1978 and had perished of disease and exhaustion midway on the journey to the Philippines. The present owner of his name had been on the same leaky craft, although he had been a major official of the National Liberation Front, the so-called Vietcong. This was known only by Freddy Phat, Marlene Ciampi, and the girl who now jumped up and ran to him and threw her arms around him. He held her tightly. They had not seen each other in two years, and both of them were somewhat surprised to discover that she was now as tall as he. She pressed her face into the leather of his jacket and inhaled his scent—old-fashioned lilac hair oil, cigarettes, *nuoc mam.* He held her away from him and looked into her face. "My dear girl," he said in French, "I am so happy to see you. But what is wrong?"

She was crying like a baby. "Everything, Uncle! My life is a quite complete ruin."

"I am desolated to learn it. Finish your soup and let me hear the terrible details." They sat, he ordered tea, he sipped, she slurped and told her story—the disaster at school, her mother's collapse, the money and what it had wrought. He listened, smiling, asking hardly a question, and thought, as he often did in her presence, of his dead daughter, who would have been near Lucy's age now. He was not a sentimental man, but this he allowed himself. He loved her. It always surprised him, like a radio message from a dead self.

When she had finished, he asked, "So you had not intended originally to come to see me?"

"No, I was going to Boston to be with Mary Ma. My new life." Lucy rolled her eyes to mock herself.

"Very interesting. You recall that the very first time we spoke you were also running away from school. I gave you some soup."

"Yes, soup and a Confucian lecture on studying hard."

"Which clearly had no effect whatever," he said tartly. "And now that you are here . . . ?"

Her face fell. Her fingers twiddled a packet of sugar. "I don't know. I feel stupid and wrong. But I'm just paralyzed. When I think of school . . . the boredom . . . it makes me shrivel."

"Oh, boredom. Pah! Coping with boredom is an attainment. No one unwilling to be bored has ever achieved anything grand, and I am sorry to see you have not learned how. I attribute this to your narrow genius, and to the impatience with tedium that I believe is common among people with such gifts. However, this can be corrected by cultivating the proper attitude. And you must have tutoring, in order to catch up in your studies."

"Tutoring by whom?"

"By me, it goes without saying. You will recall that I taught you how to calculate with fractions when you were eight—"

"Which I've managed to forget."

"—and your current work will pose no greater problems. As you will recall, I am a licensed teacher, and also not unskilled in the techniques of extracting information from unwilling heads. I believe similar techniques can move information in the opposite direction." He gave her one of his shark looks, and though she knew he was kidding, it still gave her a chill. She returned a hard look of her own.

"Will I have to listen to cryptic Eastern sayings that will make me a changed and better person, as in those movies?"

Tran sniffed as he had learned to in Paris in the fifties. "I assure you that my teaching methods are not cryptic at all. The opposite, in fact. I will be quite French. In any case, we will fix your school problem or kill you entirely, one or the other. Then we will see about repairing your dear mother. There is a telephone behind the cashier's desk. Please call your home immediately and tell your father of these plans."

Lucy meekly went off and did so. Meek was a relief just now. She found it encouraging that both St. Teresa and a commie gangster agreed about what she should do.

• • •

Marlene awoke and did not know where she was. This ignorance upon arising had not been unusual in recent weeks, but formerly she had, after a few moments, recognized her location as some corner of her home. This was not the case now. Above her she saw not the familiar smooth, off-white dropped ceiling of the loft, but acoustic tile, pale green. A TV hanging from the ceiling. A window, large and clean—the light said morning. A bag on a pole with a tube leading into a human wrist. A hospital? The wrist was attached to a chromed bed rail by a Velcro restraint. Her wrist, it seemed; the other was similarly tied, as were her ankles. *That* kind of hospital. They had somehow Velcroed the inside of her mouth, too, a technology she had not known existed. With effort she tore her tongue loose and croaked. Nothing happened. A call button was taped to the bed rail, within reach of her right hand. She pushed the button.

In came a large, ocher-colored woman in a pink pants uniform and pink harlequin glasses attached to a chain. She smiled and said, "Good, you're up. How are you feeling?"

"Water."

The woman applied the tube of a plastic squirt bottle to Marlene's lips. She sucked at it gratefully.

"Thank you," she said in a near normal voice. "Um . . . can I get loose now?"

"I don't see why not." The pink woman undid the restraints. "You got to promise me you won't tear up the place like you did coming in."

Marlene rubbed her wrists. "Where am I?"

"Kinney-Briard. You're in detox. I'm Dottie."

"Hello, Dottie. I'm Marlene." She stuck out her hand, and Dottie shook it uncertainly. Marlene thought most of the clientele at Kinney-Briard did not shake hands with their keepers. Kinney-Briard was one of the city's many private and expensive drunk tanks. "How did I tear the place up coming in?"

"You fought like a devil when you figured out where you were and that we were taking off your clothes. They said you were boxing them . . . you knocked Pat Lucas down with a punch in the jaw, and she's nearly two hundred pounds. And you gave Dr. Einkorn a split lip. I wasn't on shift then, but I heard it took six people to get you sedated and restrained. Where'd you learn to hit like that?"

"My dad taught me. He was a ranked welterweight in the forties." Marlene then added inanely, "I was drunk."

"You could say that. You had a blood level of point four one. Point one-o is legally drunk. Point five is when people start going into terminal comas. You were lucky your husband brought you in when he did."

"Yeah, lucky me." Marlene groaned and shifted in the bed. She could feel the initial pangs of what she knew would be one of the great headaches of the decade. Dottie was changing the IV bag. "What're you dripping into me?"

"Saline glucose with different electrolytes. You were seriously dehydrated, too. And malnourished. How long have you been drunk?"

"Not long. Weeks, not years."

"I guess. Rate you were going, you wouldn't have lasted a year."

On this cheerful note, Dottie departed, but not before dispensing an analgesic and directing Marlene's attention to the helpful brochures on the nightstand. Apparently "Doctor" would be by this afternoon to tell her about the program.

"The doctor I slugged?"

"Afraid so, dear."

"Did I hit anyone else besides those two?"

"No one but your husband."

"Oh, marvelous." Marlene pulled a pillow over her face. To her surprise, she fell instantly asleep.

And awoke to find Karp sitting there watching her, his expression neutral, tinged with apprehension. He had a purpling bruise under one eye.

She whimpered and placed her hands over her face. "Tell me it didn't happen. Tell me it was all a bad dream and I'm in here for an inoperable brain tumor."

He ignored this. "How do you feel?"

"Like I've been beaten with chains." She peeked through her fingers. "Jesus, Butch! I'm so sorry. What can I say? I don't remember any of it."

"The visit to the school?"

A pause, a shriek. She pulled the pillow over her head. From beneath it, she wailed, "No, I thought that was the d.t.'s. I really . . . Oh, God, no! That poor kid! Where is she?"

"Consorting with known criminals. She took off right after the events in question and ended up in Bridgeport. She called me last night. Apparently the plan is for her to stay up there with him until she's caught up in school. I spoke to Sister Royal about it . . ."

"Oh, God! Did she mention the . . . events?"

"Only to convey wishes for your recovery. She's a good egg. She says tutoring is a fine idea and that Lucy's welcome back if she catches up on her work."

"Did she ask who's doing the tutoring?"

"Yes. I said it was a personal friend of yours. A graduate of the Sorbonne. Take the pillow off your face, Marlene."

She did so and looked him in the eye. She reached out to touch the bruise, but he shied at her fingers. "I did that."

"Yes. A right hook, just after you coldcocked the doctor. You were also vividly negative as to my Semitic ancestry and my sexual prowess. It was quite a performance. I wasn't aware you harbored those feelings."

"It was the liquor talking," she said shortly, not wanting to consider any of that. "Am I going to have to be guilty about this for the rest of my life?"

"No, but it would be good if you fixed it so it wouldn't happen again."

"What, getting blasted? Okay, I promise I won't embarrass you in public again. I'll exercise discretion." She could feel the irritation rising. She looked at her husband's face. She blocked out the pain and love she saw there and painted it over with a smug, judgmental mask. She wanted a drink. She was ashamed of it, but there it was, not to be denied. "When am I getting out of here?" she asked, looking away.

"You need to talk to your doctor about that. When I spoke with him before, he suggested the full detox, four weeks."

The thought of Karp talking to some twerp shrink about her: a bolt of pain and revulsion, converted to rage. "You were talking to what's-his-face, Einstern? You told him all about how bad I am?"

"Einkorn. No, I told him I was terribly worried about you, that you'd never acted like this before, that I didn't know what the fuck to do. He offered me a Xanax and gave me a brochure about Al-Anon."

"Are you going to go?"

"No. Look, Marlene, I don't know fuck-all about alcoholism. Maybe I'm in denial, maybe I'm one of those enablers you read about. And if you want to know, Einkorn was kind of leaning me in that direction, but looking at this last twenty years we spent together, I honestly don't see that. I can't recall another time in all those years when you were falling-down drunk like you've been half a dozen times in the last month." He looked at her, but her face was closed to him. "I understand you're hurting from what happened. You've been hurting before, but you snap back; you get on with life. But not now for some reason." He tried a smile on. "Hell, Marlene, it's like *Invasion of the Body Snatchers,* where the Chinese guy says, 'That not my wife.'" Marlene didn't smile back. "I mean you got a problem, let's talk about it. We always talked about stuff, even when we were fighting."

"My problem is there's nothing to drink around here," said Marlene in that strange voice she was using nowadays, a flat and bored voice, not her own, something she'd heard maybe. It was eerie for him, almost flesh-crawlingly. He wanted to shake her, hit her. He'd never wanted to do that before, even back when she was committing technical felonies every other night. He suppressed the comeback line, he sensed that's what the new Marlene wanted, a little trading of one-liners, keep it light, brittle, and bitter.

Instead he said, "Speaking of the movies, you remember what the girl says to Butch Cassidy? I'll love you, I'll do anything for you, but I won't watch you die."

That got her attention. He sensed something trying to come out in her, some real thing. He ought to have been tender now, dropped his guard, opened up, broke down, but he was not good at this sort of thing, not good at dealing with the dark parts. So he said, "Whatever you want, Marlene. I'll help you any way I can. But I'm not going to just watch you kill yourself. Pull one of these again, and I'll take the kids and split, I'll walk away. That's my bottom line, just so you know."

"That sounds like an ultimatum."

"Take it however you want."

They couldn't look at each other then, both hearts breaking.

The clinic was on Fifty-third off Second. When Karp left, he walked south, just to walk. The sky was low and threatening, cold for April; the green fuzz on the trees seemed out of its time, sprayed on, not real. Karp was a good city walker; his long legs ate the blocks without feeling the pounding, his size kept lesser beings from blocking his path. He walked blindly, his mind unable to get a bite into what was happening to him. It was not real, it was like a bad made-for-TV movie. He walked for a long time.

In leaving, Karp had left a hole Marlene could not fill with the material in the brochures. Nor did Dr. Einkorn fill it with his bland line: you're sick, we can fix it for you, give us a chance, put yourself in our hands, stop denying. Marlene was surly and wished that she had hit him a couple more times. No, she decided, when he had gone, too, the poor bastard is just doing his job. I am just not the job he does. Not yet, anyway.

She got out of bed and found her clothes in a closet. The skirt and jacket and blouse she had worn to the interview of doom were unwearable, stained with vile substances, stretched and torn. It looked as if whoever had worn them had been in a fight and lost. The underwear was intact, though, one of the sets she had bought in Bloomie's that day when she had got rich and drunk, and so were the boots and the long, fleece-lined leather coat. She got into the undies and boots and coat and found her cell phone in her bag. She used it to call the limo service. They knew where Kinney-Briard was.

Marlene put on her makeup, trying as she did so not to really look at her face. It was like making up someone else in high school. Dottie came in while she was doing this.

"You going somewhere?"

"Yes, I'm checking out."

"You shouldn't. You're not detoxed yet."

"I'll detox on my own."

"I doubt that, sugar, but it's your life. Try to eat something. You won't want to, but force yourself. Bananas are good. And try to dilute it a little."

"I'm not going to drink. I mean get drunk. Like I did."

"Yeah, you are," said Dottie confidently. "I been doing this awhile, and I've seen about four million runners, and every one of them thinks they're different. I should go call Doctor, but I guess you don't want to wait around for that."

"No," said Marlene as she finished her eyes. She stood erect and fluffed her hair. With the belt cinched and the coat buttoned to the collar she looked dressed. She saw Dottie in the mirror observing her.

"How do I look?" Marlene asked, only a little sarcastically. "Like a drunk on the run?"

"You got that right. If I was you, I would go on home before you start in drinking, put some clothes on you. You go into a bar that way, you liable to end up in a cheap motel with a line of guys out to the street."

"Thanks for the advice," said Marlene stiffly. She shook hands with the nurse and did not look long into her eyes, which held far too much compassion. The limo was waiting. The driver was Osman. Marlene gave him the Crosby Street address. She slumped in the corner, hiding in her beautiful coat, flinching under the waves of psychic pain that rolled up from hell into her mind. She pinched her naked thigh under the coat hard, but it did no good. How did she get here? she wondered. This is not me. I am a solid citizen. I am not a drunk. I am not a shopomaniac. I am a good mother and a good wife. Not convincing. The memories came back, in fearsome detail; she squirmed, she writhed, she cried out. Osman's dark eyes appeared in the rearview mirror.

"Madam? Is something wrong?"

"No." No, she thought, I am not, I am not going to sit in a church basement and tell my sad story to a bunch of strangers. I can control this. Her teeth hurt from the gritting she was doing. "Stop here, pull over," she ordered. The car rolled smoothly to a curb, Thirty-second and Third. She jumped out and came back with an icy bottle of Chablis. The limo was supplied with stemware, and she had a corkscrew. Just one, make it last. She did make it last, almost to her door.

"Wait," she told the driver, and entered her building. She left the wine in the car, which she thought was okay and proof that she wasn't such a lush. A lush would never leave the bottle. In the loft there were cooking smells, something frying. In the kitchen was a woman she had never seen before, a stocky Latina not much older than she. The woman stared at her, essayed a formal smile. Marlene gave it back and lurched to the bedroom. A woman I don't know is taking care of my family, she thought. The dog was waiting for her in the bedroom, on the bed, where he was forbidden to be. He jumped off with a loud thud and fawned, snuffling and drooling. A pool of saliva ten inches wide was on the center of the duvet. Everything is falling apart, she thought. She dropped her coat, yanked off her boots, and opened her wardrobe. A cascade of pricey gorgeousness fell out onto the floor, some of it still wrapped in store tissue, other items popping from shopping bags. She grabbed a pair of tan leather pants off the top of the pile and a red silk shirt from a Lauren bag and put them on. She heard the door open.

The boys were standing in the doorway looking at her, their expressions like those of refugee children staring through barbed wire. She sat on the bed and spread her arms.

"Come'ere handsomes!"

They sat on either side of her, and she kissed them both.

"Where were you?" asked Zak.

"I was in a hospital."

"Were you sick?"

"Sort of."

"Are you going to *die?*" Giancarlo here, always cutting to the chase.

"Eventually, but not until you both learn to clean up your room or get married, whichever comes first. Who's in the kitchen?"

"Aemilia," said Zak. "She's making us fried chicken and french fries."

"Good. All the important food groups. Is she nice?"

A pair of shrugs. "Okay," said Giancarlo. "She mainly leaves us alone. Mom . . . ?"

"Yes?"

"Are we ever going to get back to regular again?"

"Regular like how?"

"Oh, you know . . . all of us together, and Lucy and all of us having dinner and fun and talking."

"I sure hope so," said Marlene. "But, look, I'm the problem here, not you or Dad. I'll be straight with you guys, okay? I made a mistake, and it got some people killed and hurt, and other stuff happened that kind of knocked me off my feet. I'm not good for you all to be around right now. Lucy is staying with Uncle Tran in the country for a while, and I'm going to take off for a little while, too."

"You're getting *divorced,* aren't you?" Giancarlo's eyes started with tears. His brother was impassive. The emotional life of the twins was not really his concern. Zik handled that end of things.

"I am not. I just need a time-out, just like you need a time-out once in a while."

"You could take it in your room."

"No, grown-ups can't take a time-out in their rooms. They have to go away for a while. But, look." Here she grasped a hand from each in her two hands. "I swear to you I will fix myself up and then we will all be regular together."

And she jollied them and got them smiling, which she could always do (skilled phony that she was), and got them into the kitchen for their meal, then threw some things into a suitcase and stuffed into a duffel bag clothes that never imagined that they would ever be so stuffed, then dashed down the hallway to her office and grabbed up a pile of mail and tossed it into her bag. She found the lead and clipped it to the dog's collar. Someone to talk to. A quick good-bye, a flurry of kisses, and she was out.

The driver goggled when the dog jumped in and curled up on the seat. He was about to say something when Marlene got in, slammed the door, and thrust two $100 bills at him.

"It's just a dog," she said.

Like a playing card snapping over, his thoughts changed from worrying whether the dog would rip the damned upholstery and get him into trouble with the limo service, to contemplating what he would buy with the money.

That accomplished, Marlene dabbed at her damp eyes with a tissue, then poured and drank off a glass of crackling dry Chablis and heard as if for the first time the voice that said, oh, hell, you've had two, you might as well finish the bottle. No, not quite yet. Osman wanted to know their destination.

"I don't know. Some hotel. The Plaza. Go up Broadway." He nodded and pulled away, out to Canal, then north on Broadway.

Just a couple of nights, get myself together. Taper off a little. These were her thoughts, and to keep her mind occupied with trivia, she started to open her mail.

There must be, she thought, a jungle telegraph that tells everyone when you get a hold of a chunk of money. She had never received mail like this before. Business envelopes from people skilled in managing money, or stealing it. Prospectuses from firms needing capitalization, in larger, thicker ones. Large, creamy envelopes, almost as rich as leather, with invitations to gather at cultural events and give money to worthy causes. This appealed to her. A worthy cause. Here was one. The New

York Foundation for the Arts. What more worthy, and it was tonight. At the Regency. She might be worthless herself, but she could still do some good. Besides, it would be an opportunity to wear some of those clothes, and there would be champagne. Here she could test her resolve. A couple of glasses, three at most, write a check, show the flag, and away. Like a regular person.

14

TRAFFIC STOPPED KARP AT A CORNER. FOR THE FIRST TIME SINCE HE HAD FLED the clinic, he looked around to see where he was. A glance at a street sign located him in Murray Hill. He knew this corner—that deli, that chicken place, that saloon, the red awning in front of the Italian restaurant. He crossed the street, went through a glass door into a tiny entranceway, found and pressed a little button.

"Yeah?" said a gravelly voice out of the rosette of holes in dull brass.

"Guma, it's Butch."

A pause. "Butch *Karp?*"

"No, Butch Stellarezze, the numbers guy. Let me in, huh?"

The buzzer sounded. Karp went through and took the creaky elevator to six. The hallway he entered was dark and peeling, lit by a single forty-watt bulb. Water stains splotched the ceiling. This was a rent-controlled building, and the landlord was not generous. Raymond Guma was waiting in his open doorway. Karp had been prepared for some changes—he had not seen Guma (and he felt the shame of it now) in over six months—but he was startled by the man's appearance. Guma had always been a stocky, fleshy man, a combination of Yogi Berra and something out of an illustration in Rabelais or Boccaccio. Now his flesh hung slackly on his frame, his once-generous belly shrunken almost to nothing. He was wearing a velour bathrobe in dark green, gray sweatpants, and a white T-shirt, none of them too clean.

"Been a while, Butch," said Guma, shaking Karp's hand. "Come on

in. Don't mind the mess. The girl's coming in tomorrow." He stood aside
to let Karp enter.

Smells of cigars and Scotch over the base pong of old apartment,
unwashed clothes, of which a pile sat on a straight chair, a stink unpleasantly familiar, reminding Karp of forced childhood visits to aged relatives. When did Guma get old? He had retired barely a year ago, after
forty-odd years prosecuting for the DA both here and in Brooklyn, and
at the retirement party, a blast of historic dimensions, he had still been
the Mad Dog of Centre Street, the Goom, grabbing women, sucking
down his Teacher's, singing in Italian, telling the old nasty jokes. Playing
the clown. A pose. He was not, in fact, a clown. Among other things, he
knew more about the New York Mob than anyone else on either side of
the law and had taught Karp rather more than Karp wanted to learn
about manipulating the legal system.

Guma led Karp into the living room, pointed to an armchair, closed
the door to the kitchen (not before Karp had seen its piles of soiled
dishes, the brown bags overflowing with garbage, the stacks of pizza
boxes), and sat down on a dingy sofa with a little sigh. It was dim in the
room; the avenue just visible through three big windows dressed with
venetian blinds, all at different heights, one crooked. The sofa faced a
large TV set, switched on with the volume a low grumble, the screen
showing thousands of white birds in some rookery. Karp recalled that
Guma was a nature-documentary fan, a surprising taste in one so thor-
oughly urban.

"Want a drink?" Guma asked. "You look like you need one."

"I'm fine. You go ahead yourself."

"Sure? Okay, I think I will." A fifth was on the coffee table among the
stacks of black videotape boxes, and Guma splashed a little of it into a
squat tumbler, raised it, said, "Absent friends," and took a sip.

"You lost a little weight there, Goom. You feeling okay?"

"You mean besides the cancer? I'm doing great. Never better."

"I'm sorry. I didn't know."

"Yeah, well, the networks didn't pick it up for some reason." Guma
shrugged, grinned, showing large, uneven teeth. "Hey, what the fuck—I'll
go out with all my marbles intact." He held the glass up, swirled its contents. "Actually, they chopped a couple parts out, they say I'm in remission.
I'm supposed to revamp my lifestyle, but I can't see the percentage in it,

you know? If it comes back, it comes back." He plucked three-quarters of a Macanudo Lonsdale from a brown-glass ashtray and relit it.

"It's funny," he said, leaning back in a cloud of pungent smoke, "months go by, I don't hear from my old pals at the office, and then in the same week I get a visit from Roland and now from you. I figure Jack'll be by tomorrow." He looked around the room appraisingly. "Maybe I should redecorate, my social life is starting to look up so much."

"Roland came by?"

"Yeah, right after you guys canned his ass. He was drunk and looking for someone to get drunker with. Which we did. We watched my Serengeti tape. I figure he wanted to see rending flesh. He's really pissed at Jack. You, too, matter of fact."

"Why me? Christ, I was on him for years to keep a goddamn cork in it. And I practically begged Keegan to let it slide."

"Yeah, well, he wasn't being that rational. He thinks he was set up."

"I know."

"Was he?"

"Probably. Why, I don't now. Not that he had any shortage of enemies."

"No. Still it's a shame. What about you? I hear you're running homicide again."

"Not exactly. He wants me to clean up the political cases, make sure nothing interferes with his coronation. If anything goes wrong, he's got someone to toss out the door after Roland."

Guma squinted at Karp through the smoke. "That don't sound like the old Butch. You were never a cleanup type of guy. You were more of a look-under-the-rug kind of guy, see what other people stuck in there. How's Marlene?"

Karp shot him a sharp look. "As usual. Why do you ask?"

Shrug. Puff. Sip. "Oh, you know. Even here in the leper colony people drift by. Such as yourself. Roland. A couple others. You know, share views, listen to the drums of the distant villages."

"Oh, yeah? And what do the drums say?"

"They say Marlene made a bundle off her firm's IPO. They say she started buying out the stores, riding around in a limo. They say she started hitting the bottle pretty good, and she fucked up and got some people killed."

"You believe that?"

"I don't know. No offense, but you know and I know your bride was never that tightly wrapped to begin with. Be honest? I never figured her for a lush, but still you got to admit she pulled a lot of weird shit back in the day."

Karp wanted to go. This had been a stupid idea, coming here. He hadn't seen the guy in a while, he was in the neighborhood, he dropped by. Guma had never been what you could call a confidant of his, not like V.T., but there were things you couldn't even say to a confidant, stuff you needed a wife to talk about, but his wife was out of action just now, occupied by a hostile power. So now he had to either get up and leave, like an asshole, or start talking about Marlene, which he definitely did not want to do, not to Guma—but he could change the subject. And, of course, Guma knew the DA, knew not only where the bodies were buried, but who had stashed them there and why, and now Karp started in on it, the whole miserable thing.

"*You* leaked that story on Cooley? *You?*" was the response when Karp got to that part.

"Yeah, I did. It was that or quit and go public with it, which for some reason I wasn't willing to do. I couldn't in good conscience ask Clay to help any more than he had already. Keegan was in the tank. I wasn't going to get any resources for doing an investigation. I was pissed, Goom. I figured if I lit a fire, make it impossible for them to bury it, Roland would get behind it—"

"Roland?"

"Yeah, I know he's a cop groupie, but there's a line. He'll blink at a little perjury, and little taint in the evidence, but he's hell on bent cops. It's a point of pride with him. Was. He was no way going to stay quiet for what's starting to look a lot like an assassination and a cover-up. Not by the cops so much, but by us. They presented us with a load of stinking fish, and we said, 'What smell? We don't smell anything.' The fucking election."

"You should've got Roland in on it from the beginning."

"Yeah, I know, I know! But I had no idea he was going to get sandbagged at that press conference or ruin himself after. It was the background I didn't count on, the racial thing. Benson, boom! Marshak, boom! Lomax, *ka-boom!*"

"You have a political-wile deficit, pal, is what it is. It's a murky pool."

"I know it. I still can't believe I took that route." Karp paused, remembering, reconstructing the origins of the debacle. "You know what it was? It was Shelly Solotoff. I had lunch with him just before, and he gave me this load of horseshit about the DA, how corrupt it was, Garrahy was a fraud, I was wasting my time—you know, the usual crap you get from people like that. God knows why they feel it necessary to shit on the system. But, anyway, he went on and on, and I just decided right after that I was going to do something crazy, just to kick-start the damn thing, bring Jack to his senses—"

"Oh, Shelly Solotoff," Guma interrupted. "He's a piece of work. You knew I got him canned?"

"You did? I thought he quit to go private."

"We let him resign, let's say. This was way back there. Garrahy's last year; Jack was heading homicide. You were doing that crazy liquor-store holdup artist, and Shelly was working the Victoria Falla case. It was his first major, and Jack had me looking over his shoulder. You remember that one?"

"Little girl, found naked, raped and murdered up in Inwood, yeah. They liked a guy for it, a bum, and then . . . didn't it turn out he was the wrong guy?"

"Right. The bum's name was Manuel Echiverra, a local drunk. Had a sheet on him for dickie-waving, annoying little schoolgirls. Anyway, you know the cops always grab up characters like that in a child sex case, and they looked at him pretty good because he was on the block a lot where the vic lived. He stayed in a box under the highway. Slept on a bag of rags, and when the cops tossed it, some of the rags turned out to be little Victoria's clothes."

"Uh-huh. It's coming back now. You got the indictment."

"Of course, but some stuff didn't fit. Not a hint of violence in the record. The guy could barely walk around. He was crippled up some way, I forget how, and he had the syph, too: the guy's brain was cheese. On the other hand, after claiming he found the clothes in a Dumpster, he made a full and free confession after a couple of days in custody, ho-ho. Okay, the bottom line was that the cops also looked at the vic's step-dad hard, too, but since they had Manuel—you know how it is. They filed and forgot. It ain't like in the movies, as you well know. Shelly was all set to nail Manuel, but wonder of wonders, there was a serious player on D, Jerry Felkes; you know Jerry? . . . Right, he's a judge now. A terrific lawyer, and Shelly was getting spooked a little. So it comes time to hand over the *Rosario* material, he doesn't hand over the incriminatory stuff on the stepdad. I mean, why cloud the issue with another guy who also attracted the attention of the cops? Reasonable doubt, shit, we don't want any of *that*."

Guma finished his drink, reached for the bottle, hesitated, put it down, thus demonstrating that he could still leave it alone. "Armand Figuroa, the stepdad. A real prince. He was fucking the other daughter, too, as it turned out. Seven years old. By the way, Shelly didn't vouchsafe us any of this stepfather business when he presented the case to the bureau. Just the Manuel stuff, and it looked solid."

"When did you find out?"

"Felkes called Jack. He actually hired a PI out of his own pocket, and the guy came up with the missing police records. Jack and me talked about getting Shelly disbarred, but we decided not to. A high-profile case, the scandal . . . Jack reamed him out and gave him the boot. He hated you, by the way, Shelly. I mean back then. Maybe he still does."

"What? Why the hell did he hate me? I never did anything to him. He invited me to *lunch*, for crying out loud."

"And was he a pleasant companion?"

Karp did not need to think. "No, it was pretty clear the whole thing was set up to make me feel like an asshole and a loser. I didn't cop to it then because . . . Christ, who the fuck knows? I guess I couldn't really imagine why anybody would go through that much trouble."

"Shelly is strange. He used to ask me about you, obsess practically. You were the fair-haired boy, you were winning all those cases, looking good. How did you do it? You must've been cutting corners." Guma took a last puff on the Macanudo and placed it neatly in the ashtray. He splashed another quarter inch of whiskey into his glass. "Some guys never get it, the line. The biggest case he was ever on, and he cut some corners to win it because he assumed you and me and everyone else was doing it, too. Especially you. And now? Let's face it, the guy's a high-priced pimp living on a rich wife, draping himself in a lot of liberal causes, bitching about the corruption of the district attorney's office . . ."

"That he got canned from. The scales fall from my eyes. Guma, I'm a college graduate, I'm not a dope. Why didn't I see that about him? Back then or recently?"

Shrug, smile, hands out, palms up. "What can I say? You got a blind spot. You're a fucking superstar in a very hard business, and you got no idea that people could look at you and be jealous, and hate you, and smile at you while they hate you."

"He's Sybil Marshak's attorney."

"I know. And he's going to walk her and spit right in your face. I'd give odds that's why he took the case in the first place."

"But he wouldn't have faced *me*. I had nothing to do with homicide until *after* Roland pulled his boner in the elevator."

Guma grinned, extended an index finger, and slowly tugged down on his lower left eyelid.

"Oh, *please*," cried Karp. "You're not suggesting he set that up to get Roland out of the way so he'd have a shot at me! How could he? How'd he know that Roland would shoot his mouth off?"

"Hey, he worked in the bureau. He knew Roland had a tendency to unload all kinds of unpopular shit when he thought no one from the outside was listening. The press conference was common knowledge. He took a chance, and he lucked out. And who else is Jack going to turn to, a case like this Marshak thing? Butch, the Fireman, Karp is who. Matter of fact, it's a wonder Roland's lasted so long. If that hadn't've worked, Shelly would've tried something else. An underage girl would've been my personal choice, I wanted to shaft Roland Hrcany. You find that guy in the elevator, a hundred bucks says he's linked up some way with old Shel."

"I can't believe it."

"Then don't. Meanwhile, he's going to cream you in Marshak. If it ever comes to it."

"Unless I find out about the watch."

"Come again?"

Karp explained all about the watch. Guma's face seemed to take on more life as Karp talked, his body becoming more erect, fuller, as if someone were inflating it with a pump.

"What do you think?" Karp asked when he was finished. "Am I crazy or what?"

"No, you're not crazy. Jesus, Augie Al Firmo! He's connected up to his ears, you know. With the Gambinos."

"I didn't know. We ever catch him?"

"Never, and he's been in business now for a long time. Shit, he might even be older than me. I don't know how many times they've tried to sting him, but he always slips away, or someone else takes the fall for him. I remember back in '84, Ray Cooley tried to take him down. They had a sting set up over two years. A bunch of detectives were running one of the biggest fake burglary rings on the East Coast. I mean they were pretend ripping off shipping containers and pretend fencing stuff all over the place. They were paying off the Mob. Half a dozen of them liked it so much they were doing it for real. You remember that . . . the Mollen people were real cranky behind it."

"Yeah, now I do. That was Ray Cooley?"

"Yeah. He really wanted Augie Al, but no soap. They picked up a bunch of his associates and a couple of the *cugini,* but they couldn't make anything stick to the man. Nobody ratted him out either, which is unusual. But Augie Al's always been a big carrot-and-stick guy. Nowadays he's semiretired, only handles high-end ice, watches, opticals, like that. Guns, too. Fancy stuff they truck in from those Second Amendment–type states." Guma stopped, scratched his head. "You know, now that I'm thinking about it, there was a thing back then where he was using street people to move stuff around. Smart, really."

"Why smart?"

"Hiding the shit in plain sight. You got a guy in an army jacket with fifty fake Rolexes, who's gonna think three of them are real? There's five cutouts between Firmo and the skell."

"And he doesn't get ripped off?"

"Hey, probably all the time, same like the dope guys. It happens once, the skell gets toasted, and move on. A cost of doing business. He buys wholesale, he sells retail. What can I say, it's a living. So to bring it back, probably the guy Marshak shot was a mule for Firmo. I don't see what that buys you on your case against her."

"I don't either. It was just a loose end." But Karp's mind was vibrating with notions. The watch. Ramsey shot. Firmo. The Cooleys, father and son. The father failing to catch Firmo. The son chasing a skell named Canman. Bent cops. Skells muling hot items. An unusual number of skells found with their throats cut. *Toasted.* Canman a suspect. Cooley chasing Canman. Cooley killing Lomax, whom he knew. How?

Lomax, a sheet for fencing, theft. Connection between Lomax and Firmo? Don't know. Cooley on a gun-running stakeout the night of the Lomax shooting. Connection? Don't know. Firmo linked up with Cooley? Don't know. Cooley linked to the bum slashings? Don't know. How to find out?

"Ah, shit!" Karp snarled.

"What?"

Karp shook his head. "Nothing. Just that I need an investigative apparatus to figure out something, and the one supplied by the taxpayers for just such purposes seems to be out of order." He explained the tantalizing connections.

"Do like Felkes—hire a PI," said Guma.

"Be serious."

"Hey, why not? Your wife's rich. Come to think of it, your wife's a PI. Hell, you want to, I'll ask around. I take it you think Cooley's dirty."

"Filthy. Got to be. Why else would he take a chance like that, a big public shooting, to get Lomax? What, you don't think so?"

Guma waggled a hand, palm down. "Hey, anything's possible. The pope could be hocking the Vatican silver. But Cooley being dirty I would tend to doubt."

"Why, because he's a hero?"

"No. But I knew Ray. I knew all of them, matter of fact. Did you know they were from south Brooklyn?"

"No. But you know everybody."

"I don't know Donald Trump. I don't know Jennifer Lopez . . ."

Karp ignored this. "How well do you?"

"Ray Cooley was a year ahead of me in Cardinal Hughes. We were on the same teams. He was a pitcher. The 'Two Rays of Sunshine,' as the *Brooklyn Eagle* had it. Neither of us had the stuff for the bigs, but we fucking burnt up the parochial-school league. I hit .387, he had like fifty strikeouts his senior year."

"And that's why Brendan Cooley isn't dirty?"

"The Cooleys," said Guma portentously, waving an admonitory finger, "are not as you and I. If you're interested, I could probably find out whether anyone on the cops got a bad smell off the kid. And I could talk to Connie Sassone."

"Who is . . . ?"

"Brendan's ex. She's a niece of *my* ex's. My first ex. Nice kid. I was there when they got married."

"Would you?"

"Sure, why not? Dying don't take that much of my time."

Karp let that pass. To fill the silence he asked, "Remind me what happened in the Falla case. I recall you got a conviction."

"Yeah, I did. Felkes did great, brought the bastard stepfather up there, but he couldn't break him, hammered the cops, but they did their usual 'Hey, it's routine, we talk to the relatives in a child case,' blah blah. Felkes got the confession tossed, but it didn't do him a lot of good. The thing was Manuel didn't help himself, the way he looked. Fucking hulk, fat, greasy hair, pockmarked, falling asleep at the trial. Guy looked like Frankenstein in a suit. One time he was actually drooling. Every mother's nightmare, right? They were only out forty minutes and convicted on the top counts, rape and murder two. Felkes didn't give up though. He was running out his appeals when science marches on, they invent DNA, and it turns out Manuel doesn't match the semen they found in the kid. He did eleven years anyway, they turned him loose, and he dropped dead within a week. We got the stepfather though. I did him, too, as a matter of fact. Twenty-five to life. It was when you were out private." Guma laughed, raised his glass. "The fucking system, right? Gotta love it."

Drag enough folding money through the lobby of a pricey hotel, Marlene found, and you can get your two-hundred-pound drooling mastiff into your suite. She ensconced herself, hung up her clothes, had the concierge take her crystal jacket and other drunked-over garments out for cleaning and repair, made an appointment at Danilo's for hair and at Lamy's for a complete overhaul, killed time until the appointments by playing with the dog and watching cable, and did not drink even one of the charming little bottles in the minibar. At three she kissed the dog good-bye and walked over to Lamy's on Madison and Sixty-third, where she got boiled, seared, stripped of exfoliations, mud-packed, massaged, oiled, plucked, waxed, and manicured. She felt pretty good until her hostess told her she shouldn't wait too long before beginning plastic surgery. Mildly depressed by this news, she went over by limo to Fifty-seventh, where Danilo gave her a $300 haircut so skillful that after it her hair looked just as it had when she went in. Then she shopped some, an evening bag and some perfume, and a few things for the office, to assure herself that she was going back to the office, someday, and then back to the hotel.

At around six-thirty she called home.

"It's me," she said when Karp answered.

"Where are you?"

"At the Plaza."

"Uh-huh. What're you doing?"

"Having a vacation from my life."

"Drinking much?"

"I might. Are you going to send a spy to find out if I do?" she asked, and immediately regretted it.

After a silence, Karp said coolly, "Well, do what you need to do, Marlene. You'll keep in touch, yes?"

"You're pissed off at me."

"Yeah, I guess I am. I kind of thought we were a family. One of us has a problem, we're supposed to duke it out, not run away."

"You'd be happy if I was in a twenty-eight-day program with Dr. Eichmann though, wouldn't you?"

"Einkorn. Frankly? Yeah, I would. But you're not going to do that, so why should I even mention it?" A long pause. "So . . . what are you doing?"

"Right now? I'm getting ready to go to a rich people's party over at the Regency."

"A party, huh? Wear some of those clothes you bought."

"I guess. Look, Butch, this is not a permanent thing. I mean I *love* you. I just need to be away for a while. When I have to be around, you know, people I care about, I just want to die, I'm so ashamed. I know *you're* not like that, but I am. I can't bear the idea that I'm draining energy from everyone making everyone miserable. I want to crawl into a hole until I'm better."

And more of this. Marlene was not entirely sure if it was true, the words were just coming out without much reflection. It *was* unbearable to see him and the kids, but it was also unbearable to be alone. She did not say that, however, and the conversation rattled to a close, as such conversations will, on square wheels.

Once off the phone, Marlene went to the minibar and drank down two Baileys, to line her stomach, and then, remembering Dottie, ate a banana from the fruit basket the hotel had provided. The valet service knocked, and there were her things, the crystal jacket shorn of a few inches but otherwise perfect. Then she dressed in her white Valentino outfit, strapped white Manolo spikes on her feet, spritzed herself with Chanel, snatched up her new bag, a confection of silver and bronze links over black silk, threw the jacket over her shoulders, and after a quick doggy kiss, left the room.

The do for the New York Foundation for the Arts was familiar ground for Marlene. People who provide security for the rich log a lot of hours at such affairs, and she had been to many, but as security rather than as a guest. There was a discreet table where one gave in one's invitation and passed over one's hefty check; Marlene stopped there, gave and passed, got a smile from a couple of old face-lifts, and moved on. She spotted a number of familiar people as she entered the ballroom, for it was the usual gang: old money, media moguls, a scattering of bored-looking art makers, New York movers and shakers, a sprinkle of Eurotrash, a few pretty-boy crashers who owned dinner suits and little else, half a dozen people who had achieved the nirvana of first-name identifiability, with their retinues, and a small group of nouveaux being allowed to buy entry into the good side of the red velvet rope. Of whom Marlene imagined she was now one.

She snagged a glass of champagne from a passing waiter, drank it down, and cast her eye across the crowd. Who cast back, for Marlene in full rig was a spectacular sight. Everyone was wearing crystals that season, but Marlene, being a parvenue from Queens, had more crystals than anyone else. Everyone in the place was to some degree well-known, but Marlene was notorious—not exactly the same thing. People came up to her, anorexic women with rigid golden hair helmets and couture gowns, men of moderate size spraying ego from their tanned or pig-pink faces, blank-eyed supermodels on the arms of debauched stockbrokers, they were all dying to meet her, a heroine, someone who had actually killed people. How did it feel? Were you scared? Are you carrying a gun now? To which she answered: It made me vomit. Yes. No. And every time the waiter came by, a glass of Krug. That made three, her limit this evening.

She wandered over to a table of little yummies, but was repelled by the creamed crustaceans, the tapenades, the caviar, and salmon mousse. But there was a large cornucopia made of pastry, from which spilled a mass of real fruit, and she selected a banana to go with her fifth champagne.

She felt a presence close at her side and turned. A young man, red-haired, thin, good-looking in the way she happened to like, with clever blue eyes.

"That's quite a jacket," he remarked.

"Yes, it is. I feel like I should be stationed in front of an auto dealership on Linden Boulevard, slowly rotating."

He laughed. "You won't get far with this crowd if you make fun of expensive clothes. Eating a banana is also not the done thing, although I love the way you do it."

She chomped another section of the fruit, chewed, said, "Is that right? You're an expert?"

"No, just another working stiff like you, but with less money. A private dick, too." He held out his hand. "Peter Walsh."

She took it, squeezed, warm and dry, good, and he didn't try to hang on to it, which she always hated. "Marlene Ciampi. But you know that."

"I did. In fact, I spotted you when you came in, and I've been working up my courage to come over and slip in and talk to you. In between the beautiful people in my rented tux."

"Really. About what?"

"Oh, a job, I guess. I'd like to protect the famous and get stock options."

Marlene looked him up and down while she drained her glass. Miraculously, a tray and waiter appeared, and she replaced the empty with a full. "You don't look like a private dick, Walsh. You're too pretty."

"You're pretty."

"Yes, but I'm hard as nails. Are you hard as nails?"

"Hard enough, in the right circumstances." He had moved closer. She wanted to sag against him, sag against something, but she held back. A good thing she had kept the champagne down to four hits.

"You're not an ex-cop, though, are you?"

"No. I'm an actor. But I played a cop once."

"Anything I would've seen?"

"Not unless you're a connoisseur of New Jersey community theater. If you watch TV real late, you can sometimes catch me demonstrating the amazing multiwrench."

"An unusual background for a PI. Most of them are ex-cops, ex-military. Sometimes ex-DA, like me. Where did you learn how to investigate?"

"Oh, off a matchbook. Good jobs at high pay. No, what they hire me for is hanging out, blending in with a crowd, seeing what you can pick up."

"Impersonation."

"Not necessarily. If you show up at a place in the right clothes, with the right look and speech, people assume you belong there. In a factory, they assume you're a worker. In a DA's office they assume you're a DA. At a function like this, they assume you're a rich art lover. People say things, do things, they wouldn't ordinarily do in front of an outsider."

"So you're working now?"

A shrug. "Not really. A client of mine passed me a ticket. Since I don't have any stock options, I appreciate the free eats. And, of course, you never can tell when you might pick up something." He waggled his eyebrows theatrically, and she laughed.

"Oh, Walsh, you are too smooth for me, too smooth by far. I need more traction nowadays. I don't like to skid out of control." She gave a tiny tug at his cummerbund, presented her gaudiest smile, finished her . . . what was it, fourth? . . . glass of champagne, and flounced away.

A dull gong sounded, and she found herself caught up in the flow of people. The dinner. Did she want dinner? Not really, but it was too much trouble to fight the flow. Besides, she had to sit down—the marvelous jacket felt like a full combat load on her shoulders. She felt her elbow gripped. It was a large man, beautifully barbered, tanned, with deep, dark eyes. "You're at table four," he said.

"Am I? How do you know?"

"I know because I arranged it." A little squeeze on her upper arm. "I'm Shelly Solotoff. I'm an old pal of Butch's. He's not here tonight?"

Somehow Marlene suspected Solotoff already knew that. "No, he's home with the babies. Besides, he has no interest in being nouveau riche."

"But you do?"

She yawned. "Excuse me. Three champagnes and I'm off my feet.

Do I? I don't know. It serves to pass the time and show off one's taste in clothes."

They arrived at the table. He held her chair; she sank gratefully and slipped out of the jacket.

"I used to work with your husband, back in the stone age, when the sainted Phil Garrahy was still in charge."

"That must have been before I got there. Do you do this kind of service for all the wives of men you worked with twenty years ago?"

He chuckled. "That would depend on how many wives they had. But only when they're beautiful, exciting, and dangerous."

"And rich?"

"That comes under excitement. The poor are so dull, don't you think? Noble maybe, but dull."

Marlene fanned her face. "Gosh, Shelly, all this charm. I'm quite overcome. Now tell me about the time shares in St. Bart's you're selling. Or mutual funds."

He grinned. "Nope, no deals at this table. This is the laid-back table, right, Jimmy?"

This was a cell phone magnate, who seemed disappointed when Marlene did not immediately recognize his name. He obviously knew Solotoff. They exchanged some good-natured ribbing as between men who have little to say to one another. Also at the table: one of the one-name people, whom Marlene thought looked older than she appeared on TV, with her boy toy, sculptured from bronze and clearly coked up; and two rubicund middle-aged men with silvery toupees and women young enough to be daughters. Laid-back, indeed. The star cooed when Marlene was introduced to her and wanted to know about shooting people and pouted when Marlene declined to expatiate on the delights thereof.

Silent waiters brought the heavily worked and barely identifiable food of the rich: cuttlefish cannelloni with morel-asparagus puree; lobster bisque with carmelized truffles; terrine of baby lamb, roasted foie gras, Scottish salmon, ambergris, cocaine, uranium . . . Solotoff gorged and was excessively knowledgeable about the food and wine. Marlene picked at the food, longed for a banana, drank the succession of wines. Also gorging: the boy toy, the daughters, although Marlene felt sure they were scheduled for an after-dinner barf in the ladies'. Their men ate lightly and conversed about possessions and exotic and strenuous vacations. The cell magnate flirted with the one-named star. Solotoff had eyes for no one but Marlene, however, which Marlene thought was flattering, considering the lookers at the table. Something about the guy was off, however; there was more than the instinctive drive to try to seduce an available woman, although she had enough of a load on for that not to matter too much. She was having a little vacation was all, nothing wrong with that. Solotoff, though, seemed inordinately interested in her husband. Every other sentence seemed to be fishing around about Karp, and there were insinuating remarks, backhanded compliments. Even partly anesthetized by drink, Marlene did not like it and said so.

"Why're we talking about Butch? Butch is fine. Butch is home with the babies."

"What I said, he's a great man. Watches babies. Bestrides the legal system like a colossus. Beautiful wife, who he doesn't mind is running around town. Total confidence, Butch. I mean who could compete with the almighty Karp? It must be hard, though, married to perfection."

Marlene giggled. "He's far from perfect, believe me."

Solotoff leaned closer. She could feel his breath on her face and smell his winey exhalations. "Oh, yeah? Tell me some of his imperfections." Under the tablecloth, his hand fell upon her thigh.

"He's more perfect than me, that's the main one," she said, and then the waiter was there with a wine bottle, and Marlene found that her hand had moved without conscious will to cover the glass.

Solotoff's hand increased its stroking pressure. "Oh, go ahead. It's Chambertin. A very good year, too."

"No." She closed her eyes. Something bad was happening. There were hidden messages in the sounds of the banquet, the murmurs and the clink of implements. Her skin felt clammy, and the rich food roiled in her belly. There was someone she had to see, someone she had to talk to, a friend . . . who was it? Who had the answer? Or the question?

Someone was talking into her ear, things about Butch. About a different Butch, a cheat, a hypocrite, corrupt and manipulative, which made kind of sense because she was a different Marlene. What had happened to the real ones? She didn't know. A shudder ran through her. She shook her head, and the room reeled around her in slow motion, the chandeliers making long, slow circles. The one-named star had her head thrown back, cackling, showing the little face-lift scars under her ears. The waiters passed out peach bavarois with goat's-milk ice cream, swirled with semisweet chocolate. Hieroglyphics in the swirls. The message . . . horrible, *horrible.*

"I have to go now," she said, and rose to her feet and fell hard against Solotoff, who rose, too, and grabbed her around the waist. She felt the crystal jacket being dropped on her shoulders, and she floated through the room, leaning into the man. Butch? How did Butch get here? Butch didn't like these kind of things. Maybe the different Butch, the monster.

Now in a car, a limo, dark. Far away, someone was doing stuff to her body, fingers probing up her skirt, plucking at her underwear, squeezing her breasts, breath on her neck, a leech of some kind there sucking away. She let it go on; she had no strength, and besides, she was not even sure it was her, whoever she was now.

Brightness, a hotel lobby, an elevator, more grappling. Pausing before a door, the man was probing through her purse, finding the key card, the little light going green, into the room. Marlene saw the bed, its coverlet turned down, the green-wrapped chocolate on the pillow. Oh, good, once she was in bed, everything had to stop. She took three steps and flung herself on it, facedown.

Solotoff looked at the prone figure with satisfaction. Her skirt had flown up, exposing the full length of her thighs and one buttock, enclosed in patterned silk. He took off his jacket and tie, unhitched his cummerbund, and kicked off his pumps. He had drunk a good deal of wine, but knew that it was not enough to keep him from screwing Karp's wife. She was a little older than he liked for strange pussy, but she could have been a hundred and he would still have gone for it. He slipped his suspenders off his shoulders and dropped his trousers. Too bad he didn't have a camera, but who knew he would luck out this way? In his mind he anticipated his next meeting with Karp. I fucked your wife and now I'm going to fuck you in court. No, too crude. Had to be subtle, make it last, make it hurt more. Things had not worked out well for Solotoff in recent years. He had the practice, he had the rich wife, but something was missing. There was a nasty ache where contentment should have been. But this, somehow this was going to make up for a lot of it. This was going to be sweet. Maybe she'd even like it. Maybe she'd like it from him better than from Karp. His groin stirred. That would be a bonus.

He took a step toward the bed. Yank those panties down and fuck her like a dog. A set of heavy thumping steps sounded behind him, and then a sound, like some machinery starting up, a low growl. He spun around, his heart pounding, and tripped over his pants. From the floor the dog looked as large as a grizzly bear. It growled again and came a step closer, moving to put itself between Solotoff and the bed.

"Easy, boy, good boy." Solotoff looked wildly around for a leash or something. How did the goddamn thing get in here? He got slowly to his feet. Lock it in the bathroom, that was a plan. The thing looked stupid as shit. Holding his pants up with one hand, he made shooing motions. The dog didn't budge. He went to the bathroom, opened the door.

"C'mon, boy," he crooned, walking slowly around to get behind the monster. The dog held its ground, the great head swiveling to follow him. A little nudge with the toe to give the fucking animal the idea . . .

Thirty seconds later, Shelly Solotoff found himself in the hallway outside Marlene's room, shaking and sans shoes, sans jacket, sans tie, sans cummerbund, sans the seat and half of one leg of his trousers (these remains well-soaked with urine) and now divesting himself of an expensive meal and a good deal of slightly used Chambertin. Yet another thing to blame Karp for.

15

THE MORNING AFTER, ONE OF A SERIES: ACTUALLY, IT WAS EARLY AFTERNOON before Marlene awakened from a hideous dream of being smothered by jellyfish, to find her dog licking her face with a tongue the size of a washcloth. The usual raging thirst, pounding head, disorientation in time and space. The usual panicked thoughts: What did I do drunk *now?* Then a *really* awful thought, as the events of the evening just past surfaced like corpses rising from a shipwreck. No, I *couldn't* have, not even drunk, I absolutely refuse to believe that I took that jerk back here and . . . But now she registered that she was fully dressed, and that her luxurious underpants were intact, bone-dry and in place. What now, false memories? He *had* been here—there was his jacket on the chair. She rose slowly from the bed and looked around the room. Trained detective that she was, it took her hardly any time to cop to what had happened; the torn strips of tuxedo trousers stiff with dog drool told all. It made her feel better than she had in ages, and she hooted and hugged the dog and immediately called her good friend the concierge and ordered a large pepperoni pizza and a bottle of merlot.

So they brunched together, Marlene sucking abstemiously on the wine and slipping warm, greasy, spicy triangles down the animal's maw; *schlup, schlup,* they vanished like dollar bills into a change machine. Her career as a drunk seemed to be entering a new phase. The first shock was over; the deep, embarrassing scenes would not happen again, she told herself—that was like the shaky, wobbling start of a kid on a new two-wheeler. There would be rules now: a little pick-me-up in the morning to get her through lunch, when she would deserve a couple or three for being good, and then cold turkey for the P.M. while doing useful work, and then the evening when she would keep a comfortable level until it was time for oblivion, the nightcap, as they called it. Plenty of people, she knew, even famous and successful people, did it for years, and so would she. This way she could go back to work, face them all down, go back to her family, discharge her responsibilities, for as long as her liver held up. Not quite ready to go back home yet, though, wait a while for the routine to kick in, not quite ready to face Butch, *definitely* not ready for the daughter. But soon.

So she went to work, in her new outfit, a neat little black suit with a cream silk blouse sporting a demure black ribbon at the throat. So she was welcomed back: by Lou Osborne, who looked nervous now, having sold his baby. He had to worry about becoming a takeover target, about the stockholders, about the latest Nasdaq quotes (45¾, down a quarter for the week), about growth targets—message, pull your load, Marlene; by Harry Bellow, who looked at her with a sad eye, from his own dryness, and tried clumsily to talk to her about it, but she put him off with a barrage of funny one-liners; by her staff, who were happy to cover for her. Which she needed. She did not go out anymore, no poking around with the clients. She sat in her office and moved paper while the expensive watch counted off the hours until lunch, until quitting time. They wrote her speeches, which she gave to frightened women. They made sure she did not interview new clients in the afternoon. Good old staff. Oleg was out of town, she learned, which was a pity. Oleg was always willing to go out for a quick one. He did not have the new American attitude toward drink. Good old Oleg. But in the long afternoons she had plenty of time to think. Her thoughts were not particularly clear, but they were vivid and disturbing. The money, root of all evil. The money came from the stock. Why had the stock gone through the roof? The publicity about the Richard Perry rescue. How convenient for Osborne! Still, that was life— good luck, bad luck. What had Oleg said that day, before the kidnapping? Something about events make market. And hadn't Oleg been a little evasive that day, some meeting or other that she hadn't heard about. Of course, *evasive* was Oleg's middle name. She turned to her computer and brought up Osborne's intranet. Every call that came into the phone system was logged and digitally recorded in compressed form.

Everyone's call file was protected by a twelve-digit password known only to the user and to the system administrator and his staff. That's why she couldn't find out what Oleg had been up to on the phone in the weeks before the kidnapping. She typed out a message for Wayne Segovia, encrypted it, and sent it out. Wayne couldn't work in the field anymore, at least not for a long time, but he was a bright kid. They had put him in the computer department.

Then she called her husband. She spoke with Butch every day. He told her how the boys were doing, and she talked to them, too, sad little conversations with long pauses. When Karp asked her when she was coming home, she said, "Soon, a week." She said, "Pretend I'm in Chicago." She said, "I miss you," which was all true. And he said, "I miss you," too, but he did not mean the same thing by it.

For Lucy, the days started at five. Her tutor lived not, as Lucy had supposed, in a godfather-type mansion with an iron gate and extensive grounds, but in an ordinary, if large, brick, five-bedroom house in an old neighborhood in north Bridgeport. The neighbors were local bourgeoisie, people who owned insurance agencies and car dealerships, and Tran seemed to fit in well. His lawn was immaculately mown and tended, and the shrubbery was minimal, low, and perfectly shaped, affording, as Lucy was not slow to notice, excellent fields of fire in all directions. Four people lived in the house besides Tran. Dong drove the Mercedes, Vo kept up the house and grounds, Dinh seemed to be some kind of accountant or business manager, and Mrs. Diem was the cook and housekeeper. All three of the men had the quiet, hooded look of soldiers, and Lucy knew that they were not just domestic workers.

When Mrs. Diem knocked at her door at dawn, Lucy arose with alacrity because if she did not, Tran would arrive and deliver a blistering lecture, with quotations from *The Analects, The Tale of Kieu,* and Chuang Tzu, about the vital importance of duty. She would wash herself and dress in pajamas and go down to breakfast, which was tea and congee or noodles and fish. Then she and Tran would go out into the back garden and do tai chi. Lifting Water. Flying Diagonally. White Crane Flaps Wings. All the twenty-four patterns of the simple set, for an hour, rain or shine. Lucy had done some of this in Chinatown, but never as seriously as she did now; she had not known Tran was an adept. His strong, scarred hands moved her body through the evolutions. The *chi* started to flow again in its secret channels; it settled in its proper home below the navel. She breathed more easily; the impacted garbage began to drain from her head.

After that, study all morning with Tran, math and science. He was a good teacher. Use your strengths, he said, math is a language, science is a language. She saw that it was true. The quadratic equations, the sines and cosines, the chemical formulas started for the first time to make sense, like Chinese. The boiling of foreign tongues in her head slowed to a mild bubbling. She spoke French to Tran, Vietnamese to the others. In the afternoons she would be driven to the University of Bridgeport to do research for the papers she owed. Then back home, where after dinner she would work on papers and do the assignments Tran had given her. After a few days of this she called Dr. Shadkin at the lab, another duty. He was appalled.

"Lucy, for God's sake," he cried, "you're sweating high school? High school? Okay, let me fix this—by the authority vested in me by the trustees of Columbia University, I hereby grant you a Ph.D. Now, come back here."

She laughed, she said she would be back when she got this worked out. Her parents wanted it, she had let them down, she had to do it.

"What is this, some kind of Confucian thing?"

"Yes, something like that," she said.

"I'll send you stuff."

He did, tapes and books on Lithuanian. At night, after she had finished her schoolwork, she dived into that language with relief, as a runner finishing a distance race walks easily for a while to cool off. Lithuanian was important to the Indo-European project, being the closest living language (they thought) to the mysterious root language from which nearly all the tongues of Europe had sprung. Pitch accents; richly case-inflected nouns; three rather than the usual two number designations. Fascinating!

Thus, she succeeded in occupying her mind entirely with work, leaving barely a fragment for thinking about her family, or about David Grale. Only momentarily, just as she drifted into sleep, did the shadow come back again, the one around David Grale, the secret and never-examined fear. She had a dream once about the tunnels: She was running through darkness, lit intermittently by sparks, full of the roar and screech of the trains. A figure leaped out at her, the electric discharges shining on the long knife in his hands, on his mad saint's face.

Weeks passed in this way for the divided family, and Karp waited, something he was good at. Like all first-class athletes, he understood that sometimes, for mysterious reasons, you suddenly couldn't sink the shot, hit the ball, find the inside corner of the plate. Some people railed and went a little crazy when this happened and sought doctors and witch doctors and changed how they did what they did, and beat up on their loved ones, but not Karp. It was Karp's instinct to stay the same, to be the unmoving center around which the bad luck or juju or *mishegoss* fluttered or screeched, in confidence that if he did that, it would all come back to the way it had been before. Or not. He could live with that, too. Meanwhile, he was not idle. He had a number of lines in the water, and from time to time he would give them a twitch or two.

One morning he summoned his favorite twitchee. "Murrow," he asked, "what are you doing with yourself these days?"

"Oh, mainly *coram nobis* petitions. Things seem kind of dead on Marshak."

"They do seem that way. Handling petitions is good training, though."

"Yeah, but what I don't understand is how come we convicted all these guys who didn't do it. Something's not right."

"Or else some of the convicted prisoners who're petitioning are not telling the truth. They're just trying to get out of prison."

"Really? Gosh, I never thought of that. My boyish heart is shattered. What's going on with the big cases?"

"Oh, not much. Jack's going to run out of time before he has to decide on the death penalty on Benson, which means he'll have to decide sometime next week."

"He's going to go for it?"

"Assuredly."

"And you're going to prosecute it?"

"Mine not to reason why. I've given him enough stuff that he can pretend to discover after he wins the June primary so that he really doesn't have to make a jackass of the office by trying to actually hang

Benson. Of course, if McBright wins, he's probably going to go ahead with it anyway, just to show he's an equal-opportunity oppressor of the innocent."

"I've been following his campaign with interest. I notice he doesn't include Benson in the justice-is-color-blind speech anymore. He heats up Marshak and Lomax, though, in compensation. As to Marshak, do you know a Detective Paradisio?"

"The bum-slasher task-force guy?"

"That guy. I'd like you to go down and see him, and tell him . . . get out your little book, Murrow, this is a little complicated."

Later that day Karp could, therefore, in good conscience explain to a judge that he should not summarily dismiss the case against Sybil Marshak, as her counsel had moved, because the crime in question appeared to be part of a larger criminal conspiracy subject to a continuing investigation, which was expected to throw a clearer light on the claims of self-defense. Shelly Solotoff was livid. Surely, this was something for a grand jury to decide. Why had the DA's office declined to bring this case before its grand jury? Ms. Marshak was a public figure; it was inconceivable that she would be involved in anything criminal. She was enduring enormous pain and suffering by having this felony charge hanging over her head. Dark conspiracies were hinted; the phrase star-chamber was used more than once. Judge Frederick North Davis, a portly and phlegmatic gentleman the color of wet coffee grounds, was not overly impressed by these arguments. He pointed out that Ms. Marshak had, in fact, killed a young man with a firearm, and that her pain and suffering might well be assuaged by the fact that she was still living on Central Park West rather than Rikers Island, where almost all of the many other people who had killed young black persons with firearms were presently languishing. In the interests of evenhandedness, the judge also looked sharply at the people's rep and asked when this investigation might be expected to conclude.

Karp reached deep into the back of his trousers and pulled out a date. "No more than two weeks, Your Honor."

Solotoff followed Karp out of the courtroom and accosted him in the hallway.

"Up to your old tricks, huh, Butch?"

"What old tricks are those, Shelly?"

"Spreading confusion, looking for an angle. You know as well as I do that there's no ongoing investigation here. You just can't stand the thought that a grand jury might refuse to indict in a clear case of self-defense. This one is a lot more blatant than Bernie Goetz. The guy came at her with a knife. End of story."

"Did he? We'll see."

Solotoff laughed pityingly. "I hate a sore loser. Actually, I hope you do indict. I'm looking forward to creaming you in court."

"Me, too," said Karp amiably.

"Also, telling fibs to a judge . . ." Solotoff waggled an admonitory finger. "You could get into trouble, assuming I wanted to press the issue."

"It's not a fib. There is an investigation."

"Oh, horseshit! There is absolutely nothing going on in Marshak and you damn well know it."

This was said in so forceful a manner that passersby looked over, and Karp seemed to notice Solotoff in a different, far more interested way. He turned the famous gaze up a notch. "No, I don't, but I was kind of wondering how come *you're* so positive. Got a pal in the DA, hmm?"

Solotoff realized what he had done and tried to cover it by saying, "Come on, Butch, you know *you're* my only pal in the DA," followed by a hearty, patently false laugh. Karp did not join him, continuing only to stare, as at a cockroach of unusual size. In the blank seconds thus occupied, Solotoff found that instead of thinking what to say now, to recoup his advantage, his mind was playing over the images of that horrible night: creeping down the back stairs, calling a limo, sneaking out the service entrance of the hotel, stinking, in rags, shoeless, creeping into his apartment where, by miserable chance, his wife was up and entertaining some of her old school friends. He'd said he'd been mugged, an absurd story, which was accepted, if not believed. And the bitch must have told him all about it (she had not, in fact), and he was gloating over it right now. He thought briefly of just bringing it up (Speaking of pals, your wife's a friendly girl; I was squeezing her tits the other night . . .), but no, especially as he hadn't scored, better forget the whole thing. The key was to distract Karp from this particular line of questioning, but as it turned out he did not need to, for Karp glanced at his watch and distracted himself.

"Yeah, well, I'd love to stay and chat, Shelly, but I have an appointment. A former pal of yours in the DA. You remember Ray Guma, don't you?"

"Oh, yeah. Good old Ray. Send my regards," Solotoff said, still smiling, but with a fading voice. Karp shook his hand and strode off. If Solotoff had hold of his client's pistol, he would have shot Karp right there in the courthouse hallway.

For his part, Karp wasted little time thinking about Solotoff as he took the elevator down to street level. The weather had changed within the last few days, and it was warm enough now to venture out without a coat. A presage of spring, and Karp took it as a sign. Maybe the ice would break up now, maybe Guma had something to go with. He walked up Baxter to the China Palace, as unimperial a place as could be imagined despite its name, a red-daubed, dark, and dingy joint smelling of oriental greases, with a dying snake plant in the front window. It was favored by bail bondsmen and an older generation of courthouse workers for its dimness, its quiet, and its cheap food; more important, like most Chinese joints over a certain size, it had a full bar.

Guma was sitting in the back at a table he had frequented for over twenty years. He was wearing a powder blue knit shirt and a check jacket, which made him look more like a minor Mob guy than he usually did. He had a Scotch started, and Karp ordered an iced tea to keep him company.

"You know," Guma said, "I'm gonna do this, I should get a PI ticket. Then I could charge expenses. I must've blown a hundred bucks on cabs alone. Not to mention the drinks I had to buy."

"I'll take care of it. You find out anything?"

"A little. I'll give you the bad news first. You ever know Bud Cropsey?"

"Rings a bell. He was a snake, wasn't he? One of the guys Mollen used."

"You got it. Bud started out as a field associate, then he got blown on that case up in the Two-six where the cops were running a bunch of whores, '89 or so, and then he went inside and went right up the line, retired captain, head of Confidential Investigation Unit One. His specialty was OC connections to the cops, so I saw a lot of him. Anyway, like I say, he's retired now, got a place out in Great Neck. I got him to make some calls for me. Not a whisper. Zilch."

"Cooley's clean? He can't be!" said Karp with a sinking feeling.

"What can I say? That's what the man told me. And he's got no reason to lie. The man's a snake for thirty years, he's got no friends in the department. I tried to tell you that before. The Cooleys are their own breed—they don't take shit and they don't take money."

"Okay, okay, I believe you provisionally. Crap! Was there any good news?"

"Yeah, that shooting, Lomax. There *was* a smell on that, and it got up pretty high in the department. One PP got involved. Chief Battle, our old pal, handled it personally."

"He got to Catafalco."

"Yeah. The funny thing is, it was a straight-up report. Steve Amalfi did the homicide. He noted the funny stuff. The skid marks and the traces on the guard rails were wrong for the story Cooley was telling, and so were the bullet wounds, which you picked up when you read the abridged report."

"Abridged?"

"Must've been, unless you left something out when you told me about it. I went to see Amalfi, too. He wouldn't talk to me, but he said the report speaks for itself, and it does, if you get the whole thing. It's adding up the little bits that knocks Cooley's story all to shit. On the surface it's just barely plausible. A DA who wanted to find something would've said, whoa! Hell, a DA who was above room temperature would've seen it."

Karp was not really interested in why Catafalco had not seen it, more likely, seen it very well but had declined to act. Karp understood that part of it perfectly. What he still did not understand was Cooley. He asked, "Why did he do it then? Amalfi have any ideas? Or Cropsey?"

Guma shook his head and drained his Scotch. "Not a clue. Cropsey thought it might be something personal. The Cooleys got hot tempers, and they hold grudges. Speaking of which"—here Guma checked his watch—"we should get going if we want to beat the rush to Jersey."

"We're going to Jersey?"

"Yeah. Oh, right, I didn't tell you. Connie Cooley said she'd meet with us. She's over in Harrington, her house. It's forty-five minutes if we miss the traffic."

"Guma, how're we supposed to get to Jersey? The bus?"

"What, they don't give you a driver anymore?"

"Yeah, I have a driver, but this whole thing is off the books. And the driver is a DA squad cop, and the DA squad works for Norton Fuller."

Guma shrugged. "We could rent a car."

"We could, but . . . wait here a minute."

Karp got up and found a pay phone in the hallway near the men's room. A crazy notion, but something about it seemed right, a way to break some of the Lilliputian threads that were tying his life to the ground. He called her private number and after some preliminary chat, he blurted out, "Marlene, I need to borrow your limo. Me and Guma have to go to Jersey."

"Uh-huh. What's wrong with your driver?"

"We're visiting a brothel, Marlene. Look, I'll explain later. Just make the call, okay? And, Marlene? Order something kind of discreet."

The limo, when it pulled up in front of the restaurant twenty minutes later, was a superstretch Caddie large enough for all the Spice Girls, white with smoked windows.

"I always wanted to ride in one of these," said Guma, sinking back contentedly into the pillowlike upholstery. "I especially like the way little honeys stare in the windows. Look at this trifecta coming up here. You could fit all three of their butts in a grocery bag, like casabas." He grinned horribly, waved. "Yes, girls, it *is* Brad Pitt, but it's my day off." To Karp he remarked, "We should make quite a splash out in Harrington."

"A lot of cops live in Harrington, I hear."

"Yeah, there's quite a population. Connie hasn't been too happy there since the divorce, but he won't let her sell the house. A funny guy, Brendan."

"How so?"

"He has his little ways, she tells me. But I'll let you hear it from her." Guma leaned forward and switched on the television, flicked through channels, and got the third inning of the Mets game. He poked around in the built-in bar and found that someone had filled the tiny refrigerator with Bud. He cracked one, offered one to Karp, who declined, took a long swallow, and sat back with a gratified sigh. "This is the life. You could get used to this."

"Yeah, you could, but then it wouldn't be the same. It's great because we're *not* used to it. If we rode around in one of these things every day, it'd get old fast, and then we'd feel like shit in a regular cab, forget about a bus or a subway."

"Yeah, well, you can say that because you're rich. Look at that fucking guy! He should've had that ball. You notice nobody can field nowadays?"

Karp was about to say that he wasn't rich, his wife was rich, and only paper-rich at that, but he let it go and watched the game companionably with Guma as the gorgeous vehicle took them north to the Washington Bridge, over the river, north again on the Palisades Parkway, and then through smaller roads lined with suburban trees coming into leaf, past a school, a shopping center, then through still narrower roads, until they came to the house.

Karp got out and stared at it. It was remarkably like the house he had grown up in, a good-sized split-level, clapboard painted pale cocoa, set on a little hill with a sloping lawn bordered with low shrubs. A blue Voyager sat in the driveway. Above it hung a basketball hoop. Two bikes leaned against the garage door. The woman who answered their ring was petite and dark, with remarkable, large black eyes, and glossy black hair cut in a jaw-length shingle. She looked about thirty, but seemed younger because of her slightness, and at the same time older because of the circles under her eyes and the deep lines under each one, tear trails, Karp thought. The woman was a crier. She looked as if she had recently been crying. She wore a tan tracksuit with blue stripes up the seams and Adidas. She smiled at Guma and kissed him on the cheek and showed Karp a graver face as she shook his hand.

The living room was spotless, almost unnaturally clean for a house with at least two kids in it. A beige wall-to-wall was on the floor, and the furniture was medium-quality department store, bought out of model rooms, on credit, or with the envelopes the bride got at the wedding: modest and respectable. Karp thought the room looked unused, like an old-fashioned parlor; the family must do its living not in this living room, but in a basement or the kitchen, where the TV was. He took in also the expected picture over the mantel, the colored photographic portrait of the whole family in a gilt frame: Cooley looking proud and satisfied in his dress blues with the green bar of the medal showing over the head of a towheaded boy of about five. A younger Mrs. Cooley with a smoother, less stress-worn face held a baby girl. The current version pointed them to a tweed sofa and offered coffee, which they declined, then beer, also declined, and she sat in an armchair opposite.

"Thanks for seeing us, Con," said Guma. Karp nodded agreement and wondered why she was seeing them. The continued presence of the portrait argued against postdivorce hatred.

"I'm doing it for Brendan," she said.

Guma said to Karp, "Butch, I told her about your interest in the Lomax shooting, about how some things about it didn't add up."

"Yes, we really appreciate it," said Karp. "It must be difficult . . ." His eyes went to the portrait.

She saw that and said, "I don't want him hurt. He needs to stop what he's doing, where he's going, but I don't want him hurt. Just so you know, I will never testify against him in court. They can't make me, can they, Ray?"

"Not if you're his wife, Con. But technically you're not anymore."

"I'm still his wife. I'll always be his wife. The decree isn't final. I keep losing the papers."

After a moment, Karp asked as gently as he could, "Connie, do you actually know anything about the circumstances under which your husband shot Mr. Lomax?"

"You mean specifically that? No. I don't know anything about my husband's life on the job. That was part of the problem." She flapped her hands helplessly. "I don't know where to begin."

"Begin with the Cooleys," Guma suggested.

"Oh, right, the Cooleys! I could talk about the Cooleys all day, maybe not as much as they could, but pretty good. You have to learn if you want to be in that family. Not that I ever could really be in that family because my dad works for Con Ed, not on the job, so I couldn't really ever understand. According to Rose. That's my mother-in-law." Connie shook her head like a dog shaking off a flea. "No. I'm starting wrong. I don't want this to be just complaining, like on a TV show. Okay, first of all, when I met Brendan, he wasn't like he is now. We dated in high school. We were high school sweethearts. I never thought he'd join the cops. Brian was in the cops, and Brendan figured that was enough Cooleys. He got a job at Newark, with Continental, he thought he might go into flying, that or air traffic control. Anyway, not the cops. And they let him, I mean Ray did, but I could tell Ray was disappointed Brendan was outside the club. I mean all their friends, everyone they know is in the job. We'd get together at their house, when Brian was alive, and I could see how they closed Brendan out. Nothing obvious, but I could see it, and it hurt him. He loves his family. He loved his brother, worshiped him practically. Not that they ever talked about that. The Cooleys don't talk, not like me. So I guess this was building up under the surface, for years, Brendan thinking that his family thought he was, I don't know, a wimp for not being a cop. Anyway, we lived with it, we even joked about it sometimes, about the job, cop jokes. We were happy, I thought. Brendan passed the air traffic controller's test, he was going to start training. He was all pumped about it, and then Brian got himself killed."

She sighed and pulled a wad of tissues out of her tracksuit pocket and blew her nose, then let out a harsh, forced laugh. "God, look at me! I feel like one of those jerks on Sally Jessy Raphael."

"You're doing great, Con," said Guma. The two men waited, hardly moving. They both had heard a lot of confessions.

She sniffed, dabbed, resumed. "Okay, Brian got killed, shot in the street. Do you know this story?"

Karp said, "He was killed protecting one of his informants."

"Yeah, he gave his life for a junkie snitch. That's what he was like, Brian. A hero. The funeral was huge, delegations from all over, the widow and the three kids, the flag-folding thing. And all the time I kept thinking, I couldn't help it, even though I was ashamed, you know? I'm so glad it's not Brendan. And I thought he should've been thinking about his family, Brian. I mean it's one thing to go through a door or chase a guy down an alley, up fire escapes. That's part of the job, but not take a bullet to protect a . . . a skell. You think I'm awful to think that, right?"

"No," said Karp, "it's natural to think things like that."

She gave him a long look to check him out, and she saw that he was sincere, that he'd been there, too.

"And after that, it's hard to explain, it sounds stupid, but Brendan wasn't there anymore. It was like someone else was living in his body. He quit his job and got into the cops. No problems there. Graduated top of his class in the Academy. No more jokes about the job. Practically no jokes about anything. And he was always angry. The Cooleys have all got this Irish temper, especially if they think someone is trying to shaft them, and he started to blow up all the time, at me, at the kids . . . and when we got together at parties, now I was the one who was left out. He was in there with the cops, and I was in the kitchen with the cops' wives. And I thought it was my fault. I couldn't stand thinking of him out there on the streets. He'd work a graveyard shift. I couldn't sleep, waiting for him to come home. He started taking risks, too. About six months after he joined up, he tackled an armed robber by himself. He would've been killed except the guy's gun jammed. So they made him a detective, and then he did that thing with the hostages, going in there without his vest, unarmed. You heard about that?"

Both Karp and Guma nodded.

"Well, after that I told him I couldn't take it. It would've been one thing if he really loved it, if it was his life, I would've been prepared for it, like the other girls, like Rose was. But he *didn't* love it, it *wasn't* his life. It was someone else's life. We started fighting all the time. I was awful, I admit it. I threw stuff, I scared the kids. I wanted to shake him back to being Brendan, *really* Brendan. This doesn't make any sense, I know . . ."

"No," said Karp, "it makes perfect sense. That's why you split up?"

"Yeah, he beat me up one night. My fault, again. I hit him with a candlestick, and he punched me a couple of times and packed a bag and left. And later he said he was afraid he might hurt me if we lived together. I mean he never touched me before that. He's not that kind of man. He said we could talk about our problems later, after this Firmo thing was over. But it was never over." She threw up her hands. "And here I am. A PD widow and I don't even have a folded flag."

"The Firmo thing," said Karp carefully. "What was that about?"

"Oh, that was the only thing he'd talk about, I mean from the job. A big criminal, a Mob guy, some kind of thief or fence. Ray was always talking about Firmo, too. The One That Got Away. It was like a family joke. Like when are you going to take the trash out? Just wait, I gotta get Firmo first. Ray tried to catch him for years and couldn't, and now Brendan was going to. He was going to show his dad that he was as good as Brian . . . better, in fact. Better than Ray was himself."

"What, he said this?" Karp asked.

"Oh, no. Are you kidding? A *Cooley* thinking about why they're doing something, ruining their life, getting killed? That's not the Cooley way." She hung her head, picked at her fingernails. Karp noticed they were bitten like a child's. "We went for marriage counseling. Our priest set it up, a nice Catholic social worker. Brendan went one time. I went to her some more, by myself, because I wanted to understand: How could this happen? I wanted to know. We're good people. We both love our kids. How could this happen to us?"

Karp knew it was a rhetorical question, but he said, "I don't know."

She looked up at him. "Yeah, neither do I. She, I mean the social worker, Mrs. Ruffino, she said it's the unconscious. When you have kids, you take all the negative crap you haven't dealt with in your life and put it into them, and then they go and do the same to their kids. We don't like to deal with the dark stuff. We want to be nice, and we want our kids to be nice. But we're not nice, or not all nice, like we think we are. And we lay it on our spouses, too, that shadow. I can feel that Cooley stuff working in me, too. That need to be totally, like, upright, clean, that outrage at the bad guys. I don't know if I follow all of it, but it's a point of view." She laughed, that same harsh sound. "It's not the kind of thing we talked about when I was growing up."

"Me neither," said Karp. "But back to Firmo. Brendan didn't get him either, did he?"

"No. He had an informant. He was working him for nearly a year . . ."

"This was Cisco Lomax?"

"I didn't know his name," she said quickly. "I wasn't privy to the details. I mean this was incredibly secret. He didn't even register this guy as a CI because he thought that Firmo had some cops on the payroll, which was how Ray's case got wrecked back then. Maybe he thought I was working for Firmo, too, I don't know. He was a little nuts on the subject. But I heard him talking to Ray about it. My guy, he called him, just 'my guy.' They set up this scam, some big shipment of stolen gold watches, diamond watches. Brendan was really out on a limb with the department on it. I think Ray was backing him on it, or they never would have let him take it on. It was one of those things like the job does. If it works, great; if not, you're shafted. He couldn't sleep the week before it went down, hardly ate at all. And what happened was his guy screwed him on it. I don't have the details, but I got the impression that this informant leaked the scam to Firmo's people, and they pulled a switch at the place where Brendan expected to catch Firmo with the hot watches. Firmo didn't show, and when Brendan opened the package, the watches in it were cheap copies. The real ones were gone."

There was some more after that, and they listened. She made some coffee and they drank it. Guma and Connie talked about people they knew, the family. They heard the hiss of a bus stopping down the street, and soon after that a blond kid rushed in, a little older than the one in the picture over the mantel. He stopped short and gave the two men a hard look, then went over and stood next to his mother, who rose and put an arm around him. Karp and Guma stood, too, and made their good-byes. Connie Cooley came to the door with them.

"Nothing is going to happen to Brendan, is it?"

"I don't know, Connie," said Karp. "I'll be honest with you, like you just were with us. I think he broke the law, but I don't have anything yet I can make the case with. I may never have."

"But . . . if it came out, he'd be through in the cops, wouldn't he? They'd make him leave."

"Yeah, that's probably true." Karp said it because that's what she wanted to hear. That's why she had agreed to talk with them.

Back in the white limo, Guma cracked another beer and said, "Poor kid, huh?"

"Yeah, a sad story. You marry someone and they change."

"Or they don't, which is probably worse, as my second wife never got tired of pointing out. Anyway, it sort of clears up why Cooley did what he did."

"To an extent. Lomax was clearly his rat. He thought he'd turned him, but Firmo was playing Cooley for a sucker, with Lomax's help! Cooley saw him on the street that night, took off after him, and blew him up. That's clear. Probably he's killing these homeless guys to cover his ass on that."

Guma knotted his brow. "Killing . . . ? What, you think *Cooley* is the bum slasher?"

"Some of the later vics, anyway. I got my guy down at the cops checking out if any of the people who died, the vics, had ties to Firmo's organization, like this kid Ramsey did, the one Marshak shot. What I think happened was there *was* a nut going around killing homeless, and after Cooley shot Lomax, he had to get rid of anyone who knew about his connection to Lomax, so he adopted the nut's MO. What's a few bums more or less? It fits."

"It might," said Guma, "but right now you can't even show the connection between Lomax and Cooley. If you're right that Lomax was the snitch there, you got no one to testify. The only people who knew about it are Firmo, obviously, and maybe Cooley's partner, neither of whom are going to be witnesses for you."

"There's the Canman."

"That's the bum he's been looking for, the one Lucy knows."

"Yeah, the first time she told me about Cooley looking for him, the thought crossed my mind that he might have something to do with the homeless murders."

"Why the hell would you think that?"

"I don't know. Just a vagrant thought. I knew he'd assassinated one lowlife already, and I knew he wasn't assigned to the bum-slasher task force. Why would he be looking so hard for the one homeless the cops were most interested in as a suspect? Why would he want to rough up people who the regular task-force cops just talked to? I mean it's not characteristic of Cooley. He's got absolutely no history of brutality, as you found out yourself. But now we know a little more about Brendan Cooley. We know he's a little nuts about being the perfect cop. We know his brother died protecting a snitch, and that made him change his life, become a different person. He develops a relationship with a snitch of his own, but this particular snitch betrays him. Cooley goes crazy and kills Lomax. Now he has to cover it up or his whole life is going to collapse. He takes out the homeless guys who knew the story. Maybe only one is left, Canman. According to Lucy, the Canman's a pretty smart guy. He runs all over the city with a cart full of cans, which could make him a perfect courier and stasher for a theft-and-fencing ring. We know about the connect between Cooley, Firmo, and Lomax now. What if there's one between Lomax, Cooley, and Canman? Now Cooley catches a break because the cops have Canman as a suspect in the slashings. Cooley finds the guy, and it's heroic cop shoots and kills bum slasher, case cleared and closed."

Guma rubbed his jaw and snorted. "Oh, *that's* a stretch."

"Maybe. But Cooley's going out of his way to find this guy, and he seems to have started just after he shot Lomax. That's significant.

Maybe finding and whacking Canman is a twofer for him. He shuts up the last witness to the fact he knew Lomax and clears the other killings he's done. In any case, I'd sure as hell like to find Canman before Cooley does."

"How are you going to do that without using the cops, or cranking up Keegan? Because I can tell you right now, the Goom is not going down those tunnels looking."

"Oh, I'll think of something." Karp reached for the telephone.

16

LUCY'S FINGERS SNAPPED DOWN ON THE KEYS, AND THE WORDS SNAKED across the screen. Ten past three in the morning and she was pulling an all-nighter. She had heard the phrase often enough but had never actually done one herself until now. Pulling an all-nighter, a deed dense with scholastic virtue, and she felt good about it, an unexpected attainment of the new her. She was writing an essay in French on the subject of Paul Claudel's *Cinq Grandes Odes.* Tran had suggested the theme, somewhat ironically, as being suitable for a Catholic schoolgirl. He had, in fact, known Claudel in Paris in the late forties, if *known,* as he said, was not too strong a word for the relationship between a Vietnamese student busboy and a literary lion. Lucy liked the poems anyway, full as they were of homages to the glories of creation and expressions of longing for God. She loved the line about the girl in the white palace who felt no regret for home but was like a little tiger ready to spring, and whose whole heart was lifted by love and by the great force of laughter. One of the great advantages of fluency is that one has perfect access to poetry in the original. She had not thought about this much before, not being, she had thought, the kind of person who liked things that other people demanded she read, but she had to admit she had changed her mind about this. She had, almost without knowing it, become an educable person. Not quite the little tiger girl yet, and she did regret her home, but she could now see that she could become someone like that. She could be open to joy.

She finished a page, mashed the save button, got up, stretched. A reward was due, a fresh cup of coffee and a cigarette. Everyone in the house smoked like coke furnaces, and she had taken up the habit in a desultory way, more for self-protection than because she enjoyed it. Although the taste of tobacco, the first toasty puff, was delicious, she could do without the trays full of butts and the constant acrid stench. She went into the kitchen and stood for a moment at the sink, enjoying the ticking silence of the house. She filled the coffeemaker, poked in the refrigerator, ate a couple of cold spring rolls, licking fish sauce from her fingers afterward. The smell of coffee filled the room, and something other than coffee, a sweetish, heavy odor, something burning. She sniffed; it was coming from the door that led to the finished basement that Tran used as his office. She sniffed again. Burning insulation? She opened the door, walked down a couple of stairs. The smell was overpowering. She trotted down the rest of the flight and came into the room.

The overhead lights were off, and the room was lit only by a tiny blue flame that hovered like Tinker Bell near the far wall. Something flashed copper-colored in the glow, a pipe of some kind. As her eyes adjusted, she saw that Tran was lying on his side on the brown leather couch, holding a long, brass, small-bowled pipe. His eyes were closed, and his face was more peaceful than she had ever seen it. He looked ten years younger. His eyes opened. She felt a flush of embarrassment.

"I'm sorry, Uncle. I thought something was on fire."

He smiled and beckoned. She walked over and sat next to him on the couch.

"Now you know my secret vice. Are you shocked?"

"I am scandalized, Uncle. Why do you do it?"

"Take opium? To assuage my grief. It is very effective." He spoke slowly, with long pauses between the phrases, as if each one required substantial consideration. "Have you finished your work? It is very late."

"It is. I can't imagine how you are up every morning so early."

"Oh, I don't sleep. Perhaps a short nap in the afternoons. And the work . . . ?"

"I think I have the math and science down. The history paper is done, as you know." She had written about the effect of the battle of An Loc on American and Vietcong diplomatic and military policy, including some insights not at that time known to the CIA, much less the

American-history teacher at Sacred Heart. "Also, I'm almost finished with the Claudel paper. I intend to work through the night."

He smiled and nodded and upended the bowl of the pipe over the flame of the alcohol lamp. He took a deep breath of the fumes, released it, and sighed. Raising his eyebrow, grinning, he offered Lucy the mouthpiece, which she could now see was made of amber.

She giggled. "Maybe later."

A deep chuckle. "An excellent, virtuous answer. Also, it avoids my being shot by your mother or put in jail for a hundred years by your father. I believe it is time for us to return."

"Us?"

"Yes, I am coming with you. Your mother requires more service."

"You talked to her?"

Another long puff and a longer silence. "Of course. I talk to her almost every day. It is a benefit of the telephone."

Lucy gaped, she grinned.

"Surely, you did not imagine she was unconcerned about your welfare, or that I was in any sense helping you to hide from your family."

Lucy was offended and felt betrayed. She was, on another and more genuine level, delighted and relieved. She was silent for a while as these feelings fought among each other, with the latter gradually triumphing.

Tran inspected the bowl of his pipe, scratched at it with a fingernail. "I am going to prepare another pipe. You may watch and see how it is done. Perhaps one day you will be the mistress of an Asian warlord, and the skill will be a useful addition to your many other talents."

"Do you think that is at all likely, Uncle?"

"With you, one cannot tell. Life is full of surprises, which is why I am not teaching French literature at the Lycée Chasseloup Laubat in Saigon, as my father planned."

So she watched as he manipulated the *yen-hok* needles, twirling and roasting the tarry ball over the flame, and carefully placed the fuming pellet into the pipe. He drew heavily and lay back. She was dying to ask him about the service her mother wanted, but he looked so relaxed and peaceful that instead she kissed him quickly on the cheek and returned to Claudel.

It cost Marlene a nice lunch and a lot of guilt, of which she could afford the former a good deal more than the latter, but Wayne Segovia seemed genuinely happy, and that might count for something in the halls of purgatory. He had lost twenty-five pounds, and his normally olive skin was the color of old dishwater. She watched him eat a whole lobster, a dozen cherrystones, a scoop of garlic mashed potatoes half the size of his head, and a dark brown dessert made entirely of unblended calories. She picked at a Cobb salad and drank most of a pricey bottle of Meursault.

"Lobster for lunch," he said wonderingly when he was finished. "I don't know, Marlene. I don't think I better tell my wife about this. She might think you got designs on me."

"Oh, your virtue's safe. A couple years ago maybe not, but I'm a reformed old lady now." Marlene sipped from her glass. "Actually, there was one little favor."

"Oh, ho. See, women take me to two-hundred-dollar lunches at the Palm all the time just to look at my face, so, frankly, this comes as quite a shock." He laughed, which was pleasant to see. "So what can I do for you?"

"I want to change my password."

He looked puzzled. "Marlene, that's not worth a hot dog and a Coke. You press the change-password button when you log on and just do it."

"Yes, but you have to know your old password before you can do that."

"You forgot your password?"

"Yes, this is so embarrassing. They sent a memo around the other day that everyone should change their password, and since I'm such a good girl, I did, and I used the little program that generates a random password and changed it, and then something came up, and I forgot to write it down, and when I turned my machine on this morning, it wouldn't let me."

"Yes, that's how computers make our lives easier. Okay, no problemo—we'll go back to my joint after and fix you up."

They did. Segovia sat at his chair in his tiny cube, and Marlene stood behind him. Segovia got into the root level of the Osborne system, found Marlene's password, decrypted it, and wrote it on a slip of paper.

"Tape it to your monitor," he said, handing it over.

She laughed dutifully and pulled a notebook from her bag. "I'm going to write it down right now in a safe place," she said, and did, and also wrote down the system administrator password he had tapped out several times, which she had read and memorized from over his shoulder.

She waited until the end of the day and slipped into an unused office and logged in as a system administrator using Segovia's password. It let her into any file in the Osborne system, and she was able to bring up Sirmenkov's phone records, hundreds of neatly ranked, compressed, and encrypted WAV files with the phone numbers they represented, and the time and charges. She selected a subset of these and with a few strokes dumped them all into a Zip disc, added Sirmenkov's decrypt key, logged off, and went back to her office, where she unpacked them, decrypted them, and burned them into a rewritable compact disk. She connected a headset to the machine and brought up a conversation of some length that had occurred in the right time frame. In Russian, of course. He would be talking to Uncle Fred in Minsk, or ordering a fur hat . . . or doing something extremely naughty. Marlene did not speak Russian, but that, of course, was not going to be a problem.

She pulled a CD case at random out of the rack next to her computer and saw it was Dire Straits, the *Brothers in Arms* album, and laughed. She put the CD she had just made into the Dire Straits jewel box, took a bottle of Hennessy out of her bottom drawer, and like a private eye should, poured herself a stiffer hooker and sat in her chair facing the wall that celebrated her sordid career and drank it slowly. In a while, she slipped the album into the CD slot on her machine and put the earphones on and poured herself another, and in time she got to the point where rock-and-roll lyrics seemed to be, more than the gospels and the prophets, a guide to proper living. She thought, after all the violence and double-talk you do the walk, you do the walk of life. When the music stopped, she went to the bathroom, fixed her face, sprayed some Binaca into her mouth, left the building, walked to her hotel, checked out, had the doorman hail her a cab, and headed for home.

Karp went back to the office after the Jersey expedition and hung around until the building was as deserted as a courthouse ever gets, waiting for Murrow to get back or call, but neither happened. Who called instead was his wife, saying she had come home to his bed and board. A brief call, and unsatisfactory. She sounded drunk, in fact. Karp put that out of his mind, as he was by now so skilled at doing, and continued his paperwork. The homicide bureau was operating fairly well, he thought. The city was now running at a pace of around six-hundred murders a year, of which somewhat less than half were his. A few years back it had been more like twenty-two hundred a year, with three a day in Manhattan. Now the pressure for corrupting plea bargains was a lot less. People who killed people could expect to go away for a reasonably long time, which might deter them from doing it again, or from sinking into crimes the law considered worse, such as selling marijuana. But, oddly enough, he was finding, the prep on the cases before him was no better than it had been when the same staff was working three times as hard. Not as good, even, in some cases. A mystery, one he did not expect to solve.

He worked swiftly, efficiently, peppering the files with notes, most of them pointed, merciless, finding inconsistencies, omissions, unwarranted assumptions. He was surprised that he could still do this, on autopilot almost. He could still penetrate through the fog of semiliterate police reports, technical gibberish, precedents, motions, testimony, lies and veracities, to a place where the truth lay plain. Or rather its predicate; the jury would, if the prosecutor didn't mess up, transubstantiate this tangled mess into truth, or legal truth at least, not necessarily the same thing.

Karp became aware that it had grown dark outside. It was 7:38 by his watch. He began stuffing files into the worn cardboard envelope he used as a briefcase, then stopped. Why bother? He was tired. The thought of lying in bed next to Marlene and working on cases, as they had on so many nights, she beside him reading a magazine, or a novel, companionable . . . no, he wasn't ready for that yet. Leave the office in the office. Yet it was hard, he found, surprisingly hard, to leave the place naked of legal impedimenta. Nothing to hide behind. He laughed at himself. Workaholic, not just a figure of speech, a joke. He actually felt lightheaded in the elevator; withdrawal symptoms.

The evening air was mild, damp, smelling of concrete and buses. The courthouse district was nearly deserted at this time of day, except of the homeless, moving into the vacated public spaces, the broad plazas, the architectural nooks, even here a few streets from the center of police presence. He heard a bottle smashed, a yell, and walked on, north on Centre, past the new high jail, with the Best Health Deli and the Nha Hang Pho noodle restaurant conveniently built into its street-level floor (message: we're part of the economy, too), and across Canal, where the air changed, becoming warmer and spiced with the indefinable mélange of Chinatown. Here it was not deserted, not at all; the crowds were still out shopping, looking for action; in the many lofts above, the indentured needlewomen of Fujian were just getting their second wind, moving into double-digit hours. As Karp jaywalked and reached the north side of the broad thoroughfare, the crowd parted for a young oriental woman in pigtails and a padded jacket and loose trousers, calling, "Kissamee, kissamee," as she shoved a heavy canvas cart full of cut cloth. The crowd tittered knowingly; yet another just off the boat, *excuse me* her only phrase of English, and mispronounced.

Karp crossed Lafayette onto Howard and left the crowd behind. Crosby Street was dark and nearly deserted as he approached the entrance to the loft. A man was leaning against a dark sedan, and as Karp passed, the man said, "Hey, Karp!"

Karp turned and was not entirely surprised to be looking into the belligerent face of Brendan Cooley.

"You know who I am?"

"Yeah, you're Brendan Cooley." Karp extended his hand.

Cooley ignored it. "I want you to lay off my family. That's out of line. You got something to say to me, you come see me."

"Your ex-wife wanted to see me. I went out to her home with her cousin, Ray Guma."

"That's bullshit, and you know it. And I'm gonna have a little talk with Uncle Ray, too. The pair of you were out pumping her."

"And what were we pumping her about, Detective?"

"The fuck I know! You got some bug in your head that I'm dirty or something. You're going around talking to people, making these suggestions . . . I don't know where you get this shit. . . . *I'm* the bum slasher? Why not the Boston Strangler? Maybe you think I got Jimmy Hoffa, too."

"You know what it's about, Detective," said Karp softly, but Cooley didn't seem to hear him.

"I don't understand, what is it? My dog pissed on your car?"

"Lomax."

"Lomax? *Lomax?* I went through a fucking grand jury on Lomax. *Your* fucking grand jury, as a matter of fact. I was cleared. It was a good shooting, end of story. So what is this shit about the slasher? Why am I singled out for special persecution, huh? Answer me that!"

Karp looked at the detective. He was dressed in plain clothes, anti-crime clothes, a flannel shirt (to hide the pistol) over a faded red T-shirt, blue jeans, and tan leather work boots. He looked like a typical New York artisan, which was the point. He was angry, with what seemed like righteous anger, which Karp thought was as well thought-out and authentic as his construction-guy costume.

"I live just up there," said Karp, pointing. "You could come in and we could talk about it."

"I know where you fucking live, man. And there's nothing to talk about, except you telling me you're gonna leave me alone, me and my family, *especially* my family."

Cooley took a step closer to Karp and waved a finger in his face, like a gun. The thought briefly crossed Karp's mind that if Cooley had really done what Karp thought he had, then the policeman was crazy and might kill him right here, in front of his home. Then he dismissed that thought. Cooley's anger did not look like crazy anger, but the controlled kind, a standard policeman's tool, and then another, perhaps more disturbing, thought arose: What if Karp was wrong? No one had anything but nice to say about Brendan Cooley, so where did Karp get off playing Javert to his Jean Valjean?

"Okay, Detective Cooley," Karp said in as mollifying a tone as he could manage, "I will never disturb your family again. I'm sorry my visit to Connie upset you so much."

Cooley glared at him, but still the set of his jaw relaxed slightly, and his face showed confusion, then a hint of suspicion. "You fucking better not. And what about the rest of this horseshit?"

"Lomax? Well, that's a different story, isn't it? I know you knew Lomax, and I know why you went after him that night. I know about Firmo and the stolen watches, and how Lomax screwed up your operation. I know you pursued him and shot him to death, shot him from your car, and finished him off with a shot through the passenger-side window. It was an assassination, Detective."

Cooley stared at him. His face lost its angry red and went the color of white jade under the sodium lights. "It was self-defense," he said, and choked. "It was self-defense. I was *cleared,* for chrissake!"

"Yes, and I'm going to unclear you."

"You can't prove shit!"

"Yes, I know. I'm working on that."

Karp walked away and went up the five flights instead of taking the elevator because he wanted some exercise to burn the adrenaline out of his system before, as he expected, getting another jolt from whatever Marlene was cooking up.

Cooking up indeed—a sweetish odor with a burnt undertone filled the loft; he headed for the kitchen, where he found his sons roasting sweet peppers over the gas stove. The mighty Vulcan was turned up all the way, and six-inch blue flames shot close to the intent, small faces.

"Hi, Dad," chirped Giancarlo, "we're charring peppers."

"I burned my hand," said Zak, exhibiting a tiny blister.

"Uh-huh, that's nice," said Karp distractedly, turning the flames down. "Where's Mom?"

"In the bedroom," said Zak. "Lucy's coming home, too. Mom said."

"Isn't that great, Dad?" exclaimed Zak's brother. "We're all home together!"

In the bedroom Karp found his wife lying prone on the bed amid a litter of unpacking—gaping bags, scattered hangers, open closets and drawers—with a folded, wet washcloth across her eyes. And the smell of brandy, sweet and dense.

"Have they burned the house down yet?" she asked weakly.

"Not yet. How are you feeling?"

"Horrible, like I had a rusty railroad spike through my temples. And please don't look at me like that. I can't stand it."

"How do you know how I'm looking at you? You have a compress over your eyes."

"It doesn't matter. I know you're looking at me with disapproval tinged with horror."

Karp did, in fact, have a look of this sort on his face, and he felt ashamed. He sat down on the side of the bed and took her hand. "What're we going to do, babe? You can't do this to yourself."

"I know, I know," she groaned. "I thought I could be a working drunk, but the body won't take it. Wrong genes. I'm starting to feel sick all the time; I want a drink right now, but I know if I do, I'll upchuck. I'm a failure as a wife, as a mother, as a security guard, as a millionaire, and now as an alcoholic."

"Marlene, I believe that is the single *stupidest* thing you ever said, and that's a tough league."

"Yes, but you have to say that."

"This is ridiculous, Marlene. You're not a failure, you're a success. I love you, your kids love you, your staff loves you, you have to fight the clients off, you're rich as God . . . tell me, *what is the problem?*"

"None of that is true. My daughter hates me."

"Oh, horseshit! She worships you. I hear she's coming home."

"Yes. According to Tran, she finished a whole term's work in three weeks, all the papers, and she's prepped to retake her exams. They'll be here later tonight."

"Well, great," said Karp without much enthusiasm. "But I still don't understand why she'll work for him and not for us."

"Yeah, it puzzled the hell out of Lyndon Johnson, too." She lifted the washcloth to expose her real eye. "Look, Butchie: this is not forever, okay? I sort of see the light at the end of the tunnel, speaking of LBJ. I got to do some things, and then I think it'll be all right. It'll be different, but all right."

"I don't understand."

"My company is corrupt. I have to get out of it, and I'm trying to figure out how."

"You want to give me the details?"

"Not right now. It's not a DA thing anyway; maybe SEC, but I'm not interested in whistle-blowing, just getting out." She paused and studied his face. "You look terrible! What have you been doing to yourself?"

"Oh, just fucking up right and left," said Karp bitterly. "We're a pair. Look, Marlene—I need your help."

"My . . . help? As in wifely support or something professional?" She sat up in the bed and removed the compress.

He took a deep breath. "I can't believe I'm saying this. Basically, I'm in a position where I can't use the official investigation apparatus. I need to find out stuff neither my own organization nor the police want found out. I could go public with it, get the feds or the state involved, but for a lot of reasons I don't want to do that. So I need the resources of a private army."

"This is the Marshak thing, right?"

"Yeah, and the Lomax shooting." And he gave her a quick briefing on the two cases. And as he talked, he felt a lightness flow into him, into his body and his head. It was almost like being a little drunk himself. Marlene was leaning forward now, shooting questions at him, intelligent questions. Her face had on it an expression he had not seen in some time. It was very much like real life again; not euphoria exactly, but a lessening of the dysphoria he had become used to, like the impact of daylight on a prisoner long in the dungeons.

"I see the problem," said Marlene. "You need to find Canman before the cops do, one, and you need to find some way of turning this Ralphie character. You're sure he's lying about what went down in the garage?"

"I'm not sure of anything, but it's a good bet. I need him watched, though. I need to get inside his head."

"Will Clay help with that end?"

"I think so. I think he'll help with Cooley if I can drop the whole package into his hands. He just won't conspire with me, not on this one."

"Some pal!" She studied his face. "Poor Butch! You hate this kind of shit, don't you?"

"I despise it. I'm like Giancarlo. I love it when things are regular. But you, of course, are a different kettle of fish."

"I am. Unfortunately, things being how they are at Osborne, I can't use my troops there. It'll have to be amateur hour, with a little *apparat,* as Oleg would say, running things. Let's see, who do we know who has a large body of tough guys with no discernible morals on call . . . ?"

"Not him," said Karp.

Marlene shrugged. "Okay, but then I'll have to think about it for a little while." She leaned back on the pillow. "In the interim, I haven't had a big messy kiss from my husband since 1987, so it feels."

"But from others, many?"

"Don't be legalistic," she said, holding out her arms, and he fell into them with relief. She tasted of brandy, like an expensive, warm dessert.

Then from the direction of the kitchen came a shrill cry, a crash, a howl. They were off the bed in an instant, colliding in the doorway, Marlene scooting ahead, her thoughts full of little boys flaming like torches and the presagement of *real,* rather than neurotic, unbearable guilt.

"Sweetie ate my pepper," Giancarlo wailed. Zak, the semisadist, was giggling. The mastiff was pawing at his mouth and making horrible groaning sounds. The two skilled investigators had little trouble reconstructing the events: the pepper, roasted a shade too long, had dropped off its fork, and the dog, trained from puppyhood to respond to the plop of dropped food, had raced over and sucked up an object with the core temperature of a thermite bomb.

Thereafter was peace restored, comfort tendered, cruelty chastised, the weeping hound treated with ice cubes and kisses, dinner whipped together and served, the boys cossetted into their beds by Mom for an unusually long time, it seemed, but not begrudged by Mom at all. Marlene came back to find Karp sitting on the costly couch idly thumbing through the television guide. The immense, expensive television was dark. She sat on his lap and kissed him. He noted the taste change—sausages, peppers, coffee. Not as exotic, but more delicious, *haimish*, his favorite flavor.

"I'm thinking of having some people over," she said, "a kind of welcome-home party."

"Like who?" Unenthusiastically.

"Don't grump. Real people. Tran'll be in tonight with Lucy, and we have to thank him, and besides, I have some stuff I need to talk with him about, and Mike Dugan, and your little guy, Murrow, and Guma. I haven't seen him in ages. And let's see . . . how about Clay Fulton?"

"Clay? You can't have Clay, not with Tran in the room."

"Why not?"

"Because Tran's got a fugitive warrant on him. He shot all those people out on Long Beach. Which Clay knows about."

"Yes, and he shot those people in the course of saving your daughter's life. It's not like he was a drug baron or a serial killer."

"He *is* a serial killer, and he might be a drug baron, for all we know. And our guest list is a little peculiar. This wouldn't be a working party, would it?"

"Wine and cheese," said Marlene, "sober discussion about your problem. *Your* problem, remember? I assume you still want it solved."

"Not that way. Not using gangsters. And Clay will walk out, and I'll lose a friend. Shit! I hate this!"

"I know you do, but you have to trust me. Look, if I wanted to know about some arcane point of criminal law, say the definition of conspiracy in *New York v. Patterson,* who would I turn to, hm?"

"*Patterson* has nothing to do with conspiracy. It says that the state may refuse to sustain the affirmative defense of insanity unless demonstrated by a preponderance of the evidence."

"See! I defer to your greater knowledge. In the same way, if you want to pull off a surreptitious investigation involving deception, chicanery, and a casual attitude toward the law, who would *you* turn to?"

Karp said nothing. She tickled him in the ribs. "Come on, Butch! You know I'm the man when it comes to the gray areas."

He sighed. He was so far gone in vice, he thought, that another increment could hardly damn him deeper. Besides, and not inconsiderable in itself, his wife was back. Real Marlene was sitting on his lap, her eye sparkling with the old light. It was worth losing a chunk of soul for. "Oh, all right!" he snapped. "Have your damn party."

"Good!" she said, and cuddled closer. "Now, where were we when the dog howled?"

At which point they heard the elevator crank up, and they sighed and rolled their eyes and felt each other up in a friendly way, and shortly after in came the prodigal daughter, alone. She, after greeting her parents warmly, and after a mutual exchange of apologies, went to the refrigerator and peered in. "I could kill for a corned beef sandwich on rye," she exclaimed, which, oddly enough, made Karp feel better than he had for a while: she was not entirely lost to the Orient, it appeared. This item was prepared, and she ate it, and they had a reunion. After a while Karp picked up the vibes telling him that the two of them wanted some time by themselves. This he was glad to give, for though he was a devout father and uxorious to the point of absurdity, given the typical mores of last-century New York, there was stuff, some weird gynospecific energy, that passed between the two chief females in his life that he did not care to be around. He went off to watch television.

"Where's Tran?" Marlene asked when he was gone. "I thought he was going to stay with us."

"He has a place on Bayard he stays in. Business associates, ha ha. He thinks Dad doesn't like him."

"It's my house, too."

"Yeah, well, he's not a sensitive, liberated New Age man. What can I say? He would probably deal direct with Dad and cut you out entirely as far as I was concerned except he's embarrassed about his English. Boy, but he's a good teacher!"

"Determined. I was saying the same to your father."

"Yes, but not just that. He just knows how to light something up, so you say. Oh, God, how could I have been so dumb not to see it! And he doesn't make you feel bad, except in that funny shtick he does about you're totally worthless and should be drowned so there'll be more rice for everyone else. It's so sad. That must be the saddest thing in the world—someone finds their métier, the only thing in the world they really want to do, and they're really good at it, too, but for one reason or another they don't get to do it."

"I don't know. People do what comes along, more or less. Your dad wanted to be a basketball player, but he's pretty happy as a prosecutor."

"But he's not a prosecutor," said Lucy vehemently. "That's my point. He's good at prosecuting cases, but they won't let him. He pushes paper and bureaucratizes. He hates it." Lucy looked closely at her mother. "And how about you, Mom? Still enjoying the ill-gotten gains?"

Marlene could not help a start at this comment. "Why 'ill-gotten'?"

"Oh, just a figure of speech. I guess they're not gotten too ill, in comparison."

"Actually," Marlene said after a considered pause, "they are. Wait here: I want you to help me with something. It's very important. Speaking of métier."

She left and returned a moment later carrying her Sony microrecorder. "Okay, here's the deal. You'll recall that two days before our IPO came out, your pal and mine, Oleg Sirmenkov, and a team of God knows what kind of hard boys he dug up, hit a farmhouse in Kosovo and rescued Dick Perry and his party from the grip of Serbian kidnappers. All the good guys were unharmed, and all the bad guys were killed in the assault, including two women. Osborne was all over every network in the world—you remember those shots with Perry getting out of the car with those big guys in black jumpsuits with *Osborne* plastered across their backs?"

"Yeah, they played it like continuously. What about it?"

"Just that a couple of days *before* the kidnapping, Oleg was walking around the office like the cat that ate the canary. Everyone else was gritting their teeth about the offering, but not Oleg. He was confident it would fly to the moon. And, of course, it did. I asked him why he was so up on it, and he said something to the effect that events would be in our favor."

Lucy looked puzzled. "So . . . you think he knew about the kidnapping before it happened? Then why didn't he stop it?"

"Why indeed? It's been bugging me for weeks. Also, it was only four days from the time they snatched Perry off a street in Pristina until Oleg's people sprang him, with half of NATO beating the bushes looking, with no result."

"What, you think he set it up? Kidnapped his own client?"

"No, but I think he knew the snatch was going down, and he let it happen. Dropped an agent into a Serbian extremist cell maybe. He had his rescue team all primed, he must have had the location and layout of the farmhouse before he went in. There's no other way he could've done that operation the way it went down, to pull out four people without injury, and kill eleven kidnappers. Oleg's good, but not *that* good. And all the bad guys dead, by the way, that's significant, too. No tales afterwards."

"But that's horrible!"

"Yeah. And the more I tried not to think about it, the worse it got. Drunk as I was, I couldn't get it out of my mind. That business with Kelsie, that was just the last straw." Marlene let out a large sigh. "Anyway, I lifted all the international-call recordings—all the calls to Russia or Pristina for the relevant time period I mean—off his computer and decrypted them." She tapped the tape recorder. "I played them out onto tape. They're in Russian, of course. I could go to a commercial translation service, but who knows what Oleg's contacts are in the local Russian community? I'd like you to listen to them and make me a transcript."

Lucy stared at the thin tape recorder with a peculiar expression on her face—repugnance mixed with fascinated delight. "Sure. When do you want it?"

"Now. As soon as possible. I'm not enough of a computer jockey to hide my traces. If Oleg's got some kind of snooper program on his machine, which he's bound to, being Oleg, he'll know someone was in his files. And it won't take him long to figure out who it was. I want to go in there Monday all loaded and ready to kick butt."

"What're you going to do?"

"I don't know exactly. Something nasty and unreasonable, I guess."

Lucy smiled at her mother. "This is your métier, isn't it?"

Marlene grinned back. "Being nasty and unreasonable? I guess."

"No, I mean figuring out the right thing to do and then doing it regardless of who it hurts, even if it hurts you."

"That's a moral stance, not a métier. I really don't know what mine is.

I can do a lot of different things pretty well, but none of them seem to make me particularly happy." Marlene laughed. "But enough of me. What about you, baby? You know what you're going to do with your life more than any of us."

"Do I? Oh, yeah, the languages—obviously, I like to learn them, but for me that's like walking or breathing. It's not life's work, and also obviously, you don't see me bursting at the seams with joy."

"No, we don't. It's depressing, too, and guilt-making. You know I always think every downer in the family is my fault."

"Well, it is, Mom, and you better believe we hate you for it."

"Thank you, darling. But I wish, I don't know, I wish you were more gay."

"What!"

"Oh, Christ, I don't mean *gay* gay! I mean lighter, more like a teenager. I mean you *are* only seventeen. I mean when *I* was seventeen . . ."

Lucy put her hands over her ears and said, "La la la la la . . . !"

"Oh, stop that! You know very well what I mean."

"Yeah, I do." Lucy sobered instantly and bit nervously at a ragged fingernail. "How can I explain this without sounding like a nut? Look, you know the story of the Tower of Babel in the Bible?"

"Of course. What about it?"

"Well, you know the right-wing fundamentalists, that's an important story to them. They claim God wants different people to stay different, and that's their interpretation of the story. It's why they object to the UN, and racial mixing."

"Okay, but they're crazy. What does that have to do with you?"

The girl looked down, tapped nervously on the edge of her plate. Then she raised her head and looked directly at Marlene with eyes that were like hot copper pennies.

"Right, it's symbolic, it's a metaphor, but there's also something real under it. Language is . . . I don't know, a mystery, and partly it's a religious mystery. 'In the beginning was the Word,' you know? What does *that* mean? And like the Pentecost, when they all spoke in tongues. Language comes from meat, but it's not meat itself. No one understands why there are so many of them or what that means either. But, Mom, the thing is, I think God is putting Babel together again. In my head. That's what I'm

for. I'm an instrument, for some use. And I don't know what it is. I'm supposed to wait to be told. You can see why that would make it hard to get
into teenage chitchat and hanging out. I mean it takes all my energy."

Lucy rose and picked up the recorder. "Let me get going on this."
She started to leave, but before she could, Marlene stood up, too, and
gave her a long, silent hug and kissed the shorn head, half-terrified of its
contents.

It was not a cheerful group that gathered in the Karp loft the following day, a Saturday afternoon, the guests having been selected for quali-
ties other than congeniality. Tran and Marlene were in a kitchen corner,
speaking low in French; Father Dugan was talking with Lucy, catching
up with her academic exploits of the past weeks and drinking a good deal
of better wine than he was used to. Somewhat later, the four of them
were huddled in the living room, speaking in low voices, in both French
and English, with Lucy jumping in as occasional translator. Dugan and
Tran had, of course, both heard a good deal about one another, but this
was their first vis-à-vis. To Marlene's great relief, they seemed to get
along, both of them being basically conspirators. Plots thickened.

Karp, Clay Fulton, Guma, and Murrow were meanwhile sitting
around the dining room table, amid a litter of beer bottles, drinking and
swabbing tortilla chips through Marlene's salsa. Fulton loved Marlene's
salsa, but did not like what he was hearing, the business with Firmo, the
gold watches, the hookup between Cisco Lomax and Firmo, and how
that connected (they thought) to bullets flying down the Henry Hudson
Parkway in the middle of a rainy night. Fulton was silent and glowering
when Karp finished with the story of the visit to the Cooley home.

After half a minute or so, Karp asked, "Well? What do you think?"

"What do I think? I think you got a lot of nerve dragging me in here
for this horseshit."

"It's not horseshit, Clay," Karp relied. "It's the only story that explains
the facts. Cisco Lomax screwed Brendan Cooley out of the collar of his
life, the collar his father couldn't make, and when he saw him driving by
in the night, he lost his head, took off after him, and blew him up."

"You want to think that, fine! There's a thing called a grand jury you
use for checking out if someone maybe did a crime. You think you got a
case, take it to them. That's the way the system works."

"I know how the system works," snapped Karp. "The problem is the system isn't working in this case, which is why we're having this cocka-mamy meeting. There's only one person we know about who can testify to the connection between Lomax and Cooley before the parkway shooting, and that's John Carey Williams, aka Canman."

"No, you only think that. You don't actually know shit. And, anyway, what the hell do you expect me to do about it? Crawl through the tun-nels and catch him myself? The guy is already the subject of a major search, for chrissake. He's the chief suspect in the bum slashings."

"If the cops catch Canman, he'll never see a courtroom."

"Oh, right, your theory about Cooley knocking off bums to cover his story. I mean really, Butch. Take a breath and just think that through. You're off the rails there completely."

Karp said, "Think what you want. Meanwhile, you asked me what I want you to do. Well, what I *really* want you to do is start a full-scale inves-tigation of Brendan Cooley, a real one, not another half-assed whitewash."

"That's out of the question."

"I know. And I'm sorry about that, I really am. How about this, though? You've got access to personnel records. Find out where he was the days those victims got it. It shouldn't take long, and if you're right, an alibi should turn up. On the other hand, if he was off-shift and unob-served at the time of every single one of the six killings . . ."

Fulton gritted his teeth. "All right, I guess I can do that. Is that all?"

"No. When we pick up Canman, I want to turn him over to you personally."

"You know where Canman is?" asked Fulton in a tone and with an expression that made his astonishment plain.

"Yeah, we do. We have contacts, let's say, in the tunnel community. Father Dugan does, I mean. You make the arrest and keep him in your sight until we can get him in front of a grand jury. How about it?"

Fulton scowled and thought for a long moment. "Okay, you got it. But I didn't hear any of this other shit. And—last time—that is all I'm going to do in connection with this abortion." He stood up. "Thanks for the beers."

"There's one other thing," said Karp.

"I *told* you . . ."

"No, this has nothing to do with Cooley. You said you had responsibility for locating high-crime areas on the computer and reinforcing the cops there, drug corners and that sort of thing."

"Yeah, I do. What about it?"

"There's a character, a person we'd like to see some pressure put on."

"A dealer?"

"Well, he's into a lot of things," said Karp smoothly. "Name's Ralphie Paxton. He's at 542 West Forty-fifth, apartment 3B. We want a lot of cops on the street for a week or so, busting people, frisking the usual suspects."

"Uh-huh. Well, a neighborhood like that, we wouldn't need much excuse. I can do that, no problem. You want to tell me what it's about?"

"Do you want to know?"

For the first time in a while, Fulton favored Karp with his familiar toothy grin and deep chuckle. He waved a big finger in Karp's face. "You're getting too smart for your own good, Stretch. I'm going to have to lock you up one day."

"I learned it all from you. You're an accessory."

Still waggling his head and chuckling, Fulton left.

"Well, that went well," said Guma after a significant pause. "Do you think he'll rat us out?"

"It's not ratting out. Clay is Nash's rabbi in the cops, he's supposed to look out for him. Now we told him we know where Canman is, he'll tell Nash that Cooley may be going down, and why, and try to find some way to cover him. Nash is Cooley's partner, so he'll tell Cooley, although I'm sure that Clay will tell him not to. That's the cops, that's the Blue Wall, only it's not a wall. It's a bunch of little castles, defended against the outside, but also from each other, the bosses jockeying for power and the little guys all working their own game with their rabbis, and IAD working against all of them, except where they're not, and the whole thing dipped in enough chickenshit regulations so that the bosses can burn anyone they want to, almost arbitrarily. And the secrets: Clay Fulton is practically my best friend, but when I deal with Inspector Fulton, I can't be out-front, and frank. It wouldn't be fair to him, it would rip him up, so we have to go around the barn, like I just did." Karp looked disconsolate as he sucked on a beer.

"But, meanwhile, you think this will draw Cooley out?" Guma asked. "You think he'll follow Dugan into the tunnels?"

"He'll have to. And we'll be there, too. But not you, Murrow, even though you're small and could wriggle through any narrow ratlike passages. How have you been doing with Paradisio?"

"He's still laughing in my face on the Cooley theory."

"And?"

"I reasoned with him. He's fixated on Canman, and I told him we had evidence that Canman was linked to Firmo, and maybe he was acting as a hit man, and that the victims were stolen-goods couriers who'd dipped some items. He said he'd check it out. The other thing he said was the cops are planning a big drive through the homeless areas underground. Three, four hundred troops. They intend to roust everyone down there and flush him out."

"When is this?"

"He said next Wednesday."

"Shit! Then we better get moving. Meanwhile, he already leaked our interest to Cooley, which was the point. Cooley came after me once already. The pressure's building on him, too. Goom, on the Mr. Ralphie, the lying-douche-bag front, you're okay with that? What you have to do?"

"Yeah, I'm cool. But it seems like the weakest part of this whole business. It sounds like something your bride dreamed up."

"It was a mutual effort, thank you. It's the product of two highly trained criminal-justice minds, one of which is only loosely connected to reality. But you're wrong about that."

"About what?"

"The weakest part," said Karp. "The weakest part is, we have no fucking idea where Canman is."

17

THE GRAND JURY ROOMS OF THE NEW YORK COUNTY COURTHOUSE ARE furnished like movie theaters, with comfortable theater-type seats upholstered in fuzzy beige and arranged in three concentric, concave rows. No drinks or popcorn, and the show is usually duller even than the typical Hollywood epic, but it is still a show, and the spectators, twenty-three citizens chosen at random from the electoral rolls, are usually good-natured about paying attention. Aside from the seats, the furnishings are sparse: a table for the witness, who faces the twenty-three as a lecturer administering to his class. There is no judge and no defense attorney, for the grand jury is the prosecutor's show—producer, director, and star.

Karp stood in back of his audience but facing the witness and ran through his questions more or less on autopilot, eliciting from a bored police officer that he had on a certain date and time at a certain place, within the borders of the present county, found the body of a human he had later identified as Desmondo Ramsey. Karp had the man describe the scene in the garage, then thanked the cop and dismissed him. The next witness was a medical examiner, a former citizen of Pakistan, and this person was made to say that Mr. Ramsey, otherwise in the pink of health, had met his end through the medium of a bullet that had pierced his heart. Thank you, Doctor. Then came a police ballistics technician who said that he had identified that same bullet as having come from a nine-millimeter Colt pistol registered to a Ms. Sybil Marshak. The pistol itself was produced, in its plastic sack, and duly identified.

These witnesses established the essential facts of the crime. A person had been killed in the present jurisdiction, by Ms. Marshak's pistol. It remained to be shown that Ms. Marshak had wielded the pistol, and for this purpose Karp called the next witness, Ralph T. Paxton. The grand jury foreman swore him in. Karp moved from the rear of the grand jury room and stood before him, slightly to his right so as not to obscure him from the jury. A thin man, Paxton, about thirty, mustard-colored with oiled hair swept back. He had a wary expression, eyes darting, his tongue over his lips, shoulders hunched. He was wearing a brown jacket, a tieless, clean white shirt, tan slacks, and Nikes, new ones.

Karp gave him a friendly smile and took him through the events surrounding the death of his pal Desmondo Ramsey. As he told the story, he became more confident; his voice, which had been low and hesitant, became louder. Karp gave him his head, only occasionally prompting him to be more definite, and the story emerged: He had been in an alcove of the garage, with Ramsey, who had been doing wine and pills. He had been talking about a score, a big score. They had been baling up scavenged magazines, and Ramsey was cutting twine with his knife, a six-inch hunter. They heard footsteps, high heels, a woman came into view, she couldn't see them, but they saw her go toward a black Lexus. Ramsey said he was going to take off that white bitch. Those were his words? Yes, those were his words. Do you know the name of this woman? No, not then, but later he had identified her from a photo array: Sybil Marshak. Ramsey had proceeded toward the woman, still holding his knife. Karp held up a plastic bag with a knife in it, and Paxton identified it as the one in Ramsey's possession on that day. Then what did Mr. Ramsey do? He went up to her. He brandished the knife. He *brandished* it? Yeah, like he showed it to her, waved it in her face. He told her to give him her bag, her watch. And what did Ms. Marshak do then? She took a gun out of her handbag and shot him. Just like that? Yeah, just like that. It was all over so fast.

In all, a good witness, and well-rehearsed, although not by Karp. That *brandished,* for example, had appeared in the original Q&A, and so did long stretches of descriptive prose. Karp thanked Paxton, and Paxton walked out of the room. Karp noticed Paxton had more spring in his step than he had had when he entered. Now a final police witness, a detective and a forensic expert. Karp elicited from him that two sets of fingerprints had been found on the hilt of the knife in question, Paxton's and Ramsey's, and dismissed him.

Turning to the grand jury, Karp informed them that this concluded the presentation of the people's case against Sybil Marshak. He explained again about probable cause, that they were not deciding whether Ms. Marshak was guilty of the crime of manslaughter in the first degree, but only whether there was sufficient evidence to bind her over for trial on that charge. Then he recited to them the statutory definition of the crime: with intent to cause serious injury, causes the death of another person. Ms. Marshak, he said, had intended to cause Mr. Ramsey serious injury by shooting him and had caused his death. He then explained the self-defense justification for a homicide. If they believed that Ms. Marshak was correct and *reasonable* in supposing that she was in immediate danger of death or grievous bodily harm from Mr. Ramsey, and that Mr. Ramsey was unlawfully attacking her, and if they believed that the use of deadly force was *reasonable* and necessary to avoid this danger, and that she could not in her circumstances resort to the law, then they could bring in a finding of justifiable homicide rather than sustain the indictment for manslaughter.

There was a little murmur then: this was a new one for this grand jury, rather more intellectual effort than they were used to putting out. It is extremely unusual for grand juries to decline to indict. (A different grand jury had, of course, found that Brendan Cooley had shot his man in self-defense, but Cooley was a cop and Lomax was a fleeing felon, no problem there.) There were some questions. Did he actually have to stab her? No, but the threat had to be immediate and *reasonable,* and it was up to them to decide that it was. Couldn't she have shot the knife out of his hand? Karp kept a straight face, nor did his eyes roll skyward. That speaks to the reasonableness of the force, he explained. You all have to decide if what she actually did, shooting him through the body, was reasonable in that circumstance.

He left them to their deliberations and sat down on one of the plastic chairs that lined the little room outside the jury room, where witnesses waited. The plan was unfolding, but whether it was the one he had hatched, or the one Marlene had, or some strange amalgam of both, he had really no idea. This present farce was part of the plan. Remarkably, Keegan had actually ordered him to do it, in the presence of an almost preening Norton Fuller. Karp recalled the surprise in both faces when he had agreed without demur.

He waited. He was used to it. A good portion of his professional life had been spent in waiting—for a jury, as now, for a judge to decide, for some piece of paper to trickle through the system. The wait for grand juries was usually short, but this one was taking its time. The little ante-room was crowded with witnesses and prosecutors for pending cases. Some of the ones who were cops looked at him coplike, a wary assess-ment, and there were conversations in low voices. The word had spread obviously: the NYPD grapevine was the fastest in the world. Karp didn't care about that. He had never courted popularity with the police, although he would greatly regret it if he had harmed his friendship with Clay Fulton. There were reporters outside, too, with TV cameras. He would have to make a statement later, an important case such as this. He had no friends in the press either, probably a mistake, but too late to cor-rect now. If he'd had friends in the press, he might not have had to con-coct this silly plan. Like everyone else in society, it seemed, he could then have created an alternate reality, putting a lot more subtle pressure on Keegan, and if he had not gotten his way, he could have blown the whistle. As it was, if he blew the whistle now, he'd just be fired, branded an incompetent sorehead, and forgotten. The old racist thing would not help there either.

The little amber light over the door to the grand jury room lit up, indicating they had reached a decision. Karp got up and went through the door.

Ralphie Paxton left the courthouse feeling pretty good about his performance, so good that he decided to treat himself to a cab ride home. He was supposed to call the lawyer right after he got finished, but he figured that could wait. Man wasn't paying him any money now, he could just hang for a while, fuckin' Jews thought they owned you. There was a cab, a woman climbing out of it with a briefcase and long, stockinged legs and one of those little skirts they wore now where you could see practically their whole business. Ralphie positioned himself so he could see most of it, got one of those hard looks those bitches liked to give you, and replaced her in the cab.

The driver was a rag-head, like most of them nowadays. He wasn't too happy with Ralphie as a fare, but fuck him, what could he do? Ralphie caught him staring in the rearview, his foreigner eyes clouded with suspicion. "No Brooklyn," the driver said.

Ralphie gave him the address, although he considered for a moment telling the rag-head to go to Canarsie, just to jack the fucker up a little. It wasn't worth it, not for the money. There was starting to be a problem with money. Five grand when he'd got it from Solotoff seemed to be all the money in the world, infinite riches, far more than Ralphie Paxton had ever seen in his life, but it was proving to be more ephemeral than he had ever imagined. He was drinking Scotch now, not Night Train. He was buying a better quality of sex now, no more blow jobs behind a Dumpster from a skanky crackhead transvestite, no, now it was actual girls, young ones, too, in a bed. He liked that, the lush life, but it was expensive. He had been on the streets for years, rent-free. Paying some guy just so you could live someplace was novel and irritating. And the crack, that was expensive, too, especially when he had to pay for partying. People came around a lot when they knew you were flush. He liked that, being the big man, having a roll to flash around. The girls liked it, too. So it flew out of his pocket. He didn't really know how much he had left; he was sort of afraid to count it, but it wasn't more than a grand now, maybe less. The thought of having to go back to the street was not pleasant. He liked taking a shower whenever he wanted, with hot water, and watching TV like a regular person. That he could continue this life by obtaining employment never occurred to him.

He should have held out for more money, he was thinking now. Five grand was chump change to a rich Jew lawyer. He should have had that watch, too, that was worth almost five grand on its own, that fucking Desmondo, although, of course, Firmo would've come after him pretty soon, like they said he did, and that would've been it for old Des. He really was lucky that bitch had capped him like that; at least it was quick. How to get more money. The lawyer really owed him, but that was a problem, too; he was connected, or so he said. He said that was it, the five grand, payment for information, strictly legal, deductible, he said, but if Ralphie tried to get smart, he'd make one phone call and Paxton would end up under concrete somewhere. Was he telling the truth?

There were two blue-and-whites on Forty-fifth when the cab entered the street. They were double-parked with their doors open and their flashers on. Another bust. Paxton paid the driver what was on the meter and got out. The guy gave him a look, but fuck him, the rag-head, if he expected a tip. Paxton walked up the street to his apartment house, but he hadn't taken ten steps before a couple of big guys in plain clothes with badges hanging off their necks on chains grabbed him and tossed him against a car and patted him down. He was clean, and they let him go, no apology, like he was a piece of shit. He wanted to tell them he had just testified before a grand jury on a big case, but he let it go.

"Hey, Ralphie!"

Paxton turned. It was Real Ali. Paxton felt a surge of relief. Real Ali was company and didn't do dope or drink.

"What's up, Ali?" The two men shook hands.

"Not much. I was just going by, you know. You live around here?"

"Yeah, up there. I got a place now."

"Yeah, I heard you lucked out behind that Desmondo shit. It's a ill wind, right?"

"Yeah, you got that right. You still down by the tracks?"

"Still there." Ali looked both ways and said in a lowered voice, "Look, my man, it's lucky I run into you. You wouldn't be interested in a little business proposition, would you?"

"What kind of business?"

"Holding."

"Holding? What you mean, holding?"

"Holding. Guy wants to leave some stuff in your place, he pays you rent. Like you a locker in the Port Authority, but a lot more than fifty cents. But, hey, if you're interested, let's not do business on the street."

They went into Paxton's apartment. Ali looked around and, with an approving whistle, agreed that it was pretty sweet. Paxton poured himself a Scotch, although he badly wanted a pipe. He played the genial host, recounting some of the details of his new life. Then they turned to business.

"Here's how it works," said Ali. "Man hands you a package. You don't touch, you don't smell it, and you don't look at it. A little later, the man tells you take a walk, see a movie for a couple of hours, leave the door open. The man brings in his people, and they cut the shit up. You come back, the package is history, and you got a grand sitting on your table. That's it."

"Who's the man?"

"You heard of Benny Mastracci?"

Paxton had not. He said, "Sure."

"Yeah. Call him the Hammer. Benny the Hammer. Man you don't want to fuck with. But his money's good."

"How come you know him? I thought you were through with that shit."

Ali laughed. "Yeah, that's what everybody thinks. That's how come Benny likes to use me, you dig? That's the fuckin' point."

After a brief pause, Paxton laughed, too. Fuckin' Ali. It was nice to have friends.

Ralphie Paxton met Benny the Hammer late on the following day, a knock on his door and there he was. He looked just like those guys did in the movies, in a sharp black suit, an ugly, hard-faced little white guy, with two big white guys with him, also in suits, with open collars and gold chains. They barged in and checked the place out, noting with approval the grilles on the windows and the police lock on the door. The stuff was in a duffel bag. One of the big guys stuffed it into a closet.

Benny had a gravelly voice, also as established by the movies. He said, "Ali tells me you're a straight-up guy, or I wouldn't be here. But let's understand each other. There's six plastic bags in there, and I know what's in them down to the gram. I know what's in them, and when we come back, the same thing's gonna be in them as what's in them now. If not, for any reason, Rocco and Vinnie over there's gonna stick your head in a tub of cement until it dries. No warning, no second chances, no excuses—that's just the way we work. You understand what I'm telling you?"

The man's little ape eyes bored into his, and Ralphie Paxton understood.

Guma's voice on the phone was artificially low and conspiratorial: "The package is delivered. The eagle has landed. The plume of my aunt is in the second shelf."

Karp laughed. "You love this shit, Guma."

"What can I say? I missed my calling."

"Did you scare him?"

"He was pissing himself. I brought Rocco and Vinnie Luna for effect. I thought Vinnie was gonna crack up, but he managed to turn it into an evil grin. I hear it was no bill on Marshak."

"Like we expected. A black guy comes at you with a knife in a parking garage, the classic nightmare of scared America. Thank God she had a gun is the usual response."

"You got anything else you want me to do? Besides crawling through tunnels."

"No, nothing right now—and thanks, Goom. I owe you big."

"You bet you do. I'm sending you a bill."

Karp turned off the cordless and put it down on the coffee table. "That was Guma."

His wife put down her headphones and paused the tape she was listening to. "Did he do it?"

"So he says."

"You don't look very happy about it."

"I'm not," said Karp. "I want this to be over. This is hell. But I don't want to talk about my legal daintiness anymore. How's your stolen phone calls going?"

"The kid did a good job. It was like I figured. Oleg had a positive tip this kidnapping was going down. He had a man in the group that did it. These here are conversations with his man on the scene, Ilya, who that guy reported to. Oleg knew the time and the place of the snatch and where they were hiding Perry. He declined to intervene. Result: an international incident, beaucoup press, and he goes in and gets them out two days before the IPO, guaranteeing all the bozos who make up the bull market will buy the stock: 'Duh, Osborne, I heard of them, think I'll buy a thousand.' Basically, it's what happens when the KGB discovers capitalism. They love the money, but they don't *quite* get it."

"So you're going to blow the whistle?"

"In a manner of speaking," said Marléne in a tone that did not encourage probing. "You'll be interested to know we have a line on Canman, or Mike Dugan does. Lucy's going over to Old St. Pat's tonight to get the scoop from this guy who's apparently the king of the mole people."

After a considering pause, Karp said, "I'm not sure I like Lucy getting involved in this. Why don't you go?"

"Because I have other stuff to do, and because Lucy is quite competent enough to collect some information."

"But that's it, right? Just information."

"She really wants to find Canman. He's a friend."

"He's a serial killer."

"I thought Cooley was the serial killer."

"There are enough killings to go around for the two of them," snapped Karp. "You need to back me up on this, Marlene. I don't want Lucy going anywhere near those tunnels."

"She has Tran to watch her."

"Yet another serial killer. I mean it, Marlene."

"I know you mean it, but we've been through this I don't know how many times before. You want to be protective and a good daddy, but the choice is either backing her up when she wants to do stuff you think might be risky, or forbidding her and making her feel guilty when she goes ahead and does it anyway. She's seventeen now and it's only going to get worse. At least she's not riding every Saturday night in the back of a pickup driven by a drunk teenager, like half the kids her age in America."

"That's not the same thing."

"No, it's a lot *more* scary than looking for a guy in a tunnel while holding hands with the most dangerous man in North America and his numerous associates."

"I want her right next to me, then."

"Good. It'll be a family thing, then, like the magazines are always telling us to do," Marlene said with finality, and slipped on the headphones.

It had taken Lucy some time to get used to the man's stench, compared to which Jingles's fierce pong was that of a baby fresh from the bath. The man had to actually be rotting, or have dead animals trapped between the layers of his clothes. He was playing chess with the priest in a room in the basement of the church. They were playing slowly and silently, and after the first half hour she gave up following the game. Lucy was the worst chess player in her family. She had never beaten either of her parents, and recently even Zak had knocked her off, amid merciless laughter. Whatever brain cells were used for chess in normal people had clearly been displaced in her head by those devoted to language: the tricky tonalities of Hmong reigning in place of the King's Indian defense. After a brief greeting, Father Dugan had returned his attention to the board. The other man had not responded to her at all, which miffed her, and so she passed the time staring rudely at him. There was a good deal to see. He was big, for one thing; his head was like a slightly deflated basketball, covered with a wool cap that was kelly green under the grime. The ear she could see was only a fringe of greased cartilage around a black hole, for the man had clearly been in a bad fire at some time. His face, riven with scars and discolored grafts, was tugged subtly out of place so that one side seemed to smile as the other frowned. Lucy was on the frowning side. He had an untreated cleft palate and a harelip, too, and his eyes were of two different colors, one black, the other a misty hazel. Spare Parts, indeed, although the priest called him Jacob.

"'Eck," said Spare Parts.

The priest let out a regretful sigh and a low chuckle. He moved a piece. His opponent responded. Then a brief flurry of moves and the man said, "'Eck 'ate."

The priest toppled his king, winked at Lucy, rose, and said, "Good game. Thank you, Jacob. Why don't I make us some tea? I think there's some old doughnuts left from a committee meeting, too."

Dugan left. Spare Parts said nothing, but slowly replaced the pieces on the board. His hands were huge and showed red in fissures where the skin was not black with filth.

"You're a good chess player, huh?" said Lucy, oppressed by the silence. "I'm not. I can't play for beans. Where did you learn how?"

The massive head turned, and he looked at her, into her eyes; she felt an actual jolt, and into her mind came the line from the Yeats poem her mother was always quoting, the one about the creature with a gaze blank and pitiless as the sun. Tran sometimes looked at her like that, in moments of distraction, when the kindly persona he had constructed for her benefit fell away, and she looked into more pain and loss than human beings were really designed for. There was nothing of society in it, only the horrible truth of existence. It took all her will to keep her eyes on his. Finally, he said something, a series of honks with most of the consonants stripped out.

I've heard of you, he was saying. *You work at the church.*

"Yes, Holy Redeemer. Do you go there?"

No. I only come here. I like to play chess. He gives me books. The man drew a deep breath, as if this much language had exhausted him.

You're looking for Canman.

"Yes," she said eagerly. "Do you know where he is?"

The great head nodded twice.

"Will you take me there?"

What do you want with him?

"I'm his friend. I want to help him. We think people are looking for him, the police, and also a policeman who may want to hurt him. We can help him, but we have to find him before they do."

They won't find him.

"They will. They have sweeps of the subways, of the homeless. You know that! They're planning a big one on Wednesday because they think Canman is the bum slasher, and they'll look until they find him. We need to find him first."

He's not in the subways.

"He's not?"

Not in the subways. He's in Rat Alley.

Father Dugan entered the room then, carrying a tray.

"Here's our tea," he said cheerfully. "I see you're getting along."

"Jacob says the Canman's not in the subways."

"Yes," said the priest, "we were discussing that before you arrived. Apparently there's a disused railway tunnel on the West Side that intersects some kind of derelict sewer system. It's sealed off from the tunnel proper, or was. Rat Alley, as they call it down there. Do you know that line from *The Waste Land*? 'I think we are in rats' alley, where the dead men lost their bones.' No? Jacob must know it, though. Jacob reads a lot of poetry."

"In 'A Game of Chess,'" said Spare Parts.

"Yes," said the priest. "The section of the poem in which the line appears, he means. Yet another strange conflation of art and life." Dugan leaned over as he poured tea into Lucy's cup, caught her eye, and mouthed, "Keep your eyes on me; don't watch him eat."

"Yes, Rat Alley," Father Dugan resumed, "it doesn't appear on the city's maps, not that that's unusual—there're fourteen hundred miles of sewer line under New York, apparently, besides unbelievable numbers of pipes and tubes and ducts of various kinds. This particular one seems to be the place where people go to escape when the tunnels get too cozy. They also toss garbage in there and an occasional corpse."

Lucy was, as instructed, keeping her eyes on Dugan, but she could not similarly restrict her ears. Spare Parts when eating sounded like a large fish trapped in a mud puddle by the retreating tide. These sounds paused, and he said, *It's very dangerous. Canman is crazy. I think he'll be dead soon, anyway. He is half in love with easeful death.*

"Is he sick again?" Lucy asked, alarmed.

After a horrible slurp, the deep voice went on, *I don't know. It doesn't matter because they will get him soon. They get them all in Rat Alley.*

"Who will get him? You mean the rats?" With this, Lucy forgot herself and looked at Spare Parts.

He stared back at her. Crumbs and powdered sugar were around his horrible maw, and his thick, purple tongue swooped out to grab them up. He said, *There are no rats left in Rat Alley.*

Then he stood up and strode over to a pile of cartons full of donated paperbacks. Lucy had expected him to have the lurching walk of a horror-movie monster, but his stride was strong and athletic. He knelt, selected a book, shoved it into a pocket, and left without another word.

Lucy found herself gasping, and Father Dugan chuckled. "Yes, we don't breathe too deeply around Jacob."

"Good Lord!"

"Uh-huh. Stinks like a desert father. What did you think?"

"Of him? Horrible, but not actually scary. He's very hard, but not evil, like an animal. What's his story, do you know?"

"Not much. Bits slip out occasionally. Apparently he was born down there. His mother was an illegal of some kind, and probably not all there upstairs. She made her living . . . as you would expect. God knows how he survived, but he did. He got big early, which I guess was a blessing. I have no idea how he learned how to read—he certainly never went to school. I found him one night outside, going through the trash, a pile of books that were too messed up to send anywhere, and I invited him in. He's bright—you saw him beat me just now—but not exactly with a human intelligence." Dugan sipped some tea and lit another cigarette. "It makes you count your blessings, doesn't it?"

"Will he help us find Canman?"

"Oh, he already has. Before you got here, he gave me explicit instructions on how to find this Rat Alley. But he wanted to meet you."

"Me?"

"Yes, and no false modesty, please. You have quite the rep among the unhoused. Several instances of miraculous healing have been reported." He wiggled his eyebrows and looked upward.

She giggled and blushed. "Oh, stop it!"

"The pope's been informed."

"No, really . . . so we're really going down there."

"It looks that way. The sooner, the better. What do your folks think about it?"

"Oh, Dad's going to object, but he always objects. My mother, of course, is fine with it." A pregnant silence. "I should go home."

"I'll walk you out."

At the steps leading up from the church basement he asked, "Still having the visions?"

"Few and far between now, although St. T. nearly got me arrested on a train. The message seems to be to study hard and wait. I guess they're not going to tell me to crown the Dauphin at Reims."

"And a good thing, too." He laughed. "And, Lucy? About this whole business . . ." He pinched his lips.

She nodded agreement, hugged him good-bye, and trotted off down Mulberry Street. It was dark at this hour, although the street was lit by the windows of shops and galleries. Banners flapped over the centers of culture and commerce. Just past Kenmare, she spotted a familiar figure moving swiftly in the opposite direction.

"David!"

But Grale did not seem to notice her, or anything else. He was walking rapidly, his tattered jacket flapping like one of the gallery banners, an intense and fixed expression on his face. She moved to intercept him, clutched at his sleeve.

At that he stopped and turned to face her. "David, what's the matter? Are you okay? You practically ran over me."

"Oh, sorry." His face went through a peculiar contortion, as if he were painting David Grale onto something else. But there he was again, the kindly, amused eyes, the angelic expression, the lovely mouth curved into a smile. "Sorry, I was just distracted. What are you doing out? Clubbing? Living the high life of the rich?"

"Oh, right, I'm so much in demand at the more exclusive boîtes. It's my supermodel face and fashion sense. What's up with you?"

His smile faded. "More bad news. They found Doug's body down by the tracks. It's another one. That makes seven. I'm going over there now, see what I can do. He might have effects or relatives who should be informed."

Lucy had an unbidden, uncharitable thought that in this particular case the slasher had done society a favor, followed by a spasm of guilt.

Grale seemed to see this transition on her face. "Yeah, I know, I had the same thing, the slasher's good deed. It shows how far we are from perfect love. Still, it's a kind of mercy. He had the virus, you know."

"I didn't know." She recalled the fight she had been in with Doug Drug, the blood spilled, and could not help a thrill of loathing.

"Yeah, he had it, and it made him angry. He seemed to go out of his way to share needles with his pals. It's funny, I know that the rain falleth on the just and the unjust, but wouldn't it be a kick if like the bad guys got their desserts right here in front of everyone, and the innocent didn't get raped and murdered? What if there were saints who stuck it to the bad guys in the same way as Mother Teresa took care of the miserable and poor."

"They wouldn't stay saints for long, would they?" said Lucy, thinking of her mother. "I mean, if there's one thing the Church has learned in all this time, it's that violence and power are corrupting."

Now he fixed her with his eye and spoke with intensity. "Yes, but don't you think God gets tired of all this suffering? In Sudan I saw stuff . . . you can't imagine what people did to each other there. There were times when I wanted to grab an AK and finish off the bunch of them. Not just the bad guys either, all of them, just to make an end, just to let them fly off to heaven or hell or wherever."

"But you didn't."

He seemed to deflate a little. "No. No, I didn't. But sometimes when I think of people like old Doug there, I have my doubts." Grale grimaced and shook his head. "Old Doug. He must be getting a stern talking-to right about now."

"With pitchforks."

Grale laughed. "Uh-huh, like in the cartoons. But, you know, there's a theory that hell is completely empty. I mean, figure it out: You die, and all things are revealed. You have absolutely no doubts anymore. God is good, the devil is evil. And God's mercy extends everywhere, even into the pit. How many souls do you think reject His mercy at that point? Not many, I bet."

"I don't know. What about the people who like torment? Or the people who'd never admit they were wrong even if it meant ten thousand years in hell? And what if you don't like harp music?"

Grale smiled again, but this time in a sadly disapproving way. "You've been hanging with the Jesuits again. How is the good father?"

"He's fine. We found out where Canman is."

"No kidding! That's great news. Is he okay?"

"So we hear. We're going to try to . . . you know, find out more about how he is." Stupid! she yelled at herself in her head. David was the last one to tell about this. He didn't have a guileful bone in his body, and he talked to absolutely everybody. All at once she was uncomfortable, wanting to be away home, far from the conflicting and delicious and annoying feelings the man roused in her, and so she made a hurried excuse about having to get up early and practically ran off down the street, her mind full of mortification and all the clever, mature words she never managed to get out in real life.

"Are you really going to do it?" Karp asked, embracing his wife the next morning at the door to the loft.

"I'm going to give it a try," she said. She was wearing an old black Karan suit, something she had bought in a consignment shop before the money came, and a pair of Jil Sander's she'd got on sale in what seemed another age. She looked severe and felt the same.

"This is all beyond me," said Karp.

She laughed. "It might be beyond me, too. I'll call you."

She took a cab to the office, went in, and sat behind her desk and waited. The call from Osborne came at a little after ten. She picked up her loaded briefcase and went in.

They were all there, sitting along both sides of the table, with Osborne at the head: Oleg Sirmenkov, sitting next to the boss, then Bell, the lawyer, and Harry Bellow, and Deanna Unger and Marty Fox. They stopped talking when she came in, then started up again, pretending that they hadn't stopped talking. She took a seat at the foot of the long table, placing her briefcase on the table in front of her. She looked at Harry. He was confused, which was good, she thought, because it meant he hadn't been involved. Everyone else was staring at her, with expressions ranging from fear to contempt to (in Oleg's case) cold rage.

Osborne began without preamble. "People, this is a security firm, and the worst thing that can happen to a security firm is a breach in its own security. I'm sorry to tell you that we've experienced such a breach. Late on Friday night, Oleg informed me that someone had entered his confidential files and removed some highly sensitive phone records, digital recordings of conversations. I immediately contacted Marty, and he brought in a team to try to find out who had penetrated security and where the files had gone, if possible. The team worked all weekend and found that the intrusion had taken place from a machine on our own intranet. They started looking for traces of the missing files on every hard drive in the office and were eventually successful in locating the intruder."

Osborne looked at Marlene. "I've been thinking it over half the night, and I can't, for the life of me, figure out why you'd want to do such a thing. Maybe you'd like to explain yourself, Marlene."

"Gladly. First of all, just for my own personal curiosity, were you in on it yourself? I mean the scam."

"I don't know what you're talking about," said Osborne. "What scam?"

Marlene reached into her briefcase and withdrew a stack of neatly stapled documents. She handed a short stack to Fox and to Harry, and they automatically passed them around the table.

"This is a translated transcript of conversations in Russian between Oleg and a man in Pristina, Kosovo, named Ilya. They demonstrate that not only did Oleg know the identity of the people who kidnapped Richard Perry, but also he knew, considerably in advance, the time and place they had planned to carry out the snatch. Which occurred as planned, as we all know. Further conversations concern the rescue. Oleg was at some pains to make sure that it went down two days before our IPO."

Osborne had gone pale, which Marlene thought was a hopeful sign. She liked Osborne. Which didn't mean much, since she liked Oleg, too.

Osborne turned to the Russian. "Oleg?"

Oleg made a little shrug. He smiled winningly. "Well, you know, Lou, truthfully, I think Marlene is maybe a little carried away here. This kind of operation is more complicated than watching out for girl singers, make sure no one sneaks into the dressing room. What you say on the phone to whoever, this is not always what you mean."

They all looked back at Marlene, who guffawed and said, "Oh, horseshit, Oleg! I got you nailed and you know it. But, hey, you don't want to believe my version of the story, I'd be glad to hand this package over to the press and let them play with it for a while, send a bunch of investigative reporters over there and let them poke around. The SEC is bound to be interested in it, too, especially the paragraphs on page twenty-one of the transcript where our boy here says"—she flipped through the pages and read—"'This is most important, Ilya; you must go in on the sixteenth.' And then Ilya says, 'We could do it tomorrow, we're all ready.' And Oleg says, 'No, the sixteenth. There is a business reason. Let them sit there for a while, it won't do them any harm.' Yeah, I think the SEC would be very interested in that part. It's probably even worse than messing with Rule 174."

At this the table erupted with angry noises, directed at Marlene. Osborne had to restore order by pounding his fist on the table and bellowing, and in the following hostile silence he asked, "Assuming you're correct in your allegations, what do you intend to do?"

"Not much. This is a good firm, more or less. There's no reason for you to lose all you've worked for because one person didn't quite get it. But I want out. I want to be bought out, now, today."

"That's impossible!" said Unger. "We can't trade in stock for six months after IPO."

"I don't mean a public trade. You all have margin accounts. It shouldn't be hard for you to raise the cash, especially with stock as the collateral. Interior trades are perfectly legal. "We closed at fifty-five and a quarter on Friday. That's sixty-six point three million that my piece of Osborne is worth. You can divide my stock up among you however you like, I could care less. But I want a check for that amount net of strike price, taxes, and charges, and I want it today."

"How do we know you won't release this material anyway?" Fox demanded. "What guarantees can you give us?"

"My sacred word of honor, one, and two, if I blew the whistle, Oleg would kill me. Right, Oleg?"

Like automatons, every head swiveled to look at Oleg. They all thought they were pretty tough people, but they all cringed a little at what they saw in Oleg Sirmenkov's eyes just then.

Marlene continued, "And then Harry would kill Oleg, wouldn't you, Harry, even though you might be a little pissed at me now?"

"Yeah," said Harry, "I guess I would," in a tone and with an expression that he hadn't used much since he became a corporate guy, but which was absolutely convincing.

"Which would not be all that good for the firm, either. I just mention that in case Oleg is thinking about killing me *anyway*," said Marlene with a bright smile around the table, which was not returned.

Lou Osborne asked Marlene to leave the room, which she did, then walked back to her office, to find Min Dykstra standing guard, embarrassed but resolute about not letting Marlene into her own office. She wanted to know what was going on, and Marlene told her that it was better that she didn't know. Marlene left and went to the ladies' room and sat in a booth and used her considerable reserves of self-control to resist tears and actually made a small dent in the steel wall of the booth with her fist. Then she went back to Osborne's office and hung around, in the invisibility of the corporate pariah, until Bell came out and took her into his office, and they began to negotiate.

Three hours later, Marlene signed her name to an agreement. In it she promised that she would not compete with Osborne by opening her own international security firm or by working for an Osborne competitor, and also that if she ever made public anything whatever having to do with her career at Osborne International, said firm would have the right to strip her of all she possessed, parade her naked through the streets in a cart, transport her to a deserted island, and stake her down in the sun, to be devoured by ants and crabs, or words to that effect. In return she received a certified check for $50,823,000. Then she cabbed downtown and had a long conversation with Ms. Lipopo. If Ms. Lipopo was amazed, she did not show it. Marlene imagined that the banker had experienced all manner of financial eccentricity, and that Marlene's was nothing much in comparison.

Back on the street, she recalled the first time she had walked out of Ms. Lipopo's elegant suite. Then she had been heavy, plutonic, rich, as they say, beyond the dreams of avarice. She was still richer than 99 percent of the planet's people, but she was about to become very much poorer, and she felt light, Apollonian. She stepped off the curb to hail a cab, then stepped back and dropped her arm. Instead, she walked through the money-intent throngs to the subway and took the Lexington Avenue line up to the Hunter College station. The train was not crowded. She found a seat and observed her fellow passengers. She estimated that not one of them had been born in the United States, which obscurely cheered her. On the platform at Hunter College, where she left the train, she found a hairy kid with a guitar singing "I Shall Be Released." She paused to drop a twenty in his case and tripped up the stairs and to the garage that held her battered Volvo. In it she drove downtown, happily cursing the cabdrivers and truckers, and after stopping off to pick up some supplies for the tunnel expedition, she returned home, changed into worn jeans and a T-shirt, fixed herself a wine cooler, and telephoned the archdiocese about a donation she wanted to make to the Church. And, no, she told the secretary, she couldn't just put it in the box.

18

MARLENE HAD BOUGHT THEM ALL YELLOW COVERALLS OF SOME PLASTICIZED material, and white hard hats and Motorola two-way radios, and black gum-boots. The twins had been shipped off to their grandmother's. The dog was straying no more than four inches from his mistress's knee, well knowing some interesting events were in the offing. The four donned their outfits in the loft, and Marlene looked them over like a sergeant major on parade and distributed to each a four-cell Kel-light, the policeman's choice for both illumination and tuning up the skulls of malefactors. Father Dugan appeared the most authentic in the costume, oddly enough, more authentic than he usually looked in a surplice. His roughneck Irish face fit right in with the sandhog getup. He also seemed to be the most enthusiastic, which was perhaps not so strange since he was the only one who knew where they were going. He had spent the day in the chart room of the Department of Public Works, working out a rough map based on the instructions he had received from Spare Parts. It was a very approximate map since either Spare Parts was crazy or he knew a lot more about the underground than DPW did. The priest hoped it was the latter. As for the others, Marlene looked like the plumber's daughter she was; Lucy, pale, thin, and floating in the helmet and gear, resembled a breaker laddie sent down the pits at eight years old; Karp looked like a disguised distinguished attorney, miserable and awkward, and felt the same and said so more than once.

"Oh, stop," said Marlene after one of those comments. "Where's your sense of adventure? Didn't you ever read boys' books when you were a kid?"

"I did," said Karp, "and by the age of twelve I had identified them as unrealistic fantasies, never thinking I would marry someone who hadn't."

"How do you pee in these things?" Lucy asked.

"You let it run down your leg," answered her mom sweetly, "and then remove your boot to drain."

"I can't believe I'm doing this," said Karp almost under his breath. "All we need is a map that's been browned in an oven. And some peanut-butter-and-jelly sandwiches."

"The sooner we get started, the sooner we'll be finished," said Marlene in a leadership tone of voice, and headed for the door. Karp came close and said sotto voce, "Where's your guy?"

"His name is Tran. After the fuss you made, and on further reflection, I figured you would not be comfortable acknowledging the presence of someone you knew to be a suspected felon. You will not have to take cognizance of him."

"That's extremely and unusually considerate of you, my darling. But he'll be there? Backing our play if need be?"

"I have no idea what you're talking about," she said with an airy flip of her hand.

It was a dark, rectangular hole in the western flank of Manhattan, down among the shadows of old dead piers, just south of Seventy-second Street, guarded by a loose and rusted gate. They entered, switching on their lights, Father Dugan in the lead, then Karp sticking close to his daughter, and Marlene last, descending damp slate steps, stumbling on the many broken ones.

"This is an emergency exit for the crew that built this tunnel," Dugan explained at the bottom of the stairs. "It's a railway tunnel and not used anymore, which is why it's popular. I think we should switch these lights off now. I don't want to upset the residents."

They did so. At first the blackness was absolute. Karp reached out without thinking and squeezed Lucy's hand. Gradually, however, they became aware of a distant, ruddy glow, and as their eyes adjusted, they made out shadows moving across it. They passed through a sparse water-

fall dropping from a great height, and beyond that they found themselves in the midst of a considerable settlement. The railroad had cut
deep bays out of the rock for storing equipment, and these had been
converted into apartments with beds and furniture and rooms separated
by curtains. The place had a zoo smell, mixed with smoke from the several fires. A huge figure came out of the gloom and approached Father
Dugan. As the figure came closer, Karp thought he was wearing a cheap
Halloween mask and then, with a shock of revulsion, saw that it wasn't a
mask. Lucy said in a whisper, "That's Jacob. Spare Parts."

"Our faithful native guide."

"He's okay," said Lucy reprovingly.

"If you say so," said Karp, suppressing the bourgeois in him who was
recoiling from the knowledge that his little dearie was hanging out with
people like this. The big man finished his honking conversation with the
priest, of which Karp could understand not one word, and strode off into
the tunnel, which debouched after a few minutes into a larger tunnel,
with two sets of rusting railroad tracks on its floor. They all turned their
lights on, but the narrow beams, strong as they were, did little to dissi-
pate the blackness or to give any sense of scale, for they had to direct the
light at their feet in order not to constantly trip over the uneven ties.
Spare Parts, in the lead, was setting a brisk pace. He didn't have a light
and didn't seem to need one. Father Dugan had his light angled to keep
track of the guide's legs. He was feeling better than he had since leaving
Salvador. This was why he had joined the Jesuits, to go into dark and
dangerous places in the service of God and humanity. Nevertheless, his
lips moved in prayer.

Karp followed the circle of light in front of him and kept his own lit
circle small and tried, not always successfully, to keep his footing in the
clumsy boots. In the part of his mind that was not controlling his feet or
cursing, he was trying to put in order the chain of events that had led to
his being here in a dark, wet tunnel with his wife and daughter, guided
by the Son of Frankenstein into who knew what. He was angry, mostly at
himself, but also at Brendan Cooley and the district attorney.

Close behind him, Lucy was feeling guilty about her father, sensing
what he was going through, wishing he would stop worrying about her.
She was fine. They were fine. She had absolute confidence in the ability
of her mother and Tran to get them out of any conceivable problem.

Bringing up the rear, Marlene was watching the lights of her family before her, thinking of nothing much but the current situation, in full action mode for the first time since the debacle at Kelsie Solette's, and starting to wonder when Tran would show. As she walked, she flicked her light beam from side to side, casting long shadows of her companions against the curved walls and vaulted roof. From time to time she spotted a scurrying shadow along the walls and thought that it must be some trick of light because, although she had heard that tunnel rats grew to prodigious size, she had not imagined anything quite *that* size. The dog trotted along by her side, snuffling when the rat smell hit his nostrils, perfectly content. He smelled and heard the people following them, but he had not been put on guard and so made no complaint.

Marlene felt the tap on her shoulder and let out a short, involuntary yelp.

"My God, Tran, you scared the shit out of me! Where have you been?"

"Following," he said, and something odd about his voice made her hold up her light to get a better look at him. She was shocked by what she saw. The always calm, competent, imperturbable Tran was sweating and wide-eyed and actually shaking. The plastic raincoat he wore made a slithering sound, and as she watched, he hugged himself tightly in an attempt to make it stop.

"Tran! What's the matter? Are you sick?"

"No, not sick. Or only in my head. I am devastated to have to tell you, Marie Helene, that since the war I am not very able beneath the ground, in the tunnels."

At once, and with a rush of shame, Marlene recalled the story he had told her years ago, of being buried alive for five days and then dug out and informed that his family had been vaporized by a bomb.

"Oh, you poor man! Why didn't you tell me?"

A shrug, a weak smile, a side-to-side movement of his head. "I thought I might have improved. It has been a long time. But I find that, despite the proverb, some things time does not heal. I cannot seem to control my limbs down here, and the deeper I go, the worse it gets."

"Christ! What are we going to do?" She shone her flash back the way they had come. A rat ran from the beam into the darkness, but otherwise the tunnel was empty.

"Where are your guys?"

"I did not bring them. They . . . it is a matter of face, you understand. They cannot see me like this. I am truly sorry."

She patted his arm. "Okay, no problem. Look, you go back topside and get yourself together. We'll be fine."

"I have a pistol. Do you want it?"

Marlene did, very much, but she declined. "Oh, hell no, we're just going to bring in some poor fool. He's not being held for ransom or anything. Really! Go on up, we'll be fine."

And more cheery words of this sort, which were interrupted by the crackle of the radio in her pocket. She took it out and held it to her ear.

"Marlene!" came her husband's voice. "Marlene, come in. Shit! This fucking thing doesn't work for . . ." She waited during more of this until his finger came off the button and she was able to talk.

"Butch, I'm fine. I'll be there in a second."

"What's wrong?"

"Nothing, I just got a little tied up. Are you there yet?"

"We're at a switch—the tunnel branches off to the right, and Mike says that's the one we're going to take."

"Okay, be right there." She put the radio away. To Tran she said, "Go now. We'll be fine."

"There are two, at least two, other men in the tunnel besides your party. They are moving without lights, but I heard them. They passed me while I was sitting there paralyzed. I had to tell you . . ."

He looked as if he was about to collapse, and this sight was far worse than the thought of going into Rat Alley without him at her back.

She embraced him and kissed him on the cheek, then trotted off down the tracks and found the branching and took the right-hand tunnel. In a few minutes she saw the lights of the others ahead. They had stopped and were looking at the ground.

"This looks like it," said Father Dugan, indicating the floor with his beam.

Marlene saw that the floor and part of the wall had collapsed, making a pie-slice hole a few inches wide at the tip, swelling to no more than three feet at the widest.

Karp knelt and shone his light down the hole, but could see nothing but sparkling Manhattan schist.

The priest said, "According to Jacob, this goes down about twenty feet, and then you're in the old sewer tunnel. Canman lives up a side tunnel that branches a couple of hundred yards down."

"Is he going to lead us there?" Karp asked.

"No," said Father Dugan, "this is as far as he goes."

"So . . . just the one branch in there," said Karp, looking down the slit.

"No, a lot of them, he says. It's a sewer, or was."

"Then how will we know which branch is right?"

"Apparently, it's unmistakable."

Spare Parts let out a series of honks and grunts.

"What did he say?" asked Karp.

"He said, 'I fled Him, down the labyrinthine ways,'" answered Lucy.

"What does *that* mean?"

"I don't know. It's from a poem called 'The Hound of Heaven.' Oh! He's going."

The tunnel king was indeed going, as usual without a kiss good-bye. They watched him move out of the circle of light and vanish.

Karp was by that time in a state that often occurs in unlikely adventures, in which everything seems giddily amusing and like a bad movie. Our cast, he thought: here was the kid who never got killed, and Marlene, the female star, ditto, and there were two guys, one of whom had to be eaten by the slime monster while the other rescued the ladies. Karp wondered which one he was. He said, "It's quiet. Too quiet. I don't like it." They all stared at him, but he was gladdened to see Lucy's teeth flash into a grin. Without further thought he eased his legs into the wide part of the slit.

"I'll go first."

"Why?" said his wife. "I got you into this. I'll go first."

"No, because I'm the biggest, and if I can't get through, *no one* else is going." Cutting short further discussion, he slid deeper until only his head and shoulders showed. "Stay five yards apart and watch out for the Nazis," he said, and vanished down the hole.

Karp found that the hole led to a narrow shaft just a little wider than his shoulders, descending at an angle of about forty-five degrees, so that he proceeded downward in a kind of controlled slide. His flashlight was on, but useless, as he could not lift his head enough to see where his feet were going. The ceiling was two inches from his nose to begin with, and it got closer for a breathless while and then receded, as did his incipient panic. He tried not to think of New York pressing down upon him, or of getting stuck or being buried alive. Time seemed to slow down. He could hear the blood pounding in his ears. He thought, I'm a lawyer, this is not what lawyers do, and then he imagined a professor in a law school class saying something like, yesterday, you'll recall we discussed the difference between strict and vicarious liability as expressed in *Liparota v. United States;* today we'll deal with sliding down your ass through a narrow, gravelike passage down to a sewer to find a crazy witness.

Giggling uncontrollably, he suddenly found himself falling through a blackness pierced by the wobbling beam of the flashlight. Something smashed against his thumb, and the flashlight was gone. Something grasped and skittered across the top of his helmet, and then his feet hit solid ground. The flashlight, still lit, had rolled some distance away. He went to get it and cast the beam around. He was in a cylindrical, brick-lined vault, perhaps eight feet high. The bricks were old, and the mortar was crumbling; there were heaps and spills of brick within the range of his beam, the results of abandonment and perhaps shoddy work—a typical grafting bid of the last century. There was a sound of flowing water and a penetrating stench he could not identify—decay maybe, and earth, and something sharper, a burnt odor on top of that. The air was absolutely still, cold and clammy against his skin. A noise attracted him to the hole he had come in by. He saw booted feet emerging and something else—some playful soul had jammed a skeleton's arm and hand into a crack. That was what had struck his helmet when he'd come down.

He pulled the thing out of the wall and was in time to grab Marlene's arm as she dropped. He offered her the skeleton.

"Need a hand?"

She gave a gratifying shriek. "Oh, stop! I can't take you anywhere."

"Bag it—it's important forensic evidence," he said, tossing it away. "Where's your guy?"

"Tran. He's not coming."

"What! Jesus, Marlene! You mean we're down here with just us? Where is he?"

"I don't now!" she said curtly. "Maybe he had to go to a bar mitzvah. We'll be fine. Who's this, Lucy?"

Yes, and then the dog, and Father Dugan brought up the rear. After determining that everyone was all right, the priest marched off to the left, the rest following, Karp staying within arm's reach of his daughter, who did not object. Marlene hung to the rear, occasionally turning and casting her light back the way they had come. She saw nothing unusual, except for the complete absence of rats. They moved in silence, clambering over brick-falls, jumping cracks. Their path seemed to go downward, although it was hard to tell.

The sound of flowing water gradually grew louder, and then water itself glittered in their light beams. They saw that the brick casing of the sewer had been shattered, and the farther end displaced by several feet, as if some sideways force had pushed it over. Naked rock showed through in the gap, and a deep cleft in the floor was partially filled with cracked boulders, over which flowed a stream of dark water at least ten feet wide. What looked like tree limbs stuck up here and there among the rocks.

"This can't be right," said Marlene. "Trees? We must be sixty feet below the surface."

"I've read about this," said Father Dugan. "When they excavate for tunnels in the city, they occasionally come across tree trunks. They're the remains of a preglacial forest, squashed into the earth by the ice. What this looks like is that someone was blasting up above and the shock waves cracked the casing there and released a buried stream. It's really quite wonderful. This must be one of the original—"

Marlene interrupted him and in a curiously flat voice said, "Look, there are human bones down here." She pointed her beam, and there they were, dumped in the ravine, like something out of Cambodia: skulls and bones, and not only dumped, but arranged; skulls on fossil tree limbs, leg bones neatly stacked. As the priest voiced a prayer and started to clamber down toward the ossuary, the tunnel ahead was lit by a bright flash, followed an instant later by a painfully loud blast. They all ducked instinctively as small, hard objects flying at speed whined and clattered.

"That's Canman," cried Lucy.

"What? What?" they all gabbled.

"He makes bombs, booby traps to guard his stuff. It's him!" She had scuttled down the ravine, forded the stream, climbed the other side, and was away down the tunnel before they could stop her.

Both Karp and Marlene raced over the gully; both tripped and scrambled up the other side, their boots sloshing with water. The mastiff cleared the obstacle in a bound and ran alongside Marlene, panting. Lucy was a winking yellow figure ahead, leaping like a doe over rubble. Both of her parents were in reasonably good shape, but they could not close the distance. The tunnel curved slightly, and the yellow blur with its light vanished.

As Lucy rounded the curve, she saw the ruddy glow of a fire. She slowed and turned off her flashlight. She saw the shapes of people milling around and the sound of angry shouts and screams of pain. The people were waving sticks and what looked like spears. The fire was not in one place, but scattered around in burning clumps. Acrid smoke stung her nose.

She saw one of the people pick up a brand and fling it toward the tunnel wall. It bounced and became a shower of sparks, but in the instant before it did she could see that the wall there was pierced by a narrow conduit, not more than four feet wide. This was barricaded two-thirds of the way up by what looked like bales of newspaper. In the opening thus formed she saw a face she recognized only briefly, for it ducked down to avoid a shower of missiles from the group below.

Steps behind her, and the stabbing bright beams of flashlights. She spun around. "Turn off your lights," she called out in a hoarse stage whisper. Too late. The beams illuminated the scene, the figures frozen for a moment like a tableau vivant in hell.

Lucy, like all Americans a veteran of innumerable horror movies, found herself surprised at how normal they looked. Except for their weapons and the expressions on their faces, they could be waiting in line at any soup kitchen in the city. Karp, Marlene, and Dugan snapped off their flashlights.

For a moment they were almost blind. Karp groped for his daughter's arm and missed. Then a bright red spark appeared above them, flying in a parabolic arc over the heads of the mole people and landing ten feet away from them with a dull, metallic clatter, still sparking merrily.

The word *fuse* popped into Marlene's head, along with a colossal terror. "Bomb!" she yelled, and dropped to the ground. Karp made a grab for Lucy's arm, clutched a fold of nylon, and did the same. A flash filled the chamber, followed instantly by the blast, and the hum of shrapnel overhead.

"Oh, Jesus! Oh, God!" That was Dugan. Marlene switched on her light. The priest was on his back, writhing and clutching his thigh. Bright blood was spurting from between his clenched fingers.

"Someone give me light!" Marlene shouted. Lucy rushed to her side and did so. Marlene knelt by the stricken man, unzipped her coverall, tore off her T-shirt, made a pad of it, and pressed it to the spurting wound. The fabric was black with blood in ten seconds. Marlene slipped out of her bra, wrapped it around Dugan's leg near the groin, knotted it, and used his flashlight barrel to wind it tight. The blood stopped spurting, but there was still a steady dripping from the wound.

She zipped herself up and said to Karp, "We've got to get him out of here. He'll bleed to death. Do you think you can—" She stopped because just then the dog snarled, half a brick spun by her ear and shattered against the sewer wall, and the mole people attacked. There were about fifteen of them, armed with bricks and lengths of sharpened rebar and pieces of steel pipe. Marlene shouted, "Sweetie! *Ocideti!*" which is "Kill!" in Sicilian, the mastiff's command language, an order never before received but one he knew well how to handle. The dog charged.

The Kel-lights made good clubs, except that after a couple of solid hits the bulbs went out, and they fought in virtual darkness, lit only by the dying fires reflected off the curved ceiling. Karp was in his home-plate stance, batting two-handed, wailing away, smashing faces and limbs, and all the time possessed by a sense of unreality: this is *not* really happening. Lucy was on his right, covering his right, covering his back. Marlene was on his left, standing over Dugan, striking at anything that came within range. Somewhere out in front the dog was doing good work, its progress indicated by shrieks of pain. The attack was uncoordinated—the attackers were not soldiers—but there were far too many of them. Karp felt something smash against the side of his knee, and he went down. A ragged, blood-spattered man stood over him with a weapon raised over his head. Karp found he could see remarkable detail, as in slow-mo in the telecast of a sporting event. The man who was going to kill him had chosen a piece of rebar about three feet long with a lump of concrete on the end of it.

There was something strange about the light now, and Karp could see more detail. The man's face, he was missing two teeth. He wondered if this was an effect of incipient death, or whether he was already dying. Karp tried to kick at the man to throw off his aim, and marvelously his attacker staggered back and disappeared. Karp's ears had been ringing since the bomb blast, but thought he could make out a series of flat explosions. More hallucinations? He lifted himself up on his elbows. No, someone was holding a flashlight and shooting at the shapes in its beam. He saw men fall, and flee, until there were no more. The echo of running feet died away.

The man with the flashlight came closer and shone his light onto Karp, who shielded his eyes with his hand. The light fell onto a corpse at Karp's feet: the man with the rebar club. A familiar voice said, "How about *that* shooting? You gonna indict me for that one, too?"

"Cooley," said Karp.

"Yeah, Cooley. What a fucking mess! Where's Canman?"

Karp was silent.

"Oh, for fuck's sake, Karp! He's the fucking slasher. Where is he?"

Marlene stepped into the light and pointed. "He's up there, in that side tunnel. We've got a man badly hurt here. He needs medical attention."

"Oh, Jesus!" cried Cooley after a brief inspection of the wounded priest. "You fucking people! Look, can the two of you get him out?"

"No," replied Marlene. "We'd never get him through that crack we all came down. Someone has to go out to the surface and get help—paramedics, lights, stretchers . . . Cooley, where's your partner?"

"Somewhere else, I don't know—I'm down here alone."

"Alone? But . . . I . . . there was another man following us."

"Lady, I don't know what you're talking about," said Cooley. "I came down here by myself."

Karp shot to his feet, his knee on fire, his heart leaping. "Where's Lucy?"

Cooley shone his light around, cursing. She was gone.

Lucy woke in pain. Her head hurt, and she couldn't remember anything after hearing the first explosion and running down the tunnel. Canman, and he was throwing bombs at . . . she remembered the men, the mole men. She opened her eyes. There was light, reflected off brick, electric light, dim with moving shadows. Someone was tugging hard at her coverall, and every time he did it, her head bounced against brick and a rocket of pain went through her head. She tried to sit up, but a weight was pressing her down. She felt air on her arms. A man was kneeling over her, pulling her coverall off. She could smell his stink, like the monkey house at the zoo, or maybe it was coming from the other man kneeling on her shoulders. The coverall was down to her waist. The word *rape* popped at length into her head. She started involuntarily and squirmed and kicked so that the man who was yanking her boots off fell over with a loud curse. The man kneeling on her punched her in the mouth. She blacked out again, and when she came to, her T-shirt had been ripped off, and one of the men was pulling down her jeans.

Lucy's hand moved over the ground, feeling for a loose brick, some weapon, but found nothing that would do. It hardly mattered. Given her mother's trade, she knew a lot about rape, about violence generally, and she understood that it was hopeless, that a thin, unarmed girl, however clever, could not keep two average-sized men from doing whatever they wanted to with her body.

Her jeans were off. She felt a tug at her waist, heard a rip, and she was naked. The man stood up and dropped his pants, then dropped the other pair he had under that. Lucy closed her eyes and started to pray. She didn't pray for rescue, but properly for the strength not to despair and to survive with her spirit intact, and if they were going to kill her afterward, for God's mercy and the forgiveness of sins. And she also prayed for the souls of the men.

He was kneeling now, and she felt her legs jerked roughly apart. She knew it was going to hurt terribly. The man gave a peculiar bubbling cry, and Lucy felt drops of hot liquid fall on her thighs and belly. She knew what that was; her skin crawled.

Then a shout, a sudden violent movement, a yell. She felt a heavy weight fall across her lower legs, and suddenly the man was no longer kneeling on her shoulders. She opened her eyes. The man who had just been about to rape her was flopping about like a landed fish, gurgling and clutching his throat. The gush of blood pouring past his hand looked black in the dimness. He arched his back once, collapsed, and lay still. There were noises behind her, grunting, gasping, the sound of feet on loose stones. Men, fighting. She could see the moving shadows of their struggle cast onto the ceiling by the glow of the flashlight lying there near the corpse. She rolled onto her knees and crawled until she found her coverall and clumsily dragged it on, willing her shaking hands to behave. She found a boot, put it on, hopped around to find the other one, stumbled, fell.

A cry of pain from the darkness, and she also heard a little pattering sound as of droplets falling on something hard, and then the soft thump of a body falling. She snatched up the flashlight and was not entirely surprised when David Grale walked into its beam.

Cooley said, "I better go look for her. One of you should stay with Father Dugan, and the other one should go back and get help. I got a radio, but it won't work here."

"I'm coming with you," said Karp and Marlene, almost as one.

Cooley knelt and pulled a Smith Airweight .38 from an ankle holster. "Whoever's gonna stay should take this. But there's no point in anyone coming with me to look. It'll just mean another person I got to watch out for."

"Butch, you should go for help," said Marlene. "I'll take the gun and stay with Mike."

Karp rose to his full height and said in a loud voice, articulating every syllable, "I am not leaving this fucking tunnel without my daughter. Let's go, Cooley!"

With that he walked off in the direction in which the mole people had retreated. Cooley gave Marlene the .38 and stalked off after Karp.

She sat down next to the priest, checked his tourniquet, examined his face. He was pale and clammy. "Mike, how do you feel?"

"Not that great. I'm cold."

"You're getting shocky from loss of blood. I have to get you warm. Close your eyes."

She unzipped the coverall and pulled it down to her waist, then lay partly on top of him, her naked breast pressing against his chest, her cheek against his.

After a long moment he remarked, "They warned us about this in the seminary."

"I bet, and it's every little Catholic girl's fantasy, too. Meanwhile, I won't tell the pope if you don't."

He sighed. "Speaking professionally, do you think I'm going to die down here?"

"No, provided we can get you out of here and you don't go into shock. You'll think this is nuts, but I can't stop worrying about my dog. My daughter is God knows where, you're bleeding like a pig, but I'm worrying about my dog. I must be some kind of monster." She whistled again, provoking weird echoes.

"No, that's natural," he said. "I once saw a woman embroidering a dress, working very carefully, like it was the most important thing in the world. That afternoon two of her children had disappeared. This was in Salvador. Everyone has their own way of coping with the enormities of life." He was quiet for a while. "Speaking of which, I always imagined myself dying outside, looking up at the stars. If I start to fade, I want you to hear my confession."

"Can I do that? I mean, is it legit?"

"Well, we're a priestly people, including you. As an added bonus, though, you'll get to find out what I did to get busted out of the upper zones of Jesuit-dom and stuck as assistant pastor for life in a little parish under the eye of a conservative archbishop."

"You're not going to die, Father," she said confidently. "You can't, not when I just gave you forty-six million dollars."

"Are you okay, Lucy?" asked Grale, concern in his tone and expression.

"I've had better days. Are those guys dead?" She saw that Grale was carrying a six-inch fillet knife with a heavy wooden handle, the kind they sell in little supply shops down by the fish market. He was wiping it absently with a rag.

"Oh, yeah. It's very fast, that way." He sighed and grinned. "They know for sure now, the both of them, if it's all true."

"How did you find me?" she asked.

"Oh, I was hanging out in the Spare Parts people tunnel trying to get a line on where Canman was, and I saw you come through, and I waited, and then that cop came by and then some guy who looked Chinese. It was a regular parade." He looked around and gestured to the space, smiling. "I've been hearing about this place for years. It's incredible, isn't it? A whole little world that no one knows about." He finished cleaning the blade and stuck it carefully into a leather sheath, then into the pocket of his jacket. His face and clothes were heavily spattered with blood.

She took a deep breath and said, "David, you're the bum slasher, aren't you?"

He nodded. "Uh-huh. Anyway, I came down the railroad tunnel, and the Chinese guy spotted me, I think, but I ducked into where it forked and lost him. Then I came through that hole in the floor, and I was there when those bombs went off. Was that Canman?"

She nodded. "Yes."

"I figured. Then the mole people jumped you all, and I didn't know what to do, and a couple of them grabbed you and dragged you away, so I followed them. And"—he hesitated, pulled uncomfortably at his chin—"I figured with two of them, I'd better wait until they were, you know, involved with you, so I could take one out right away. It worked out okay, but I guess it was worse for you. I'm sorry."

"That's all right, David. Thank you for rescuing me," she said as calmly as she could manage. She had started to shake, and the shaking got worse, as did the thoughts dashing themselves to fragments in her head, this Alice-in-Wonderland conversation she was having with good and beautiful David the mass murderer, down here in the tunnels with the cannibal rat people. He was good, he had saved her from, he was evil, I'm losing it, this is crazy, crazy, I will never, never . . .

It came out in a scream that echoed like screams do in horror movies, and she threw herself against him, sobbing hysterically. He hugged her and stroked her head, murmuring there, there, it's all right, no, it's all right.

When the sobbing had exhausted itself into disgusting, heaving snuffles, and she felt she could once again articulate language, she asked, "Why do you do it?"

"I'm not sure, really," he answered calmly. "I guess I just know. Not voices in my head or like that. I just know I have to. They're so miserable, they're suffering so much. It's mercy. Or they're evil, they're going to do bad things to the innocent. Like Doug. He was after little Lila for weeks."

"David, killing people is wrong." The phrase sounded absurd to her, but he seemed to take it seriously.

"Is it? I guess it depends who's doing the killing. God kills people all the time. St. James was called Matamoros, so it was okay to kill Moors back then and still be a saint. So many dead people. I saw whole villages murdered in Africa, kids, old grannies, chopped to pieces. And I couldn't do anything about it. It drove me crazy." He laughed. "I guess you think that's literal. I don't know. I don't *feel* crazy. And I prayed for guidance after Africa. Honestly, Lucy, I was so messed up. Give me something to do, I prayed, use me some way. I had a job on Fulton Street for a while, cleaning fish, so I had this knife, and one night I just followed this man. He was going through garbage bags, looking for pieces of food, and then I saw him picking up crack vials and crushing them and scraping the tiny grains that were left out so he could get enough to get high. But it was really *low*, not high. And it hit me: this soul would be better off released. And a kind of glow. I saw him kind of light up. I saw the soul part of him that hadn't been polluted by his life, and it wanted out, it wanted to be free, and I let it go. It's no pain, the way I do it. Just a little thrashing and then peace. I felt I was an instrument of God, like the kind of predator that takes sick animals that are suffering. Gosh, Lucy, you look awful. Your mouth is all bruised, and you're shaking."

He touched her lips delicately with his bloodstained hands.

"Are you going to kill me, David?"

She saw the startle, the shock on his face. "My God, no! Why would I want to kill you? You're beautiful and good and everyone loves you."

"Well, usually when you find out who the serial killer is," she said carefully, as to a small child, "he kills you to shut you up."

He seemed to find this amusing. "Is that what I am? I guess everybody has to have a label. But what if you're something that doesn't have one? You, for example. Or your mom. Is she a serial killer? No, you can tell them what you want. And I have no intention of hurting you. After you rest a bit, I'll take you back to the main branch. You can find your way back to your parents easy from there."

"Then I'd like to go now," she said, and struggled to her feet, wavering as dizziness washed through her. He gripped her arm.

They found her other boot under the corpse. He pulled it out and helped her on with it. Then they walked in silence down the dark passage.

"This is it," he said. "Just go to the right and you'll be—"

"Lucy!" came a shout. Her father. He'd seen her light.

She answered the shout. They heard running steps.

"I better go," Grale said. "Good-bye, Lucy."

"But what will you do?"

"Oh, I think I'll stick around here for a while. I like it down here. It's a simple life." He laughed. She could see his shining teeth, that glorious smile. "In fact, I think maybe I've finally found my ministry."

She kissed him then, on the mouth, pressing hard, and after a second or two of teeth-clunking surprise he kissed her back, and it was really her first real kiss, and very good it was, too, although the circumstances were not what she had dreamed of, and the person, while the right person, was not whom she had imagined him to be.

Then she was in her father's arms and crying again, but not for long. The cop hurried them back. When they arrived, everyone pretended to ignore Marlene's state of dress, but she was soon relieved of warming duties by Cooley's fleece-lined jacket.

"I should get that guy out of there," Cooley said, staring at the newspaper fort across the tunnel. "He could start tossing bombs again."

"Why would he do that? We're not attacking him," Lucy objected.

"Yeah, but a psycho killer like him, you can't tell what they'll do."

"He's not a killer," said Lucy. "David Grale is the bum slasher."

Simultaneous expressions of shock, surprise, and disbelief from the three adults standing.

"No, really," said Lucy over their objections, "he told me so himself. A couple of the moles had me in a side passage, and they were going to assault me, and he killed them both with his knife. And then he told me." She started to cry, then bit her lip to suppress it.

Marlene said, "In that case, Canman can stay there forever, for all I care. I'm going for help. Give me your radio, Cooley. I'll put in a call as soon as I reach the river gate. Keep looking for the dog."

After a moment's hesitation, Cooley handed her his radio, and she ran off.

Lucy went over to sit with Father Dugan. Cooley and Karp settled some distance away. The only light came from the wounded man's flashlight tourniquet, and it was growing dim. Time passed in silence but for the quiet conversation between Lucy and the priest. Karp's watch did not glow in the dark, so he lost track of time. It could have been twenty minutes or an hour. He was thirsty, and his knee hurt. Now Cooley was walking around flashing his light in both directions, and on the ground. He came back and sat down again. "There's four of them dead. No sign of the dog."

More silence. Karp cleared his throat and said, "Interesting development about Grale." Karp was glad that Cooley couldn't see his face, and that he couldn't see Cooley's. He was angry, embarrassed, and confused, angry at Canman, at Grale, at Cooley, at Marlene for concocting this expedition, at Tran, whose heavy artillery would have come in handy for once, but most of all at himself. He had gone down the wrong path many times before—it was a hazard of his occupation—but never as badly as this, and never in a way so void of the constraints built into the system, constraints designed to keep nasty prosecutors such as himself from screwing up the lives of the innocent. That the system had let him down badly was small comfort at this point, and certainly not to a seasoned self-flagellator like Karp.

"If it's on the level," said Cooley after a long silence.

"I think it is. Lucy wouldn't invent something like that, and if you noticed, the legs of her coverall and one of her boots are covered with blood, globs of it."

"Yeah, I guess. Does this mean you don't like me for it anymore?"

"Okay, Cooley, I was wrong," Karp snarled. "If you want, I'll kiss your ass in Macy's window. But I still like you a lot for the other thing."

Cooley made a disgusted noise and stood up. He switched on his flashlight.

"Where're you going?" Karp asked.

"I'm going over there and grab up that asshole."

"I'm coming with you," said Karp, getting up, too.

"No, you're not."

"Oh, yes, I am. I don't want my witness conveniently shot while escaping."

Karp heard a curse and a rustle of fabric, and suddenly he was looking at the butt end of a Glock 17.

"Take it, you fucker!" Cooley shouted.

"Don't be stupid, Cooley. Sit down, and we'll wait for the cavalry to get here."

Cooley took a step forward, and Karp put up his hands defensively, but the detective only grasped Karp's coverall and jammed the weapon into the big patch pocket on its breast. Then Cooley strode off, becoming a bobbing circle of light and the sound of trodden bricks.

"What's going on, Dad?" Lucy was standing by his side, only a voice in the dark.

"Cooley's gone off after Canman, the idiot!"

"No!" Lucy cried, and in an instant all Karp could see of her was a running silhouette against Cooley's light. Without thinking, Karp ran after her, stumbling on the uneven surface and on the dead mole people.

Cooley's beam made a white circle on the newspaper barricade. He tossed a chunk of brick at it and yelled, "Canman! You crazy bastard! Come out of there!"

Nothing. Then a scrabbling sound from behind the barricade.

Lucy came up and stood next to Cooley. "Let me go up there. He knows me."

"Are you nuts! Get the hell out of here!" Karp came staggering up, and Cooley yelled at him to take his daughter away, which he had every intention of doing, and taking Cooley as well.

But she ran away from Karp, and only stopped when Canman's head popped over the bales of paper. A red glow sprang up, lighting his face like a fun-house devil's. He stepped over the barricade, and they saw that he had a highway flare in one hand and a can grasped in the other. The flare was bright enough so that they could see that the can contained two pounds of Hercules Red Dot smokeless gunpowder, and that a short fuse was sticking out of the top of it.

"Get away!" yelled the Canman. "Get away from me or I'll light this off. I swear I will." The flare hovered around the tip of the fuse. Karp and Cooley instinctively backed away, although they knew at some level that if a pound or so of powder went off in this place, a few feet was not going to make any difference.

But Lucy went right up to him. "What are you doing?" she cried. "What *are* you doing? Haven't enough people been hurt?"

"Get out of my way!" he yelled.

"No! Where are you going to go? You're already in the most horrible place in the world. Living in a sewer! You idiot! Look at me! Do you want to kill *me*? Why do you think I'm here? Do you think I'm a cop? A social worker? I'm here because of you, John Carey Williams. I care about you, and you know it. It drives you crazy, but it's true."

And she lowered her voice and kept talking. Karp couldn't hear what she said, but the guy wasn't moving. He was listening, his mouth slightly open, his eyes fixed on Lucy. Karp didn't want to move either. None of them did. They were all fixed to the floor like stalagmites. It went on, Lucy talking quietly to the madman, the flare fuming, inches from the fuse, but not moving either. Something uncanny was happening, something outside Karp's experience, something out of a half-remembered myth: the Virgin and the monster in the deep cave. He tried to remember how it came out, what its deeper meaning was, but he could not. It was not his department, this sort of thing.

Then he became aware that Cooley was no longer by his side, although his flashlight was still there illuminating its circle of wall. It had been propped up on a pile of fallen brick.

A scuffling sound, and Lucy's scream, and Karp saw that Cooley had crept up behind Canman and grasped him from behind. The flare wavered and fell. Cooley and Canman went down in a heap, and Karp saw a tiny spark separate itself from the struggling men and roll toward him. It rolled almost to his feet. He could read the label by its sparkling red light. Time stopped. He thought about running, but there was nowhere to run, and there were Lucy and the others to consider. He could pick it up and throw it, but it looked heavy, and how could he be sure of the blast radius of such a bomb? It might bring down the whole rotten tunnel, burying them all under tons of brick. He could throw himself down on it, but he did not really want to do that.

Another second expired. He picked it up instead. The spark had almost vanished into its nail hole. There was no way to pinch it off. Karp lifted the thing to his face and stuck out his tongue. He felt a jolt of intense pain and heard a brief sizzle.

19

THE NYPD DOES NOT STINT ON RESOURCES WHEN ONE OF THEIR OWN IS IN trouble, especially when one of their own happens to be Brendan Cooley. They sent SWAT teams and bomb squads, and detective chief inspectors and crime scene units and paramedics and canine teams and generators, and thousand-candlepower lighting rigs, and there were guys from Public Works with hard hats, yellow slickers, and rolled-up maps, and others with pneumatic drills, and they would have brought in the helicopters had they figured out how to get them down in the tunnels. Fulton was there, too, and on Karp's insistence took charge of John Carey Williams, the artist formerly known as Canman, not before informing Karp, with some satisfaction, that Brendan Cooley had alibis for every one of the bum slashings. Which Karp already knew. Fulton was short with Karp, and the police brass were even shorter, but it was also the case that the district attorney is formally in charge of every police investigation. The actual ADAs almost never pressed this point, but it was there to be pressed, and Karp knew it, and so did they. Fulton's career was probably damaged by it—another doleful burden for Karp to carry.

Father Dugan was rushed off to the hospital along with Lucy, who did not want to go, but Karp insisted with a ferocity that surprised even him, and Marlene went along with her. Karp was happy to observe that an assaulted and beat-up daughter trumped the lost dog. You could never tell with Marlene. The cops had sequestered a pier and brought in a trailer for their operations center, and Karp hung around drinking bad coffee and being treated with correct frostiness by the cops. They were bringing out bags now, stretchers with the dead, and bags of remains. Cooley had apparently killed four men outright, and one had died later of wounds received. There were also two corpses with their throats torn out. What there wasn't was live people. No cannibal moles, no David Grale. And no large dog, dead or alive. Karp assembled a picture of what was happening below as reports filtered back to the command trailer. The old sewer, it turned out, had numerous unmapped branchings, and there were any number of passages broken into subways, real sewers, utility tunnels. Tracking through all of it would take weeks, and by that time the fugitives could be scattered anywhere in the thousands of miles of the city's catacombs.

Toward evening, there was a sense of anticlimax among the command cops. The press was avid for a statement, and there were no perps to parade except for a bunch of homeless, whose major crime was being poor. There were grisly human remains (some of them cooked, but they weren't anxious to let that out) and a new prime suspect in the bum slashings, but that was not going to advance anyone's career. Karp didn't feel he had to be present while they concocted their plausible untruths, so he left and ran right into Brendan Cooley, about to come in.

They looked at each other for a moment, and Karp thought that Cooley was thinking of pushing right by without a word, so he stuck his hand out and said, "Look, Cooley, I didn't get to thank you for saving me and my family. I mean it—thanks."

Cooley took the hand and gave it a brief, reluctant shake. He said, "No problem. I should say the same. That was a fancy piece of work there with that bomb. With your tongue. I got to say, you got a pair on you, man. I thought that was fucking farewell and adieu for sure. And that's quite a girl you got there. I never saw anything like it. Fucking guy's holding a bomb, and she just goes right up to him and gives him hell. Hypnotized the bastard like a goddamn chicken."

"Yeah, I don't know whether to be proud of her or lock her in her room forever." Karp shook his head ruefully. "I'll tell you, it never for one minute occurred to me that I would have a daughter like that. My heart's up around my collar half the time. Yours are still young—you got time to prepare, but the day will come."

Their eyes met, and a certain understanding passed between them. Cooley said, "I got to go in there and talk to the chief."

"Yeah. Look, we got stuff we need to discuss. Why don't you come by my office tomorrow, say around ten? We'll talk."

"Should I bring my lawyer?"

"That's your right, of course. But I thought it would be good if we just talked informally, just a couple of heroes shooting the shit. You know how fucked up lawyers can be."

"I'll think about it," said Cooley, and went into the trailer.

Past the cops on guard, and the yellow tape and the gabbling barrier of reporters, Karp was gratified to see his driver and Murrow leaning against a dark sedan. In the car, to Karp's relief, Murrow did not ask for a thrilling replay of the tunnel adventures, but instead conveyed information.

"The thing went down about two hours ago. Paxton's in custody at the One-six."

"Good. Any problems?"

"No. They called your office as arranged when they scooped him up."

"The bust was legit?"

"Oh, yeah. Half the people on that block are snitches. Three Mob-looking guys carrying a duffel bag into a building, the lines were humming half an hour later. Meanwhile, everyone's glued to the tube back at the office. Your exploits. The DA wants to see you as soon as you get in."

"He can wait." Karp looked out the window at the city. It looked the same—people, cars, buildings, all oblivious to what they walked, drove, and stood over. It seemed wrong somehow that only hours had passed since he had descended into the underworld. Like all people who have experienced the remarkable and terrifying, Karp wanted the world to have been changed and was irrationally annoyed that it was going on in its accustomed way, like ants in a child's ant farm.

"What's wrong with your face, Murrow?"

"My face?"

"Yeah, you look like you stepped in dog shit. I stink, don't I?"

"You might want to change your clothes," said Murrow delicately.

They went to the loft on Crosby Street, and Karp stripped and tossed the sewer gear into a trash bag and took a long, hot shower. Bruises he had not felt at the time were blossoming like flowers after a rain, blue and purple. Dressing, he found he had to sit on the bed to get into his trousers. I am getting too old for this shit, he thought.

At the precinct, Karp found Ralphie Paxton in an interview room, looking gray and frightened. Karp gave him a smile.

"So, Mr. Paxton, we meet again. You've got yourself in some trouble now, haven't you? Have you been read your rights?"

"Yeah. Look, I don't know nothing about any bag of dope. Someone must've laid it on me, in my place, while I was out."

"Yes, and I see here on this paper that you have waived your rights. Are you absolutely sure you don't want to talk to an attorney?"

"I don't need no attorney. I didn't do nothing. I told you, they dumped that shit in there when I was out. How do I know what's in the back of some damn closet?"

"I see. The problem with that story, Mr. Paxton, is we have witnesses say you were there when the package was delivered. We even have a witness who says you set up the whole thing for money."

"He's a goddamn liar!"

"Uh-huh. Mr. Paxton, are you aware of the penalties this state provides for possession of narcotic drugs? Under Section 220.21, possession of more than four ounces of narcotic drugs is a class A-one felony. That carries with it a mandatory fifteen-year minimum sentence upon conviction, and then sentences can go as high as twenty-five years. We don't like drug lords in the state of New York."

"I ain't no drug lord, for God's sake! Do I look like a damn drug lord?"

Karp ignored this and went on calmly, still smiling. "On the other hand, we often make allowances for people caught in a squeeze. You don't have to be charged with anything. I can't make you any promises, but sometimes when a person comes forward of their own volition and helps us out, we can help them out. You know how the system works."

"You mean like I tell you who gave me the stuff?"

Karp pretended to think this over. "Well, yes, sometimes that's possible. But in this case, we know very well who gave you the stuff. So we don't need you for that. Can you think of anything else?"

Paxton thought. He knew nickel-dime dealers he would be glad to sell, but he sensed that these would not lift the load for a major-quantity dope bust. It was unfair. He had never even had a taste of the stuff, he had been good as gold, had taken the warnings seriously, and now this. The guy was staring at him with those funny eyes. He remembered them from court, how he could hardly stand looking at them while he told the story of Des and that woman. Really, that was all he could think of, and he didn't think it would be enough. Despairingly he said, "I got that thing, that thing I was in court for?"

"Yes?" Karp exhibited the mildest interest.

"Yeah, what went down with Des and that Marshak. That wasn't exactly what happened."

"I see. And you would be willing to tell us what did happen?"

"Yeah, if I can get a little help off of this dope beef."

"Well, that's certainly possible, but first I'd have to hear your story."

Paxton nodded. *Possible* was a good word just now, a lot better than *fifteen mandatory.*

Karp made a gesture to the one-way glass, and a police technician walked in with a video camera on a tripod. A clerk came in and placed a typed paper on the table and left. Karp said, "Okay, Mr. Paxton, this document here reiterates your waiver of your rights and expresses your willingness to freely give a statement without legal counsel, and it also expresses your willingness to be videotaped doing it. If you'll just sign there at the bottom."

Paxton signed without reading. The camera whined into action. Paxton looked into the camera like a good American and told the truth. With very little prompting from Karp, he described how Des Ramsey had approached Sybil Marshak. He had been using a knife to cut twine, but he did not have it with him when he approached her. He had been polite. He had said, "Excuse me, lady. Do you have the right time?" And she had pulled out a gun and shot him, just like that. Paxton had run. He hadn't even checked to see how Ramsey was, he had grabbed up the knife and run. Then later, he'd seen the flyers about five grand for any information about the case, called the number, spoken with a guy named Peter Walsh, and told him the story, the truth, just how it happened, and mentioned what they were doing when the thing went down, and the knife business, which seemed to interest Walsh a lot. And then Walsh had taken him to see Mr. Solotoff, and he had shown Mr. Solotoff the knife, and Mr. Solotoff had said that he must have been mistaken, that his client had told him that Ramsey had come at her with a knife, and he had said, no, Ramsey just asked her the time. And Solotoff had said that wasn't a $5,000 story. The five-grand story was Ramsey had the knife. And Paxton had agreed to tell it that way. Ramsey was dead, it wouldn't hurt him any. And Solotoff had rehearsed Paxton, over and over, and Solotoff had told him he was connected, and if Paxton told anyone, he was going to get whacked. Paxton looked at the camera, and then at Karp, imploringly. "So . . . am I gonna get protection?"

"You won't need protection," said Karp. "He was bullshitting you."

Paxton looked doubtful for a second, and then he relaxed and tried on a smile. "I guess. He must've been bullshitting about you all, too."

"In what way?"

"He said the whole thing was wired with the DA. He said you all wanted it like that, on account of Marshak being such a big fucking deal, politics and shit."

Karp felt a peculiar chill at this statement, but kept his face blank and his voice neutral.

"Did he mention anyone specifically? In the DA's office?"

"All you all, he said. The DA, Keegan. And his main guy, what's his face?"

"You don't happen to recall his name, do you?"

"Feller? Or Puller, something like that. But his first name was Norton. I remember that because he had him on the phone while I was there to impress me or some shit. Norton this, Norton that, like they were buddies. He even showed me he had a tape recorder of them talking, make sure the guy didn't back away from it. He said it was a done deal. But it must've been a scam. I mean, like you say, the man's a bullshitter."

"Why do you think it was a scam?"

"Because he also said you was in on it, too. Matter of fact, he said it was all your idea."

Karp closed off the interview by having Paxton recount the various dates involved and was not surprised at how good he was at this. Scavengers, he knew, typically have a keen appreciation of calendrical time since their livelihood depends on knowing when different neighborhoods have trash picked up. Paxton would make an even better witness than he had as a perjurer.

Karp had the technician turn off the camera and leave. "Mr. Paxton,

I want to thank you for being so forthcoming. I'm going to have your statement transcribed and have you sign it, and then we'll be done."

"What about me? What about my case?"

"Well, there's the matter of your perjury before the grand jury. That's a serious matter, and we're going to hang on to you until it's resolved. What we do about it will depend on your testifying truthfully when we reindict Ms. Marshak."

"No, I mean what about the dope? The fifteen years?"

"Oh, that. I think we can go easy on you there. I just want to say that I hope your baby recovers from its constipation."

Paxton goggled. "What the fuck you talking about, man? I ain't got no baby."

"You don't?" said Karp, miming vast wonder. "Then why did you have twenty-two pounds of baby laxative in your apartment?"

Karp called the DA's office and was connected immediately.

"We need to talk," said the DA.

"We do, but not today. I'm beat and I'm going home."

The DA didn't acknowledge this. "The press is going crazy. What the hell were you doing down in those tunnels? And whatever possessed you to take along your family and that priest?"

"It's a long story, Jack. There was an important witness hiding down there, and for a number of reasons I didn't want to involve regular channels."

"Regular channels? What the devil are you talking about? Why do you think we have a DA squad?"

"I'll talk to you tomorrow, I promise. But I can't even think straight right now."

"And why was Cooley down there? Jesus, Butch, if you're fucking with that case after I warned you off . . ."

"Jack, really, I'm practically falling off my feet. I'll see you in your office tomorrow."

"With good news, I hope."

"The best, Jack."

Karp was, in fact, falling off his feet, and hurting besides, but he did not go home. Instead, he went to Bellevue with Murrow in tow. After checking in on his daughter, he went to the locked ward, where he found a large, black detective sitting outside a room. This was Mack Jeffers, one of Clay Fulton's people from his days as a Harlem lieutenant. Clay had been true to his word. No one who shouldn't was going to get past Mack Jeffers. Karp exchanged a few words with the cop, and they went into the room.

Bellevue had washed John "Canman" Williams and trimmed off some of his hair. He had been battered by his struggle with Cooley, but he looked more like an undernourished professor than anything resembling the fire-faced demon of Rat Alley. Karp wondered whether the transformation was due to the hospital's cleanup or to something his daughter had accomplished. Canman was thirty-something, Karp estimated, although his skin had the thickened look common to those who lived rough. His eyes were blue, intelligent, wary, proud.

"How's Lucy?" were his first words when Karp entered, which Karp took as a good sign.

"She's not badly hurt. Her body, anyway. They're checking her over. You seem okay."

"Are you charging me with a crime?" Light on the pleasantries was the Canman.

"Well, I guess I could charge you with any number of crimes, but just now we're holding you as a material witness."

"Witness to what?"

"To the relationship between Detective Brendan Cooley and Shawn Lomax. Cisco Lomax."

"What if I don't know anything material about that?"

"If I think you're lying, which I do, you would be in serious legal trouble."

"And if I tell you what you want to know?"

"Then I can be accommodating."

"Great. Just write out a statement of what you want me to say, and I'll sign it."

"Don't be a wiseass, Mr. Williams. I just want you to tell the truth."

"Oh, the truth. Excuse me, I thought you were a lawyer."

Karp had few real prejudices, but one of them was against lawbreakers with brains and education. He had far more sympathy for the Ralphie Paxtons of the world. So when Karp spoke, he turned the lasers to stun and put an edge in his voice.

"Yes, and we could sit here all day and trade brittle one-liners about the corruption of society. But, frankly, I am bruised and tired, and so is my whole family, which is more or less your fault, nor do I forget that you nearly murdered me and my daughter this afternoon. So you'll forgive me if I cut to the chase. It is not often that I lead Leviathan out of his cave and let him feed freely on a citizen, but I am inclined to do so in your case. If you play with me, Mr. Williams, I promise you that I will indict you on three counts of attempted murder, which is a class A-one felony, and I will convict you, and I will use every chip I have to get you the maximum sentence the law allows and make sure you are placed in the toughest cell block in the nastiest prison in this state. You think you're a tough guy, but, believe me, inside of two weeks you'll be wearing frilly nightgowns and eye shadow, and I will personally attend every parole hearing you get to make sure that it goes on and on and on. Have I made myself absolutely clear?"

A sullen nod. "Yeah."

"Good. The alternative is to pretend for a few minutes that you're the mensch my daughter apparently sees in you, and forget your epic battle against bourgeois America, and tell me the fucking truth."

Which Canman now did, concisely and articulately, with little prompting, and, to Karp's immense relief, the story was the one Karp had constructed over the past months, out of hints and guesswork. Cisco Lomax had been the fence Firmo's man. Lomax had arranged for packages to be transported by the more responsible class of street merchants, including Canman. Canman had seen Lomax with Cooley many times, and Cooley had seen Canman, because Lomax had also been a snitch for Cooley, cultivated slowly over a year. Lomax had helped set up a bust at a site where Firmo would actually take personal possession of a looted shipping container.

"And what went wrong?" Karp asked. This was the crux.

"I don't have the details, but what I heard was that Cisco was just, like, stringing him along. Cooley was paying out serious money, maybe some of it his own, to keep Cisco on board. It could be that Cisco made the whole thing up, the big deal in the warehouse. He was that kind of guy. Anyway, the night it was supposed to have gone down, Cooley gets to the warehouse with a whole army of cops, and nothing's there but a crate of Taiwan watches. He came down later to the yards and routed everyone, looking for Cisco. And me. As it happens, I wasn't there. He must've thought I was in with Cisco on it or something."

"Were you? Where were you that night?"

"At Cannes for the festival. I don't know, man—somewhere across town, negotiating for bags of empties. That's what I do. I'm a fucking homeless. I don't check in at night, all right? The next night was when Cisco got it. Then Cooley started to come around looking for me. So I got small. That's it, that's all I know."

"Okay, you got all that Murrow?"

Murrow looked up from his pad. "Got it."

"We'll have you sign a transcript," Karp said, pausing at the door.

"Can Lucy come by and see me?" asked Williams.

"No," said Karp, looking down at the man with distaste. "Let me ask you something. How can you settle for the kind of life you're leading, living on the street in cardboard boxes? You're smart, you're skillful, you're educated. You could have a real life . . ."

"I had a real life once. I was an engineer. First, I made toys for people to kill with, and then I made toys to keep rich people from being bored. And I had to take pills to help me forget what I was doing. And after a while the pills made it impossible for me to do that stuff anymore. A self-correcting system. What I wonder, though, is how a bastard like you ever produced someone like Lucy."

"A question I ask myself all the time," said Karp, and shut the door. He sent Murrow back downtown and went to find his wife.

Who was with Father Dugan, just back from surgery.

"Marlene," said Dugan groggily, "was it a figment of my fevered imagination, or did you tell me down there that you gave me an obscene amount of money?"

"Not a figment. Forty-six mil."

He groaned. "Why would you want to do a thing like that for? I thought I was always so nice to you."

"It's tainted gold, Father. I couldn't think of anything else to do with it. Besides, I discovered I wasn't cut out to be quite that rich. It wasn't good for my liver."

"You do realize I'm under a vow of poverty."

"Not a problem. The arch was very understanding. There's a foundation being erected as we speak, the Lucia Foundation, to dispose of the income. I'm the chairman of the board, you're the executive director."

"I see. And what is this foundation supposed to do with its money?"

"To be decided. Good works. Righting wrongs. We'll think of something."

"I'm sure. Could I have a long white limo with darkened windows?"

She laughed. "Only if you take to wearing green spectacles, a Charlie Chan panama hat, and to carrying a malacca."

"Done. Well, well. So the arch swallowed the black sheep getting out from under?"

"Yes. When you give someone forty-six million dollars, your suggestions tend to be treated with respect, I find. Tell me what happened after I left the sewer. Butch was excessively brief."

"I wish I could. Canman had a bomb, and Butch managed to put it out. All I saw were moving shadows. But I heard snatches of what Lucy said to him, some trick of acoustics in the vault. It was quite remarkable. You don't need the actual words, although for an impromptu sermon I wish I could do as good on my best day. No, it was the tone. We say we hate the sin but love the sinner, but we hardly ever bring that into the light. It's so hard to make the distinction so that it's clear to the sinner. But she did that. I've never heard such a combination of wrath and love. It raised the hair on my neck. The Holy Spirit, or I'm a Methodist."

"My poor baby!" said Marlene.

And after he had drifted off, she went outside and saw her husband walking toward her in the hallway, looked toward him expectantly, and saw how it was by his face before he even said, "I'm sorry, baby, he's gone."

Marlene whirled and slammed her fist into the hard plaster wall, and once again, hard enough to leave a smear of blood, and he grabbed her before she could break her knuckles. She wailed then, a long, crooning cry, loud, too, so that hospital staff came out of their stations, and a neuropsych team was discreetly marshaled. But not used, for Karp carried her away and picked up Lucy, who, when she heard, howled, too, in a slightly higher key. Karp wisely made no effort to stop this duet, nor did the words *It's only a dog* approach his lips as he escorted his very own Italian opera to a waiting cab.

● ● ●

"Are you all recovered now?" asked Karp. It was later. They were in bed.

"Oh, I guess. He was eleven. That's old for a dog. And he went out fighting instead of in a vet's office. I guess I should be happy for him. You think this is dumb, right?"

"Not at all. Man's best friend. The emotion does you credit, I guess. We never got into pets in my family. I don't have the feeling for them."

"Yes, and I love you anyway. Isn't that strange?" A pause here. "I gave away all my money. To the Church. Well, actually to a foundation Mike Dugan's going to run. Forty-six million. Easy come, easy go. Do you think I'm crazy?"

"A nice question. It should be put, 'Do you think I'm crazier than you already did,' and the answer is no, not really. I didn't like the way you behaved when you had all that money, and it wasn't in any way real to me when you had it. What did you do with the rest of it?"

"Oh, well, I'm crazy, but I'm not stupid," answered Marlene with a sniff. "The rest will take care of the kids' education and a stake in life and so forth, and to tide me over until I decide what I'm going to do with the remains of my miserable life. I'm thinking vaguely of getting some acreage, maybe breed and train mastiffs. I seem not to be able to get along with people very well, poor or rich."

"Was that why you were always drunk?"

"You noticed? Yes, well, there was that business at Solette's, that didn't help. And I also recall noticing that the rich guys my age all had girls with them fifteen years younger than me, and I realized I was not a babe anymore, and that the only guys who were ever going to hit on me were ones who wanted me to help them get rich, like Peter Walsh. I realize that I have faithfully toed the feminist line all these years—don't make me a sex object and so forth—which is a lot easier if you have a face and you wear a six, so I felt like a hypocrite in the bargain . . ."

"Peter Walsh? The PI?"

"You know him?"

"His name came up. What's your connection?"

"He came on to me for a job at Osborne. Came in for an interview, too. Apparently he worked for your old pal Shelly Solotoff. He was the one who set up that sting on Roland. Talked about it quite cheerfully. It's all on tape."

"Is it?"

"Yeah, Osborne tapes all their interviews."

"I'm surprised he admitted it. Doesn't he know in some of the jurisdictions Osborne has offices it's illegal to record conversations without other-party consent?"

"Well, he's a cocky little bastard. Maybe he thought it would be louche and impressive." Marlene pouted. "But we were talking about *me*. Why is it every time I start to pour my heart out, we wind up discussing felonies?"

"You want me to say that despite our advanced age and disabilities, I still consider you the most desirable of women?"

"It would be a start."

Karp rose early the next day and arrived at an almost empty office. On his desk, from Murrow, were two copies of the Canman transcript. He walked upstairs to the DA's office and laid one of them on Keegan's desk. At a little past nine, Karp called the general counsel's office at Osborne and had a brief conversation with William Bell, at which Bell agreed to send over a copy of Peter Walsh's interview tape. Karp did not have to threaten to subpoena the tape as evidence of a crime. Osborne wanted to keep Karp, and any other of Marlene Ciampi's relatives, very happy. A courier brought it in forty minutes later. After checking it out in the AV suite, Karp walked down to the chambers of Judge Marvin Peoples, the hardest-working and earliest-arriving and only black Republican judge on the Supreme Court in and for the County of New York, and gave him a condensed version of the tale of Marshak and Solotoff, and the judge duly issued a warrant for the search of the offices of Sheldon Solotoff and the seizure of certain recorded telephonic communications.

Ten minutes after he returned from handing the warrant to a couple of DA squad cops, his secretary buzzed him and said that the DA wanted to see him right away. He went up and found, not to his surprise, that Norton Fuller was there. Both he and the DA were looking grim.

The DA flipped the pages of the Canman transcript. "Would you mind telling me what this is all about?"

"Not at all," said Karp. "This statement demonstrates that Cooley knew Lomax, and that he had a serious grudge against him. His story that he was in pursuit of a stolen vehicle that just happened to contain Shawn Lomax is therefore false. This is confirmed by the fact that Cooley didn't know the vehicle was stolen when he set off in pursuit. The stolen-car call didn't come in until after Lomax was dead. A simple examination of police records will bear that out. A similar examination of the crime-scene analysis will demonstrate that the chase did not go down as Cooley and the other police witnesses testified. I refer to the complete analysis, not the mere excerpt on which our grand jury presentation was based. The complete analysis is quite competent. It shows that at no time was Cooley in danger of being rammed by Lomax's vehicle. The tire marks and damage to the vehicles don't add up to that at all. In fact, Lomax was so incapacitated by gunfire that he couldn't have threatened the detectives at all. Incapacitated by fire from the rear, by the way, and he was shot through the head by Cooley while Cooley was on the ground less than ten feet away."

"A police cover-up," said Fuller, trying the phrase out for the first time.

"No. The police report is complete and accurate. The grand jury verdict was the result of incompetence encouraged by political expediency. They guessed correctly that we would give Cooley a pass, and we did. It's our bad."

"Wait on that—" began the DA, but Karp said, "No. There's only one way out of this now, and that's to take our lumps and move on. Speaking of which, I want you to look at this videotape. It concerns a different but curiously related case."

Karp went to the large television in the corner, switched it on, and slipped the videotape into the VCR on top of it.

They watched the interview in silence.

When the tape ended, Fuller said, "What a load of bullshit. What did you threaten him with to get him to say that?"

"Quite a lot, as it happens, but it's true nevertheless," said Karp.

Fuller turned to the DA. "This is ridiculous, Jack. He concocted this whole thing to get back at me. It's palace politics pure and simple. I mean really! The idea that anyone would take the word of some piss bum against the word of me and Sybil Marshak . . ."

"And we have confirmation, or will have before long, from Peter Walsh, Solotoff's PI, the man who found Mr. Paxton there. He will testify that the original story Paxton told him is the same in every respect as the one you just saw. Solotoff made the whole thing up and conspired with you to suborn perjury. And it would have worked if there hadn't been that watch. No one carrying a watch that expensive would have gone for a cheap mugging. That's how I knew that Paxton's story had to be phony. And you did your part, Norton, by releasing Ramsey's juvenile record, making him out to be a violent criminal. And you got Jack to push through a grand jury whitewash, which worked out okay, by the way, because now I have a perjury charge to hang over Paxton's head, to make sure he behaves when we bring Marshak up again."

"I can't believe you're listening to this . . . this vile conspiracy, Jack. I would never dream of conspiring to suborn perjury."

The DA maintained a stony silence, but Karp could see a faint grimace of disgust blossom on the noble face. Karp said, "You weren't paying attention. Shelly taped you, just like Nixon. The conspiracy is an open book."

"It's not! There is absolutely nothing incriminating in any conversation I ever had with Solotoff . . ." Fuller froze and stared at Karp, then at the DA. The disgust was in full flower now.

"I rest my case," said Karp, wishing more than anything that he knew for sure whether that look was born out of revulsion for the act, for Fuller's compromising the integrity of his office, or because the weasel had been so stupid as to get caught.

Fuller was pale now, sweating, and his words came out in a high-pitched jabber quite different from his normal voice. "Jack, I swear there is nothing there, nothing they can prove. Of course, I talked to Solotoff. It's our most politically sensitive case. But at no time did I say or do anything even remotely suggested by these charges. Solotoff will back me up on this a hundred percent."

Karp laughed and said, "Oh, Norton! The absolute index of your incompetence for this kind of work is the fact that you still don't understand that when I put the hooks to Shelly Solotoff, you will be the very first bit of meat he throws me."

The DA said, "If you'll excuse us, Norton."

Fuller said, "Jack, you want to be very careful now. The primary is nine weeks away and—"

"I *said,* if you'll excuse us, Norton. I will attend to you in a few minutes."

Fuller left. Karp had read about people slinking out of a room, but he had never seen it actually done until then.

The DA's lips had disappeared into a rigid horizontal line. "So," he said after a long time. "Where are we?"

"He has to go, immediately. I have no great interest in prosecuting either him or Solotoff, but at a minimum both Fuller and Solotoff get disbarred. I'll let you decide what should be done with both of them beyond that. I can indict Marshak behind this new material, and I intend to go forward with it. Cooley is a little more problematic, but I intend to give the grand jury another crack at him, too."

The DA was shaking his head from side to side like an old clock's slow pendulum, and his expression was the kind that rare and spiny fish see from the other side of the glass.

He said, "I can't believe it. You still, at your age, want to be the white knight. It's preposterous. It's like still wanting to be a cowboy. I should have gotten rid of you years ago. I don't know, it must be a brain lesion. You simply never learned how things get done."

"I guess not."

"Then let me give you some advice. The problem with the white knight is he comes to the castle and they send him off to slay the dragon. And he slays the dragon. Then there's another dragon, and he slays that, too. And another. Sooner or later, though, there'll be a dragon so big that the white knight's going to get chewed up and fried, you can put money on that. So the moral of the story is, when you grow up, you don't want to be the white knight. You want to be the guy that sends the white knight out to kill the dragon. Get it?"

"Is that you, Jack?"

"Yes, it is. Or was. This little drama you produced just lost me everything I worked for my whole life."

"Well, you know, I don't know about that. People might like to see a DA who's not afraid to clean his own house and take some political risks. McBright is the pol in this race, and he's good. I might even say he's better than you at working a crowd. In a political race, an ethnic race, a special-interest race, he's going to whip you. But if you demonstrate integrity and courage, maybe people will decide they like that better than having someone in here who's always telling them what they want to hear. If not, maybe the office isn't worth having."

"That's your opinion, is it?"

"Yes, it is. And while you're soliciting my opinion, you should cut your losses on Benson. As I pointed out earlier, he's not convictable on capital murder. I mean while you're starting to do the right thing without fear or favor . . ."

"Oh, terrific. The police vote, the West Side liberal vote, and now you want me to dump the Jewish vote, too. You think I can get elected by the Ukrainians?"

"I'm Jewish, and I'll vote for you."

"Oh, get out of here!" Keegan growled. "I'm sick of the sight of you."

Karp bristled at Keegan's tone and leaned over Keagan's desk, placing his face inches away from his boss's. "Don't you ever talk to me like that! If you can't handle truth anymore, and want to break faith with everything we're really all about, just tell me and I'm gone for good." Karp pulled back.

Keegan peered into Karp's eyes and suddenly slumped in his chair, now appearing like a half-filled laundry bag set on a subway seat by a seasoned strap hanger. While staring down at his desk, Keegan spoke in a depressed, steady monotone. "OK, OK, you're right. Maybe I'm the only prick around here, but it's tough. It's tough sledding. I just want to be DA."

Karp went out. He found Brendan Cooley waiting for him in the hallway outside his office, alone.

Karp ushered him in, sat him down, settled himself into his chair, and gave the detective a long, searching look. "What are we going to do with you, Cooley? It's not very often I get to jam up someone who saved my life. Read this!" Karp tossed over the transcript of Canman's Q&A and waited as Cooley paged through it.

Cooley flipped it back across the desk. "It's just talk. He doesn't know anything. You got nothing solid."

"Actually I do. The problem with a scam is that it might look good on the surface, but it never stands up to serious poking. The simple fact is that you lied, and your partner backed your play, about chasing a stolen car. We can absolutely prove that wasn't the case. That knocks the blocks out from under your testimony. Then we have the crime-scene analysis, and the medical forensics, neither of which confirms your story. Then you have the witnesses, the patrol cops, and your partner. They're caught in a lie. Okay, cops stretch it all the time, especially to cover an excess of zeal by a brother officer, but when we put it to them that they're covering up an assassination, will they hold up? When they're looking at dismissal and prosecution for perjury? I don't think so. I know I can indict, and I'm pretty sure I can convict you, if not for murder, then for manslaughter one." Karp waited. Cooley stared at him, his face stiff. He said nothing. A smart guy.

Karp continued, "I actually think you're guilty of murder. You might be thinking, in a trial who knows how it would go? A popular heroic cop, the victim a lowlife. The right jury might give you a pass. You know and I know that we don't ever really try the crime that's in the statute books. We try a particular defendant against a particular victim, which is why you're always better off killing a black person, God help us. Or maybe that's changed. The jury pool isn't what it was when we were coming up. You might get convicted, which would be twenty-five to life, hard time. On the other hand, while I'm not corrupt enough to give you a pass, like some of my colleagues here, I am corrupt enough to recognize that you're basically a decent man stuck in a job he hates."

Cooley snapped out of his trance. "What? What're you talking about?"

Karp held up a meliorative hand. "Cooley, I'm not going to insult you by trying to psychologize here. But I met your wife. I know your story. Your dad, your brother, the whole cop thing. What you should do now is look at where you are and where your whole life is going. Right now, you got Dad and the cops and nothing else. You lost your wife and kids. It's not what you wanted out of life. You're never going to be able to replace your brother, or show your father that you could bring down the bad guy that got away from him."

"Goddamn it, leave my family out of this!"

"Right. But just look at it, is all I ask. Now, like I just said, I'm twisted enough to take into account what you did down in the tunnel and the kind of person you really are. You're not someone who needs to be off the streets forever. So your choice is, what I'm giving you here is, on the one hand, a trial for murder, a huge scandal, incredible heartbreak for your family, and the real possibility that your life could be completely gone. I will try that case myself, and I am very, very good at prosecuting homicides. The other thing to keep in mind is that we could have a guy in here next year who wants to make his rep by showing that white cops don't get to blow away African-Americans whenever it strikes their fancy. He will want to drop the jailhouse on your head. Or, on the other hand, I will offer you a plea: manslaughter in the second degree. That means you will have to stand up in front of a judge and admit that you were reckless in pursuit of a fleeing felon and killed a man. That's not a lie, even you'd have to admit that. You'd serve the minimum in a low-security facility along with crooked accountants and corrupt assistant district attorneys and lawyers, eighteen months, twenty months, something like that. Don't answer me now. Talk to your lawyers, talk to your family. But don't take too long, okay? I don't know how long I'm going to be in a deal-making position myself."

Cooley sat frozen for a full minute. That was good, Karp thought. He was thinking seriously, not going in for histrionic denials. And for an instant there Karp thought he had seen relief on the man's face. Then Cooley snapped his head down once and rose to his feet. "I'll be in touch," he said, and walked out.

Karp sighed and looked out the window for a while, twiddling a pencil against his teeth. The phone rang. His secretary said it was Sheldon Solotoff, and it was urgent.

Karp told her to hold the call. Then he dialed his home.

"How did it go?" his wife asked.

"Terrific. Can I have a job on the dog farm?"

"Send me a résumé. Really, though. Did you smite the evildoers, as always?"

"I smited, but I think my smiter is wearing out." He gave her a rundown on the events just passed, including the interview with Cooley.

"Do you think he'll go for it?" she asked.

"I have no idea. I like to think of him a few years out, back with his family and flying around in little airplanes or talking in jetliners. I shouldn't be thinking that, the guy killed a man and all, but there it is, I'm being honest. For a change."

"Oh, don't be silly. You have innumerable faults, as I know to my cost, but dishonesty is not one of them. I say that as an accomplished liar."

"Then how do I know you're telling the truth?"

A raspberry sound over the phone. He asked, "How's Lucy holding up?"

"Oh, shattered, shattered. She cares so much and sees the good in people. It knocks her down when it turns out they're all too human. What she needs is a nice kid with piercings and blue hair and a heavy coke habit. Then we could be real parents."

"Well, she's got a do-good foundation named after her. That should take some of the sting out."

"Oh, the Lucia Foundation isn't named after Lucy, or not directly. It's named after the person she was named after. You know, Nonna Lucia, my mother's grandmother."

"I don't know."

"You do! I've told you that story a million times."

"Nope."

"Yes, but you never listen to a word I say. Lucia di Messina, a sprig of the old aristocracy, which is where I get my classy bearing, if you noticed. She ran off with the gardener's boy, around 1890 this is, ran off to Naples. Her father sent heavies after her, and she scooted all over Italy with the guy, hiding. They caught up with them in a hill town in the Abruzzi. By that time, my grandfather Paolo was around, a little kid, I guess."

"Oh, right, now it's coming back. They killed the gardener."

"Uh-huh, the handsome Lorenzo, and as the family legend has it, she stood in the doorway of her house, in her blood-spattered shift, over the dead body of her husband, and blew them both away with a shotgun. Split to America with the cops on her heels, and the rest is history. Pazza Lucia to the family, a real character. I'm sorry I never knew her."

"Look in the mirror," said Karp.

"Oh, yeah, it's been noted." Marlene laughed. "But really, blood will tell, don't you think? I've tried to be respectable, you can't say I haven't, but *au fond,* when all is said and done, I'm just a thug. I can't imagine where Lucy comes from. Were there any really good people on your side?"

"I doubt it. Maybe a *tzaddik* slipped in on my mom's side way back in Bessarabia. As a matter of fact, she was the only person in my family no one had a bad word to say about."

"Anyway, Lucy was moping so much that I dragged her out of the house and took her grocery shopping."

"What about the little elves who kept the refrigerator stocked with overpriced food?"

"Things of the past, my dear. While I yield to no one in my ability to lounge about all day in a silk peignoir, there is something about walking down Grand Street with a net bag breaking my shoulder that's really kind of terrific. The rich have no idea."

"Did she perk?"

"Yeah, she did. And then we had lunch out, at Heavenly Sanitary Noodle Company, and Lucy spotted one of Tran's henchmen and got to talking to him, and he said Tran was practically suicidal with shame, and so we went to see him in this tacky place he stays at on Bayard."

"And did the magic work?"

"Of course. She said something to the effect that we loved him because he was human, because he had failings, and it wasn't his fault, and we knew he wasn't perfect all the time. I thought he was going to burst out crying, the poor old bastard. And I said more or less the same. I do love him so, and how weird is that? My fatal weakness for heroic, brilliant, perfectionist, self-flagellating men."

"Ahem," said Karp. "Although I don't feel particularly heroic."

"No, really, anyone would have picked up a sparking bomb and put it out with their *tongue!* Jesus, Butch, give yourself some credit once."

"Well, I am a lawyer. My tongue is highly trained. Speaking of lawyers, I have Solotoff on hold."

"Waiting for his new asshole to be reamed, I assume."

"Yeah. You know, I still can't figure it out. Cooley is like an open book to me. I actually like the guy. I sympathize with him even while I'm holding him responsible for what he did. But Shelly . . . ? This whole ridiculous business, the thing with Roland, the perjury. It makes no sense."

"To you, no, because you're not like that. I think he wanted to somehow involve you in corruption, to show that, yeah, he left the DA not because he got kicked out, but because it's all a big scam anyway. If he'd pulled it off, he would have waved it in our face, ha ha, the outfit you worked for is shit, and you're a jerk for believing in it."

"I don't know. There are some sewers I won't go into, I guess. Maybe a career as a kennel person would brighten my outlook. Do you think there's really a place for me?"

"I intend to be very selective in my staff. Tell me, do you have any experience shoveling piles of dog shit?" said Marlene.

"I worked for the New York criminal justice system for twenty years."

"You're hired."